EMBRYO

EMBRYO

Keith Barnard

SOUVENIR PRESS

ISBN 0 285 62993 X

Printed and bound in Great Britain by
WBC Ltd, Bristol and Maesteg

To my wife, Ann

Acknowledgements

The author would like to thank for their advice, support and assistance in the production of this book:
My wife, Ann
Dennis and Sylvia Stuart
Gretta and Bill Robinson
John and Eileen Naylor
Dr Roger Seagger, FFARCS
John Landaw, FBCO
Min

Author's Note

Much of the action in this story is set in a fictitious teaching hospital in Bournemouth, the Princess Marina Hospital. Bournemouth does not have a teaching hospital, and there is no intended similarity between the hospital in this book or the characters associated with it, and any medical establishment or members of staff of any medical establishment, in Bournemouth or elsewhere.

1

The out-patient clinics in the Gynaecology Department at the Princess Marina Hospital, Bournemouth, were held on weekday mornings, but the Wednesday clinic was the one that the Senior Registrar Simon Robinson, FRCOG, enjoyed the least. The patients at this clinic were all referred from GPs with requests for termination of pregnancy, or TOPs — in other words, abortions.

It was a joint clinic, which meant that responsibility was shared between several consultants who took it in turns to see the patients. All referrals from the General Practitioners were pooled, rather than allocated to a named consultant. The reason for this unusual arrangement was that the attitudes of the consultants to requests for TOPs inevitably varied, and if one was perceived by the referring doctors as being too harsh or too lenient with his decisions, it could have meant that the work-load was unfairly distributed. The system had led to this particular clinic being given the rather unfortunate name of the 'Abortion Pool'.

Simon was doing the TOP clinic that morning on behalf of his boss, Mr Roger D'Arcy, who was at a conference in London. There had been 23 patients, ranging from a girl of 15 who had become pregnant by a 29-year-old man on a one-night stand at a drinks party, to a 44-year-old woman with grown-up children, who had thought she was safe from pregnancy as her periods had ceased a year previously, and had stopped taking precautions.

These ladies were fortunately in early pregnancy, and Simon had agreed to every request except one.

Feeling rather weary, and looking forward to the start of his half-day off, he said goodbye to the last patient, and leaned back in his chair. He had been up in the night dealing with an ectopic pregnancy, and needed to relax.

The Sister in charge of the Out-patient Department put her head round the door.

'I'm very sorry, Mr Robinson, but there's been a mix-up.' She came into the office and closed the door. 'We seem to have got another patient for you.' She was clutching a manilla folder, the case notes. Simon tried not to show his irritation.

'Oh dear. Just when I thought I'd finished.'

'I know, I'm sorry. It was the appointments clerk — she thought she'd done the right thing. This girl was down to see Mr Greenwell, but of course he won't see the TOP requests as a rule.'

Jeremy Greenwell was the one consultant who did not take part in the 'Abortion Pool' at all. He was a Roman Catholic, and his colleagues recognised his right not to be involved on religious grounds.

'It certainly seems as though someone's made a mistake,' Simon had to agree.

'That's what the appointments clerk thought, so she changed her over to this clinic. I've only just been told about it.'

'I don't suppose we can put her off?' the Senior Registrar asked hopefully.

'Oh, no, poor lass. She's waiting right outside, and she looks in a bit of a state.'

Simon sighed with resignation.

'OK, send her in.' He was due to meet his wife, Kate, at the squash club for lunch. Oh well, she was used to him being late.

'Thank you, Mr Robinson.' Sister put the notes on the desk, and ushered in a slim, fair-haired girl, her hands clasped anxiously in front of her.

Simon could see how agitated she was, and tried to put her at her ease. He came round the desk, gave her a smile, and asked her to sit down. He brought his own chair from behind the desk so that he could sit nearer to her, more informally, without the desk being a barrier between them.

He glanced at the notes. 'Gemma Randall. Is that right?'

She tried, not very successfully, to return his smile.

'Yes, that's right.'

'And you've come to talk about an unwanted pregnancy.' He tried to sound gentle, but the girl looked away, at the floor.

'It's all right, I'm not here to judge you. I just want to talk to you about it, so we can make sure you understand what's involved, and then help you make the best decision about it.' He paused, looked at the notes. 'You're 21 and a student at Bournemouth Polytechnic, I see.'

'Yes. I'm reading mathematics.'

He gave her a broad grin. 'Ah, one of the clever ones. I never could get on with advanced maths. Even differential calculus was completely beyond me. I suppose you find it easy?'

That got a more genuine smile from her. Gradually Gemma relaxed, and told Simon her story. Despite her modest account of herself, it was apparent that she was a brilliant student, and this pregnancy was going to threaten a promising career. Simon wondered at first why such an intelligent person should run the risk of ruining everything for the sake of unprotected sex, but it became obvious that that was not the case.

10

She had a steady boyfriend, and they made love regularly. But they used condoms, and Gemma also used a spermicidal foam. They were clearly being conscientious and responsible with contraception. Furthermore, as Simon knew from the notes, she had not long before had a cervical polyp removed. She had been in this same hospital for a few days, and had assumed that because she had also had a D & C she would be unlikely to get pregnant for a while. There had been an incident, some seven weeks previously, when a sheath had come off before withdrawal was complete, although she had been using the foam. That might have been enough. Since then she had missed two periods.

As she related these events, Gemma became more and more upset, and was obviously fighting back the tears. Simon was experienced enough to know that this was no act. The girl's promising academic future was in jeopardy, and he felt a great deal of sympathy for her; by the sound of it she had been very unlucky. He felt she satisfied the terms of the Abortion Act. And although personal feelings shouldn't come into it, he liked her and wanted to help.

By the time he came to examine the girl, he had almost made up his mind.

'Let's have a look at you, then.' He called the Sister in, who took her to a side room and prepared her for examination.

Simon started by putting his hand on her abdomen, and immediately realised something was not as he expected. He could feel an enlarged uterus easily. That shouldn't be possible until a woman was at least twelve weeks pregnant — certainly not at seven. Gemma caught his look of consternation.

'What's wrong?' She looked up at him anxiously from the couch.

'Well, nothing really, but are you sure about your dates?'

'Positive. Why?'

'This bump of yours seems to suggest you're a lot farther on than you think.'

'Does that mean that — that you can't do it?'

'Not necessarily. But we ought to clear this up right now.' Simon turned to the Sister. 'Let's do a scan on her straight away.'

The nurse looked worried. 'I'm afraid the ultrasound technician's already gone for her lunch. She thought we'd finished here.'

Simon wasn't bothered. He often did scans himself, in fact he preferred it if he had the time. The three of them went along to the technician's room and he set the machine up. Sister went off to prepare for the ante-natal clinic that followed in the afternoon, and left him to it.

He settled down alongside his patient and gently began to move the probe over the girl's lower abdomen. The screen was facing him where she could not see it. Usually he liked the mother to share in the

11

experience of seeing her baby outlined in this way, but he did not think it appropriate for patients anticipating termination of pregnancy.

Simon felt quite relaxed. This was the last patient of the day, and he quite enjoyed using this advanced piece of technology, in which the scanned image was digitised, translated into pulses that could be interpreted by a computer. The computer then enhanced the picture, improving contrast and clarity of detail, giving an excellent 'real-time' view of the contents of the womb.

He moved the probe around, and got an increasingly clear picture of the baby. There was only one, not twins, which had been his first thought when he found Gemma large for her dates, and it was lying transversely, or across the uterus, which was not unusual in early pregnancy. He recognised almost immediately that this was much more than a seven-week foetus: it was nearer fifteen weeks, as he had suspected from his examination. Although the girl had only missed two periods, it was possible that she was this far advanced, as some women, albeit rarely, do continue to menstruate in the early months of pregnancy.

He reached for the measure by which he could calculate the width of the widest part of the baby's skull — the bi-parietal diameter. This measurement gave a very accurate indication of how old a foetus was, certainly to within a week. Sure enough, it was 32 millimetres, equivalent to a fifteen-week pregnancy. He was watching the movement of the baby's heart, which always fascinated him, when his eye was caught by a movement of the head. As it turned towards him, the face seemed to be shown in astonishing detail. He looked on, spell-bound; but then his interest turned to a sensation of ·shock, he felt cold, his scalp prickled.

As he looked at the fifteen-week-old face, it seemed to be staring *straight back at him*. He felt that it was gazing right into his soul.

Then the impossible happened. As he watched, the expression changed — he was sure he was not mistaken. The baby gave him a malevolent grin.

* * *

Simon watched Kate through the glass at the back of the squash court. He needn't have worried about being late — his wife was still playing. They had arranged to meet at the squash club as they both had a half-day. He looked down from the elevated balcony which was actually part of the bar, and admired the efficient way she moved about the court, obviously dominating her opponent, keeping command of the 'T' the whole time. She was serving, and her opponent managed for once to produce a return that Kate had to chase right up near the front wall. She reached out and flicked the ball

12

with her wrist; it floated up in a long loop, over her opponent's head, and died in the back left corner. It was a superb shot, and fittingly was match point. Kate turned smiling to her opponent and held out her hand. They walked off the court together, chatting animatedly, Kate demonstrating a shot as the door was held open for her.

Simon smiled to himself. She was quite a girl, his Kate. Self-assured and competent at most things, excellent at others. She enjoyed sport, and squash especially. She was technically better than Simon, and when they played together he always had to work hard to win. After a few moments Kate came up the stairs into the bar, saw Simon, and walked across, smiling broadly. She was flushed, and radiated health and energy. Her white sports shirt stuck to her, revealing pleasing curves. Simon was conscious of two men at the bar sizing her up appreciatively as she strode past them.

'Good game?' he asked as she approached.

Kate wiped sweat from her forehead with the sweatband on her wrist. 'Terrific! Have you been here long?'

'No, I got a bit held up at the Abortion Pool. I only saw the last few minutes of the massacre.'

Kate was modest. 'It wasn't a massacre.' She grinned. 'But I wasn't under too much pressure, I must admit.'

'What was the score?'

'Nine love, nine three.'

'In my book that's a massacre!'

'You're looking at it through the biased eyes of a proud husband. Now, where shall we go for lunch?'

'I thought we were eating here.'

'I fancy a change.'

'All right. How about that place on Poole Quay?'

'Fine by me. I'll just have a quick shower.'

'I'll wait here. And make sure you're not long — you know you're almost pathologically incapable of having a quick shower!'

An hour later Simon was looking out across the water near Poole Bridge. They had just had a ploughman's lunch and a glass of beer. All manner of sailing craft were moored above and below the bridge, and a small collier waited at the far end of the quay. There was quite a bit of activity, this being one of the first fine spells of the year, but Simon didn't notice. His mind was still trying to get rid of the image of that grinning face, like an animated gargoyle, looking out at him from the screen.

Kate watched her husband gazing distractedly into the distance. She could tell something was bothering him. He should be happy and relaxed; she didn't like to see him like this, just when everything seemed to be working out for them.

13

They hadn't been in Hampshire long. Only four months ago, at the age of thirty-four, he had made the most important move yet in his career, getting the post of Senior Registrar in Obstetrics and Gynaecology at the Princess Marina Hospital in Bournemouth. In four years or so he was virtually assured of becoming a consultant, thus securing his professional and financial future. On the strength of this appointment and his increased income, they had bought a larger house in Holdenhurst, a small village a few miles north-east of Bournemouth, near the River Stour. Now that he was a more senior member of staff he did not have to live so close to his work.

Despite all this, Kate could see that her husband was troubled.

'Penny for your thoughts.' She reached out to touch him, and he jumped. 'Sorry, love,' she said, 'but you were miles away.'

'I'm the one who should be sorry. I haven't been very good company for lunch, have I?'

'Want to tell me about it?' Kate was grateful that Simon did not often bring his work problems home with him, and when he did, he rarely spoke of them in detail. However, she always made sure he knew she would lend a sympathetic ear if needed.

Simon gazed out over the sunlit water again. He couldn't tell his wife what he'd seen, she would think he was going round the bend. He had already tried to persuade himself that he must have imagined it, but it had affected him badly. When the poor patient had seen his ashen face and shaking hands, she had become nearly hysterical, convinced her doctor had seen something terribly wrong — which in a way he had. It was hardly surprising that his attempted reassurances were not accepted. In the end he had had to agree to admit the girl there and then, to be sedated. He arranged for the ultrasound technician to do another examination that afternoon, and had decided to keep her in overnight and get his boss's opinion in the morning.

He realised his wife was still waiting patiently for an answer. 'It's just something that happened this morning,' he said, turning to her with a weak smile. 'I never like the Abortion Pool at the best of times, and D'Arcy was away today, so I had to make all the decisions . . .'

Kate understood her husband's dislike of the responsibilities of requests for termination of pregnancy. He was a sensitive man, and could not take the ending of a potential human life lightly. But he was compassionate, too, and always wanted to try and help his patients if he could. It was an infrequent but real dilemma in gynaecology and obstetrics — to help the mother, destroy the child.

The mother usually won with Simon. She was there, in front of him, vocal, pleading, tearful, desperate. The foetus was just a little clump of cells hidden away in the darkness of the womb, and could not state its case. The mother was an entity that might come back to

14

haunt him if she delivered a malformed infant, or attempted suicide because her request was denied, or if her boyfriend or husband deserted her, leaving her to cope with the unwanted baby alone. The tiny foetus could not exert those pressures.

At least, not until now. He had looked this one in the eye. He felt as if, somehow, it seemed to know him. Would its spirit remember him if it was destroyed? Would Simon himself remember *it*? He knew the answer to that, beyond doubt.

Kate interrupted his reverie. 'My, you are thoughtful today.' She stroked the dark hair at the back of his neck. 'Was it as bad as all that?'

'Sorry. Again. I'll be all right. Let's go for a walk, and choose our next gin-palace.'

Simon was tall, nearly six feet, and his arm went comfortably around Kate's shoulders as they strolled along the quay. They both liked the sea and ships, and when they came down here they often played a game of choosing the grandest motor yacht or ocean-going racer on view, and planning a round-the-world voyage in it. One of their ambitions was to own a sailing cruiser and travel abroad in it, but establishing career and income had to come first.

There was another ambition they shared which helped explain Simon's ambivalent feelings towards the abortion clinic: Kate was desperate to start a family, and Simon himself was almost as keen. For reasons of finance and career advancement, they had taken stringent precautions against pregnancy earlier in their marriage. Kate was a midwife, and her income had helped them get a good start on the housing ladder. They had stopped using contraception nearly two years ago, and, like many couples, had not thought about any problems in achieving pregnancy. That Kate had failed to do so as yet made it all the harder for Simon to agree to discard all those unwanted progeny without some thought.

His heart wasn't in the gin-palace game, and Kate soon sensed that it was time to give up. 'Look, my love, this is no good. You're so distracted. What are you thinking about now?'

They had stopped by a tall bollard near the end of the quay. Simon leaned on it, his arms resting on the top. Kate put her arm across his back. 'Tell me what's worrying you. Please.'

He told a half-truth. 'I was thinking about you having a baby.'

'It'll happen soon, don't worry.'

Simon admired his wife's stoicism, but worried that she might be hiding her true feelings to protect him.

'I've been thinking,' he began slowly, 'that perhaps you might like to give up your job, now that my salary can cover our outgoings and a bit more. Help you concentrate on the task in hand, so to speak.'

Kate looked at him sharply. 'You ought to know me better than

that,' she said. '**I'm capable of doing a respon**sible job well, **and I'd**
much rather be doing that than sitting around at home wasting my
training and my abilities. Many women would give their eye teeth to
do a job like mine. I'd be letting them all down if I just wasted my
opportunities and sat around at home.' She thought for a moment
and then went on. 'When I eventually do get pregnant I'll want to go
on working and being normally active for as long as possible — at
least until I can't get into the uniform. If Fergie can go skiing, I can go
on working and playing squash.'

Simon had to smile. 'Sorry I spoke.'

Kate smiled back. 'Well, really! Give up work? And do what? Take
up needlepoint and sit on my backside watching TV all day?'

'It's just that it's been a long time now that we've been trying.'

'I'm all right, Simon, honestly.' She was trying to make light of it.

'You don't have to pretend, love, I know how much you want one.
And so do I.'

'It'll soon be all sorted out, you'll see. A quick blow up the old
tubes, and — bingo!'

Simon shook his head at her light-hearted description of the
investigation she was due to have the following week. Jeremy
Greenwell, the anti-abortion Consultant Obstetrician, was going to
do it. It was the next step along the line in getting the reasons for her
infertility sorted out. They'd had some tears and laughter along the
way already, but this would be the 'big one'.

For eighteen months they had put off asking for medical help, since
Simon knew that most consultants don't entertain investigating delay
in conception until after about two years of trying. But although they
had done all the right things, still nothing had happened. Each
morning for the previous six months Kate had taken her temperature,
looking for the sudden rise about mid-cycle that would indicate
ovulation. Most times it was not very obvious, certainly not the clear-
cut jump in temperature shown in the example in the front of the
book of charts.

On one occasion, however, about three months ago, it had been
very obvious. Kate had a day off, and had rung Simon at work. He'd
gone in to the hospital in the small hours to deal with a difficult
forceps delivery and had planned to stay on there, but Kate was
insistent he come home.

'This is it!' she shouted excitedly down the phone. 'If there isn't an
egg there just ready and waiting, I'm a Dutchman! And — ' her voice
dropped to a seductive whisper — 'I want you to come and fertilise it
right now!'

And so he did. It seemed a bit strange, coming home at 9.30 in the
morning and getting into bed with his wife for a purely clinical act of
insemination. Simon didn't think he was going to make it at first. He

16

got very agitated, and was about to get up and go back to work. But Kate wasn't going to give up that easily.

'Come on, husband,' she urged, and gently coaxed him into action. In anticipation of the situation, they hadn't had intercourse for several days as the middle of Kate's menstrual cycle had approached. Simon therefore eventually achieved a particularly satisfactory ejaculation.

'Well,' he said, 'mission accomplished. I gave it both barrels! If that doesn't do it . . .'

'You're telling me,' said Kate, lying back.

Simon smiled. 'You look like the cat that got the cream.'

'I just did!' They both chuckled for some time at that.

Kate was three days late with her period that month, and when it started, just as she was beginning to get her hopes up, she was bitterly disappointed. Simon came home the afternoon she started bleeding and found her crying on the bed. That was quite out of character for Kate, who usually dealt with life's more difficult moments philosophically. He decided then that the time had come to use his influence and get some tests done. Kate already knew Simon's new boss, D'Arcy, too well socially to be comfortable with him in such an intimate matter. They had elected to approach Jeremy Greenwell because he seemed gentle and sympathetic, and — equally important — he took a special interest in fertility problems. He used to joke that as a Catholic he was bound to be dedicated to increasing the population. He knew his stuff, and although he was rather remote and a bit pompous, he seemed to know how to promote positive attitudes in his patients. In many hospitals, sessions devoted to difficulties with conception were called 'Infertility Clinics'. Greenwell would not have that. They were the opposite, he said, and woe betide anyone who did not refer to them as 'Fertility Clinics'.

There had been other amusing, and embarrassing, moments. First, Simon had to provide a sample of his semen. Clearly it was no use investigating Kate extensively if the problem was with him. He was given a plastic pot, and endured lots of jokes about retiring to the bathroom with a copy of *Playboy*.

He felt very awkward about it, and it gave him fresh insight into how his patients must feel. He had given countless men instructions on providing semen samples, but had never really thought in any detail about actually doing it. He knew it was no good collecting the sample in a condom during intercourse, because the sheaths were impregnated with spermicides that would ruin the test.

In the end Kate, good old understanding, down-to-earth Kate, had done it for him. Well, in a manner of speaking. Simon remembered thinking, as he spurted into the container, that he hoped it was a decent quantity. He didn't want his pathologist friend to think he was in any way inadequate. He arrived at the laboratory at the appointed hour, sheepishly carrying his specimen, to be greeted by a bawdy cheer from the lab technicians. There was no anonymity for the medical staff in a hospital; sometimes being part of the team made things harder, not easier, he reflected.

His sperm count showed he had no problems. 'A drop of good stuff,' a friend from the Path Lab told him later that day. So next it was the post-coital test.

For this the couple being investigated had to have intercourse at an appointed time, the woman attending a clinic at the hospital soon after, when samples of the male ejaculate would be taken from her vagina. The object of this was, firstly, to make sure the semen was ending up in the right place — not everyone knew what they were doing, as Simon had found out on more than one occasion. Secondly, by seeing what percentage of the sperms were still active, the chance of their survival during the long journey through the uterus and into the fallopian tubes, where they would meet the egg coming the other way, could be assessed. For some reason, some women secreted mucus from the neck of the womb, or cervix, which was hostile to their partner's sperm and seemed to kill them off, or at least slowed them down so much that they could not make it to the meeting with the egg.

The post-coital test was therefore useful, as Simon knew well enough, but it was hardly romantic. It was a good thing that they both had a sense of humour, and were not embarrassed with each other where their bodies and sex were concerned. They frequently walked around naked, they never wore anything in bed, and they always made love with the light on. Neither of them could understand why anyone would want to do otherwise, although they knew friends who did.

On the appointed morning, at the appointed hour, they lay in bed looking at each other. Kate was the more anxious this time, as it was she who had to go through the subsequent intimate examination. Although as a midwife she had done enough vaginal examinations herself not to be embarrassed about it, somehow the association of the examination with recent intercourse made it different. She had learnt from both doctors and nurses alike that any internal examination was regarded as something quite asexual; but somehow she felt there was a sexual aspect to this examination, although she could not explain why.

Simon moved close to Kate, so that their bodies touched along their whole length. He gently began to caress her breasts, squeezing her nipples gently, trying to arouse her. As he reached down, expecting to feel her moistness, she was quite dry.

'I'm sorry, love. I keep thinking about the examination. I know Jeremy Greenwell is very nice, but . . .'

18

'He *is* very nice, and he's a gentleman — and an innocent.'

She turned to him, curious. 'What do you mean, an innocent?'

'Well, he never tells jokes, not smutty ones, anyway, and doesn't recognise one even when he's made it.'

'You obviously have an example in mind.'

He had. 'I was helping him in theatre last week — you remember, when John Dunston, his Registrar, was away at that interview, and he was talking to a woman in the prep room. He always likes to have a word with the patients before they go under, to remind himself of the person behind the case, as he puts it. He likes to tell his new doctors how easy it is to get a distorted view of people when you only look at them from one end.'

'Do get on with it, love.' Kate was now beginning to worry about the time, as well as her failure to respond.

'OK. This lady, who is not the most cultured of women, goes on about her vaginal problems in graphic detail. When she's finished, Greenwell says to her, all smooth and reassuring, "Don't worry, my dear, I'll look into it." The woman gives him a grin and says, "Well I hope you don't fall in, duckie." We were all in tucks, but he just didn't see it! "Did I say something amusing?" he says, and stalks off into the theatre.'

Kate had to smile, and then they both got a fit of the giggles. As they settled down again she was more relaxed and this time responded to Simon's advances.

The post-coital test showed nothing wrong. The next stage, therefore, was to test the patency of Kate's fallopian tubes. She was producing eggs — biochemistry tests on blood and urine proved that — and there was nothing to stop Simon's perfectly healthy sperm getting to her uterus. So — were the tubes that linked the ovaries to the womb open or blocked? If they were blocked there was no way eggs and sperm could meet. To find out, a dye that showed up on X-ray would be injected into the uterus through the neck of the womb, and if it filled the tubes and spilled out at the other end — then there was no blockage.

This, then, was the 'quick blow', as Kate had so flippantly called it, that was scheduled to be carried out by Greenwell the following week. If that was all right, then they had just been unlucky so far and there was no reason why she should not conceive — sooner or later.

Simon had been quiet a long time, gazing over the water.

'Come on, love, let's go home.' Kate turned Simon's face towards her, a hand on either cheek, and gave him a gentle kiss. 'It'll all be all right, you'll see. Mr Micawber, remember?'

He smiled at her. 'Well, he hasn't let us down yet.' Over the years, like most ambitious young couples, they had overcome a number of problems — some financial, some practical, some political. Whenever they were struggling and there seemed no way to make progress, they always quoted Mr Micawber, and told each other that 'something would turn up'. So far, it always had, and mentioning him was like touching a favourite talisman.

That night they made love, slowly, gently, free from thoughts of conception. Kate had only just finished her period, so this was just for the pleasure of it, without the nagging feeling that crept into Simon's mind of late whenever they had sex about the time of Kate's fertile period — the feeling that he was performing a service of insemination rather than an act of love and enjoyment.

Simon seldom dreamed, or at least if he did he could hardly ever recall anything. This night was one of those rare occasions. He awoke to find Kate shaking him. At first he thought it was a part of his dream. He was trembling with fear and anger. The light blinded him for a moment when Kate switched it on, making him shield his eyes. She smoothed his hair and was surprised to find it wet with sweat.

'Are you all right, love?'

He tried to reassure her, heart still racing.

'Yes — yes, I'm OK. Just a bad dream, I think.'

'Must have been pretty awful. Whatever was it about?'

'You know me, can't remember. Falling down a hole or something, I expect.'

Kate fussed over him a little more, then put the light out, snuggled in to him, and went back to sleep. Simon lay there in the dark for some time. In fact he could for once remember his dream in stark detail, but he had been unable to bring himself to tell Kate what it was.

He had been dreaming that her tubes had been tested, that she had quickly become pregnant and they were both radiantly happy. He was at her bedside, holding her hand, urging her on as she finally pushed a daughter out into the world. The midwife wrapped their baby in a sheet and handed it to him with an anxious look on her face. Simon looked down at the face of his child, and his feelings of pride and happiness changed dramatically. It was the same face he had seen on the ultrasound screen that morning.

2

Gemma Randall, her long blonde hair straggled about her face, sat in her bed that first evening in hospital trying not to cry. She was frightened and confused. She was quite convinced that there was something terribly wrong with her. The look on the doctor's face as he watched the TV screen had really alarmed her. She was certain he did not mean his reassuring words, and when the proposed second scan was put off because of a 'malfunction in the machine', she was not fooled. They were hiding something, that was obvious. What could worry the medical staff so much in a young woman? She had convinced herself of the answer: it could only be cancer.

At about 8.30 her boyfriend, Mike, who was also a student, came to see her, and she confided her fears to him. He became angry and immediately went to find out more about it. He approached the staff nurse on duty.

'Your girlfriend is only in for observation,' she said reassuringly. 'There's nothing down here in the cardex about cancer.'

He was unconvinced. 'Look, she's getting herself in a right state. Are you sure there's nothing else?'

The Staff Nurse looked resentful, then relented.

'I'll look in the medical record if it'll make you feel any easier.'

'Please. I'd be very grateful.'

'No,' the nurse spoke emphatically after she'd scanned the notes. 'Nothing out of the ordinary. No mention of anything unusual.'

Her boyfriend's assurances were not enough to convince Gemma, however, and she cried herself to sleep despite the two capsules of temazepam given to sedate her.

Simon set off for the hospital the next morning, impatient to discover the result of the second ultrasound scan he'd ordered on the girl who had caused him so much consternation the day before.

He rushed up to the ward to speak to the Ward Sister.

'I'm sorry, Mr Robinson, but another ultrasound wasn't done.'

Simon was exasperated. 'Not done? Why?'

'The technician came back in the afternoon and said there was a fault on the machine.'

Simon's annoyance, however, soon turned to a feeling of relief. If the machine was malfunctioning, that might explain the strange

21

image he'd seen the previous afternoon. He left Sister's office and went to see the girl. By the time he reached Gemma's bedside he'd made up his mind how he was going to play this one. The girl wanted a termination, and he had to offer her some sort of explanation for his behaviour the day before. He'd got one ready.

He pulled the curtains around the bed and gave her what he hoped was a reassuringly warm smile. Poor kid, she looks awful, he thought, settling himself on the edge of the bed. Many of the senior nurses frowned upon his habit of sitting on the bed, but he felt it was much better than towering formidably over his patients so that they had to squint up at him, and he liked any informality that helped them to relax.

It was obvious to Simon that Gemma had been crying and he waited for her to compose herself, but she kept dabbing at her eyes, refusing to meet his gaze. He reached out and gently pulled her hand away from her face.

'Come on, it can't be as bad as all that.'

She sniffed, gave him a brief glance, and said almost accusingly, 'No one will talk to me.'

'Well, I've come to talk to you.' He gave her another smile. 'So — what's been upsetting you?'

Gemma knew she was afraid to ask. There was a long pause.

'Have you changed your mind?' Simon prompted.

Gemma was momentarily confused. In her ceaseless agonising about her own fate, she had almost forgotten what had brought her here in the first place. 'Oh, the baby. No — it's not that.'

Simon was puzzled. What the devil was it, then? Boyfriend not standing by her? Parents finding out? He coaxed a little more. 'Just tell me about it. Perhaps I can help.'

Help! Of course you can help! What a stupid question! Gemma's feelings were anger now as much as worry. Her self-control deserted her. She looked at him and shouted, forgetting that others beyond the curtains could hear. 'I want to know what in God's name is wrong with me!'

There was a momentary silence in the activities of the ward, before one of the staff nurses put her head round the curtain. 'Do you need me, Mr Robinson?'

He held up his hand. 'No, thanks, I'll sort it out.' He turned back to the girl, who was now sobbing helplessly. 'I'm not sure I know what you mean, Gemma, but let me assure you there's nothing wrong with you apart from the pregnancy.'

She looked at him defiantly. 'Come on!' She blew her nose noisily. 'What about the scan, then? I saw the look on your face. And the technician was even too scared to come and do another one in the afternoon.'

Simon grasped the situation immediately. He cursed himself. He should have realised before! So often patients get hold of the wrong impression and build up the wrong conclusion in their minds, and if no one acts to correct that impression, an almost impenetrable barrier of confusion and mistrust arises. Communication with the patient was so important — he always emphasised that when he was teaching students. 'Always tell the patient what's going on,' he'd say. 'They're not daft. They'll understand, better than you might think, and then they'll trust you all the more.' Yet here he was, not listening to his own advice. He had left this poor girl in the dark, and she had assumed there was something terribly wrong with her.

He put his hand on her forearm and looked directly at her. 'Believe me, Gemma, there is *nothing* wrong with you. I promise. Honestly, the only reason another scan wasn't done was because the machine packed up.' He took a deep breath. Oh well, here we go. All the more reason now to go ahead with his version of the truth. The girl was looking at him, a glimmer of hope beginning to show in her eyes.

'Tell me something, and be honest. It's important.'

Gemma sniffed. 'What?'

'Are you quite sure you want to have this pregnancy terminated?'

She thought for a long moment, going over once more the ground she'd covered several times already. Was she being selfish? Was it really 'taking a life' like the anti-abortion people were always saying? Would she spend the rest of her life feeling guilty? Then her thoughts turned to hopes of a career. She wanted to be married, to have a family. One day. But not yet. There was so much learning, so much living she wanted to do first. She knew that if she had to give up all those hopes and dreams now, she would spend the rest of her life wondering about the might-have-been. She might grow to resent the child, hate it even, for denying her the chance to find out what she might achieve. And Mike — he would feel he had to marry her, and would he too perhaps grow to resent her for stifling his own ambitions? One day she would be a wonderful loving mother to a much loved and wanted child. But not now. Not yet. There was only one answer.

'Yes.' She looked directly at the doctor. 'Yes, I'm quite sure I want this pregnancy terminated.'

'Then this may help you a little.' He spoke gently, trying to make sure that what he was about to say was put in the right way. 'I understand now why you're so upset, and it's really all my fault, and I truly am very sorry.'

Gemma looked at him in surprise. She had not had that many dealings with doctors, but her limited experiences and the media images had taught her that this particular species were not like ordinary mortals. They generally thought their word was law and

23

would not countenance any criticism. And yet here was one who admitted he was at fault, and was apologising for it. Before she could frame a response, he continued.

'What I saw on the screen yesterday was not something wrong with *you*. It was the baby.' That at least was true.

He had her complete attention now. 'The — the baby? What was — is wrong with it?'

'I should have said something then. It would have saved you all this worry. I was waiting for the second scan, so I — '

'Please, what's wrong with it?' Another pause.

'It has a malformation. Of the head.' Well, that's what I thought, Simon told himself as he tried to justify his course of action.

The girl looked at him for a long time, then hung her head. 'What you're trying to tell me is that I ought to have a termination anyway.'

Simon had never been anything other than totally honest with his patients in the past. If a woman looked him in the eye and said, 'Tell me what's wrong. I want to know,' he always told her, whether it was something trivial or whether it was cancer. He wasn't finding this easy. He made himself look directly at her. 'That's about it.'

'Can you show me — are there any pictures . . . ?'

Simon hadn't expected that one. Damn! He hadn't thought this through carefully enough. It was true that they often took polaroid pictures of the screen to keep a permanent record, and on such an occasion of finding a malformation he would certainly have done so. The fact was, he had been so distracted by what he saw that he had completely forgotten about taking a picture. 'I'm sorry, but the camera wasn't available.' That sounded terribly weak. 'We — we'd run out of film.'

Another long silence. Gemma was an intelligent girl, and was trying to rationalise her situation as much as possible. 'What sort of malformation was it exactly? I did "A" level biology so I know something about foetuses and embryology.'

Simon felt himself begin to sweat. This was not working out at all as he had planned. He had expected the girl just to breathe a sigh of relief, be grateful even, that she was absolved of the responsibility of the decision. He was offering her a cast-iron reason for termination, while at the same time explaining away his reaction of the previous day. He had thought it would be simple. Yet here he was, having told one little white lie, and now having to tell several more, each one getting a shade darker.

'It was microcephaly.'

'Oh.' She frowned and looked up at him. 'What does that mean?'

What devilish spirit had made him choose that particularly unpleasant abnormality? Simon asked himself. This was getting ridiculous. He could scar this girl for life here if he wasn't careful, give her a fear of giving birth to some sort of monster if she ever became pregnant again. He'd have to play it down. 'It's a condition where the brain doesn't form properly. It's rather small, and so is the skull — hence the name.' He assumed she'd understand that. He went on quickly and earnestly. 'But it's not hereditary. It's a chance in a million, and it couldn't happen again to you.'

She looked at him for a moment, then gave him a sad smile. She reached out and took his hand, her eyes still wet with tears. 'Thank you. Thank you for telling me. It helps more than you know.'

Bloody hell! Here he was telling the poor kid a load of crap like this, all because he had let his imagination run away with him, and she was thanking him for lying to her. He didn't know how to respond, so said nothing.

Looking suddenly self-conscious, Gemma pulled her hand away. 'What happens now?'

God, yes, what does happen now? Have to get on with it, close this nightmarish episode as soon as possible, Simon decided.

'As you're already in here, we might as well keep you, and put you on the list for tomorrow morning.' Another thought struck him. 'One more thing — I can't remember if I told you yesterday — you're much farther on in pregnancy than you might have thought: about fifteen weeks, in fact.'

'Fifteen weeks! But that's impossible!'

Simon gave her a crooked smile and shrugged, palms outwards.

'In medicine almost anything's possible. Ladies getting their dates wrong happens all the time. Especially if they menstruate in early pregnancy, as a few do.'

Gemma bit her lower lip. 'Will it make any difference to the — to the operation?'

'Not much — a little bit more to it, that's all. And all the more reason to get it done as soon as we can.'

Gemma relaxed. The decision was made. She wasn't going to die of cancer, there was a good reason for the termination to be done, and it would all be over tomorrow.

'Thanks again, doctor. I'll sleep easier tonight, I know that.'

Which is more than I will, thought Simon as he walked away. At the door to the ward he turned to give Gemma an encouraging wave, when a thought struck him. It made him feel so faint that he had to get quickly to the visitors' waiting room and sit down. His mind had just looked into the network of deceit he had woven with his fabrications, and seen that he had ensnared himself.

Microcephaly was a rare disorder. He would never be able to persuade his boss to undertake the termination without seeing this most uncommon abnormality for himself on a scan, perhaps even wanting to write it up for a paper in one of the medical journals. And even if he could talk him out of that, the pathologists would certainly want to get their hands on it. He sat there in a cold sweat for several minutes, wishing he had never got himself into such a mess. He had never done anything like this before, never been dishonest or untruthful, yet here in the space of 24 hours he was deceiving patients and colleagues alike. All because of what? Because of something he *thought* he had seen at the end of a busy Abortion Pool. But dammit, he had seen it, and he wanted to get rid of it — from his mind and from the body of this poor girl — whatever it was.

He worked out what he would have to do now. Two doctors who had seen the patient were always needed to authorise a termination of pregnancy. This they did by both signing the 'Green Form', a statutory document on which both doctors confirmed that they had seen and examined the patient and also confirmed that the requirements of the Abortion Act were satisfied in that particular case. Often the referral letter from the General Practitioner was accompanied by a Green Form, with Part I already signed by the referring doctor. This speeded things up and showed that the GP considered it a *bona fide* case. Simon knew there was such a signed Green Form in Gemma's notes. He only had to add his own signature to Part II to make it legal, so that the termination could go ahead. There was only one other proviso. He would have to do the termination himself. Quickly and quietly.

3

It did not take any great powers of observation on Kate's part to tell that Simon was still preoccupied with something the next morning.

'Is everything all right, love?' she asked when she came downstairs in her dressing-gown to find him helping himself to breakfast a good three-quarters of an hour earlier than usual.

He looked up from his cornflakes. 'Fine. Really.' He finished swallowing. 'Why?'

'You didn't say a word when you got up. And here you are rushing off.'

'Got an extra case on the list.' He drank some coffee, and nearly spat it out because it was too hot.

'That's no problem, is it?' She considered a moment. 'Are you sure no one's upset you?'

'Kate, please, there's nothing wrong.' He tried not to sound testy.

Kate detected the signs. 'Sorry. Just trying to help.' Simon stood up, wiped his mouth and gave her the briefest kiss on the cheek. ''Bye, love.'

Kate watched him grab his coat and rush out of the door. *Something's* bothering him, she thought. I'll ask him about it tonight. She went back upstairs to prepare herself for her own day's work.

On Friday mornings Simon and his boss, Roger D'Arcy, used the two main theatres for one of the two major lists of routine gynaecological surgery carried out each the week. They always planned the lists carefully beforehand. Simon, now an experienced surgeon in his own right, would operate in Theatre Two with the house surgeon assisting, while D'Arcy would operate in Theatre One with the Junior Registrar. If there was some unusual or complex procedure, Simon would arrange to assist D'Arcy himself, as he was still in effect in a training post and would anyway welcome the chance to broaden his experience. On these occasions the Junior Registrar would operate on some minor cases in Theatre Two so that it was not idle in Simon's absence.

The proposed operating lists did not always work out as planned. A patient might not turn up, a doctor might see some urgent case in the out-patients that could not wait its turn, or there might be a complication with a patient on the ward who needed to go back to theatre. So on this particular Friday morning it was not too unusual or

27

difficult for Simon to arrange with the Theatre Sister to start his list half an hour early. The extra procedure was the TOP on Gemma Randall, and the reason he gave was that she was already fifteen weeks, and that she was also very emotionally distressed and could not wait until the usual TOP list the following Monday.

Simon stood in the theatre, already scrubbed and gowned, waiting for his patient. The anaesthetist, a normally cheerful red-headed Welshman, Gwyn Reece, was late. Simon's desire to make an early start had affected the whole theatre team, from porters to nurses, as well as the anaesthetic staff. Gwyn had indulged in a hard night's drinking at the Rugby Club the evening before, and although he and Simon got on well together, he was not too happy at being deprived of some of his recovery time.

He slipped the needle expertly into a vein on the back of Gemma Randall's hand and automatically asked her to start counting to ten as he pushed in the plunger. Gemma got as far as four.

'Morning, Gwyn.'

As Gemma was wheeled in Simon tried to sound relaxed and cheerful, which was far from the case. He was sweating nervously, and his mouth was dry from the excess adrenaline that was circulating in his bloodstream.

'Morning, you keen bastard.'

Such a form of address was not unusual for Gwyn, but Simon was surprised at the vehemence of his friend's reply.

'What's up with you, then?'

'Oh, nothing much,' he said mournfully. He had a just discernible Welsh accent. 'Just that you've dragged me out of bed early for this.' He nodded at the unconscious Gemma, who was now also paralysed by a muscle relaxant. Gwyn had inserted a tube into her trachea, the main airway into her lungs, and now she was dependent for her breathing on the Welshman squeezing a black bag attached to the hoses delivering the mixture of anaesthetic gas and oxygen. 'It's just that I could have been lying in bed letting my liver metabolise the remaining poisons in my system after last night's session.'

The porters had by now transferred Gemma to the operating table, and the Theatre Sister and a student nurse were putting up the lithotomy poles. These fitted either side of the operating table and towards one end. They were about eighteen inches high, and towards the top of each was a small sling in which Gemma's feet were now suspended. This meant that her legs were held apart with her feet and knees up in the air, so that her vaginal area was fully exposed and accessible to the surgeon. Finally, the part of the table on which her legs had been lying before they were put in the slings was folded down, so that her bottom was right on the edge of the operating table.

It is hardly surprising that after such contortions, sometimes maintained for long periods of time, patients often complain of aching hip joints.

When Gemma was properly set up in this most inelegant of positions, the Theatre Sister and her nurse assistant draped green linen towels like huge loose stockings over her legs. Finally another dressing towel was placed so as to cover the area between her legs. This towel had an opening cut in it, so that when it was in place, the only part of Gemma's lower body to remain exposed was the vulva, or outer part of the vagina.

While all this preparation was going on, Simon's imagination was running riot, and he tried to suppress fanciful ideas of what he might find when he removed the foetus. He was normally reasonably relaxed about operating: he was competent and confident, and knew he was good without being arrogant about it. But this was something altogether different, and he did not like the feelings of anxiety that were sweeping over him. The last occasion he had felt like this was the first time he had performed a hysterectomy completely unsupervised, which was now many years ago. Then, however, the anxiety had been tempered with a feeling of excitement and eagerness to show what he could do. Now, he only felt nauseous, a little shaky, and had trouble controlling his breathing.

His tensions must have shown, because he was brought back to the situation in hand by Gwyn calling across to him. It was a moment or two before Simon realised he was being addressed.

'Hey! Is there anybody there?'

Simon was uncharacteristically flustered as he tried to marshal his thoughts.

'Sorry, Gwyn, what were you saying?'

'Are you all right, old chap? You look as if you've seen a ghost.'

That was a bit too near the mark for Simon, who felt slightly weak. 'No, I'm OK, thanks.'

'Are you sure?' There was a distinct edge of concern in his friend's voice.

'Yes, I'm sure, really.'

Simon sounded positive enough, and reassured by this, Gwyn reverted to type.

'In that case, get your arse in gear and let's get this done so I can pour another cup of coffee inside me!'

Simon moved over to the operating table, where Gemma Randall's external genitalia were exposed awaiting his attentions. As he moved in close, holding his hands up to make sure they didn't touch anything unsterile, one of the operating theatre nurses positioned a stool behind him so that he could sit down. He could not do this himself without contaminating his sterile gloves. Satisfied that he was in the correct position and at the right height, and feeling increasingly tense, he began with much trepidation what should have been so routine a task that normally he hardly thought about it.

He began by swabbing the vulval area with an antiseptic solution, then, parting the lips of the vagina with the thumb and index finger of one hand, he inserted a metal speculum with the other. The operating light was positioned over his right shoulder, and was adjusted by a theatre technician until it illuminated clearly the neck of Gemma's womb. The small opening in the cervix was what Simon was looking for, and, using a pair of long-handled forceps which expanded at the end into small oval pads, he inserted one pad into the canal of the cervix so that the other was left outside. By carefully closing the forceps he was able to grip the neck of the womb and pull it gently downwards, thereby bringing it more fully in view.

Simon began to sweat as he asked for the dilators. These were a series of graduated probes, each one a little larger than the last. By inserting them into the cervical canal, starting with the smallest and using successively larger ones, he was able slowly to stretch and enlarge the cervical canal without damaging it, and thus gain access to the cavity of the womb itself. He was normally quite dispassionate about terminations, but now he found his mind was thinking things that did not usually bother him. In there, he thought, as he passed the last dilator, the foetus lay, unsuspecting, waiting to be destroyed. He paused for a moment, and to try and help himself get away from his thoughts, he spoke to Gwyn at the other end of the table. 'Everything all right up there?'

'Yes, fine. What are you faffing about at, mate? Get on with it, will you?'

'Sorry.'

'I should bloody well think so. Booze always gives me a diuresis and my bladder is about to burst. If I don't get a break soon I'll have to ask our pretty young Sister here to hold something besides that instrument she's got in her hand.'

The Theatre Sister, who was far from being young and could not even charitably be described as pretty, frowned at this male chauvinism, but there was a snigger of amusement from the other theatre staff.

Simon took a deep breath and picked up the curette, a long-handled instrument that had a small spoon-shaped depression in one end. The edge of the 'spoon' was sharpened. Its purpose was to be passed into the womb where it could be used to macerate and break up the contents, scrape off any attachments, including the placenta or afterbirth, from the wall of the uterus, and by repeatedly inserting it and removing it with a scooping action, encourage the contents of the uterus to come out. He also had a suction catheter ready to help evacuate any residue.

30

It was a messy business, and one of the few times Simon had thought he might faint in an operating theatre was when he had witnessed his first abortion. The mixture of congealed blood and thankfully unrecognisable foetal parts pouring out of the patient's uterus and into a receptacle held between the surgeon's knees had made him feel sick and weak. He had seen plenty of blood and gore before — that didn't bother him; but there was some psychological overtone in this business that troubled him. He had got over it now, of course. It was just another job. This, at least, was what he was telling himself as he prepared to insert the curette.

He had paused while these thoughts raced through his head, and once again the anaesthetist's impatience brought him back to earth. 'For Christ's sake, get on with it, man!'

'Sorry — don't know what's the matter with me this morning.' He noticed the Theatre Sister, who was standing next to him, giving him a curious look.

'You're sweating, Mr Robinson. Are you sure you're all right?'

Good grief, thought Simon, I must look rough if the old dragon's noticed. He braced himself, and plunged the curette into the cavity of Gemma Randall's womb, through the sac of the watery amniotic fluid which immediately flowed out, and then penetrated the resisting tissues of her unwanted baby.

He felt an extraordinary sensation go up his right arm. His first and only thought was that he must have had an electric shock. His vision went grey, then black, and he felt his hand twitching uncontrollably.

The next thing he was aware of was fighting against an oxygen mask in the recovery room, where he was lying on a trolley with Gwyn looking anxiously down on him.

He tried to get up, but Gwyn pushed him back again, put down the oxygen mask and leaned over to turn off the flow from the wall-mounted supply. He was white-faced and as agitated as Simon had ever seen him.

'What's up?' Simon's mouth was dry, his voice weak. 'Did I faint or something?' He looked anxiously from the anaesthetist to the young nurse who was standing well away by the door.

Gwyn turned and put his hand up against the wall, resting his forehead on it, paused a moment, turned abruptly back. 'I don't know what in God's name you did, but this is one hell of a mess!'

Simon sat up, and this time Gwyn did not try and prevent him.

'What's going on?' He felt sick, light-headed, sensed disaster. 'What's happened to Gemma?'

'Christ, what were you *doing* to her?'

'What do you mean? I was doing a TOP! Is she all right?'

'All right?' Gwyn almost shouted. 'Bloody hell!'

Simon swung his legs over the side of the trolley and put his feet to the ground. His head swam for a moment, then cleared. He started for the operating theatre doors.

Gwyn moved across quickly, barring his way. 'Wait! For Christ's sake let them sort it out.'

Simon looked at his friend's eyes, full of alarm, darting quickly to the theatre doors and then back to his face. He felt afraid.

'Who the hell are *they*?'

'D'Arcy and Cohen, of course.'

His boss and a consultant anaesthetist. 'Oh, shit! For God's sake, what the hell is going on?'

'You perforated her bloody uterus, you dull bugger!'

Simon was stunned. He sat back on the trolley and thought he was going to pass out again. Gwyn was telling him that somehow the curette had punctured the wall of Gemma's womb. The consequences could be disastrous. A uterine blood vessel could tear, leading to profuse bleeding. Nearby bowel could be perforated, leading to peritonitis and shock. Even the bladder might be damaged . . . But how? He went over what he could remember. He recalled dilating the cervix, then being given the curette, passing it into the cervical canal, then — what was it? He thought he had received an electric shock. But after that . . .

'Tell me what happened, Gwyn,' he said, almost in a whisper. 'I — I can't remember.'

Gwyn looked incredulous. 'You can't remember? What do you mean, you can't remember? Your hand was pushing that curette in and out of her sodding uterus like a piston on the Coronation Scot!'

Simon felt another wave of nausea, and covered his face with both hands.

'Oh, my God! Honestly, Gwyn, I don't remember anything after I inserted the curette, except I thought I got an electric shock.'

'Electric shock? It was more like a bloody epileptic fit!'

'Please, Gwyn — just tell me exactly what happened.' His friend looked at him, heard the desperation in his voice.

'Please!' Simon repeated.

Gwyn stopped his agitated pacing and sat on the trolley next to Simon. He pinched the bridge of his nose with his fingers as if to help the recollection, then looked up at his colleague.

'OK. You asked the old dragon for the curette, and she gave it to you. I wasn't really paying much attention to what was going on at your end, and couldn't see much, but suddenly Sister shrieks out, "Mr Robinson!" and I look up and she's grabbing your right hand, which is going crazy, jerking backwards and forwards. I was coming round to see what the hell was going on, when you just went rigid, your eyes wide open, though they didn't look as if they were seeing anything. Then you just flaked out. Hit the floor with quite a thump, despite the old gal's attempts to break your fall.'

Simon hung his head and looked dazed. Without looking up from the floor, he asked almost inaudibly, 'What happened to Gemma?'

Gwyn took a deep breath and wiped his mouth with his palm. 'Well, as soon as we had you stretched out on the floor and it was apparent you were breathing spontaneously and had a fair pulse, I went back to check her. Her blood pressure was in her boots, pulse very rapid, she was beginning to sweat. Obviously in shock. It seemed impossible she'd avoided any internal damage the way that curette was digging in her. So I pressed the button. Got the resuscitation team in here, and then sent for D'Arcy.'

'How is she now?' He hardly dared to ask.

'I'd just been back in before you came round,' Gwyn told him. 'D'Arcy had opened her up. Said there were at least three perforations, and a ruptured uterine artery. They were running in her second unit of blood. Good job you did a routine cross-match, they had three standing by. He'd repaired the artery, thought he might get away without a hysterectomy. He was starting to check the bowel when nursie here said you were stirring.'

Gwyn was beginning to regain some of his composure. He put his hand on Simon's arm. 'I'm sure she'll be OK, mate. But Gordon Bennett, did you give me the fright of my life!'

The implications of all that had happened were beginning to flood in on Simon. He could already feel his career slipping away. 'How long was I out for?'

Gwyn looked up at the clock on the recovery room wall. 'About fifteen minutes, I'd say.'

There was a long moment of silence. 'That's an awfully long time for a vaso-vagal attack.' He used the medical term for a simple faint. Gwyn looked at Simon, and saw the fresh anxiety in his eyes, knew what he was thinking.

Simon spoke again. 'You said earlier, it was more like an epileptic fit — you were joking, weren't you?' He could tell from the worry in his friend's eyes that he wasn't. Even so, the anaesthetist tried to make light of it.

'I don't know, old fruit. It certainly wasn't like any *grand mal* fit I've seen before, but I'm no expert. Could have been Jacksonian. But cerebral anoxia can precipitate what looks like a fit.'

Simon knew that well enough, and it was a straw worth clutching at. The lack of oxygen that occurs during a faint can occasionally trigger off an electrical discharge in the brain that produces an epileptic-like fit, but the brain shows none of the electrical instability of true epilepsy. The distinction was of the utmost importance: to be diagnosed as having epilepsy could be the death-knell of any further advancement for him in the medical profession, quite apart from the

33

consequences of the damage he had done to the poor girl still on the operating table. But what if it had been a Jacksonian fit, as Gwyn had suggested? In this form of epilepsy, instead of the whole body going into spasms and twitching, only one limb is involved, the spasms starting in one arm or leg, sometimes spreading to involve the whole body, but usually confined to one part. What had happened to him could well have been a Jacksonian fit.

Then there was the little matter of his deception over his reason for hastening Gemma's operation, the strange ultrasound, the concocted foetal abnormality, all to be explained away. A few days ago he had felt on top of the world. Now everything seemed to be falling to pieces. How could this be happening? He realised he was close to tears, and fought to suppress them.

'Thanks, Gwyn.' He stood up again. His mouth was still dry, and he felt a bit weak, but he thought he could face the music now. He really had no choice, anyway. As he turned to go back into the operating theatre, his friend close behind, D'Arcy came out, having finished with Gemma Randall, and left via the recovery room.

'I'll send for you later,' he said as he swept by. He looked like thunder, and avoided looking at his Senior Registrar. Gwyn tried to make Simon go to the common room for a coffee, but first he insisted on going to see Gemma Randall. He found her in intensive care, where she had been taken straight from theatre. He was aware of some curious glances from the nursing staff as he approached her bedside, and wondered if some of the looks were hostile or whether he was just being paranoid.

Gemma was unconscious, or at least asleep. She looked very pale, and a unit of blood was running into the vein in her left arm. A small oscilloscope monitored her heart-rate and electrocardiogram. It looked normal. Her heart and circulatory system seemed to have weathered the storm, thought Simon, but what about her brain?

Whenever the brain is kept short of oxygen for more than a few minutes, there is a risk of brain damage — especially so if the patient is anaesthetised. How long was it from when he caused the internal bleeding and shock to when Gwyn was able to start resuscitating her? How long was he out for? Gwyn had said fifteen minutes. Christ! He started to sweat with anxiety. He felt afraid: for Gemma, in case he had been responsible for turning her into a cabbage, and for himself, because he would have to live with that knowledge and its consequences for the rest of his life. He was about to go and ask the ICU Sister if she knew what Gemma's neurological state was, when his bleep went off. He went to the nearest telephone, feeling weak and shaky. It was the District General Manager, asking him to come and see himself and Mr D'Arcy at 2.30 that afternoon.

Simon spent a miserable three hours just hanging around. The

General Manager had politely told him on the phone that he should not present himself for work 'until this matter has been resolved'. He couldn't face the company of his colleagues in the common room, or in the canteen, and anyway he couldn't face eating. He spent most of the time hidden in the depths of the hospital library.

He arrived a few minutes before half-past two, and knocked on the door, heart thumping. James Featherstone, the District General Manager, was there, and so was D'Arcy. Featherstone was not a medical man. He was one of the new breed of managers brought into the National Health Service in an effort to improve the efficiency of the running of the hospital. He had come from a position in industry some eighteen months ago, and was undoubtedly good at his job. However, to Simon's mind he still did not fully appreciate that the needs of patients, doctors and nurses were not easily equated with those of a conventional labour force, machinery and production targets.

Simon knew that to say this incident would not go down well with Featherstone would be putting it mildly. It was bound to disrupt the department; there would probably have to be an inquiry, questions would be asked. If Featherstone thought his financial bonus, awarded to higher management as an incentive to improve cost efficiency, was threatened, he would be positively hostile.

'Sit down, Mr Robinson.' He sounded pleasant enough. 'Now, I think you'd better tell us as much as you can about this unfortunate incident.'

Simon had been giving considerable thought to this question while he was waiting for D'Arcy to finish in theatre. He wasn't sure how to explain his actions, which at the time had seemed so well-intentioned but now seemed frankly deceitful. He decided he would simply say that he felt particular sympathy with the girl's case, that he had made up the story of foetal abnormality to make it easier for her and to remove her fears that she thought something was wrong with herself. In a sense it was true enough. He certainly thought this baby was abnormal, but he could not bring himself to say to a fellow professional what he had seen, or thought he had seen, on the ultrasound scan. An abnormality was one thing, but to try and say what he really thought he had seen . . . He had contemplated this. What did he really think? At first he was convinced he had seen something — something *evil*. It had completely overwhelmed him, distorted his usual rational thinking. Instead of acting like the scientist he was, his emotions and the circumstances — like forgetting to make a photographic record and the fault preventing a second scan — had contrived to make him follow a course of action which had led to disaster. It was bad enough that he had experienced some sort of episode this morning that had injured a patient, but for

35

that event to expose his secretive attempts to help a girl because he thought she had some evil monster inside her . . . it seemed so implausible now as to cast doubts on his very sanity.

He was holding his forehead, trying to clear his thoughts.

'Well, doctor, we're waiting for your explanation.' That was D'Arcy, and he didn't sound friendly at all. Simon supposed he couldn't blame him.

He related his version of the events over the past few days, emphasising that his motivation was to help the girl, regretting the deception over the abnormality and apologising for acting without waiting to consult his boss. As to the events in theatre that morning, he had no explanation. He told them how he had felt what he thought was an electric shock, but could remember nothing after that until he came round in the recovery room. He assured them he had never experienced anything like it before, and he appreciated the implications. He tried to anticipate one line of action by saying that he would like to see a neurologist and have an electro-encephalogram. He knew that this measurement of the electrical activity of the brain could help clear up the question as to whether he suffered from some hitherto undiscovered tendency to epilepsy, a thought he knew would already have occurred to D'Arcy.

When he had finished, D'Arcy and Featherstone looked uneasy and exchanged glances. Before they could ask any more questions, Simon put one of his own.

'Before we go on, please, can you tell me how Gemma Randall is doing?'

D'Arcy raised his eyebrows as if this was not an appropriate question just now, but Featherstone nodded his encouragement for an answer.

'All right.' D'Arcy spoke rapidly, unemotionally. 'She had three perforations of the uterus, a ruptured uterine artery, a perforation of the descending colon and a tear in the anterior fornix of the vagina which went to within an ace of extending to the bladder. Hardly surprisingly, she was in severe shock. She appeared to respond well to resuscitation, but her pupils seemed very slow to come down. There is obviously a possibility of cerebral anoxia, but we don't know yet if she's suffered any brain damage.'

He paused to look at Simon, who was sitting bowed, with his hands over his eyes. A hint of sympathy entered his voice as he sensed the devastation of his colleague.

'My God, man, what were you trying to do to her?'

Simon left the room a few minutes later, his world torn apart. He needed to get out of the hospital, he needed Kate. She wouldn't be home yet. He wished she were there, waiting for him now. He drove around for a while, but became aware that his concentration was poor

36

and he was increasingly weary. He decided to go home before he had an accident, and wait there until his wife returned. She would comfort him, help him hold on to his sanity.

4

It was after four by the time Simon got home. He wanted to see Kate, pour his worries out to her, have her soothe the wounds to his psyche. He felt a twist of annoyance that she was not there to greet him. She was of course at work. He desperately wanted to collapse physically and emotionally into the arms of his wife, but he had to hold back his feelings and wait for her. She worked on the district, not in the hospital, which meant that she spent a lot of her time visiting patients in their homes and holding ante-natal clinics with local General Practitioners. It was a good arrangement for Kate: it gave her a measure of independence and freedom, and she had a certain amount of flexibility over her hours of work.

He went to the sofa in the lounge, and lay back, closing his eyes. Despite the tension within him, he felt overwhelmed with tiredness and exhaustion. Within minutes he was deeply asleep.

Kate came home at 5.15. Simon's car was in the drive, and she was surprised but pleased that he was home early. Must have been a quiet day, she reckoned, for him to be back at this time. She found him soundly asleep on the sofa. Poor man, this job must be wearing him out. She smiled fondly as she looked down at her husband. Better leave him to sleep if he's that tired, she decided, and went to take a shower. She had spent two hours in the poorly ventilated and over-heated delivery room at the Maternity Unit during the afternoon, with a woman who made very heavy weather of the birth of her second baby. She needed to freshen up and get out of her uniform.

Simon woke with a start, momentarily disorientated. He felt acutely anxious, and then remembered why, a wave of nausea washing over him. Oh, God, if only it were all a dream. He looked at his watch: 5.30. He got up and went to the door. As soon as he opened it he heard a familiar noise.

If Kate had a fault, it was that she liked to bathe and shower. That was what he could hear now, the shower. His pleasure at realising she was home changed irrationally to annoyance. He started to mount the stairs, striding upwards aggressively, brooding. What did she think she was doing? When he wanted her, needed her, she was pampering herself under the shower, not knowing or caring what he was going through. He knew his thoughts were unreasonable, yet he could not suppress them.

He reached the bathroom door and wrenched it open. His wife had still not heard him, due to the noise of the water and because she was singing softly to herself. The glass shower cubicle was opposite the door, against the same wall as the bath in the unusually large bathroom. Steam obscured the air. He could make out her form through the glass, which was clear apart from a few horizontal stripes. On a different occasion he would have had to suppress the urge to go to her, as he often had in the past, to run his hands over her body made even smoother with the slippery soap, caressing her nipples into hardness even as he hardened himself.

Now there were no such thoughts. He shouted her name again and again, as loud as he could, a harsh, rising, angry sound. When Kate eventually heard the shouting, she did not recognise it as her husband. Momentarily overcome with fear and panic, her first thought was that an intruder was out there intent on robbery or rape. She jumped and turned at the same time, slipped, and fell against the glass door of the shower. Being held shut only by a magnetic strip, it swung open under her weight, and she dropped backwards out through the door and sprawled, naked, onto the floor. She rolled over, terrified, looked up, and felt both surprise and overwhelming relief at seeing it was Simon. Her shock returned immediately when, instead of rushing to help her, he stood over her and ranted.

'What the hell are you doing? You're always in that bloody bathroom!' He moved forward threateningly, the blood vessels and muscles in his neck standing out. Kate scrambled to her feet and backed away. He raised his hand, and for a moment she braced herself for a blow. His closed fist shook as he ground out a final plea through his clenched teeth.

'Don't you care about me?'

Kate had recovered enough to detect the desperation beneath the anger. She started to speak, put out her hand tentatively. 'Simon, please, what — ?'

He turned on his heel, went into the bedroom, and flung himself face down on the bed. Kate was trembling with shock and cold. The shower was still running, splashing through the open door and making an ever growing pool on the tiled floor. She reached in and turned it off, took a large towel and dried her hair roughly, then her face. She wound the towel around her body so that it covered her from breasts to mid-thighs, and went slowly into the bedroom.

She wasn't sure what to do. She had no idea why her normally placid and never-violent husband should behave like this. He ought to be in a good mood, coming home so early. Was he trying to catch her in some imagined infidelity? When he'd left that morning he had seemed a little preoccupied, but it was early, and she had thought nothing of it.

There was no point in ducking the issue. She had never had cause to be afraid of Simon in the past, and she wasn't going to start now. She spoke firmly.

'Simon! I want to know what all this is about.'

There was no response, and as she moved forward to insist on his attention, she noticed a movement of his shoulders. She went a little closer, cautiously, then more quickly as concern overcame her. She reached the side of the bed and sat on it next to him. His body was shaking more obviously now. She placed a hand on her husband's shoulder, felt the tremor, heard the moist indrawing of breath.

Simon was sobbing as if his heart would break.

* * *

Kate tried in vain to console her husband, who seemed quite unable to tell her what was wrong. He clung to her, kept saying he was sorry, but every time he tried to tell her what had happened he started to sob again. In the end she decided she would do her matter-of-fact nurse's act.

'I'm going to make a cup of tea.' She stood up. 'I'll come back and talk to you when you've got control of yourself.' She tried not to sound too unkind.

As she went through the automatic motions of boiling the kettle, she briefly entertained the thought that Simon might be suffering from some hitherto hidden mental illness, but immediately dismissed it. She was just stirring the pot when the sound of her husband's voice made her jump and nearly knock the pot over. She turned swiftly to face him, half afraid of what she might be confronted with. Simon was white-faced and red-eyed, but seemed calmer. In fact he had a rather shame-faced look.

'I'm sorry, love. I'm all right now, I promise.' He wiped his eyes with his fingers. 'I really do think I could do with that tea.' He tried a laugh. It was no more than a brave attempt.

He sat down at the kitchen table. Kate poured the tea, passed him a mug, and sat opposite him, a mixture of hurt and sympathy showing in her eyes. Simon saw this and looked down at the table for a long moment.

'Kate, whatever you think about what I am going to tell you, I am not going mad.' Her stomach lurched and she gave him an anxious glance. 'It's very important you believe that.' He spoke emphatically.

Kate looked directly at him and studied his face, his eyes, his look. This was her husband, she told herself, upset and emotional, but definitely the same man who had got out of her bed that morning, not some different or altered personality. She had done enough mental nursing to feel confident that she could recognise if someone she knew well had become psychotic, detached from reality. She felt so sure of her assessment that she gave a half-smile of relief.

'Have I passed?' asked Simon, returning his own attempt at a grin.

'Yes, my love. All present and correct. Now, for God's sake tell me what the hell is going on.'

Simon sipped his tea, took a deep breath, and began to relate the events of the last few days. He told her everything. When he mentioned what he'd seen on the ultrasound screen Kate gave a little gasp, and looked at him intently.

'It's true, I swear it. Christ, I wish I'd photographed it.' He began to get agitated. Kate tried to calm him.

'It's all right. I believe you. It does sound fantastic, but I *do* believe you.' She spoke reassuringly, even though she was feeling a glimmer of doubt, and was trying to reassure herself as much as Simon.

When he went on to relate the events of that morning, Kate became very pale and still, a hand held to her throat as she tried to take in the horror of what had happened. She realised at once the implications of it all. He might have killed a patient, he might have epilepsy, he might be the subject of litigation — it all went through her mind even as Simon described the subsequent events and his interview with D'Arcy and Featherstone.

He looked up at Kate as he ended his narrative. Her face was creased in concern, and she was shaking her head slowly from side to side in her anxiety.

'What did they say is going to happen to you now?'

Simon bit his lip hard to try and keep himself under control. 'I've been suspended.'

'Oh, love, no!'

'They said I can't even go to the hospital, let alone work there — or anywhere else.'

'Oh, God! How long for?'

'Indefinitely.'

5

Simon spent two miserable days at home, waiting for news from the hospital — waiting to hear what was to happen to him and how poor Gemma Randall was doing. And, perhaps worst of all, wondering if he really did have epilepsy and was likely to be struck with another attack such as he had had in the operating theatre. He had never really been ill, or even threatened with illness, before, and although he always tried to be sympathetic towards his patients, he knew that in future he would look entirely differently on their worries about themselves — if indeed he did have a professional future.

Kate had tried to take his mind off things by encouraging him to go out, to think about buying things for the house and garden, to enjoy making love. It wasn't much use. Simon was totally preoccupied. He felt terrible: his constant anxiety made him feel sick all the time, and he couldn't eat. He didn't sleep much either, and both nights Kate was aware of him getting up in the small hours and going downstairs to make tea and read.

The morning of the third day was a complete contrast. Instead of getting up and pacing around almost as soon as it was light, Simon stayed in bed. He refused any breakfast, and the toast Kate took him was left untouched. She came and sat on the bed and chatted to him about some news items. Simon hadn't attempted to look at the paper.

After a few minutes he turned his back on her, pulled the duvet up over his head, and said, not very pleasantly, 'Kate, for God's sake leave me alone, will you?'

Kate was upset and worried as she went off to work. Simon was very unhappy, which was understandable and only natural in the circumstances. But now he was exhibiting classic symptoms of withdrawal, and she knew that was often one of the early signs of the transition from just feeling down to being pathologically depressed, and hence in need of treatment.

As she drove around between her home visits, she kept going over the problem in her mind. Simon was so level-headed, she kept telling herself. She had known him go through some bad times before, and had seen him under stress — mostly about passing exams and promotions, and of course about Kate herself and her as yet unfulfilled desire to have children. But he was always resilient, never down for long.

She had never seen him like this. Again and again her fair knowledge of mental nursing came to torment her. She had done a year of it before she decided she really wanted to be a midwife. She had been interested in the subject at the time, and had read widely about it. The thought which kept coming back to haunt her this morning was that many successful suicides involved intelligent men who hid their distress until the act itself. The shocked family's reaction was nearly always, 'I didn't know he felt so bad.' They were always doubly stricken with guilt and remorse, wondering why the loved one had not confided in them, wishing they had probed more, asked more questions, been more sympathetic . . .

Don't be ridiculous, Kate told herself. Simon's not like that, and besides, it's only been a couple of days: he couldn't possibly fall into such profound despair in that short time. Or could he? The doubts returned again, but before she could ride that particular carousel round once more she had arrived at her next call.

In late morning one of her visits took her back near Holdenhurst and home, so she seized the opportunity to call in to see how Simon was. The phone was ringing as she opened the front door. She waited to see if Simon would answer on the extension in their bedroom. On the eighth ring she answered it herself.

It was Gwyn.

'How is he?' There was concern in his voice.

Kate felt an unfamiliar warmth towards this rather coarse Welshman, who had made so unfavourable an impression when they first met. He was, if nothing else, considerate and understanding, and she knew now why Simon liked him so much.

'He's not good, Gwyn. Not good at all. I'm really worried.'

'Why, what's he done?'

'That's just it. Nothing, yet. He's just spent the morning in bed and doesn't want to have anything to do with anybody, including me. He just doesn't seem interested any more in what happens.'

'That doesn't sound too healthy.'

'That's what I thought.' For a moment neither of them could think of anything to say. Kate broke the silence.

'Gwyn — ' She hesitated, then continued. 'Gwyn, will you come over and talk to him?'

'Well, yes, of course, if you think it'd help. But — '

'But what?'

'Look, do you think you could persuade him to talk to me now, on the phone?' His voice was unmistakably anxious.

'Gwyn, what's the matter?'

He avoided the question. 'Let me talk to him, please?'

Kate put down the phone and went up to the bedroom. Simon was where she had left him, the duvet still over his head.

43

'Simon, love, it's Gwyn on the phone. He wants to talk to you.'

There was a long pause.

'Simon!' There was no movement from the bed. Kate pulled back the covers, trying to suppress an irrational feeling of dread.

Simon opened his eyes, and, without moving, asked gruffly, 'What does he want?'

'I don't know.' Kate tried to keep the relief from her voice. 'But it sounds important.'

Simon sat up, throwing the covers away as he did so. He sat still for a few seconds on the edge of the bed, then, with a short, deep sigh, picked up the phone.

'Yes?' He snapped out the word.

Poor Gwyn, he deserves a better greeting than that, thought Kate as she went back downstairs. She could hear Gwyn's voice talking urgently as she picked up the phone in the kitchen. She was tempted to listen in, but felt disloyal somehow. She hung up.

The call was short, and after a few moments she could hear Simon moving about. He was getting dressed! Well, that's something, she thought. She wondered what Gwyn had said to motivate him to this effort. At least he wasn't so withdrawn he couldn't respond to his friend. She looked up and tried to smile cheerfully as her husband came down the stairs. My God, he still looks rough. She hoped her dismay didn't show in her face as she looked at his unshaven chin and glowering expression.

'I'm going in to the hospital,' was all he said as he went through the kitchen and into the hall, where he picked up an old coat and some car keys.

'Will that be all right? You said that you weren't supposed to — '

'I don't care. I've got to see it.'

'See what, Simon?'

He opened the front door, and turned to her. His eyes looked a little wild, his expression strained.

'Gwyn's got it.'

'Got what, for heaven's sake?'

'The lab report on the foetus.'

He slammed the door. Kate listened to his car being driven off too fast, and felt a heaviness settle over her.

* * *

Gwyn was waiting for him in the car park behind the Pathology Laboratory, as they had arranged. He hurried over when Simon drove up, and got into the car before Simon could get out.

'Just drive off again, will you?'

'Whatever for?'

44

'Don't argue, just do it!' Gwyn was tense and angry, and looked around him almost furtively as Simon, still grumbling, drove out into the tree-lined avenue that led away from the back entrance to the hospital.

'What the hell is all this cloak and dagger stuff?'

'OK — you can pull over now. Look, there's a space just ahead.'

Simon pulled in, stopped, put the hand-brake on, and turned to his friend. 'Well?'

'Sorry about all that. It's just that — ' he stopped, seemingly embarrassed.

'That I'm *persona non grata*. Not the man to be seen with?'

Gwyn gave him a self-conscious grin. 'Well, sort of. And also because I wanted to have a word with you before we go in there.'

'Go in? To the lab, you mean?'

'Where else would they have lab reports, you bonehead?'

Simon looked nonplussed. 'I thought you'd have a copy of it for me to read. Something simple like that. You know, good old-fashioned stuff, like words written down on a piece of paper.'

'Ah, that's better.'

'Now what are you talking about?'

'You. Trying to be sarcastic. That's a bit more like it.'

'A bit more like what?' Simon gave an exaggerated frown.

'From listening to Kate just now, I thought you were about to stick your head in the proverbial gas oven. At least you sound alive.'

Simon nodded thoughtfully. 'To tell you the truth, I did feel pretty desperate this morning.'

'Look, don't think I can't understand how you must feel. If I had the worry of losing my job, or even my career, and added to that the possibility that I might have epilepsy, then I'd probably be near-crazy too — especially as I've got a head start on you, being slightly mad anyway! Although . . .'

'Although what?'

'Well, I haven't been mad enough to go fiddling about with operating lists to hide things from my boss, even if it was with the best of intentions.'

'Don't you believe that my intentions were to serve the best interest of my patient?'

'Yes.' Gwyn nodded earnestly. 'Yes, I do. But — it's such a bloody balls-up. It's not like you.'

'Not like me?'

'You know — good old steady Mr Robinson, all that crap.'

Simon was getting annoyed. 'All right, so I've been a bloody fool. I'm only too well aware of it, you know.' He turned away from the young anaesthetist and found himself fighting his emotions again. God, what's the matter with me? he thought. Surely I can cope with

45

this without getting worked up every five minutes. He sat hunched up, biting his knuckles, staring out of the window.

Gwyn reached out and put a hand on his friend's shoulder. 'Sorry. Are you OK?'

Simon swallowed. 'What about this bloody report, then?' He kept his face turned towards the side window.

'I couldn't show you a copy, because there isn't one.'

This time Simon did turn to look directly at his colleague. 'Isn't a what? Report, or copy of the report?'

'Christ, you can be a dull bugger. No copy of the report.'

'Now just a minute. On the phone you said you had the report.'

'Correction. I said I had *seen* the report. But it was just by chance. I went to the Histology Lab to see if they'd still got some frozen sections from this morning's list, and Janice — she's the one with long black hair and big knockers — was typing at the VDU in the secretaries' office. I looked over her shoulder, hoping more for a glimpse of cleavage than anything, when I noticed she was typing in the report on Gemma Randall's foetus. Obviously D'Arcy had completed the termination when he was patching her up, and sent the specimens over. Which is no more than I'd expect.' He looked sideways at Simon. 'I was just trying to make out what it said when old Tin-ribs came in.'

Simon looked up. Tin-ribs was the nick-name given to Walter Ironside, the dour and dull Senior Consultant in Pathology.

Gwyn paused and looked out of the window as a girl showing a lot of leg walked by, then turned back to Simon.

'So I thought I'd better get going, and asked Janice if she'd send me a copy of the report. Tin-ribs evidently heard me and in his best "You're only a worm and if you're not careful I might step on you" voice, told me there would be no copies available to me.'

Simon was astounded. 'No copies! There are always copies of path reports after a termination!'

This was true, as they formed an essential part of the case notes, both for the further management of the patient, and from a medico-legal point of view. Such reports were equally important, whether it was after a simple D & C (the procedure often carried out when investigating some disorder of function of the uterus), or after a natural miscarriage, or termination.

The implications were considerable. In an ordinary D & C, the examination of the scrapings from the uterus gave information on the patient's hormone status, as well as excluding disease of the uterus itself. After miscarriage, such material would show if the miscarriage had been complete, and sometimes whether some abnormality of the tissues in the womb had been responsible. In the case of a TOP, in early cases the report would commonly just state 'Products of

Conception seen', meaning that at least some of the the contents of the uterus had been successfully removed, and that the pregnancy therefore could not be expected to continue. It was possible for an inexperienced operator to miss the early pregnancy stuck to the wall of the uterus, and if the histology was negative, the patient had to be carefully followed up. The consequences of sending someone out of hospital, thinking they were no longer pregnant when in fact they were, were obviously very serious.

'Didn't you say something?' asked Simon.

'Of course I bloody well said something. I said the report would have to go in the patient's records, so why not give me a copy now? He nearly had a fit. I don't think I've ever seen him get so worked up. Swore at me, told me it was none of my business, told me to get out. I acted all casual, told him to keep his hair on, or what's left of it, and said I was in no hurry and would read it when it was in the case notes. When I went out I could hear him slobbering over poor Janice, saying that there were to be no copies, repeat, no copies, of the report made available to me.'

'It's just incredible. What does Tin-ribs think he's doing?'

'No idea, chum.'

'So what am I doing here? And what are we — just a minute — you said you saw Janice typing it out! Come on — what the hell did it say?'

'I honestly didn't see much. I was trying to take it all in at one glance. I saw "severely macerated", so you obviously chopped it up pretty good with your curette plunging in and out the way it did.'

Simon shuddered. 'Anything else?'

'Yes. I could swear I saw the words "abnormal tissue".'

Simon felt his stomach lurch. He hadn't expected that. He had fabricated the story of microcephaly. Was it possible there was some *other* abnormality? Nothing gross, surely. The ultrasound would have shown . . . He felt slightly faint, and his breathing was becoming more rapid. The image of the grinning foetus leaped back into his mind. He had more or less come to accept that he had imagined this almost surreal experience, but what if there really was something? He had to find out. He had to see that report for himself.

'Are you all right?' Gwyn sounded anxious.

Simon turned to him. 'Yes, fine. Let's go and get a look at that bloody report.'

'The only way we can do that is to look up the computer file.'

'Then let's go and do it.'

Gwyn hesitated. Simon tried to reassure him.

'It's OK. If I'm seen in there by anyone who matters, I'll tell them it was my idea. Better still, you go and chat up Janice, and I'll access the file through one of the terminals in Biochemistry — there's bound to be one free, most of their results from the auto-analyser go straight to the central computer now.'

Simon was quite familiar with computers, having one of his own which he used as a word processor to write his medical papers. He also knew how to operate the laboratory machine, as even in the short time he had been at the hospital, he had on occasion gone to access the computer directly rather than wait for written reports to arrive, especially urgently needed ones at weekends.

Gwyn reluctantly agreed. 'I'll go first.'

They left the car where it was and walked back, so that they could enter the laboratory complex by a side entrance. There were no senior staff around as they moved down the brightly lit corridor that linked the various pathology departments together.

Janice was still in her office, fingers flying over the keyboard as she typed in reports. 'See you later,' said Gwyn with a lewd grin as he went in.

Biochemistry was the next door but one. He went into the outer office where the terminal was situated, and sure enough it was unattended. All the technicians were in the larger inner area, operating the various high-technology machines that did most of the work. The days of boiling up reagents in test-tubes to do individual investigations were long since past, the new devices doing a dozen or more tests at once on tiny samples of blood or serum.

Simon had already worked out his excuse if he were 'caught in the act'. He would say he had recalled an important biochemical investigation on a patient that he wanted to check up on, and he was very sorry, he knew he shouldn't be here, but it was vital and in the patient's best interest. He had a name and a test all ready. This lying game was getting easier, he thought ruefully.

He sat before the computer terminal. Although this particular screen and keyboard was in the Biochemistry Department, he knew that he could get into any part of the system from here. He entered the code for histology, and a menu came up on the screen. He chose 'Obs & Gynae' for his speciality, and the screen changed to one with a series of boxes on it. The cursor winked at him from a box inviting him to enter the patient's name, surname first.

Simon realised his palms were sweating, and wiped them on his thighs. He looked nervously about, then turned back to the keyboard. He typed in RANDALL, and a window appeared in the screen listing three Randalls. None had the Christian name Gemma, or a date of birth that matched.

Damn! thought Simon, annoyed at the extra time it was taking him. He asked the computer for lists of reports by date, and by subject-matter. No Gemma Randall. He looked at the door to the Biochemistry Lab. Still no imminent interruptions. He applied some of his computer knowledge. Leaving the part of the program he was in he typed in DIR. This asked the computer to show him the directory of all the different files in its entire memory. He didn't want to go through them all, there would be thousands. He wanted only histology files, and he wanted only those that had been set up that day. He asked the computer appropriately. It began to list the histology reports it had for that day. There were only six. None of them referred to Gemma Randall.

There was only one explanation for this: somebody had deleted the file. Not only was there no written record, but there was no memory of it in the computer either. Simon swore under his breath, cleared the screen, and went to fetch Gwyn. He was in full swing with Janice when he knocked on the door to attract the anaesthetist's attention. Gwyn reluctantly made his excuses and came out into the corridor.

'Got what you want?'

'It's not there.'

'What do you mean, it's not there?'

'There's nothing in that computer about Gemma Randall or her histology report. I checked the directory. There is no such listing.'

'That's ridiculous. I saw Janice doing it myself not an hour ago.'

'Let's go and ask her.' Simon went into her office, and stood to one side as he pushed Gwyn forward.

'Go on, ask her.'

Janice turned her ample proportions and sunny smile towards them.

'Ask me what?'

Gwyn looked momentarily embarrassed, which was something new to Simon. He prompted. 'Gwyn wants to ask you about a report you were typing this morning.'

Janice turned on the charm. She obviously fancied the young anaesthetist. 'I'm sure I'd do anything to help *you*, Dr Reece.'

Gwyn cleared his throat. Simon was forced to the conclusion that Gwyn did not like his 'performances' with the ladies to be closely observed by an attentive audience. He smiled to himself at his friend's discomfiture, and watched and waited for the show to begin.

'Well, it's like this, look you — ' Simon just managed to suppress a laugh into a smothered snort at Gwyn's exaggeration of his normally mild Welsh accent. Obviously part of the act, he thought, as Gwyn gave him a filthy look.

'You were typing up a report this morning when I happened to be in here, and well, we'd like to have a look at it.'

Janice beamed, crossed her legs slowly and deliberately to give a generous glimpse of thigh, and took a deep breath designed to stretch her satin blouse even more tightly over her breasts.

'Just give me the name, doctor.' She put her hands down on either side of her chair and tossed her hair back. She was giving Gwyn the full works.

Gwyn hesitated, coughed again. 'Er, Randall. Gemma Randall.'

Janice's attitude changed immediately. She sat bolt upright, uncrossed her legs rapidly, and went pale. 'Isn't that the girl who had the abortion the other day, the one who . . .?' She looked accusingly at Simon.

'Yes, that's the one.' Gwyn moved a little closer, spoke soothingly. 'Just a quick look.'

Simon sensed they would draw a blank, and Janice confirmed it.

'No, no, I can't do that.' She seemed actually frightened now. 'And you —' she looked at Simon again — 'I heard — with respect, sir, you shouldn't even be in the hospital, Mr Robinson.'

Gwyn tried again, Welsh accent broader than ever. 'Whatever's the matter, Janice, love? We only want a quick peek.'

'No, no. I — I can't. Dr Ironside issued instructions that there were to be no copies sent out. I tried to ask him about it, and he was — was almost — ' She suddenly seemed near to tears.

Gwyn oiled his way a little nearer, and spoke even more soothingly in his best understanding bedside manner. 'Was almost what, my dear?'

Janice looked up at him, and a tear overflowed. 'At first he was all nice, you know how he can be.' Gwyn didn't. 'You know — smarmy.' She gave a little shiver of distaste. 'Then I said it was very unusual, and asked him why. He got ever so angry. He shouted at me, and said if I wanted to keep my job I'd do as I was told and not question his authority.'

She sniffed, and reached for a tissue. She was recovering enough now to play for some sympathy, looking up at Gwyn with fluttering eyelids. He reached out and held the hand with the tissue in it.

'It's all right, Janice, love. Don't get upset. We don't want to get you into trouble or lose you your job. You don't have to show it to us. Just tell us where it is on the computer.'

Janice thought for a moment, and in the pause Gwyn gently stroked the back of her hand with his thumb. She weakened. 'It's — it's where you'd expect it to be — filed under histology. You can call it up by typing in the first four letters of her surname.'

'No, you can't.' Simon was getting impatient, and increasingly anxious that they would be disturbed. 'I've already tried, using the Biochemistry terminal. It's not there.'

'Don't be daft. Look!' Without having to think about it, her hands danced over the terminal keyboard, typing in the commands.

She stared at the screen, and after a moment said to herself, 'What's happened to it?' She cleared the screen and tried again. Nothing. She called up the directory as Simon had done. When she had scrolled through the list of files in the directory she turned to the two doctors, her eyes wide and frightened. 'It's gone! Dr Ironside will kill me!'

'D'you mean to say *you* didn't delete the file?'

Janice looked at Simon, horrified. 'Me? No! No, of course not!'

'But you're the only one who uses this terminal.'

'All I know is it wasn't me. And it wasn't done from here. It must have been done from one of the others.'

Gwyn looked both puzzled and annoyed. 'So who did delete it?'

All three exchanged glances. Janice began to look afraid again. 'No, no, it wasn't either of us,' Gwyn assured her.

Simon's anxiety was growing. Someone was bound to come along soon. 'Look, thanks, Janice. We won't get you into any trouble, we promise. Thanks for trying.' He started towards the door.

'Janice — ' Gwyn was looking thoughtful. 'Janice, Ironside didn't do that report himself, did he?'

The girl was scornful. 'No, of course not. He hasn't looked down a microscope for years. It was Dr Ravensbourne.' She bit her lip, worried that she had been indiscreet.

'Don't worry, Janice. I've said we won't let you down. Now come on, Gwyn.' Simon was at the door, holding it open. He heard the outer door leading to the corridor close noisily. 'Someone's coming. I'll see you outside, Gwyn,' he called as he rushed to the other end of the passage and the outside. He glanced back to see if Gwyn was following, and saw Dr Ironside striding purposefully towards Janice's room. Gwyn came out as the pathologist approached the door, said something to him, then turned and walked away quickly. Simon didn't think he had been seen, and waited outside for Gwyn to join him. When he emerged, they walked smartly back to the side entrance of the hospital and towards the street where they had left the car. They were silent until they were out of the hospital grounds. Simon looked at the heavens.

'Phew! That was close!'

Gwyn did not reply, but just regarded Simon with great concern.

'What is it, Gwyn?'

'Wait until we get into the car.' They walked, almost ran, to the vehicle, and as soon as the doors were closed, Simon turned to Gwyn. 'Well, come on, for Christ's sake.'

'Before Tin-ribs turned up, I asked Janice where Dr Ravensbourne was. I thought we could simply go and ask her about the report.'

'And?'

'She said she's gone.'

'Gone! Gone where?'

'On holiday.'
'Oh, come on! When?'
'This bloody morning.'

6

Janice Marshall had a lot to think about on her way home from work that evening. As she sat on the bus that took her to Moordown and the small 'starter home' she owned jointly with her boyfriend, she daydreamed about Gwyn Reece, the 'gorgeous gasman' as she liked to refer to the anaesthetist. He really is so nice, she thought, and he was so attentive today. And he's obviously attracted to me. He likes women with big breasts, the way he kept looking at them.

Janice was used to men admiring her bosom, but she treated most such appraisals with disdain, knowing full well she was the object of lechery, not aesthetic appreciation. Many women would have looked upon such an endowment as a great attribute, but she often wished she was not quite so big.

She gazed out of the window, not seeing the rather drab streets go by, and began to imagine what it might be like to be the wife of a hospital doctor. She did not feel any guilt about this fantasy, even though she was as good as married to Sean Donaldson. They had a mortgage, that was commitment enough. They knew that neither of them would have been able to afford a home without the help of the other, and as much as anything, it had been their mutual desire to escape from living with their respective families that had driven them together. They both had to work, so there was no question of a family, and Janice took her contraceptive pill religiously, even though it had made her breasts even larger.

She was letting her thoughts roam into her overglamorised perception of the world of medicine, when she remembered again the matter of the missing report. That brought her swiftly back from the land of make-believe, and her stomach knotted uncomfortably with the anxiety she felt about it. Old Ironside was probably making empty threats, but Janice, in her lowly position and dependence on her essential earnings, felt vulnerable, and there was no way she was going to challenge his authority. She knew she shouldn't have said anything at all to the two doctors, but she so wanted to impress 'Dr Gwyn' with her helpfulness. And now the report was missing! Her palms became sweaty as she recalled what had happened upon Dr Ironside's return, and was so lost in her troubles that she did not notice a passenger move from the back of the bus to sit almost opposite her and study her more than casually.

Dr Ironside had been very angry that she had been talking to Dr Gwyn again. He had wanted to know what the younger doctor was after. She had felt so intimidated that she had mentioned the presence of Mr Robinson. She was stricken with worry that he would find out that the report was no longer in the computer, and thought it best to tell him then, rather than conceal the fact and perhaps get into more trouble later. He was angry, and muttered something about someone having to read the slides again.

Although not particularly intelligent, Janice was well known for her outstanding memory, which helped her to be such a good secretary and typist. She knew she would be able to retype the report almost verbatim, despite the fact that she didn't know what half the words meant. She had offered to retype it there and then, as it was one of only seven she had done that morning. The senior pathologist did not seem to listen. He started to shout at her, and said he supposed she had told the two doctors what was in the report. At this point Janice was reduced to tears. She said over and over again that she had not told them, and as her sobs subsided, Dr Ironside turned on his heel and left without saying another word. She hadn't seen him again all day.

Her reconstruction of the day's events was interrupted when the name of her stop was called out, and she only just got off the bus before it set off again.

Her thoughts turned to more basic matters, like getting something to eat that evening. She went into a small grocer's shop near her house. She didn't like going there, because the two young men who usually served always nudged each other when she came in and sniggered behind her back when she went out. But it was handy, so she ignored their innuendoes and bought a pie for Sean and some salad and yoghurt for herself, as she was making yet another forlorn attempt to diet.

Janice let herself in through the front door, which opened directly into the lounge-diner area. The stairs rose up from close by the door, leading to the two bedrooms and tiny bathroom. She went straight through to the small kitchen, putting her bag on the work surface, before going to open the back door. She had a cat, a mostly black tom she called Hercules. As expected, he was waiting outside and rushed in, pressing himself against her legs in anticipation of food and milk. She saw to the cat's needs, then plugged in the jug-kettle for a cup of tea. While she was waiting for it to boil, she ignored her conscience and took a chocolate wafer from the fridge, switched on the radio, and flopped down on the two-seater sofa. She took a bite, put her head back, and closed her eyes. It had been a difficult day.

Her foot was beginning to tap to a Beatles 'Golden Oldie' and she was trying to imagine 'Dr Gwyn' singing it to her, when she heard a noise from the kitchen. She lifted her head to listen. Probably the cat. She began to relax again when, coinciding with a break in the music, she heard the closing of a door. Her first thought was that it must be Sean, before she remembered he was doing a late shift that evening at the DIY superstore where he worked. Anxious now, she jumped up and went to the kitchen doorway. What she saw made her gasp with surprise. She was not to know that it was to be the last thing she would ever see.

She stood transfixed with disbelief as those last messages were relayed from her retina to her brain. They formed an image focused on the jug-kettle, saw the lid removed from it and the boiling water it contained thrown towards her face. Too late she registered the danger, as the amorphous mass of steaming liquid travelled the short distance to its target. In a fraction of a second, the transparent coverings of the front of both her eyes peeled away, the lids coming down too slowly to protect them. The clear jelly beneath went a milky white, then her eye-lids swelled grotesquely as they blistered so much that the light was shut out completely.

The shock at first prevented Janice from breathing, but a few seconds later, as she clawed at her eyes and tried to make out what was happening to her through the incredible pain, she opened her mouth to gasp for the breath with which to scream. As she did so, another quantity of boiling liquid was thrown so accurately that much of it entered her mouth, and her indrawing breath sucked some into her throat and larynx. The effect was more devastating than before, the membranes in the narrow breathing tubes rapidly swelling to obstruct the passage of life-giving air. Janice's hands groped at her throat and face, dislodging large shreds of skin as she did so. Her right hand reached out in her distress, skin hanging from her fingers in long pink fronds. Her mind screamed in silent terror, her face an unrecognisable mess.

Her paroxysms of agony were observed from a few feet away by her assailant, whose only show of emotion was a satisfied smile.

* * *

After leaving Gwyn at the laboratory, Simon went over to the neurological unit at a nearby hospital in Bournemouth, to see one of the consultants there. They had trained at the same medical school and, although separated by some years, he knew Greg Barrett fairly well and felt he could talk to him freely about his possible medical problem. Dr Barrett interrupted a busy clinic to see him. He performed an extensive examination of Simon's nervous system, but it was no surprise to find this quite normal. The main diagnostic procedure in epilepsy was an electro-encephalogram, or EEG, so

Simon then took a request form Greg Barrett had signed for him to the EEG department. He saw the technician there, who arranged to carry out the test the following day.

The investigation itself held no fears for Simon. It was a non-invasive procedure in which a number of small electrodes were placed on the scalp and minute electrical currents from the activity in the brain were amplified and recorded in graphic form. What worried him was what the various patterns on the read-out would show. He was not having much luck in putting the problem out of his mind.

Soon after he got home, Kate came in from work, but only had a few minutes before going out again to her regular early evening class in French. They had a hurried cup of tea together, during which Simon told her about the disastrous visit to the laboratory and his visit to his neurological colleague.

After Kate had left, in an effort to rationalise the situation that faced him, Simon went over everything from the beginning. It all began from the moment he had seen that alien face on the ultrasound. His one hope of possible explanation of what he saw, and of determining whether it was real or imagined, lay with the pathology report on the foetus. There seemed no getting away from the conclusion that Dr Ironside was trying to keep that information to himself. He had been angry when Gwyn had asked to see it, and there was no trace of it on the computer. And now, the doctor who had made the examination had suddenly gone on holiday!

Simon knew Dr Ravensbourne really had gone *somewhere* because of a little subterfuge he had indulged in that afternoon. He had called the Histology Department, giving a fictitious name, and asked to speak to her, only to be told by the secretary that she was away. Simon expressed surprise, saying that he had arranged a meeting with the doctor for the following day. The secretary was apologetic, but said that she had gone at very short notice, and that she had been asked to take names and phone numbers of all callers for Dr Ravensbourne and would phone back when she was in a position to make alternative arrangements. Simon told her it wasn't important, and hung up.

Surely it couldn't be the case that Ironside had engineered Dr Ravensbourne's hasty departure? All to hide the result of a path report? Whatever could be contained in it that required such an elaborate cover-up? Simon's curiosity was stimulated to the extreme by all this. He could not escape the inference that it was no ordinary report, thus reinforcing his belief, his hope, even, that it might hold some answers that were relevant to his present plight.

He was clearing away the tea-cups when a thought struck him. It was so obvious he didn't know why it hadn't occurred to him before. He had been lamenting the disappearance of Dr Ravensbourne, because she clearly would know what was in the report, when it clicked in his mind that the other person who would have read it, and would have at least some recollection of its contents, was Janice Marshall. Her fear of Ironside would certainly have prevented her from telling them anything while they were in the laboratory, but if he could see her at home . . .

The adrenaline was flowing as Simon drove to the hospital, formulating his plan to get Janice's address. He couldn't find it in the phone book, and he thought his best bet would be the Accounts Department. The day staff would have gone home by now, and all he was likely to encounter were the cleaners. He took his white coat, bleeper and stethoscope, the uniform that identified him as a doctor and would allow him to pass almost anywhere within the hospital without question or suspicion. He went in through a side door near the hospital kitchens; he didn't want to risk being recognised going in through the main entrance.

The Accounts Department was in a small wing on the third floor. The cleaners were in the area, but were still working in the corridors. Simon breezed past with a nod and a smile, as it was pointless trying to speak above the noise of the vacuum cleaners. He strode confidently into the main office, and closed the door after him. He had a good idea where to look, as he had been here when he first arrived, so that all the appropriate details could be entered in his file. A smaller office on his right held the relevant filing cabinets, and they were all clearly labelled according to whichever category or department each member of staff belonged to. Laboratory staff were a distinct group, and rather to his surprise the cabinets were not locked. He located Janice and her address in a matter of moments, but as he pushed the drawer shut the sound of vacuum cleaners increased dramatically. The door to the outer office had been opened.

Simon looked around for something to justify his presence, and saw a booklet entitled 'Superannuation for Medical Staff in the Hospital Service'. He picked it up, headed for the door and waved the booklet at the two cleaning ladies with what he hoped was a confident gesture. They barely nodded in response and carried on with their task.

Only ten minutes later Simon was looking for Janice's house in Moordown. Most of the homeward-bound traffic had gone, and the road out of the town centre northwards was a good one. He turned into an estate of new small houses, mostly in terraces of three or four, each in a slightly different configuration in a rather unsuccessful attempt to make them look individual. All the little roads were named after birds, and after only one wrong turn, he pulled up outside 11, Raven Close.

His second combined ringing of the bell and loud knocking on the door brought no response. Disappointment began to overwhelm him. His spirits had been temporarily lifted by his hopes of seeing Janice.

He stepped back from the door. He could see no obvious way round the back, as the house was in the centre of a terrace of three. In any event, the building was so small that if she had been in she would surely have heard him. He walked up to the door for one last try, and paused as he was about to press the bell. The noisy surroundings had quietened briefly, and he could now definitely hear music: it was surely coming from the room into which the front door opened. He tried to look in, but couldn't, thanks to the heavily draped ubiquitous net curtains. He knocked and rang again. Still no answer.

The music suggested occupancy after all. He made a more determined effort to find a rear entrance. Perhaps she was operating a noisy kitchen gadget, or was upstairs in the bath. He walked past the next house, saw a net curtain pull back briefly as his passage was observed by a curious neighbour. Beyond the end of the terrace lay a concrete hard-standing for three cars — there were no garages. A white Transit van occupied the first space, and as he walked past it Simon could see the narrow entrance to a small passage that led behind the tiny back gardens. Each one was fenced off by six-foot high wood panelling, and in each garden's section there was a narrow doorway with the number of the house displayed on it. He entered the small area at the back of number eleven and noticed with relief that the back door was open. He went to it and looked into the kitchen.

The chaos that confronted him left him completely at a loss at first. Groceries were everywhere on the floor, broken mugs and glasses amongst them, puddles of water adding to the mess. He wondered what on earth had been going on. Taking a hesitant step forward, he called out.

'Janice!' No response. 'Janice?'

Another careful step. He jumped and nearly cried out in alarm as a cat dashed past him and shot out of the back door.

'Miss Marshall! Anyone there?' He picked his way carefully through the debris, towards the sound of the radio. 'Hello! Miss Marsh — '

He had reached the point where he could see into the lounge. He stopped, the sight before him making him feel momentarily faint, and put his hand out to support himself on the kitchen work-top. He withdrew it immediately with a jerk. He looked down and saw blood, from a cut where his hand had encountered broken glass. He paid scant heed to it, his attention riveted on the scene in the lounge.

Something — someone — was lying back on the sofa. Could that be Janice? He took another few steps, until he was right inside the room.

Could this hideous creature with the swollen red mass of a face possibly be her? Something terrible had happened here, and he realised that she had surely been raped. Her dress was torn open all down the front and her knickers hung round one ankle. Her brassiere had been pulled up to her neck, exposing her breasts.

Simon realised she must be dead. I'll have to call the police, the ambulance, he told himself. He tried to swallow, but couldn't, his throat was so dry. Briefly he entertained the thought of just going away and leaving someone else to report this gruesome discovery, but he knew that would be morally wrong as well as foolish. He had been seen coming in here, and to leave without reporting all this would surely imply guilt of some sort.

He started to look round for a phone, when Janice's body gave a momentary spasm as her chest tried to draw in a last rasping breath past her swollen larynx. The doctor in him pushed fear and revulsion aside, and he approached her to see if there was anything he could do. Her face was horrible, eyes merely slits, skin hanging from the flesh and serum oozing from a dozen places. Whatever had done this to her? He felt for her pulse at the wrist, couldn't find it. He would normally then have tried to feel for the carotid pulse in the neck, but the flesh there was also incredibly swollen and the skin fragmented. He reached forward to try and feel the apex beat, the tapping of the left ventricle of the heart which could be felt through the chest wall, and could be palpated by placing the hand just below the left breast. As his hand touched her skin, it felt clammy and cold. She must be in severe shock, with such a low blood pressure that the pulse could not have been felt at the wrist. She made another convulsive attempt at a breath and Simon concentrated intently and thought he could feel a faint pulsation beneath his fingers. He knew what he had to do: summon an ambulance, establish an airway, start resuscitation. He was about to reach for the phone, when he noticed the marks on her breasts — small broken, crescent-shaped purple indentations, several of them, mostly around the nipples. He shuddered as he realised what they were. Teeth-marks.

He started to rise, but he had barely moved when his head seemed to explode in a flash of coloured lights and searing pain. Consciousness slipped from him as he slumped forward, partly covering the once attractive body of Janice Marshall.

7

Simon became aware, first, that he was in a moving vehicle, and second, that he was in great pain. He lay quietly for a moment, trying to assemble his thoughts. The image of the bloated features of Janice Marshall floated into place. His reaction was to open his eyes to dispel the vision and to try and sit up. A restraining hand was put on his shoulder, none too gently, and pushed him down again. Simon cried out in pain as he tried to resist, then lapsed back into unconsciousness.

When he next came to he was still travelling. What was he doing here? What was going on? He saw again the image of poor Janice, then — what was next? That was it, a pain in his head. Did someone hit him? But there was pain in other parts of his body, too. What else had happened to him? The agony that had made him pass out again when he had been pushed down was in his chest, the left side of his chest, not his head. His left hand throbbed terribly, and he felt a dull and nauseating sickness in the lower abdomen as if — well, as if he had been kicked in the testicles. He lay quietly, going over his injuries again. It seemed he'd been beaten up.

Now he opened his eyes again, but this time only a little, and tried to take in his surroundings. He was in an ambulance, that much was obvious. The man sitting opposite him was presumably the one who had pushed him down so forcibly. There was something wrong about him, though. What was it? The uniform — he was a policeman, not an ambulance man. He opened his eyes wider and lifted his head slightly to see where the ambulance attendant was. The movement was noted by the police officer.

'Oh, coming round again, are we?' He turned to the rear of the ambulance, to someone Simon could not see. 'Look, Mike, Dr Jekyll is surfacing again.'

Simon tried to speak, but could only mumble. His tongue felt dry and swollen, and when he tried to trace his lips with it they felt numb and puffy.

'Got something to say, have you?' The policeman, who was stocky with a short, bristly moustache, leaned towards him in such a way that Simon felt threatened. He tried to milk some saliva into his mouth with his tongue, and moistening his lips with it, tried again:

'What happened?'

The policeman turned to address his still unseen companion, sarcasm heavy in his voice. 'Ha! He wants to know what happened!'

Simon felt desperate and not a little frightened. 'Please! What's going on? Where are we going?'

The officer turned back to him and spoke sneeringly.

'What's going on is that, although you don't deserve it, you're lucky to be alive, mate. And where we're going is the nick — with a quick stop at the hospital *en route*.'

'I wonder what his chums will think of him there, eh, Rodge?'

That must be another policeman, thought Simon, and, lifting his head with pain and effort, could just see a police cap with ginger hair showing beneath.

'Not a lot, I shouldn't wonder. P'rhaps they'll try and finish the job!' Harsh laughter from them both.

'Finish what job? What's happened to me?' Simon was feeling more and more bewildered.

'What's happened to you? You callous bastard! What about what's happened to that poor kid?' said unseen Ginger-hair.

Moustache leaned closer again. 'You were bloody lucky we didn't just leave him to it. Might have saved everyone a lot of trouble if we had.'

'You're right there, Rodge.'

Simon tried to work out what the two of them were talking about, but before he could formulate any ideas, the ambulance turned into the hospital and stopped outside the Accident and Emergency entrance. The back doors of the ambulance were opened and the driver and his partner, who must have been sitting in the front, came to get Simon out. He thought he recognised one of them, and was surprised he was not treated more kindly. As it was, barely a word was spoken, and he was unceremoniously and uncomfortably placed in a wheelchair and taken inside.

For once the A & E department was fairly quiet. He was left by reception with one of the policemen, while the other, the one with the moustache, and the ambulance driver, spoke to the Staff Nurse on duty. There were several glances in his direction, and at one point the Staff Nurse put her hand to her mouth with an expression of shock. Simon was feeling uncomfortable in more ways than one. His injuries were hurting him, and he also felt exposed and conspicuous, aware that already several people had passed by who knew who he was and regarded him curiously.

The Staff Nurse, an attractive young woman with dark hair, came over to him. Simon did not know her, but her name-tag said she was Mary Jenner. She did not smile, and she spoke very abruptly.

'You'd better come in here, Dr Robinson.'

He was taken into a cubicle, the curtain drawn, and he was left

61

alone. Simon was now thoroughly puzzled. As a member of staff at the hospital he would have expected his colleagues to be, if anything, over-solicitous and concerned, with rather more fuss than normal being made of him. He was not the sort of person to expect any special treatment as of right, but he knew that was the way it usually worked if a doctor was ill. Yet here he was, feeling abandoned and unwelcome in his own hospital. He saw a third-year student nurse through the gap in the curtains, and called her in.

'Yes, sir?'

At last a friendly smile. 'Could you do me a favour? Could you possibly see if you can find Dr Gwyn Reece for me? I'm Mr Robinson, and I'd very much like to see him.'

'I'll try, doctor.' Another smile, and she left. Before the curtain swung closed again, he saw the ginger-haired policeman standing across the aisle. As though he were guarding me, Simon thought. The third-year nurse came back shortly, and helped him undress and get into a hospital gown. It was a slow and painful business, but would make his subsequent examination much easier. Despite Simon's obvious discomfort, she seemed much cooler towards him than before.

'Did you get in touch with Dr Reece for me?' He tried to give her a reassuring smile. 'Yes,' was the terse reply, followed by a pursing of the lips. She left quickly.

After some fifteen minutes of lonely and anxious waiting, a doctor did come to see him. It was Donald Farminer, the A & E Consultant, with the Staff Nurse in tow. Now this was more like it: the man himself, not a junior casualty officer. He must have been called in especially, he wasn't usually about after five o'clock, Simon told himself. He had looked at his watch while he was waiting, and it was now nearly seven.

More disapproval was all he got, however. Without looking at him, the Consultant gruffly told his colleague to tell him where it hurt. He prodded Simon's ribs none too gently. Simon realised they could well be broken. He felt his facial bones, looked at his puffy lip, examined the swollen hand. He shone a light in his eyes, pressed around the back of his head where there was a soft but very tender swelling. Then a perfunctory look at the testicles, a cursory examination which made Simon feel slightly sick. Farminer turned to the Staff Nurse. 'All right, down to X-ray. We'll do a skull, a chest, with left lateral to show the ribs, and left hand. That'll do. I'll be in my office when the films are ready.' Without any further comment, reassurance or word of sympathy, he left.

The Staff Nurse wheeled him through to the X-ray department, and the injured doctor noticed that the policeman was still in discreet attendance. Simon actually relaxed a little whilst his X-rays were

62

being taken. The Radiographer on duty was a pleasant lass he had seen when she came to theatre to help with special procedures. He only knew her as Ros, and said hello. She recognised him at once, and was immediately greatly concerned.

'Whatever have you been up to?'

Simon had to admit he wasn't sure how he had come by the injuries. She looked more closely at his face.

'Oh, you poor thing.' She made him feel more relaxed over the next few minutes, chatting away and gently easing him into the appropriate positions for the films to be taken. It was apparent that she was behaving normally. The others obviously knew something she didn't.

He was helped back into the wheelchair and left alone in the room with the big white machines which were still gently whirring, whilst Ros went to develop the films. The outer door opened after about two minutes, but it was not Ros returning. It was Gwyn.

'Holy shit, you look a mess!'

Simon felt an immense sense of relief. He grabbed Gwyn's arm, and realised at that moment that he was near to breaking-point.

'Thank God! Gwyn — please! What the hell is going on? What's happened to me? I don't know how I've got like this! Why is everyone treating me like dirt? What am I supposed to have done?'

'Steady on now, boyo.' Gwyn detached himself and sat on the X-ray table, and he looked a very worried man.

'Christ, what is it, Gwyn? Nearly everybody has been carrying on as if I'm some sort of leper.'

'Looking at it from their point of view, I can understand it.'

'Understand what, man?'

Gwyn paused for a long moment. 'I spoke to the member of the constabulary outside just now. You've been at Janice Marshall's house, right?'

Simon looked down at the floor, then up at his friend. 'Yes. Yes, I was. The poor girl. How — how is she?'

'DOA, I'm afraid.'

Simon hung his head. Dead on arrival at the hospital. The suspicion had been forming in his mind, but he had been suppressing it. Now the inevitability of it hit him.

'And they think I killed her, don't they!' He put his hand over his eyes. 'Jesus bloody Christ!'

Gwyn put a hand on Simon's shoulder. 'All right, mate, all right.' He paused, waiting until he had Simon's attention again. 'Now,' he continued, 'look at me a minute.' Simon raised his eyes to the unusually serious face.

'This is what I've been told. Janice's live-in boyfriend, Sean somebody-or-other, came home from work early. Something about a late shift being cancelled. He says he found you leaning over Janice playing with her tits, and her looking in a hell of a mess and probably raped.'

Simon looked away, collecting his thoughts and trying to come to terms with this statement. 'Yes, that's it . . . I remember . . . I — I found her looking . . . like that . . . and thought she was dead. I was trying to find a pulse . . . trying to feel the apex beat. He must have thought I was . . . was . . .'

'Yes. Well, not surprisingly really, he loses his cool completely. Crowns you with a heavy wooden chopping board, then in a fury wades in and kicks you about a bit. He thought he'd killed you when he called the boys in blue, but you're obviously a lot tougher than you seem.'

'Gwyn — you know I couldn't do anything like that, don't you?'

There was only the briefest hesitation, then the Welshman looked directly at him. 'Yes, chum, I know it. But . . .'

'But what?'

'I just hope you can bloody well prove it.'

* * *

Simon did not enjoy the ordeal of being held in custody most of the night in the cells of Bournemouth Police Station, despite the support of Gwyn, who went with him from the hospital, and of Kate, who arrived as soon as she could when Gwyn phoned to tell her what was going on.

The anaesthetist contacted a solicitor on Simon's instructions. He chose the only one he knew, the one who had recently helped him with his house purchase, knowing that she did mostly criminal law rather than conveyancing. Her name was Pauline Jamieson; she was attractive, about 35, and he presumed single as she called herself 'Miss'. Fortunately she was prepared to consider representing Simon, and came to see him in his cell. She was brisk and businesslike, and went straight to the point.

'Dr Robinson, there is one question I must ask before we go any further.'

Simon did not reply, but waited for her to continue.

'Were you in any way responsible for the death of Janice Marshall?'

Simon swallowed hard, and looked directly at Miss Jamieson, who in return studied his face closely.

He thought he understood the reason behind the question, and realised the importance of his reply being accepted as truthful.

'No. Absolutely not, in any way.'

Miss Jamieson considered for a moment before responding.

'Good. I hope you didn't mind my being so direct. I would not accept this case if I had any suspicions that you might be guilty. I'm not that sort of lawyer.' She opened her briefcase. 'Now we can crack on with getting you out of here.'

Initial inquiries and interviews by the police soon established that a neighbour, presumably the one Simon had seen peeping through the curtains, had heard what she thought was a domestic argument going on before Simon arrived at Janice's house. Not much shouting, but a lot of banging and crashing, she told them. She hadn't paid much attention as it was nothing unusual. However, she *was* able to fix the time of Simon's arrival, and was able to recall that it was some time after all the noise had stopped.

In Pauline's presence, Simon gave his version of events to the investigating officer several times, and had no difficulty in giving a consistent story. Gwyn was able to substantiate the reason for his visit, although later in private he told Simon he was a bloody fool for going to see Janice at home.

After several hours, Pauline Jamieson challenged the police either to charge her client or release him. They decided to let him go, admitting that what had at first seemed a cut-and-dried case was by no means so simple. Shortly afterwards Simon was on his way home, physically and mentally battered, but free.

Two days later, Pauline phoned to tell him that the preliminary forensic evidence confirmed that Janice's injuries had been sustained about half an hour before the neighbour saw him arrive. Thank God for nosey neighbours, thought Simon. And for modern forensics. He knew that when a body was seen fairly soon after the moment of death, it was possible for a very accurate timing of recent events to be given. Tissue damage, such as that from bruising and burns, followed a predictable pattern of progress, and the time at which the injuries had been sustained could be determined precisely. Such high technology investigations were frequently very valuable and, in Simon's case, crucial to substantiating his own and the neighbour's evidence.

After that Simon went virtually into hiding, nursing his rapidly healing injuries and his damaged ego. The local press and television gave a lot of publicity to this particularly horrific crime, and his name frequently came up. He felt ashamed of his association with what had happened, and was aware of the embarrassment he was causing the hospital and his colleagues. The only thing he forced himself to do was to have his rearranged EEG test carried out, and his one moment of cheer was being told by his neurologist friend that it was completely normal.

His improved mood after that oasis of encouragement did not last long. His suspension at the hospital was confirmed until further notice, and his depression was not improved by a visit from Gwyn, who called after seeing Gemma Randall in the hospital.

Gwyn was hardly inside the door before Simon began his questioning.

'How is she? Is she going to be OK?'

Gwyn knew his news was going to upset his friend.

'Let's go and sit down, and I'll tell you all I know.'

Simon's stomach churned. These were no glad tidings the Welshman was bringing him.

'One good thing,' began Gwyn, 'is that she is now conscious. But —' he paused and glanced at his colleague — 'she's got a right-sided paralysis, and she appears to have a serious problem with her speech. She can understand what's being said to her, but she's got an expressive aphasia.'

Simon groaned, and put his face in his hands. It meant that the poor girl could understand what was being said to her, and her brain could formulate responses, but somewhere the nerve pathways were damaged so that she could not articulate comprehensible speech. This was probably due to a problem in a local area of the cortex of the brain responsible for speech, and her right-sided weakness was part of this same injury. Lack of oxygen during her period of shock was almost certainly the cause.

'I had a good talk to her,' Gwyn said. 'I told her how desperate you are about what's happened, and I tried to explain why you couldn't be there to visit her in person.'

Simon shook his head slowly. 'Poor kid. The poor kid. And *I did that to her.*'

'Well, let me tell you something, boyo. She's a remarkable young lady. She gave me something for you. Perhaps it'll buck you up a bit.' He handed Simon a folded piece of paper. He recognised it as an X-ray request form. It was blank.

'Turn it over, blockhead.'

Simon did so. On the other side Gemma had tried to write a reply with her left hand, and Simon wanted to weep when he saw it. In a barely readable scrawl, she had managed to write:

Dont worry

* * *

Inevitably, following his involvement in the death of Janice Marshall and his recent position as a prime suspect for murder, Simon was summoned to appear in court at her inquest. He had attended inquests before in his career, following the unexpected sudden death of a patient, or where there was a possibility of industrial injury being a contributing factor, so the actual procedure did not worry him. Pauline Jamieson had assured him he had nothing to fear, but they were both concerned about the possibility of more unwanted publicity.

As it turned out, apart from the ordeal of avoiding and refusing to speak to journalists, it was a brief affair, proceedings being opened and then adjourned. What stood out in Simon's mind, however, was the post-mortem report, a copy of which had been given to him by his solicitor. He could hardly wait to discuss it with Gwyn and Kate that evening.

'Look at this,' he said, showing them the document, 'and tell me what you think.'

There was silence for some minutes as they read the report.

'Well?' Simon was impatient.

'It makes pretty horrific reading, but I'm not sure what you're getting so excited about.' Gwyn looked puzzled. 'The cause of death was asphyxiation from tracheal obstruction caused by inhalation of boiling water. We knew that already, surely.'

'Yes, we did. But what about the rape?'

'The teeth-marks are unusual, I suppose — "small, like those of a young person", it says here. So I suppose it could be some adolescent responsible.'

'And the vaginal examination?'

Kate joined in. 'Yes, I thought that was a bit odd.'

Gwyn looked at her in surprise. 'Why?'

'Well, for one thing, it says "unusual vaginal trauma", whatever that means. And this: "The appearances of the semen suggest it was deposited in the vagina several hours prior to death." Now how can that be?'

'My question exactly.' Simon looked at Gwyn.

With barely any hesitation Gwyn responded. 'Obviously she had it away with her boyfriend that morning.'

Simon was quick and emphatic with his response. 'No, she didn't. Knowledge of prior intercourse is a vital part of these investigations, especially when a sexually active woman is involved. See here —' he pointed to a rider at the bottom of the document — 'it says that the last known intra-vaginal ejaculation occurred at least three days earlier. That must have been from Sean Donaldson, her boyfriend. Why should he lie about it?'

Gwyn conceded the point. 'All right, but it just doesn't make sense. She certainly looked as if she'd been raped right then and there in her house. You saw that for yourself.'

Simon was disappointed. 'Yes. Yes, I did.'

'However,' said Gwyn, 'there is another possibility that springs to mind.'

'Which is?'

'See who did the post-mortem?' He pointed at the signature at the bottom of the report.

Simon did not need to look. 'It was Arnold Matthews. He always does them if he's around.'

'And what is he?'

Simon wasn't sure what Gwyn was getting at. 'Well, he's the appointed Home Office Pathologist — works in Warrenchester — not exactly brilliant by all accounts — '

'And a piss-artist.'

'How do you know that?' Simon was taken aback.

'Come on, man, it's common knowledge. He's had a drink problem for years. They're always having to sober him up to get PMs done in time for the inquests.'

Kate joined in. 'So you're saying he could have made a mistake?'

Gwyn nodded. 'I think it's highly likely.'

Simon was subdued. 'Hmm. Yes, I suppose that is a possibility.'

'A probability,' Gwyn corrected him.

Kate turned to her husband. 'But you obviously had some other idea, love?'

'Well, yes, but it seems a bit far-fetched now.'

'Come on, let's have it,' Gwyn urged. 'We promise not to laugh.'

'It's just that if the semen was a few hours old, then she must have had sex with *someone* earlier in the day.'

'Like who? And where?'

'Where presents no problem in a big hospital. Who? Well, what about Ironside?'

Kate looked startled, but Gwyn, forgetting his promise, laughed. 'Don't be ridiculous! That old trout?'

'I don't see why it's so ridiculous,' said Simon defensively. 'Ironside was very angry with Janice that morning. She implied herself that he was lascivious. And if he saw me talking to her, he might have gone over the top, lost control.'

'Not right there in the office, surely. Someone would have heard something.'

'Perhaps after work, then. He might have followed her to give her another dressing down.'

'Or undressing.' Gwyn grinned.

'It's not funny, Gwyn.' Kate looked really annoyed.

'Sorry. I know, it's not a joking matter. But why wouldn't Janice have said anything about it?'

'She was terrified of losing her job — you could see that when we spoke to her.'

'But not to say anything if you were forced into unwelcome sexual relations with your boss?'

'If you can believe the papers, sexual harassment happens all the time,' said Kate.

'Jesus! What's the world coming to?' Gwyn brushed back his hair with his hand. 'But what's all this speculation about when Janice had sex got to do with the murder? Or with your predicament?'

'I know it's only wild speculation, but if anything did happen between Ironside and Janice — well, he could have gone round to her house later to shut her up once and for all. Because of wanting to cover up the rape, if there was one, and to make sure no one found out about the report.'

Gwyn looked at Simon incredulously. 'Bloody hell, man! This is downtown Bournemouth, not "Miami Vice". I think you're letting your imagination run away with you!'

Simon was not to be deterred. 'You just tell me why Ironside wants to keep the report on Gemma Randall's foetus secret, then!' He was shouting now, standing and banging his fist on the table. 'That's something that's important to me, and I want some explanation!'

'All right, all right. I take your point.' Gwyn spoke soothingly. 'The report on the foetus *is* important.'

Simon sat down, still looking angry. 'And don't patronise me, Gwyn.'

'I'm not patronising you.'

'That's what it sounds like.'

'Look, mate — I'm trying to help you. So don't get the hump with me.'

Kate was annoyed. 'For heaven's sake, you two! Please don't fall out with each other.' She turned to Gwyn. 'I know we don't always see eye to eye, but I know now what a good friend you are. Stay with us through this, please.' She put her hand on his arm. Gwyn was embarrassed at this show of affection from such an unexpected quarter. He picked up her hand briefly.

'Don't worry. I'll stick around.'

There was an awkward silence, then Simon spoke. 'She's right, Gwyn. We need you. I can't say how grateful I am for your support. Just ignore my tantrums.'

Kate stood up. 'I think a bottle of wine is in order.'

An hour later, they had drunk one bottle and were halfway through a second. They had left the subject of Ironside and the report and, relaxed by the alcohol, were talking of more pleasant things.

Eventually, Gwyn announced it was time for him to go. Simon, looking tired, nodded his agreement.

Kate looked at one, then the other. 'Wait a minute! We haven't decided what we're going to do — about the abortion histology, and all that.'

'Well,' suggested Gwyn, 'I suppose we could walk into Ironside's office and say we'll tell everyone that he raped his secretary unless he hands over the report.'

Simon tried to look annoyed but ended up suppressing a snigger. 'Or we could ask him for a semen sample. "Er — excuse me, but would you mind tossing off in here, old cock?"'

Gwyn hooted. 'Yes, I suppose his would be.'

'Would be what?'

'An old cock!' The two men clutched themselves in a paroxysm of schoolboy laughter.

Kate's first reaction was disapproval of this juvenile behaviour, but then she realised it was the first time she had heard her husband laugh in what seemed like a long time. Gwyn seemed to forget about leaving, and she left them to it. While she was clearing up in the kitchen, she could hear more coarse puns being bandied to and fro as they concocted more and more improbable situations concerning the despised Dr Ironside. She was happy to hear laughter in the house as she went up to bed.

8

Kate had set the alarm for seven o'clock. She awoke at once, as always, turning off the bell before the second ring. Simon was in bed beside her, breathing deeply and sonorously. She knew the signs: he and Gwyn had obviously polished off another bottle or two. She gave him a hard shake, but got no response. A poke in the ribs received only a grunt in return. She got out of bed and looked down at her husband. She felt love for him, but she also felt very sad: sad that he had so many troubles to bear, sad that she couldn't solve them for him, and sad that they had caused him to forget that she did have some troubles of her own. She couldn't really blame him, she knew, but it would have been nice . . .

She walked quietly to the bathroom and began to prepare herself. Today was the day she was to go into hospital to have her expectations of becoming pregnant resolved one way or the other.

Simon awoke to find Kate gone, and a note on her pillow.

> I tried to wake you.
> Come and see me, please?
> Love,
> Kate

He felt a wretched despair. He was so preoccupied with his misfortune that he had completely forgotten about Kate's admission to hospital. He knew how much it meant to her, having a baby. To him too, but not, he was sure, with the same degree of intensity, and he had left her to go and face this ordeal alone. He sat on the edge of the bed, his head in his hands. He felt an overpowering sense of guilt, and of hopelessness. It was all his fault. Why did he have to try and be so sodding helpful? It was those bloody abortions. He swore to himself he would never have anything to do with terminating pregnancies again.

He stood up and went to the window. He laughed, a slightly unstable sound. Why should he worry himself about never doing any more abortions? He would probably never do any more operating, full stop. He'd ruined his own life, and Kate's. All those years of work and study, wasted. She'd probably be better off without him. All this

71

shame and misery. He gave another, somewhat falsetto laugh. Ha! You can't even make her pregnant, he accused himself. What's the point of it all? Perhaps she'd be better trying again with someone else . . .

His morbid line of thought was interrupted by the telephone. He turned to answer it, then paused. What's the point of that, either? It'll only be more bad news. He turned away, but the ringing was insistent. It could be Kate, he supposed, and went and picked it up.

It was the Sister from his ward.

'Mr Robinson? I just thought you'd like to know that your wife is going up to theatre now.'

Simon felt tears prick his eyes. He swallowed hard, afraid to speak in case his emotions were too obvious.

'Mr Robinson? Are you there?'

He made an effort. 'Yes. I'm sorry. Thank you, Janet.'

'Are you all right?' She sounded genuinely concerned.

'Yes, yes, I'm fine, thank you.' Ridiculous, he observed, the way the British always profess they're 'fine', even if the world is crumbling about their ears. 'I'll be over to see her as soon as she comes round. Give her my love. And thanks.' He replaced the phone.

Well, you've let her down badly once today already; you can't do it again, he told himself. He had a quick wash and shave, then phoned Featherstone's office. The District General Manager was on another line, and he had to wait. His resolve wavered.

'Yes, what is it, Mr Robinson?' The greeting was not warm.

'Er, my wife is in hospital having some investigations. She's on G3. I thought I'd better check if it was all right for me to visit her.' His resolve hardened. This is crazy, he told himself. I'm like a pathetic schoolboy asking permission to go to the lavatory. Dammit, I'm going anyway, whatever he says!

'Ah, yes, Mr Greenwell did mention it. Of course that will be all right. Visits not in a professional capacity will be quite acceptable.'

Simon slammed down the phone, his temper rising. Patronising bastard!

He found his car keys and drove aggressively to the hospital.

* * *

When Kate recovered from her anaesthetic she was surprised to find herself in the private wing. She had more or less assumed she would have a room to herself, a courtesy extended to doctors and their wives if circumstances permitted, but on a public ward as she was essentially an NHS patient. Jeremy Greenwell had not mentioned anything about it. Automatically, she thought, I hope Simon will be able to find me. This minor anxiety turned to a heaviness of heart as she considered that Simon might not be *trying* to find her. He was so preoccupied, so depressed. He would probably be out on another wild goose chase like the one that had led him into the dreadful business with poor Janice Marshall. Whatever had happened to the level-headed soundness of judgement that had characterised his approach to life until now? Kate wasn't even sure why she had decided to go along with these tests at such a difficult time. Was she so desperate for a child?

Her mouth felt dry from the anaesthetic, and she was nauseated to the point of retching. She looked around for a bowl in case she should vomit, but could not see one. There was a bell push on a cord lying on the covers, and she pressed it. Almost at once a plump, cheery-looking nurse in her mid-forties put her head round the door.

'Something you want?'

'Feel sick,' Kate croaked.

The bright look turned to concern. 'Be right back.'

A few minutes later Kate was propped up in bed, her mouth freshened with iced water, and a stainless steel bowl handy. The friendly nurse, who was in fact the Ward Sister, turned to leave.

'Thanks very much,' said Kate, gratefully, 'I appreciate that. I'm a nurse, too, you know.'

The Sister smiled. 'Yes, I do know.'

'I'm honoured Sister should attend to me herself.' She tried a smile.

'This is nothing special. I do the same for everyone.'

'Really? However do you get the time to fuss over all the patients yourself?'

'Oh, it's different up here, you know. The staffing ratios are so much better — and I do enjoy a bit of practical nursing. Too much time doing administration drives me up the wall!'

The Sister had reached the door now. Kate called to her.

'Just a moment.' She'd remembered the question she had intended to ask first. 'What exactly am I doing here, instead of down in the Gynae ward?'

The Sister frowned. 'Ah, well now — ' she paused awkwardly, looked down at her feet, then glanced along the corridor and seemed to relax again. 'You've got a visitor,' she said brightly, then went out and closed the door.

Kate felt elated. Simon had come to see her after all!

She tried to push her hair into some sort of shape, hoping it wasn't too much of a mess. The door opened, and she couldn't hide her disappointment when she saw that it was Jeremy Greenwell.

He came into the room, professional concern showing on his face. 'Oh dear. Aren't you pleased to see me?'

'I'm sorry. Yes, yes, really. I — I thought it might be Simon.'

'Of course, of course.' He shook his head sadly, as he approached and stood over the bed. 'Whatever is that young man up to? Such a promising career.'

Kate didn't know what to say. She had not expected so personal a comment. Greenwell smiled down at her.

'Never mind, we won't go into all that now, will we? I thought you'd like to know the news as soon as possible.'

'The news? Oh, about my tests.' Kate fought against nausea again. 'Yes, yes, please.' For some reason she felt frightened. He was so close, towering over her. Involuntarily, she shrank away from him.

'It's all right.' He interpreted her movement as nervousness. 'It's all good news.' He bent forward, his hands on the bed, less intimidating now that his face was more at a level with hers. He smiled, and she was aware he was putting on his best bedside manner for her benefit. He had either forgotten she was a nurse or thought she was dim anyway, because he went on to explain as if talking to a child.

'Now then, we've blown some dye and some air all through your tubes, and they are as clear as can be. So your little eggs can get all the way down into your womb without any trouble. You'll find a tiny stitch in your tummy — that's where we put the little telescope to have a good look round.'

Kate realised that he had said this sort of thing many times before, and she was just getting the standard patter.

'Your ovaries look fine, with eggs growing on them, and there's nothing else about, gumming up the works.'

Kate had to retranslate that as meaning she had functioning ovarian follicles, and that there were no signs of adhesions or endometriosis. Why couldn't the silly man talk properly? Did his female patients really like to be talked to in this patronising way?

Greenwell was studying her face, puzzled at her reaction. Kate didn't realise her irritation was so obvious.

'Do you understand? Everything is all quite, quite normal.'

She made an effort to smile at him, because this really was meant to be good news.

'Yes, I understand. Thank you very much, Jeremy.' At their previous meetings he had insisted she call him Jeremy. 'I'm very grateful.'

Had he forgotten his invitation to use his Christian name, or was he disappointed at her lack of enthusiasm? He was probably used to wild cries of delight and gushing hero worship, thought Kate. Either way, she could not help noticing that he looked momentarily affronted. He soon switched his standard reassuring smile back on.

'I expect you're still a little knocked off by the anaesthetic, my dear — ' he was giving himself a suitable explanation for the lack of adulation — 'so I'll leave you in peace now. But one more thing: after this procedure, it's surprising how many of my lasses go off and get themselves pregnant straight away.' Greenwell gave her an almost conspiratorial look, then stood up and went to the door.

Kate called to him as he reached it. 'Mr Greenwell — Jeremy — why am I here and not downstairs?'

He gave her his most charming smile. 'All part of the service,' he said, and left.

Kate tried to analyse her feelings. She should have been jumping for joy. Everything was normal! So why wasn't she ecstatic? Perhaps greasy old Greenwell was right — that the after-effects of the anaesthetic were still bothering her. But she didn't think it was that, or Greenwell's irritating manner. It was because she had been almost afraid that everything *would* be normal. She had been all but wishing that there would be something wrong. Nothing major, just some simple explanation as to why she had not become pregnant. Then there would be some tangible problem to face, and to solve; almost anything was possible these days, and high-technology medicine held no fears for her. But to have everything completely normal left her in a sort of limbo, with no satisfactory explanation for her failure to conceive, no specific course of action to take, and a nagging feeling of guilt that it was all her fault.

This is stupid, she told herself as the tears welled up, you should be happy!

And then she was, as Simon burst into the room, rushed to her, and held her tightly in his arms for a long time.

* * *

As Simon left the private wing he told himself how lucky he was to have such a forgiving wife. She had been upset, naturally, by his absence earlier that morning, but he had made a genuine and abject apology, and she had said that really, it didn't matter, so long as he loved her.

Simon was very pleased that everything was normal. 'You'll be back home tomorrow, and then we can get on with it,' he joked as he left.

He had barely got to the end of the corridor, however, when all the old problems began to move in on him once more. In the lift he made a sudden decision. He pressed the button for the Intensive Care Unit. To hell with it! He would go and see Gemma Randall.

A staff nurse was on duty in the ICU. Simon did not know her well, and even after he explained who he was she was doubtful about letting him see his former patient.

'Sister said I wasn't to let her see anyone,' she protested.

Simon thought this instruction might be aimed particularly at him, but the staff nurse did not seem to associate him with the situation, so he leaned on her a little, insisting that he see Miss Randall, and assuring her that he would only be a few minutes.

Gemma recognised him as soon as he came to her cubicle. She was propped up on several pillows, with a naso-gastric tube disappearing up her right nostril, the free end taped to her cheek, and a drip in her right arm with a bottle of dextrose saline running in slowly.

He looked at her, and felt terrible. I'm responsible fot this, he thought. Gemma moved her left hand, and he could see she had a small note-pad and pencil. She concentrated hard for a moment, then held up the pad. It said:

$$\text{Hi}$$

Simon smiled, said 'Hi' back, and was rewarded with a lopsided grin. That stopped him smiling. The poor girl had a facial palsy as well. One moment an attractive, intelligent girl with everything to live for, the next, reduced to a wreck of a human being.

He couldn't face her any longer. He began to leave, but stopped when he heard a gagging sound behind him. He turned quickly, expecting to find her choking, but Gemma was trying to attract his attention with an attempt at speech. She looked at him with an expression he could not make out. She thumped the bed several times with the palm of her good hand, then when Simon did not respond, she pointed repeatedly at the floor. He went to look under the bed, but she held his hand to attract his attention again, shaking her head. A tear ran down each cheek in her frustration. Christ, thought Simon, what does she want? He pointed to the pad, and she laboriously began to write in her left-handed scrawl. He watched as she formed the words, and felt a wave of emotion pass over him as he realised what the message was. She wrote:

$$\text{please stay}$$

'OK,' he said, 'I'll stay.'

He pulled over a chair, and sat holding her hand, at a loss. What could he say to this girl who was lying there like this because of him? There was a long silence.

Eventually he asked, 'Is there anything you need?' Gemma shook her head.

'Are you in pain?' Another negative.

He looked down, then forced himself to look at her directly. 'I'm sorry,' he said.

She reached for the pad. Simon waited patiently.

I know

'This is all my fault.'

No- mine

'How can you say that? Have they told you what happened? How you came to be like this?'

She nodded her head vigorously.

'Then how can you say it's not my fault?'

More laborious writing.

me - my baby

Simon looked at her in a mixture of disbelief and admiration. She was trying to tell him that if she hadn't got herself pregnant in the first place, none of this would have happened. What was it that gave someone that sort of spirit, that sort of forgiveness? He felt he didn't deserve it. He looked away, blinking rapidly. He didn't know she was writing again until she tugged at his sleeve and handed him another note.

I know what you thinking

He smiled at her. 'That I don't deserve this response from you?'

She nodded her agreement, and gave him another crooked grin.

'But why? Why don't you just throw me out?'

You care

He couldn't bring himself to reply to that one. There was another long silence, and Simon started to worry about his own predicament. He looked at his watch, and at the nursing station, where the staff nurse was making a phone call. He had already stayed too long.

'I really ought to go.' He stood up.

Gemma shook her head furiously.

'I'm not really meant to be here at all, you know.'

Gemma shook her head again and pointed at the chair, indicating that he should stay where he was. He sat down again.

Gemma held up her hand, telling him to wait, then she started writing again.

What about abnoml fetus

Simon was momentarily stunned by the question. He tried to formulate a coherent answer. 'Gemma, this is the truth. I don't know. I just can't find out. I think someone is hiding the report. I've been trying to find out, ever since — '

'Mr Robinson!' Someone shouted his name angrily, so loud in the quiet ward that he and Gemma both jumped. It was D'Arcy, looking like thunder, and striding towards them, closely followed by the staff nurse.

'What the bloody hell d'you think you're doing here?'

Simon stood up. 'Well, I — I was visiting my wife, and I thought I'd — well, I'd look in on Gemma, that is, Miss Randall.' He felt a movement, and looking down saw that Gemma was clutching his wrist with her good hand.

'You're not even supposed to be in the damned hospital!'

'But Mr Featherstone said — '

'I don't care what he said. Don't you think you've done enough damage here? Keep away from that girl, for Christ's sake.'

D'Arcy was so angry that he pulled Simon away from the bed, unaware that Gemma was holding onto his arm. Simon was taken by surprise and lost his balance. Gemma did not let go immediately, and ·as a result was pulled halfway out of bed, nearly falling to the floor.

Simon looked on, horrified, as D'Arcy and the staff nurse struggled to get Gemma back into the bed. D'Arcy turned and all but screamed at him. 'Now look what you've done! Get out, will you! Get out!'

Simon turned and fled, but not before he had seen the desperate, beseeching look in Gemma Randall's eyes.

* * *

Simon was not surprised when later that afternoon James Featherstone rang to summon him back to the hospital. He waited outside the District General Manager's office, mouth dry and palms sweaty, the sensations reminding him of how he used to feel before a crucial exam.

D'Arcy arrived and went straight into the office, without giving his colleague so much as a glance. Simon could understand that his superior would not be pleased with him, because he had brought the

78

hospital disrepute and unwanted publicity, caused disruption of schedules, and posed unnecessary problems for his boss. Nevertheless, he thought he had had a good relationship with the Consultant and was surprised at D'Arcy's total antagonism. Couldn't he expect some support from his fellow doctors? He had committed no crime, just an error of judgement. He thought members of the medical profession rallied round each other in such circumstances — a fact often criticised in the press and by the public. So often, when one of their number was in trouble, it was a case of 'There but for the grace of God', and the recognition of this led to sympathy and assistance. Why was he not getting any?

Featherstone came to the door and called him in.

'Come and sit down.'

Simon obeyed. Featherstone took his place behind his desk. D'Arcy stood looking out of the window, his back to the room.

'I thought we'd better clear up one or two things. In particular, Mr D'Arcy has made the serious allegation that you have broken the terms of your suspension and have been trying to treat patients in the hospital.'

Simon couldn't believe his ears. 'But that's ridiculous. I was only —'

Featherstone held up his hands defensively: 'Please, let me finish. I know I gave you permission to visit your wife this morning, and I have explained that to Roger — Mr D'Arcy — and he accepts it. But what neither of us can accept is your approaching a patient and causing her great distress, acting quite contrary to explicit instructions that you are not to work in the hospital until this whole unfortunate business is resolved.' He looked grimly at Simon. 'Now, what have you got to say?'

Simon took a slow, deep breath. He wanted to shout at these two pompous asses, ask them what right they had to judge him like this, to assume his motives were dishonourable. But that would only weaken his position further. He was aware that D'Arcy had turned to observe his reply.

'I was not — absolutely not — seeing Gemma Randall as a patient.'

D'Arcy exploded with a loud 'Ha!' and turned back to the window.

Featherstone gave the Consultant a somewhat disapproving glance. 'Continue, please, Mr Robinson.'

'I feel terribly badly about what's happened to her. I just had to see how she was, to let her know how sorry I am about it all.'

Without looking round, D'Arcy spoke. 'He was grilling her about her pregnancy.'

Simon was getting angry despite his resolve to stay calm. 'I was not! I was trying to console her, help her!'

'Ah! So you admit you were, in effect, giving her treatment?'

'No! I was not! Visiting someone in hospital, to give them

79

sympathy and encouragement, may be therapeutic, but surely it doesn't constitute medical treatment?'

D'Arcy turned. 'It does when you're a doctor.'

Featherstone looked up at D'Arcy. 'Why do you say that Mr Robinson was asking Miss Randall about her pregnancy?'

'Because I saw some notes she had been writing. Something about her abortion.'

'Is this true?' Featherstone frowned at Simon.

'She had been writing notes, yes. She wanted to know whether there was anything wrong with the foetus.'

'And did you tell her?'

Simon saw an opportunity. 'No, I couldn't, because I don't know what was in the report.'

'I see.'

'No, you don't. I couldn't tell her what was in the report because there doesn't appear to be one in existence.'

'There you are!' D'Arcy spread his arms towards the General Manager. 'He admits he's been trying to interfere.'

'Yes, I take your point. But — look, I know clinical matters are not my province, but isn't such a report rather important?'

Simon took a chance. 'And shouldn't the patient be entitled to know what was in it?'

'Please, Mr Robinson. Well, Roger?'

D'Arcy looked embarrassed. 'Yes, it is important, of course, especially if there are medico-legal implications.' He looked pointedly at Simon. 'But there seems to be no record of it anywhere.'

'Really?' Featherstone's eyebrows went up. 'This sounds rather serious.'

'We've looked everywhere. The specimen was definitely processed: the technicians remember doing it. But we can't find the slides, or the remains of the specimen, and there is no record on the dictaphone tapes or the computer. We're pretty sure it was put on the computer, but with that poor Marshall girl dead . . .' He glanced pointedly at Simon again.

'Do you have any explanation for this?' Featherstone looked sharply at D'Arcy.

'No, I don't. Unless . . .'

'Unless what?'

D'Arcy looked directly at Simon. 'Unless someone around here has been trying to destroy the evidence.'

Simon grabbed the edge of the desk, made to get up, sat down again. So that was why D'Arcy was so hostile! He thought he was responsible for hiding the report. Perhaps he thought he was implicated in poor Janice's death, too, to shut her up.

'That's a very serious allegation, Roger.'

'And it's totally false.' Simon was trembling. 'Why should I want to hide the contents of that report?'

'Because of the little story you concocted about the Randall girl, of course.'

There was no denying his 'little story'. That indeed did put him in a bad light. He looked down, hesitating.

'Do you have anything else to say, Mr Robinson?' asked Featherstone.

'Yes, I do. Have you asked Dr Ironside about the whereabouts of the report?'

'He's the Senior Pathologist. Of course I have.' D'Arcy was almost contemptuous.

'And what did he say?'

'That he knows absolutely nothing about it.'

Simon was standing up now. 'That's a downright lie! Dr Reece and Janice Marshall both spoke to him about it. Dr Reece actually asked for a copy and was refused. Ironside didn't say there was no report, but that he couldn't have a copy. And Miss Marshall told us that Dr Ironside had instructed her not to make any copies of the report available. So how can he say he knows nothing about it? He's the one who's hiding the evidence, not me!'

Simon was breathing hard with the effort of his outburst. The other two men looked at him, Featherstone somewhat perplexed, D'Arcy sneering.

'He's making it up! The Marshall girl is dead, so she can't say anything, and Reece and Robinson are as thick as thieves, so you can't place much weight on what he says either!'

'Yes, yes, all right, Roger. But these, also, are very serious accusations. I think I ought to have a word with Dr Reece, and Dr Ironside.' He shook his head. 'This is all most distressing, most distressing.'

'You'll be wasting your time. It's a pack of lies.'

'Maybe so, but I can't just leave it at that, now can I?'

'Well, if you don't want to take the word of a consultant against this overambitious, conniving — '

'I just want to do what is right, Roger.'

'What is right is for you to tell this man here to stay away from my patients, or I'll be reporting him to the General Medical Council Disciplinary Committee.'

Featherstone nodded. 'I must say, Mr Robinson, that it does rather look as if you have been interfering in the case of Gemma Randall, albeit with the best of intentions.'

'Best of intentions!' D'Arcy snorted his derision. 'You should have seen the state she was in after he'd gone. He caused her a great deal of distress.'

Simon could not control his response. 'You damn fool! She was distressed because she wanted me to stay! Didn't you see how she was clinging to me?'

'Don't you call me a fool, you young whipper-snapper! You're finished in this hospital!' D'Arcy was purple with rage. 'You're finished *everywhere*! D'you hear me?'

He marched out, slamming the door with such force that the pictures rattled.

Featherstone was silent for a moment. Simon sank into his chair and covered his face with his hands.

'Well, ah, Mr Robinson . . .' The General Manager moved some things aimlessly about his desk. 'That was, er, a little injudicious of you to, ah — '

'I'm sorry.' Simon looked up. 'That is, I'm sorry to be causing you all this trouble. But I'm not sorry I visited Gemma Randall. I'm sure it was doing her good.'

'Well, I'm afraid I must insist you don't go near her again. I hope you understand.'

Simon tried to avoid making any promises. 'What about speaking to Dr Reece and Dr Ironside?'

'Oh dear, the report. Yes, we must clear that up.'

'And while you're asking questions, you might like to inquire what has happened to Dr Ravensbourne. She's the histologist who reported on the missing slides. She seems to have vanished on an unexpected vacation. Prompted, I suspect, by a certain Dr Ironside.'

'Really? Most curious.' Featherstone made a note. 'I really don't comprehend this at all.'

'Nor do I. But it seems to me there's some sort of cover-up going on, and I don't understand why.'

'I'm sure you're making too much of it. There will no doubt be a very simple explanation for the missing report. It's not as if the Path Lab have never lost a report before, I'm sorry to say. And now, Mr Robinson, you must promise me that you will stay away from the hospital and Miss Randall.'

'I'll try.'

'I'm afraid that's not good enough.'

'I'm afraid it's the best I can do.'

'Oh dear.' This was all getting too much for Featherstone. He gave up. 'I suppose I shall have to leave it at that, then. But please don't do anything else to annoy Mr D'Arcy.'

'I'll certainly promise you that.'

Simon rose to leave. As he was going through the door, Featherstone called after him.

'Mr Robinson!'

Simon stopped, turned. What now? he thought.

'I was pleased to hear about your EEG result.'

The sudden change of tack puzzled Simon for a moment. 'Sorry?'

He tapped his head. 'Your test. I'm glad you haven't got epilepsy.'

'Thank you, Mr Featherstone. So am I.'

* * *

Gwyn was waiting by Simon's car. 'Christ, that took a long time! What happened? Roasted alive?'

'More or less. How did you know I was here?'

'I have my methods; spies in the ICU — and the DGM's office.'

Simon, despite his ordeal, raised a chuckle. 'Female, no doubt?'

'We won't go into that now. Look — there's a ray of hope on the horizon, but they spent so long wiping the floor with you I'll have to tell you about it later. I'm meant to be gassing for Orthopaedics any minute.' He looked anxiously at his watch.

'What's this all about?'

'It's to do with the Path Lab computer. I've been talking to a friend of mine who's into chips and bytes and things. He's come up with something that might be of use in our search for the Randall report. But it'll have to wait now — I've gotta dash, or Theatre will be after me.'

'So why did you waylay me here and not give me a ring?'

'I thought you might need a little boost to your morale.'

'You're dead right there. Thanks, Gwyn.'

'Don't mention it. I'll call you at home later.'

Simon began to unlock his car door, then something struck a chord. He chased after his friend, calling to him to wait.

'Gwyn, one quick question. Who gassed for Greenwell on his list this morning?'

'I did. Why?'

'So *you* gave Kate her anaesthetic this morning?' He grinned at him, with relief as much as anything. Simon was as puzzled as Kate as to why she had found herself on the private wing, and despite inquiries had got no satisfactory answers.

'Whatever makes you ask that?'

'Because Greenwell did her tubal insufflation and laparoscopy this morning.'

'Christ, I'd forgotten all about that. But I didn't anaesthetise Kate. How did it go?'

'Oh, everything was OK.'

'Well, that's great. Look, I must go, chum.'

'So who did anaesthetise her?'

'I've no idea, Simon.' Gwyn looked puzzled. 'In fact, she wasn't even on the list.'

83

9

Rather than risk any further confrontation in the hospital, early the same evening Simon phoned the ward and spoke to Kate. He explained about seeing Gemma. Kate, knowing how genuinely caring her husband was, fully understood his reasons for going, and was angry at the way D'Arcy had reacted. Her ready support made Simon wish she were back at the house with him. He told her so.

'I should be out in the morning,' she said, and he promised to be waiting in the staff car park at 10.30.

After that he couldn't settle to anything. The overwhelming despair of the morning had lifted somewhat, but he still felt in low spirits, and kept thinking about the vehemence of D'Arcy's attack. He consoled himself with the thought that, despite his pomposity, Featherstone seemed a fair man who was prepared to listen to both sides of the story.

He also felt a vague unease about Kate's investigations. He supposed he should be pleased that she was being given private treatment. If she hadn't been on the NHS operating list that Gwyn was anaesthetising for, then she must have been done in the private wing's small theatre. It wasn't much used, not being well enough equipped for major procedures, but tubal insufflation was simple enough.

He opened a bottle of wine, turned on the television, and tried to take his mind off things by watching a nature programme. He was just getting interested in the rather cute antics of some strange ferret-like desert animals when the phone rang.

It was Gwyn, and he sounded urgent. 'Simon? Can you come over to the hospital immediately?'

'Christ, I don't think I should after this morning.'

'This is important. You must come.'

'I can hardly hear you. Can't you speak up a bit?'

'No, I can't. I'm in the Path Lab.'

'Bloody hell! What are you doing there?'

'For God's sake, Simon, are you coming or not?'

'Just tell me what you're up to. I'm in enough trouble already.'

'Look mate, I'm here risking my neck for you.'

'Sorry.' Simon hadn't meant to sound ungrateful. But he was very reluctant to chance being found in the hospital again in circumstances

84

which could only be construed as interference. 'Is this to do with your computer buff friend?'

'Ye Gods!' Gwyn was losing patience. He had expected his friend to need no persuading to come and share this breakthrough. 'Yes, it is! Listen, bonehead. I was telling this chap — he's a software consultant, so he knows what he's talking about — how we'd lost some data on the Path Lab computer. I was hoping he might come up with something, and he did.'

Gwyn was speaking louder now, his excitement overcoming his caution.

'He said that most database programs automatically make back-up files in case you erase something accidentally. The trouble is, once you've rubbed a file off, you can't access any back-up directly.'

'So how does this help us?'

'He told me how to find out if the lab system makes back-up files. It does.' Gwyn was silent for some time.

Simon could sense Gwyn's excitement, and began to feel his own heart beat faster. 'Go on, man.'

'All right, all right. I was just listening. I thought I heard something.' Another pause, then Gwyn spoke again, softer this time. 'No, all clear. Where was I?'

'The back-up files.'

'OK, now what you have to do to access the back-up files is to rename them.'

'What do you mean?'

'The back-up files are not readable because the computer won't recognise them. You have to get into the operating system to change their name so that it will. My chum told me how to do it. It's easy.'

'Has it worked?' Simon held his breath.'

'It certainly has. That's why I want you to come in here. Now!'

'Good God, Gwyn! You've read the report?'

The excitement in Gwyn's voice was barely contained.

'Yep! I sure have!'

'For Christ's sake, what does it say?'

'Come and see for yourself!'

'Don't be so damn mysterious. Was the foetus normal?'

'No.'

'What was wrong with it?'

'I'm not sure. It says something about tissue damage consistent with exposure to excessive radiation.'

'*Radiation?* I don't understand.'

'Neither do I. That's why you've got to come and see it.'

'Can't you make a copy?'

'I daren't. This printer makes a hell of a noise. Besides, I want a witness.'

Simon made up his mind. 'I'm on my way.'

'Good. Quick as you can. I'm in Janice's office. Park in the road and walk round to the back entrance — the one at the end of the corridor.'

'I'll be there in ten minutes.' He ran upstairs to get his car keys.

The laboratory complex was in complete darkness. Simon entered and made his way along the corridor. He knew there was a risk of being discovered, because the duty lab technician could come in at any time to process an emergency test, usually to type and cross-match blood in the event of a road accident or emergency operation. He resisted the urge to put the light on, and fought down his irrational fear of the dark. Now, where was Janice's room? Near the end of the corridor on the right, wasn't it? He could see a little better now, as his eyes adjusted to the blackness and some light glowed from a softly lit 'Exit' sign at the far end of the corridor.

This was it! He eased open the door. It was pitch black. He took a step into the darkness, and there was a loud 'clank' as two glass bottles collided.

'Damn!' Simon swore softly. He'd gone into a store cupboard. He listened, holding his breath for a moment, then slowly pushed the door shut. He tried the next one carefully, and as soon as it began to open he could see the green glow from the computer monitor. He relaxed as he opened it wider and saw Gwyn. He was sitting in the dark in front of the computer terminal, leaning forward and peering at it very closely. His face was not fully visible, but it had an eerie green luminescence, reflected from the screen.

'Right, I've made it,' Simon whispered. There was no response from Gwyn, who kept staring closely at the monitor. Simon sensed there was something wrong, a feeling heightened by his awareness of an unpleasant smell. His scalp prickled.

'Gwyn?'

He moved closer, and noticed dark blotches all over the desk and keyboard. It was dripping down from — from Gwyn's nose and chin!

He rushed to his friend, pulled him upright by the shoulders. Gwyn flopped back, his head lolling so that his face stared up at the ceiling, eyes wide open. Simon let out an involuntary shout, and jumped back. Even by this dim light, he was certain that Gwyn was dead. He felt weak, then panicky. Christ almighty! What had happened? Gwyn! Oh, God, Gwyn! His mind was in a frenzy, and he tried to calm himself. Gwyn might not be dead! There might be something he could do!

He moved forward again. Blood had been running down Gwyn's face, but there was no obvious injury. He felt the neck. Cold and clammy. No carotid pulse. He felt around the back of the head. He felt wetness, then — was it the edge of a wound? There was a gap. He

86

reached farther, and his fingers encountered some soft, sticky substance. Despite his professional training, Simon felt sick. Oh, Jesus, what's happened to him? He withdrew his hand, went to the door to find the light switch.

The neon tube stuttered twice, then flooded the room with light. Simon blinked until his vision could cope with the brightness. He could see his friend, staring up at the ceiling, blood dripping from a gaping wound in the back of his skull. The desk and keyboard were covered in blood, and the monitor was spattered with bits of greyish material. In a state of shock already, Simon looked down at his right hand. There were lumps of grey goo on his fingers. He slumped against the wall, almost losing consciousness completely, his mind screaming one thought:

'You put your fingers in his brain!'

* * *

Simon wasn't really sure how long he sat propped against the wall of the office. His head swam with revolving sensations of nausea, fear, anger and grief. Come on, he argued, you've got to be professional about this. Gwyn is dead. OK, so he was your friend, and you're upset.

Upset? Christ!

All right, but you've seen blood and gore before, that shouldn't paralyse you like this.

But I put my fingers in his brain!

Come on, you've dealt with that sort of thing, when you worked in Casualty. All those head injuries from car smashes . . .

All right, all right. I'll do something. Get some help. Call the police.

Simon stood up slowly, giving time for the accompanying light-headedness to wear off. He went to the phone on the desk, and was about to pick it up when he thought he'd better not touch anything else for fear of disturbing any fingerprints. That's better, he told himself. Thinking more rationally now.

His attention was drawn to the screen by the insistent flashing of the cursor. The report! Where was that bloody report! Hell, that was what all this — he glanced quickly at Gwyn — all this was about.

There were four boxes on the screen, one each for name, address, date of birth, and hospital number. The details were those of Gemma Randall! At the bottom right hand corner of the picture the cursor was flashing by an instruction: 'Press return for next page'.

Simon looked and saw that the return key had escaped the worst of the blood. He didn't think the keyboard would work, but he pressed it anyway. There was a promising click, and the screen changed. It was now filled with one large box, which had the heading 'Histology Report'. It should have displayed the typewritten report, but it did not. There was just one brief statement. It said:

LEAVE ME ALONE

Simon ran from the laboratory in a state of shock and fear. He went straight to the A & E department, where he asked the Sister to call the police. The staff in Casualty were more sympathetic than before, and he took some consolation from that. Gwyn had been popular at the hospital, and the anaesthetist's friendship with the Senior Obstetric Registrar was well known. They only had to look at him to see how badly he was affected.

For the second time in little over a week, Simon found himself spending several hours at a police station. Pauline Jamieson was there again, and he was very grateful. He was getting to know her quite well.

There was less initial hostility this time, despite the fact that he had no one to corroborate his story. Looking back, he thought this might have been because he was so obviously distressed at the death of his friend. He could think of no other explanation. He had fully expected to be arrested and be given a hard time. After all, he found himself in the hitherto unimaginable position of discovering two violent deaths within days of each other. Some coincidence!

After going over his story several times and making a statement that Pauline Jamieson read very carefully before letting him sign it, he was allowed home. The lawyer offered to drive him, for which he was grateful. He didn't feel safe to drive. He felt it was scarcely safe to think.

As she pulled up outside Simon's house, Pauline turned to him.

'Look, Simon. For heaven's sake don't think I'm overdoing it, but I'd like to talk to you a bit more about this business. Can I come in for a moment?'

Simon wasn't too sure; he had a longing to be left alone. However, some company for a while might do him good, stop him brooding. He desperately wanted Kate to talk to, but she would be fast asleep in the hospital, unaware of what had happened. He had declined the offer to ring her up from the police station: there seemed no point in troubling her now. She would be disturbed enough to hear about it all in the morning.

It was now one o'clock, and Simon felt strangely guilty about letting an attractive woman into his house at this hour, with his wife away. If any of the neighbours saw them . . . Despite everything, he smiled at the thought.

'Well, that's a relief.' Pauline had been watching him by the light outside the porch.

'What is?'

'Seeing you smile. I thought you looked like a potential suicide earlier.'

That struck home. On more than one occasion recently Simon really had thought himself a potential suicide. He hurried into the house, turning the lights on, keeping his face averted until he had control of himself again. He wasn't good enough for his sharp-eyed companion.

'I'm sorry. That was a bit near the mark, wasn't it? I thought I was making a joke. I was just pleased to see you lighten up.'

'I was smiling about what the neighbours might think if they saw me letting a strange woman into my house at this time of night.' He tried a grin, but failed miserably. The effort was too much. He sank down on the sofa and buried his face in his hands. Pauline could see his shoulders shaking as he wept silently. For once, she wasn't sure what to do. She wasn't embarrassed — she had dealt with many distressed clients in her time — but she felt somehow inhibited by the fact that this man was also a doctor. She had assumed that in some way he would know how to handle his own grief, as he must have helped so many others. She was surprised to find that this did not seem to be the case. She stood watching him for a moment, undecided. To go or stay? To speak or stay silent? After a few more seconds, she came to a decision, and went in search of the kitchen.

Pauline took her time making the coffee, although it was a well enough ordered place, with everything more or less where one would expect to find it. She even found the cooking brandy, and laced both mugs with it.

Simon stood up when she came back into the lounge.

'I'm sorry about that. I'm OK now.'

Pauline had to laugh gently. 'Well, you certainly don't look it!' Simon glanced in the mirror over the fireplace, and saw a face that was red-eyed, dishevelled, weary.

'Here, drink this. I raided your brandy bottle to give it something extra.'

'Thanks. I'm sorry — behaving like this.'

'Stop apologising. I think it's important to show your emotions. Nothing wrong with it. Man or woman.' She was trying hard to avoid the old cliché about there being nothing wrong with a man being seen to cry. Once again, she remembered he was a doctor. 'But you know all about that. With your patients, I mean — ' Shut up, you're getting hopelessly lost here, she told herself.

'Actually, one thing I've learnt is that it's a darn sight easier to advise other people on how to handle their emotions than it is to handle your own.'

'You really liked him, didn't you?'

'Yes, I did. He was — ' Simon faltered, and Pauline thought she had said the wrong thing. She wanted the matter to be spoken of again, hoping it would help get him over this phase of grieving more quickly. But Simon had taken the cue. He recovered himself, looked directly at her, and continued: 'He was a very good friend. And what makes it worse is that he's dead because of me.'

So that's what's making it so much harder for him, Pauline realised. It was stupid of her not to have seen it at once. She'd heard Simon tell the whole story enough times.

'Right,' she said, matter-of-factly, 'I understand. So sit down, drink your coffee, and let's see what we can do about it.'

Simon did as he was told, and sipped the coffee with his hands wrapped round the mug. 'Do you always give your clients this class of personal service?'

She gave him a wry smile. 'No, I certainly don't.'

'Then — ' he waved the mug in her direction — 'Why all this?'

'Because I'm genuinely interested in the whole business. Criminal law is not just my job, it has a fascination for me. Most of it is terribly mundane and rather petty and sordid. But this . . .'

'This is — different?'

'Yes. Look, I don't mean I'm treating this as some sort of interesting freak show that has attracted me out of sheer curiosity. I want to do a good job for you, but this case is so unusual, it's more than just another item of work. I mean — ' She realised she was running herself aground again. 'Look at it this way. You're a nice person, and you've been hurt, and you're in trouble. Gwyn was obviously a nice person too, and he's dead. There's something evil going on here, and it will give me great pleasure to help you nail the bastard that did it!'

Simon looked at her in surprise. Her vehemence, and her language, were unexpected. He was impressed. This was a forceful woman, and a useful ally. The thought that he might have another helpmate so soon after losing his main support in his troubles was heartening. Kate was of course supportive, but not in the active way that Gwyn had been. He hadn't really thought in terms of avenging Gwyn's death, indeed had not had time to recover from or reflect on his discovery of a few hours before. But Pauline's words fired an anger in him. Get the bugger that was responsible! That sounded good. He seized upon the feeling. It was better than just mourning the loss.

Pauline watched as his face set grimly, teeth clenched. She saw his head come up, his shoulders straighten. She knew what she had done.

With a few words she had redirected his emotions from inward self-critical despair to an outward force directed at a specific target. He might not recognise how she had manipulated him just now, but he would later. She hoped he wouldn't be angry with her because of it.

'All right!' Simon looked over his coffee mug at her. 'You wanted to talk to me about it, so let's talk. Anything you think might help, as you so aptly put it, to nail the bastard.'

They settled opposite each other, Simon on the sofa, Pauline in an armchair. She began.

'Three points I want to clear up in particular. First: you've explained to me about the missing report, and how your friend — ' she said 'friend' with heavy sarcasm — 'D'Arcy says that the slides are missing too. But I *don't* understand about this Dr Ravensbourne. Do you know if anything has been done to trace her whereabouts?'

'I shouldn't think so. Although the slides are important evidence, if you like to think of them as that, in the Gemma Randall affair, a missing Path report isn't the sort of thing you'd get the police involved in — to go hunting for her to bring her back from holiday, for example.'

'Yes.' Pauline nodded her agreement. 'I'm sure you're right about that. They'd just say, "What's the panic? Wait until she gets back. It's not a matter of life and death."'

'But I still think it's odd the way she left on the same morning that Gwyn and I tried to get hold of the information. The whole thing suggests an elaborate attempt to remove all traces of the histology of that foetus. It's important to *me*, but why the hell is it so important to anyone else, that they'd go to such lengths?'

'Such lengths is right!' Pauline considered. 'I mean, it now looks as if Gwyn was killed because he'd found a way of accessing the report. It must have some incredible importance to someone, that he'd commit murder to keep it hidden.'

Simon looked away. 'Yes. I've been trying to avoid that conclusion, but there's no denying it, is there? Gwyn was killed because he was trying to help me.' He smashed his fist down on his knee. 'Jesus Christ, why!'

Good, thought Pauline, I'll get more out of him angry than mournful.

'What do you know about this Dr Ravensbourne?'

Simon thought for a moment. 'Good histopathologist. Trained at Bart's, I think. Got her MRCPath. in record time, I was told.'

'No. I don't mean professionally. I mean as a person.'

'I don't know her that well.'

'What's her first name?'

'Gillian.'

'So?' Pauline shrugged her shoulders. 'You've obviously spoken to her, or heard others talk about her.'

Simon looked up, squinting with the effort of recall. 'She seems pleasant enough to talk to, but I've only really talked shop with her. Gwyn didn't appear very keen on her, though. Didn't like to talk about her, even. I thought perhaps it was because he thought she seemed to be a bit of a women's libber.' He realised he had said it in a rather derisory manner, and glanced at Pauline anxiously to see if he had caused offence.

Pauline regarded him sternly. 'And what exactly is that supposed to mean?'

Simon was uncomfortable. 'Look, I'm sorry, I didn't mean to — '

Pauline laughed. 'It's all right. I'm only pulling your leg! Let's see,' she went on, 'the second point is, what do you make of what Gwyn told you on the phone about the report?'

Simon looked puzzled. 'I haven't really had a chance to think about it — anyway, there's not much to go on.'

Pauline sympathised. 'I realise there hasn't been much time. Just give me your immediate impression.'

'Well, all I can remember is that he said there were signs of tissue damage consistent with the effects of radiation — something like that.'

'And how might that occur?'

'I just can't imagine. And I don't know what sort of tissue damage it was. If an embryo is subjected to radiation while it's developing it can have malformations. But malformations aren't usually referred to as "tissue damage". That term suggests destruction or alteration of previously normal body cells.'

Pauline was intrigued. 'And how might that happen?'

'The obvious one is the sort of thing that was seen in the victims of the atomic bombs in Japan. But we can't be talking about that type of effect here.'

'Any other possible causes?'

'None that makes any sense. She's maths student, not a nuclear physicist, so accidental exposure in a laboratory handling radioactive materials is out.'

'What about X-ray therapy? That can cause tissue damage, can't it?'

Simon looked at her appreciatively. 'Yes, that's a sensible suggestion. How do you know that?'

Her brow furrowed. 'My mother. She had cancer of the breast. It was years ago. They took her breast off, and then irradiated the area. They overdid it. The skin was damaged, and it never healed. I used to dress it for her.' She shuddered at the memory.

'I'm sorry,' he said, and meant it. 'That sort of thing used to happen

92

all too often. But it can't account for foetal tissue damage. To irradiate the baby in the womb with DXR enough to cause damage would cause terrible problems for the mother. There's no history or signs of any problems in Gemma's case, no reason for her to have been irradiated in the first place.'

'What about ordinary X-rays?'

'No, I'm sure we can count that out. There was a time when doing X-rays in early pregnancy was thought to be associated with foetal abnormalities and even leukaemia in children, but all the recent research points to this not being the case. In fact, precautions against X-raying women who may be in early pregnancy have been considerably relaxed in the last few years.'

'So what's left?'

'Nothing.' Simon shrugged. 'I have absolutely no idea what the explanation might be.'

Pauline sighed, and looked at her watch. 'Hell! It's nearly two o'clock, and I'm in court in the morning!' She got up.

Simon was tired, too, but he was anxious for her not to leave just yet. 'Hang on a minute. What was the third point?'

'The third point?' Pauline's concentration was going. She had to think hard to remember, sat down again, rubbed her eyes. 'Something about the computer that Gwyn was — of course, that message: "Leave me alone". What do you make of that?'

'I suppose one could say it was Gwyn's dying attempt to call off his attacker.'

'Is that what you really think?'

'No, that's probably rubbish. You'd hardly type a faultless message like that with a fire axe chopping into your skull.'

'So what did it mean?'

Simon looked at her, and she could see he was frightened. 'I took it to be a warning.'

'Directed at whom?'

'Me. Who else?'

They sat in silence for a while, before Pauline spoke again. 'Simon — ' She sounded tentative. 'You are quite sure about that message, aren't you?'

'Positive. I couldn't mistake it.'

'And you didn't go back to the lab after you called the police?'

He sensed the uncertainty in her voice and looked at her. 'Why do you ask that?'

She shifted uncomfortably. 'Well, it's just that no one else has seen it.'

'What do you mean?'

'I asked the police what they thought about it. They were quite certain there was no message on the screen when they got there.'

93

10

Simon came slowly awake, aware that he was very tired, and that his head ached. He felt a wave of nausea, born of anxiety, as memories of the previous day's events came flooding back to him.

He tried to face the facts. *Gwyn! Gwyn is dead.* It can't be true! But it is true, it's no use pretending. You've got to face up to it, man. Remember last night? You vowed to go and get the evil bastard that did this, the same person who is probably responsible for the mess your own life is in. So *get up!* He sat on the edge of the bed, feeling totally drained. He knew he had to force himself into some sort of action. What had Pauline said? 'When you go to pick up Kate from the hospital, why don't you — '

Kate! Christ, what was the time? He'd said he would pick Kate up in the staff car park at 10.30. He looked at his watch, and his stomach turned over. It was 10.50! He had forgotten to reset the alarm! He suddenly came wide awake, the adrenaline pouring into his blood-stream. *Oh, Kate!* He pictured her in the car park, small suitcase in hand, waiting for him, looking conspicuous and vulnerable, feeling increasingly embarrassed and angry. He threw off the duvet, and with feverish haste struggled into his clothes.

Poor Kate! What will she think of me? Will she have heard anything about Gwyn, and about my involvement? If she has, she'll be worried sick by now. He jumped down the stairs, two at a time. God, it'll take me another ten minutes to get there! He felt near to panic. He grabbed his keys, threw open the front door, then stopped dead. Kate was just paying off a taxi outside.

Simon remained silent as she marched into the house; he was afraid to say anything until they were inside. The taxi-driver obviously knew there was some problem, because he was watching with interest with his window down. Simon closed the front door and followed his wife. She went straight upstairs to their bedroom, trying to shut the door in his face.

He pushed it open. 'I'm sorry, love. I — '

Kate dropped her bag and turned on him. She was angry, near to tears. 'Where the hell were you?'

'I don't know what to say. I — I overslept.'

'Overslept! You mean you forgot! Again! Didn't you? You just damn well forgot me.'

'Honestly, Kate, I overslept. Pauline was here until gone two o'clock, and then I didn't — '

'Pauline? Who the hell is Pauline?'

'Pauline Jamieson — you know, the lawyer. She was trying to — '

'You mean while I was in hospital being poked about for the sake of us having a baby, you were here in my house with some woman until two o'clock in the morning?' Kate was shouting now.

Simon had never seen her like this. She rarely lost her temper, but now she was almost in a rage. He didn't know how to handle it. He shouted back.

'It wasn't anything like that!'

Kate turned away from him. He could see hurt and disbelief written on her face. Simon felt a sudden, overwhelming depression. Wearily, he sat down on the bed. He didn't know how to fight back against yet another downturn in his life. There had been too many in the last couple of weeks. He hung his head. 'It was only because of Gwyn,' he said softly.

There was silence for a moment, and he raised his head hopefully, looking for some softening of his wife's attitude. She moved closer to him, and he saw her eyes were hard and narrow. Her hands were in fists by her sides, her teeth clenched. She spoke contemptuously.

'Gwyn! I might have known your womanising friend Gwyn was behind this!'

Simon felt as if he had been struck between the eyes with a knife. His mind went blank for a moment, and he lost all control. He jumped up and grabbed Kate by the shoulders. He roared at her, shaking her violently like a doll.

'FOR CHRIST'S SAKE, GWYN IS DEAD!'

Slowly he became aware of what he was doing, of Kate's pale face and wide, frightened eyes, of her desperate attempts to pull his hands away. He let go, and she fell against him, sobbing. Gently he laid her on the bed and knelt over her, mumbling 'sorry' over and over again, brushing back her hair, touching the reddening marks on the side of her neck, trying to kiss away her tears. Kate lay still, staring up at the ceiling, her rapid breathing gradually returning to normal. After a minute or so, Simon put his head on her stomach, face turned away from hers, his mind a turmoil of remorse. They lay like that for some time.

He was aware of some movement. Kate was wiping her eyes. 'Gwyn — ' her voice sounded husky — 'you said Gwyn is dead?'

Simon couldn't face her. 'Yes. I thought you would know.'

'Simon, I swear I didn't. I — what happened?'

'He was murdered. Last night.'

There was a long silence. Simon became aware of the heat of his wife's body, as though she was warming to him. As if in response to his thought, he felt her hand gently stroke the hair on the back of his head.

'Oh, God.' She spoke sadly, almost a whisper. 'Poor Gwyn. Poor Simon.'

Simon wasn't sure if he could face her yet. Still looking away, he said, 'Kate, please forgive me for — for — ' He couldn't find the words. What were they? Forgive me for hurting you, nearly strangling you? No, he couldn't make himself admit to that possibility.

'I'm sorry, too. I shouldn't have doubted you. It's just that I was so disappointed when you weren't waiting at the hospital . . .'

Simon lifted himself up, turned to look at her.

'You've nothing to say sorry for. It was my fault.'

Kate took his hand and pulled him down beside her.

'Tell me what happened.'

It took Simon half an hour to describe the events of the previous 24 hours. Kate listened carefully, stopping him occasionally to ask a question. As he reached the end, reaffirming his vow to do whatever he could to help find his friend's murderer, and — equally important to himself — to find out what was behind it all, she put a further question, one that had also been troubling Simon:

'Why didn't the police see the message on the screen?'

'I don't know. I ran from the Lab to Casualty, and called the police from there. I didn't go back to the Lab. They asked me to, but I refused. I didn't want to see Gwyn again like that. Although I had to later, anyway, to identify him.'

'Could the electricity have gone off? A power failure, or something?'

'No. I'd thought of that, and so had Pauline. She got the police to check the electric clocks. They're in all the laboratories in the block — big old-fashioned ones with second hands. They run on the mains. They were put in before everything became digital and automated. They were important for timing reactions in tests. They all showed the right time.'

'So have you got any other ideas?'

'The obvious one is that between me leaving and the police arriving, someone came and erased the message.'

Kate quickly grasped the implication of that. 'You mean that whoever killed Gwyn was still there? Still in the building when you found him?'

'Yes.'

She held him close. 'He could have killed you, too.'

'That thought had occurred to me.'

'Was the report Gwyn had managed to recover still in the computer's memory?'

'No. Pauline said the police got their own computer expert to look into that. There was no trace of any record, back-up or otherwise, relating to Gemma Randall. And the preliminary forensic report says no fingerprints, either. Lots of other marks, though.'

'Marks of what?'

'Surgical gloves.'

The implication was immediately obvious to them both: that the killer could be a doctor. They talked about it for some time. Dr Ironside's name inevitably came up, but try as they might they couldn't see how they could tie him in to this crime. The more they talked, the more they felt that the assumption was wrong. Anyone wishing to commit a crime and avoid making fingerprints would wear gloves, and if freedom of movement and a good touch were needed — like using a computer keyboard, Simon pointed out — then surgical gloves would be ideal. It did suggest, however, that whoever was responsible could well have some association with the hospital.

Simon realised with considerable guilt that he had not asked Kate how she felt after her tests.

'I'm fine.'

He looked at her sharply.

'Really I am. All this — ' she waved her arm vaguely about her — 'has set me back a bit from the emotional point of view, but physically I'm fine.'

'I thought you might have been sort of — well, half hoping for some simple little problem that would explain — and solve — everything.'

She smiled at him. He knew her so well.

'Yes, you perceptive little psychologist, I rather think I was. But I've come to terms with that. We've just got to get on with it.'

Lying by her side, Simon felt his love for his wife welling up, filling his chest. He had forgotten to pick her up from hospital, they'd had a blazing row, he'd physically shaken her. Yet here she was, less than an hour later, all that forgotten, concerned only for his welfare, and dealing in a matter-of-fact way with her dearest wish — to have a baby.

He turned to her. 'You know something?'

'What?'

'I love you.'

'That's strange.'

'What is?'

'I was just going to say the same thing.' He knew she meant it, he could see it in her eyes. She turned more towards him, put her hand on his stomach. He could feel himself becoming aroused even before she loosened his belt and slid her hand down to touch him. He reached over to stroke her breast, feeling the nipple harden immediately. Slowly they undressed each other, and all thoughts of despair, death and disaster were suppressed by their physical enjoyment of each other's bodies. Kate gave no heed to the discomfort she felt as Simon entered her, soon forgotten as her intensity of feeling rose towards orgasm. They came together, Kate crying out, Simon groaning his pleasure, and then they lay, at peace for a while, in each other's arms.

Kate lay awake for an hour, the worries of recent weeks slowly returning to the forefront of her thoughts. She looked at her husband, who now lay deeply asleep, looking untroubled for the first time in days. She eased herself out of bed, her full bladder forcing her to make a move. She passed the full-length mirror and stopped for a moment, looking at her naked reflection. She had a good shape, breasts not quite as high as they were but still firm. She touched her shoulders. Bruises were beginning to appear. High-necked jumpers for a few days, she thought. She ran her hands down over her abdomen, down towards her pubis.

A thought was forming, growing, suffusing her with pleasure. She gave herself a secretive smile. Somehow she knew, beyond a shadow of a doubt. It might seem ridiculous, so soon. But in there, a new life was just beginning to grow.

11

A great deal happened over the next three weeks. Gwyn's inquest was held, at which Simon had to give evidence. The verdict, predictably, was unlawful killing by person or persons unknown. There was more unwelcome publicity for the hospital, and Simon was virtually forbidden, by the District Health Authority, to give interviews to the press. Not that he wanted to. The amount of attention he was already getting was unpleasant enough; he didn't want to court any more. The local press carried the story in fairly sensational terms for a few days, and there were two items on local television channels about Gwyn's murder. There was inevitable speculation about the fact that only a short time before Simon had been associated with another murder, that of Janice Marshall, the circumstances of which easily led to mischievous interpretation.

For several days after the inquest the Robinsons' house was besieged by telephone calls and visitors, including reporters waiting around with cameras and tape recorders. Simon found it increasingly difficult to keep his temper, angry at these intrusions into his privacy; angry too that Kate was being subjected to the same harassment. She arrived home in tears one day after being virtually ambushed by several reporters who had surrounded her car outside a supermarket.

It was four days since the inquest, and Simon sensed the media spotlight was beginning to fade. The telephone had been silent all morning, and he was trying to relax, absorbed in an article on a new technique to reduce the numbers of unnecessary hysterectomies. When the telephone rang it made him jump, then curse silently.

'Who is it?' he asked abruptly, realised he didn't sound very polite, but didn't care.

There was a pause. Simon was about to put the phone down when a precise, slow-speaking male voice spoke.

'Is that Dr Simon Robinson?'

Simon was learning to be defensive. 'Who wants him?'

'It's all right, I'm not the press or anything.' There was a slight hesitation. 'I'm a solicitor's clerk for Humbolt and Newry.'

Simon had heard of the local firm. 'What do you want?'

'You *are* Dr Robinson, I take it?'

'Yes, I am,' he agreed reluctantly.

'I am making inquiries concerning Miss Janice Marshall.'

Simon sighed wearily. 'I really think you should contact my own solicitor direct.'

'No, it's all right, this will only take a moment.' Before Simon could object again, he hurried on. 'I need a little more detail about the young woman's injuries. You saw them at first hand, so to speak. I'd like you to tell me whether her external genitalia were badly mutilated — and also about the breasts, were they — '

Simon rose rapidly to anger. 'For God's sake, man, get off the line!'

'But I assure you, doctor, my business is legitimate. I am representing — '

'I don't care who you are representing, I'm not discussing something like that over the phone with someone I don't know.'

'But, sir, please.' The voice developed a pleading tone. 'I only want to know about her vagina. Was it — '

Simon slammed the phone down, threatening to break it. 'Bastard!' he shouted to the empty room. He got up, threw down the journal he had been reading, and went to the kitchen. He had just filled the electric kettle when the phone rang again. He hesitated before picking it up.

'Yes?'

It was the same wheedling voice. 'Please tell me about the breasts and the vagina, Dr Rob — '

Simon smashed the handset down and stood there, shaking, his hand still pressing on the instrument. He could scarcely believe it when it rang yet again. He pulled his hand away as if the phone were hot, then snatched it up. He didn't speak, just listened, his mind working to try and stop this nightmare. He waited, knowing there was someone there. Eventually the same voice spoke again.

'Doctor, why won't you — '

'Listen to me!' Simon shouted. 'This phone is tapped. Do you understand me? The calls are being recorded and traced. If you call again, I can assure — '

The voice that came at him was little more than a shrill scream. 'All right, *doctor,* keep it to yourself, you pervert!' There was a click, and the line went dead.

What was happening to him in this mad world? He had lost his best friend, possibly his job, and *he* was the one being persecuted. It was an hour before he felt calm enough to resume his reading.

His peace did not last long. He was watching the news at lunchtime when the pleasant-sounding woman called. His relief at it not being the bogus solicitor's clerk enabled him to sound reasonably civil.

'Dr Robinson?'

Again the reluctant admission, having first established she was not from the media.

'It's very good of you to speak to me,' the female voice continued

100

sweetly, 'I'm sure you must be fed up with phone calls.'

Simon gave a grim laugh. 'You could just say that.'

The woman responded with her own relaxed laughter. 'You poor man. I know what it's like to be the focus of media attention.'

Simon became a little wary. 'Oh?'

'Yes. I am on the National Committee of the WAA.'

'I'm sorry. I'm not familiar with that organisation.'

'You've never heard of us?' The voice took on a disapproving tone. 'I *am* surprised. We are Women Against Abortion.'

Simon's heart sank. He didn't want to get involved in a discussion about the ethics of abortion. Not now, when he was uncertain even of his own feelings. 'I see.'

The lady detected the weariness, the disapproval, in those two words. She continued determinedly. 'I'd like to know whether the circumstances surrounding the girl Gemma Randall have made you have second thoughts about termination of pregnancy. We always try to recruit doctors who have had bad experiences with TOP to our cause. I'm sure you will be one of those who will henceforth denounce this primitive savagery.'

Simon wanted to put the phone down, but in some way needed to justify himself to this person who was accusing him of barbarism.

'I just try to do what's best for my patient.'

'So ripping out her unborn child and leaving her crippled is doing what's best for her, is it?' The voice was becoming shrill.

'You can't simplify an issue like this into a debate on one single case, however unfortunate the outcome.'

'In other words, you're like all the rest. A child murderer!' She was shouting, but now her voice dropped. 'You'll pay for this, one day. Retribution will come. I hope you can live with the consequences —'

Simon sent the receiver crashing into its cradle.

That call was one of the most upsetting. Not so much because of the threats, but because he felt badly enough about Gemma as it was, and knew he was becoming increasingly uncomfortable about the whole question of termination of pregnancy. As he was still suspended, he had plenty of time to think about such things — too much, in fact. He wondered, should he eventually get his job back, whether he could ever make himself responsible for another abortion, either by the decision to carry it out, or by the operation itself. But he didn't need some hysterical woman screaming down the phone at him to help him decide such an important and personal issue.

After that incident, he arranged for a block on all his calls until the number could be changed and made ex-directory, and for a while he was left in peace.

The one thing Simon needed the phone for was to keep in touch with Gemma Randall's progress, by ringing the ward every so often.

101

She had left the ICU after a few days, transferring to one of the main Gynae Wards. Once her surgical wounds had healed she was moved again, and was now on a Medical Ward, where her rehabilitation could continue. She was recovering well from the injuries he had inflicted on her pelvic organs and blood vessels, but was showing little signs of recovery from the damage to her central nervous system caused by the lack of oxygen. She could just about stand now, with help from the physiotherapists, but walking seemed a long way off. Her right hand was still not showing any sign of movement, and there was no recovery in her powers of speech.

If Gemma's condition had not changed much, Kate's certainly had. She had gone back to work two days after coming out of hospital, and a week after that she had insisted on having a pregnancy test. Simon thought this was purely wishful thinking on his wife's part, since they had only had intercourse on the one occasion. The worries about the inquest and the pressure from the media soon sent him back into his morose state, and he had lost all interest in sex. Kate had not bothered him, which both relieved and surprised him, because he had thought she would be anxious to try out her now proven patent tubes. Kate, however, was sure she did not need to. She seemed to *know* she was already pregnant.

'I'm sure you think it's a waste of time, but trust a woman's intuition,' she said one morning, putting a sterile glass container of urine in front of him as he ate his cornflakes.

'Please, Kate, not at breakfast,' he chided her gently. But he could see she was determined, and arranged for the Lab to do the test.

Kate insisted he call the Lab at lunchtime. He waited, holding the phone, tension mounting within him despite his certainty that this was a wild goose chase. The technician's voice was excited.

'It's positive, Mr Robinson. Your wife is pregnant.'

Simon was amazed. 'You're sure?'

Laughter down the phone. 'Yes, doctor, quite sure.'

'Well — thanks very much.'

'My pleasure.'

Simon turned to Kate, grinning broadly. 'Hello, Mum!'

Kate shrugged her shoulders. 'Well, I knew anyway.'

Simon frowned. 'Aren't you pleased?' He could feel his elation evaporating.

'Of course. But it was only a question of confirmation — of convincing you.' She saw his puzzled disappointment, and moved to him, took his hand. 'I *am* pleased, really. What about you?'

'Need you ask? After all this time? We've finally made it!' He gave her a hug. 'What shall we do to celebrate?'

Kate drew away. 'Oh, I don't think we need to do anything just now.' She started clearing the table. 'I must get back to work.'

Left alone again, Simon felt miserable, a feeling made worse by the knowledge that he should be ecstatic. Where was the joy, the eyes shining with happiness, the urge to rush out and tell the world? This wonderful news should have been just the tonic he needed to get himself out of his depression, but Kate's attitude had spoilt it for him.

Kate seemed quite oblivious of her husband's feelings, and was totally absorbed in the pregnancy in a completely uninhibited way. What was surprising was the time she devoted to getting ready for the baby.

Not for her the waiting to see if everything would be all right, to be sure her preparations would not be marred by an early miscarriage. She went out and bought a cot, nursery wallpaper, a steriliser, and piles of baby clothes. Every time she went out, it seemed, she came back with something for the baby. At first Simon ventured to question her enthusiasm. Kate gave him a very hard look, and told him to stop fussing.

'It's all right,' she said. 'I know everything will be all right.' She tried to sound pleasant about it, but she was really angry, he could see that. 'Sometimes I think you're jealous of the baby.' She referred to it as if it were already there, a person. He did not mention it again.

Simon himself became more withdrawn as the weeks passed. Partly this was because of all the unwanted publicity, the unpleasant phone calls. But there was another reason for his increasing lack of enthusiasm. He tried to put it out of his thoughts, but he couldn't. Every time he saw Kate with something new for the baby, he knew that at night his mind would switch on the picture of the midwife holding his child. Every time it was the same. The baby in his dream was a hideous monster.

* * *

A few days after Kate had her positive pregnancy test, Simon was given notice of a preliminary inquiry by the District Health Authority into the Gemma Randall affair. It was in two weeks, and he would have to appear to give evidence.

He felt at rock-bottom about this time, and was rapidly approaching despair until Pauline Jamieson started to take a further interest in the case. The attractive lawyer had come to see him to talk to him again about the Janice Marshall killing. The police were using 'genetic fingerprinting' to help them identify the rapist. This technique involved using genetic material from body cells, by looking at the DNA, which has a unique pattern in each individual. Any cellular material could be used, and they had two sources in this case, the semen recovered from Janice's vagina, and the saliva, which always contains at least a few cells from the lining of the mouth, from the

103

bites on Janice's breasts. The problem was, the two didn't match.

Although the police accepted that Simon could not have been responsible for the attack on Janice, they wanted to check his own 'genetic fingerprint' to help, as Pauline delicately put it, 'clarify the situation'. The implications were as clear as they were abhorrent to Simon, but he agreed to have a buccal smear taken, a scraping of cells from the inside of the mouth.

That awkward request over, and more to change the subject than anything, Simon decided to mention another of his worries.

'The District Health Authority have arranged a preliminary inquiry into my suspension.'

'Oh?' She looked concerned. 'Anything I can do to help?'

'Well, it's not a formal hearing. Not something where I need legal representation. I hope!'

'Don't you subscribe to some independent insurance organisation that advises you on these things?'

'Yes. I belong to the Practitioners' Protection Association, and I've spoken to them. They'll help out if I'm sued for negligence or malpractice. But what I could really do with now is just brushing up on how to present my position in the best light.' He looked at her hopefully.

She smiled. 'So — lessons in case presentation, logical argument and other salient points of advocacy coming up!'

At first Simon had little enthusiasm for the task. He thought he would just have to turn up and take what came. Pauline, however, kept urging him to 'fight his corner', and slowly he warmed to the idea that he had a chance of influencing the outcome of the inquiry.

'I dread to think what the bill for all this time and advice will be,' he said half-jokingly, after their third evening session.

She laughed gently. 'Don't worry! This is an interesting diversion for me. I'm not working in the firm's time. I enjoy helping you. Honestly.'

Simon was very grateful for her support and her generosity. He found her company intellectually stimulating, as she explained a certain course of reasoning to make a point, or a particular method of presentation designed to maximise the effect upon one's audience. His interest in life in general was now returning, thanks to this input which was giving him some purpose to his temporarily aimless existence.

His interest in sex was also returning, but as Simon's increased, Kate's diminished. He attributed this to the hormonal and psychological changes that she would naturally be experiencing, but it was frustrating nevertheless.

Kate did not seem to mind all the time he spent, mostly in the evenings, in Pauline's company. In fact her behaviour had become rather worrying, particularly her attitude to work. Simon thought she was losing interest in it. Almost every day she seemed to leave later and get home earlier. On one recent occasion he had been telephoned by a GP's receptionist who asked if he knew where his wife was. She was supposed to be doing an ante-natal relaxation class, but had not turned up. When Simon had asked about it later, Kate simply said, 'I forgot.' It bothered him, she was usually so efficient, so conscientious. And now today, the day of the inquiry . . .

He'd been worrying about it for days, had been trying to talk to Kate about it, and the possible outcome. The time came for him to leave, and Kate was still at home.

'Shouldn't you be going?' he asked her. It was already 9.30, and the inquiry was at 10.00. Kate usually left the house by 8.30 at the latest. Yet here she was sitting in the lounge in her uniform looking through a catalogue of perambulators. She glanced up absently. 'I haven't got much on this morning.'

'I thought you had a booking clinic on Thursday mornings?'

Kate glared at him, as if irritated at the interruption. 'There's no one to book. Stop fussing.'

Simon didn't want to provoke a row, especially with the inquiry to cope with. He shrugged.

'Well, if you're sure. I've got to leave now. Wish me luck.' He proffered his cheek for a kiss.

She looked puzzled. 'Leave? Where are you going?'

He straightened up. 'The inquiry. At the hospital.'

'Oh, that!' She went back to reading her catalogue.

'Well? Aren't you going to say anything?'

She looked up again, frowning, then smiled brightly. 'Oh yes, sorry. Have a nice time, dear.'

Simon turned and left the room. He heard a car horn sound outside. That would be Pauline — she was driving him to the hospital. Perhaps she'd be more sympathetic.

There was a man Simon did not recognise in the District General Manager's office. He was introduced to him as Marcus Whitehead, the Regional Health Authority's legal adviser. It was a strange sort of justice, thought Simon, that only allowed one side the benefit of expert help. However, he knew that this was common practice at these so-called 'informal' occasions.

At least he had the benefit of Pauline's advice, even if she wasn't in the room with him, and that of the Practitioners' Protection Association. They would represent him if it came to any proceedings in law, and would foot both the legal costs and, if necessary, any damages awarded against him.

D'Arcy, of course, was there, and so was Jeremy Greenwell, as head of the Obstetrics and Gynaecology Department.

James Featherstone opened the proceedings, and recounted the now all too familiar — to Simon — story leading up to the incident with Gemma Randall in the operating theatre. He outlined Simon's version of events, and at the end mentioned the fact that the possibility of epilepsy had been excluded. In one way this freed Simon from the possible limitation of his career, but in another it left his actions totally unexplained.

Once again, Simon was called upon to justify Gemma Randall's presence in the operating theatre that morning. He had debated for a long time with himself, and with Pauline, as to whether he should mention what he saw, or thought he saw, on the girl's ultrasound scan. He could not bring himself to do it. He was more convinced than ever now that there must be some explanation for what he had seen — an explanation that did not include evil little monsters lurking inside his patient! That idea now seemed so fanciful as to make him appear unbalanced. His best defence, if there was one, was to stick to his original account, emphasising the distress of his patient, her fear that there was an abnormality, and the fact that D'Arcy was away that day and not available for a second opinion. Indeed, it was because of D'Arcy's absence that he had been doing the Abortion Pool in the first place.

He tried not to sound as if he were attempting to transfer blame to D'Arcy by commenting on his absence. Pauline had suggested that, valid as the point was, it would not help him if he tried to push the responsibility onto someone else. They would be sure to round on him for that.

The first part of the interview did not seem to go too badly. They asked him some questions, much as he expected. The legal adviser wanted to know more about his failure to take a photographic record of the scan, and about his assertion that there was no technician. Simon could corroborate the absence of the technician and his claim that the machine had run out of film was accepted. He felt a little more comfortable after that, especially as the legal adviser seemed visibly encouraged by his answers. That was a good sign, because if there were to be any litigation, and if damages were awarded, it was usual in the case of hospital doctors for the employing authority to be co-defendants, sharing the burden of any costs.

The incident in the theatre with Gemma was a different matter. On the one hand it was simpler, because he honestly did not know what had happened and did not have to conceal anything or be devious. On the other, it was a far more serious occurrence, as a patient had been injured at his hands. How could he convince them it was an inexplicable accident and not due to his own carelessness or incompetence?

Once more he briefly recounted his recollection of events. D'Arcy frowned, Featherstone and Greenwell looked slightly bored. They had all gone over this several times before. However, Marcus Whitehead, the lawyer, was very interested.

'How many times have you performed termination of pregnancy?' he asked.

Simon was ready for this. Pauline had warned him the legal representative would be after two things — how best to defend the Health Authority if it came to court, and how to push all the blame onto Simon.

'More than two hundred, sir.'

The lawyer could not stop himself looking impressed. 'And can you tell me the outcome of all these procedures — that is to say, whether there have been any other incidents of this or a similar nature?'

Like many ambitious registrars, Simon kept detailed statistics on his operations, their degree of success, any complications, rates of post-operative infection and so on. His were good — very good. He reeled some of them off.

'All my TOPs have been successful. There were two cases of post-operative pyrexia which settled within four days on antibiotics. One case had to go back to theatre for secondary haemorrhage — she had a minor bleeding diathesis anyway — and in one case I had to proceed to hysterectomy because of uncontrolled bleeding. She had previously undiagnosed posterior fibroids in a retroverted uterus. That makes a total morbidity of 1.9 per cent, mortality nil.'

Marcus Whitehead turned to Jeremy Greenwell. 'Is that good?'

Greenwell nodded. 'Very good indeed. Well below average.'

Whitehead looked disappointed, and turned back to Simon.

'What about this woman who needed the hysterectomy? Was that at this hospital?'

'Yes. Not long after I came.'

'And you missed the fact that she had fibroids?'

'No. It *was* overlooked, but I didn't select the case for termination. She was just on my list.'

'So who did select the case?'

Simon hesitated. He did not want to show himself in a bad light, but nor did he want to upset his boss any more than he had done already. He tried very hard not to sound critical.

'It was Mr D'Arcy.'

Whitehead turned to see the consultant looking annoyed.

'Is this so, Mr D'Arcy?'

'How do you expect me to remember that? I see hundreds of these cases.'

'Do you remember Mr Robinson having to perform this particular hysterectomy? After all, it can't have been long ago, and I gather that it must be an unusual event — I mean having to be done after a termination.'

'Yes, yes, I remember Robinson doing the hysterectomy. At least, I can remember him telling me about it the next day. I didn't have any say in the matter. It was he who deemed it necessary to deprive the girl of her uterus.'

Simon was incensed at the implications behind D'Arcy's words. 'For God's sake, she would have bled to death if I hadn't done it! And she wasn't so much of a girl — she was thirty-eight and already had three children.'

'Perhaps she wouldn't have been bleeding so badly if you hadn't been so ham-fisted!'

Featherstone sat back, holding up his hands defensively.

'Gentlemen, gentlemen, please. This is not going to help any of us. This is not what we are here for.'

D'Arcy sneered. 'We wouldn't be here at all if it weren't for Robinson's incompetence.'

Simon was stunned. He was searching for a response to the wounding words when Greenwell intervened.

'Roger, when I asked you about Simon's abilities some four weeks ago, you remarked what a conscientious, pleasant and competent young surgeon he was.'

D'Arcy made an incomprehensible grunt and turned away.

'Do I not recall correctly?' Greenwell persisted.

'Something like that, I suppose,' D'Arcy conceded reluctantly, 'but that was before all this happened.'

Simon was surprised at assistance from this unexpected quarter. Greenwell continued.

'Surely one event like this doesn't change a competent, conscientious surgeon into a bungling idiot?'

Featherstone leaned forward again, a little more relaxed, and ventured a question.

'May I ask your interest in Mr Robinson's progress, Jeremy?'

'I'm head of the Department of Obstetrics and Gynaecology. It's my duty to see how any newcomers to my medical staff are getting on.'

'Yes, I see. Of course.' He looked at D'Arcy warily. 'He's got a point, you know, Roger.'

D'Arcy scowled and shrugged his shoulders.

'I must say that whilst there seems no rational explanation for what happened to Gemma Randall,' said Marcus Whitehead, 'there also seems to be no evidence of incompetence.'

D'Arcy felt he was being cornered.

'How can we trust the man? What about him being mixed up in the death of the Marshall girl, and that poor bugger Reece's murder!'

Featherstone looked very unhappy at this recollection. The adverse publicity that Gwyn Reece's still unexplained killing in particular had brought to the hospital was something he didn't want to be reminded of.

Simon spoke without thinking. 'Dr Reece was murdered because he was trying to help me find the histology report on Gemma Randall's TOP.'

Featherstone looked horrified. D'Arcy simply looked to the heavens. Greenwell, however, was intent and thoughtful.

'You have proof of this?'

Featherstone found his tongue. 'Look, Jeremy, I thought we agreed we'd try to keep the Reece affair separate from this inquiry.'

Whitehead agreed. 'Yes, indeed. I'm sure that's wise.'

Greenwell persisted. 'Yes, yes I know that, but I have a feeling this is important.' The others raised no further objection, so he continued. 'Well, Simon? Do you have proof of your claim?'

Simon wanted to shout at him. Couldn't he see how bloody obvious it was? But could he actually *prove* it? He struggled to sound convincing.

'I — I *know* it to be true. But no — ' His head dropped. 'I can't prove it.'

Greenwell spoke softly, but with great emphasis. 'Then I suggest we leave this subject and return to the matter in hand.'

Marcus Whitehead looked relieved.

'Yes, thank you, Mr Greenwell, we must conclude things here before we get diverted into that other most unfortunate business.' He took out a handkerchief and dabbed his lips, wiped his forehead, then blew his nose. 'I have looked carefully at the statements taken from the theatre staff, and from the late Dr Reece. It really does seem a mystery what went wrong, and whatever happened, it does not look as though one could establish a *prima facie* case of clear-cut negligence on Mr Robinson's part. I would criticise his, er, little deceit prior to the operation, but it's difficult to see, in a court of law, how an allegation of negligence might succeed.'

D'Arcy turned towards the lawyer, eyes narrowed. 'Are you saying we should forget the whole thing? This is pure conjecture. How the hell do you know what'll happen if the Randall girl sues? We'll all be in the bloody cart then, won't we? We'll all be in the witness box, getting adverse publicity. The local press will have a field day sniping at our reputations!'

So, thought Simon, another reason, and perhaps the main one, for his boss to be angry with him. The publicity of a negligence case involving him would certainly be bad news. Especially, that is, for his treasured private practice.

'I agree that it would be unusual for me to venture so confident an opinion, but I have the benefit of some further information.'

He had the attention of them all now.

D'Arcy was impatient. 'Well, man, what is it?'

'I have interviewed the young lady, Gemma Randall, on two separate occasions.'

'And — ?' Featherstone prompted.

'I have no idea why, hut she assures me — and I have good reason to believe her — that she is *not* going to sue.'

12

Pauline was where he had left her in the waiting area, reading, when he rushed out of the lift. She seemed to sense him coming, and looked up as he approached. He had wanted to play it cool, but he couldn't suppress his smile and she stood up and held out her hands to him.

'So! It's obviously good news?'

'I suppose you could say that! My suspension has been lifted! I have to operate under supervision, but I can work.'

Pauline gave him a small hug, then pulled away and beamed at him. 'I'm so pleased. I really am.'

'It's just a temporary arrangement until Whitehead has had a chance to report back. And as soon as they decide they don't want a full inquiry — and Whitehead is sure they won't — then I'll be free to operate unsupervised again.'

'And pick up your career.'

'God, I hope so. Although I should think I might have to move to do that — I don't think I'll get much of a reference from D'Arcy.'

They started walking out to the car park. 'How do you feel about this working under supervision? You can't be too happy about it — and D'Arcy won't be very pleasant to work with.'

'You're right there. Obviously he isn't very keen on the idea either. For the time being I'll be working with Jeremy Greenwell.'

'Greenwell? But you were appointed to D'Arcy's firm. Isn't that a bit unusual?'

'Yes, I've never heard of such an arrangement before. I don't know how they've wangled it. But still, as it's Greenwell, there won't be any TOPs to do.'

Pauline looked puzzled.

Simon explained. 'He's a Catholic, remember? Religious objections, and all that.'

'Yes, of course . . . and how long did you say this supervision ruling is effective for?'

'Like I said — just until Whitehead has reported back and they're sure it won't have to go to a full inquiry. And one more thing, that really surprised me.'

Pauline stopped by her car. 'Well, go on, don't just stand there grinning like an idiot.'

'I'm free to see Gemma Randall whenever I like.'

111

Simon sat back in his seat, feeling as if a great weight had been lifted from him. Looking across, Pauline saw him smiling to himself.

As they left the car park they passed a sign saying 'Anaesthetists Only'. Simon's smile left him, and his spirits took a dive, a sick feeling returning to his stomach as he thought about the death of his friend; it was unbearably frustrating to be unable to find out anything more about the reasons behind his murder. The police were, of course, 'conducting their inquiries', but could not, or would not, tell him anything. The affair had faded from attention in the media, and things at the hospital went on as before, everyone too busy with their work and their lives to dwell for long even on such unusual and sensational events occurring on their doorstep.

Pauline noticed him slipping from elation to dejection.

'It's no good wishing him back, you know.'

'I wasn't. I was wishing I could find out more about what's behind it all. I'm sure there's some connection — something that ties in with Gemma, and Janice — and Gwyn and me. It's all too much of a coincidence, all these things happening at once, and all seeming to involve Gemma Randall's report. Haven't the police chased up Dr Ravensbourne yet?'

'Even I can't get much out of them. The last I heard, she was still away on holiday, but they don't even know where. As far as Gwyn's concerned, they've found out a bit more about his personal life: it seems he was even more of a lady's man than you realised. They're now thinking the most likely explanation is a crime of passion. They know he had an affair with a married woman last year, and he was threatened then by an angry husband.'

'He never told me about that.'

'Well . . . it was before you knew him. Perhaps he just thought it was best forgotten.'

'How did this come to light? Any idea?'

'Apparently the threats to Gwyn were so serious that he sought an injunction preventing the jealous husband from harassing him. Someone at the station remembered the case.'

'Surely they've checked up on this chap — where he was at the time, and all that?'

'Yes, of course they'll have done that. But I don't know the outcome.'

There was a long silence until they turned into Simon's street. 'What do *you* think about this "crime of passion" theory?'

Pauline glanced at him. 'You really want to know?'

Simon nodded.

She grinned. 'Bullshit.'

He grinned back. 'Yeah. My sentiments exactly.'

Kate was in the lounge when Simon went in. Eager to tell his news, he was surprised and worried to find her still sitting there surrounded by sales catalogues. She had clearly not gone to work. He went and sat down facing her. She looked up and gave him a brief smile.

'What are you doing here?' he asked gently.

She gave him the merest glance. 'I phoned in. Told them I was sick.'

Simon was immediately concerned. 'I didn't know you were getting pregnancy sickness.'

'I'm not.'

'Then — I don't understand.'

'I have more important things to do than work.'

Simon was astonished. This was completely out of character. 'Whatever happened to "I'm going to keep going to work until I can't get into the uniform"?'

Kate patted her stomach. 'I can't.'

Simon looked. It was true: the uniform buttons were straining over her lower stomach. She shouldn't be that big yet, though, surely? He'd noticed her abdomen was looking swollen, but had put that down to a bit of bloating from fluid retention.

'Well, if you don't feel up to going in . . .' He supposed it would be all right; the other midwife on her district could cover for her for a few days. His mind went back to the events of the morning.

'So. Aren't you going to ask me how it went?'

'How what went, love?'

'Christ, the preliminary inquiry, of course!'

'Well, you look pleased.'

'You bet I am. I've been reinstated at the hospital! I have to work under supervision, but at least I can work.'

'That's good, dear.' Kate went back to her catalogue.

'Aren't you pleased for me?' Simon was angered by her indifference.

Kate looked up again, gave him a warm smile, and patted the seat on the sofa beside her. 'Come and sit here.'

Mollified, Simon moved close to her. His wife squeezed his hand.

'Now don't be so silly. Of course I'm pleased. You'll be working again. It's what you wanted.' She nodded to herself, as if satisfied with her statement. 'Now then — ' She pointed to a photograph of a pram — 'I prefer the grey one with the white stripe. What do you think?'

By six o'clock that evening, Simon was growing restless. He was anxious to get back to work, anxious to get to grips with doing something about Gwyn's murder, and, he had to admit it, anxious to get out of the house. The atmosphere since his return had not exactly been convivial.

He could not understand Kate's preoccupation with all things infantile. It was as if she was expecting the baby next week, not next year. He could even have forgiven her that, if there had still been room for him in her life, but it seemed there was not. Her interest in him was suddenly superficial, and in work, non-existent. He couldn't understand it. She was an intelligent woman, for God's sake, and here she was mooning about like a little girl over a new doll. He knew he must be tolerant. Professionally, he was aware that any stage of pregnancy could cause psychological problems. But this early? And this marked? And in someone whom he would have bet his life on being one of the most commonsense and stable people he knew? He paced up and down in the lounge. Kate was upstairs having one of her interminable showers. He wanted a gin and tonic, but resisted the temptation. He knew one would lead to another, and he was already angry and tense, and afraid of what might happen if he released any more self-control. He still remembered with shame the incident in the bedroom, when he'd . . . He balked at the thought. So what to do? He felt he must do something, go somewhere.

He stopped pacing for a moment and, after the briefest hesitation, went to the phone.

'Pauline?' She sounded breathless. 'Oh, sorry, have you just got in? Look, I didn't really say thank you today for all the help you've given me — and, well, I'd like to talk some more about Gwyn.' He couldn't stop himself looking anxiously towards the stairs. 'How about if I took you out for a meal, to show my gratitude?' He was surprised at the unhesitating response. 'Great! I'll be round for you in an hour.'

They settled into a corner table, which Simon had chosen for its relative isolation. He couldn't help feeling guilty, despite telling himself that there was nothing in this. He wanted to have a discussion with another professional, about a problem concerning them both, and at the same time he was saying thank you in a pleasant and civilised way. That Pauline was an interesting woman there was no doubt, but he was equally sure that he was not attracted to her, not sexually at least. She was intelligent, with a lively personality, but that was all there was to it . . .

'Where have you been?' Pauline was smiling at him.

'Been? Nowhere — well, only at home, I — '

'I mean where have you been this last couple of minutes?'

Simon was glad she couldn't see his colour rising in the subdued lighting. 'Sorry. I was just thinking.'

She didn't press him further. They concentrated on the menu. When they had ordered, and the wine had been poured, Simon raised his glass.

'Here's to you. A sincere thank you.'

'It's been my pleasure. Honestly.'

For a moment they both felt slightly embarrassed. Pauline sipped her wine, then moved the regulation candle to one side so that she could see Simon more clearly. 'You know, I've been thinking, too.'

'Oh?' Simon felt apprehensive for some reason he couldn't explain.

'Firstly, about what excuse you gave Kate for coming out tonight.'

He wasn't sure if she was teasing him or not. 'I didn't give an excuse. I told her I was going to see you. To talk about the hearing, and about Gwyn.'

'Didn't she mind?'

'No, not a bit. She doesn't seem to mind about anything much lately, she only seems interested in the — ' He stopped himself using an expletive — 'the baby. Everything else seems to have gone by the board.'

'Did you tell her you were taking me out to dinner?'

Simon looked down at his pictorial place mat, turning it round until 'The Hay Wain' was the right way up.

'I said I'd be eating, and she needn't bother with cooking my supper.'

Pauline laughed. 'You needn't look like a chastened schoolboy! But I don't want anybody, especially Kate, to go jumping to any conclusions here. We're working together, nothing more. Isn't that so?' She looked at him seriously, but Simon could see there was a mischievous quality to her expression, or was he imagining it?

'The second thing I've been thinking about,' she went on, 'is why they've said you could see Gemma Randall. Didn't that surprise you?'

Simon was taken off guard by this change of tack.

'Well, only pleasantly. What are you getting at?'

'Come on! One minute you are denied any access to her on pain of death, and now all restrictions have been lifted.'

'It is a bit odd, I must admit — but — well, I suppose they're just being reasonable at last.'

'Not so, you innocent. Whitehead is a shrewd devil. I've been finding out a bit more about him. He'll be the one behind this change of heart.'

Simon was surprised. 'Whitehead!' He looked round and lowered his voice. 'Whitehead? What's it got to do with him?'

'He was the one who announced that Gemma was unlikely to sue, wasn't he?'

'Well, yes, but — '

'He'll not be sure why, but he must know, if he's spoken to Gemma Randall as he claims, that she doesn't hold you responsible. In fact, from what you've told me, it almost sounds as if she's carrying a torch for you.'

'Don't be daft!' But even as he spoke, Simon could see the misty-eyed look Gemma had given him the last time he saw her . . .

'There you are!' said Pauline triumphantly. 'You've noticed, and it's written all over your face.'

Simon grinned. 'I deny everything. But what exactly are you getting at with your devious lawyer's brain?'

'Whitehead has reasoned that the more opportunity your Miss Randall has to see you, the more opportunity there will be for you to work your professional — and personal — charms on her. Being you, you'll try everything you can to nurse her back to normality and so assuage your guilt, make amends, or whatever way you want to put it. Am I right?'

'I can't deny I desperately want to help her recover, yes,' Simon admitted defensively.

'And the more you do, the more Gemma develops her misguided hero-worship or whatever, and the less likely she is to turn round and sue you. Result: no scandal, no adverse publicity, no big compensation pay-out — and remember the Health Authority isn't insured like you are.'

'That's very cynical, Pauline. I can't believe anyone could be that manipulative — especially with someone as vulnerable as Gemma.'

'Take it from me — Whitehead could.'

'Then I ought to try and persuade her to sue anyway. I'll explain that because of the insurance it won't bankrupt me or anything like that.'

'Don't kid yourself. She'll know it'll damage your reputation, adversely affect your career. No, whichever way you play it, Whitehead has persuaded the others to make a smart move. You've probably got your reinstatement on the strength of it.'

Simon was having difficulty controlling his anger. 'The scheming bastard.'

Pauline looked at him over her wine glass. 'Got it in one.'

They didn't get very far in trying to formulate a plan to find out more about Gwyn's death. Pauline couldn't expect much co-operation from the police, as her client's only involvement was as a witness. He felt frustration at being so powerless, but at least he would soon be back at work. That would give him more opportunity to ask a few questions.

He dropped Pauline off at her house at about eleven. She turned to him before getting out of the car, and gave his hand a small squeeze.

'Thanks for the meal, and the company. I enjoyed it.'

Simon gently pulled his hand away. 'So did I.'

'Want to come in for coffee?'

'No, thanks. Maybe another time.'

'I'll look forward to it.'

As he drove home, Simon thought about the way Kate had been behaving. She had become pregnant so impossibly quickly after her tubal insufflation that it seemed almost an anticlimax. And now she seemed to be shutting him out. They had always had such a close relationship, and particularly over the question of her failure to conceive. They had faced it together, discussed it, shared their anxieties. Now it seemed that she wanted to continue her experience alone. Simon knew he ought to be happier than he had been for many weeks. He was reinstated at work, his wife was expecting a longed-for baby; his life, which a week ago had seemed to be falling apart irretrievably, was coming together again.

But he *wasn't* happier, and it wasn't just Gwyn. Something, he couldn't tell exactly what, was wrong.

As he went quietly upstairs he resolved to make a big effort to get through to Kate. Perhaps it was his fault that they had not been communicating. He had, after all, been very preoccupied with his own troubles. Perhaps she felt as rejected as he did.

Kate had fallen asleep with her bedside light on, one of the ever-present catalogues open on the duvet. Simon picked it up to put it on the floor, and as he lifted the weight from her she stirred, moving from her side onto her back. The covers slipped down as she did so, exposing her breasts. Simon looked down at her, feeling himself becoming aroused. She looked so warm, so inviting. He undressed quickly and got into bed. Kate woke, bleary-eyed, and Simon cuddled against her warm softness.

'You're back, then,' she said sleepily.

'Yes. I've missed you.'

Kate felt his erection. 'You've brought me a present, I see.'

The return of a spark of her old humour encouraged him. Soon she was responding to his caresses. Their lovemaking was brief but satisfying, for Simon at least. But even as he climaxed, he was aware that Kate was not having a genuine orgasm. He'd never known her fake it before. As their breathing settled, he felt he had to ask her. 'Was that good?'

'Yes, love, of course.'

'Honestly?'

'Honestly.' She paused, then turned to him. 'Simon?' He could hear the questioning, the anxiety in her voice.

'What is, Kate?'

'I hope Mothercare have got some of those blue Baby-stretch outfits left.'

Simon lay quietly for a few moments. He wanted to shout at her, but tried to control his anger. Think, he told himself. This is an opportunity to talk about this preoccupation, this virtual obsession.

'Kate, I don't want to sound critical, but all you seem to talk about these days is the baby.'

Her reaction surprised him. She started to sob, her face creased, her body shaking. Through her tears she only managed to say: 'I know.'

Simon held her, tried to console her. 'Hey, what's all this? I only made an observation.'

She sniffed, tried to get herself under control. 'But it's true. I can't stop myself thinking about the baby. All the time. I've neglected my work, and I know I haven't been nice to you, included you . . . I — I just feel . . .' She was sobbing again, unable to speak coherently. Simon waited patiently for it to subside, holding her tight, stroking her hair. When she seemed settled he spoke again.

'Try and tell me. You just feel what?'

'It's so silly. I should be the happiest woman on earth. But I feel so depressed.' She looked at him, eyes full of tears. 'I can't shut out these thoughts about the baby. They're there all the time. When I try to think about your problems, or going to work, or even simple things like preparing meals or going shopping, these thoughts push in, intrude, like some inner voice that tries to drown out my own consciousness. It's like . . .' She bit her lip, to stop herself from crying again.

Simon was listening to her, watching her, his thoughts a mixture of fear and astonishment at these revelations. He prompted her gently. 'Like what, love?'

Kate took a deep breath. 'It's as if any time I have some thoughts about you, the baby is — taking over from me.'

'The baby is — ' Simon felt the sickening clutch of anxiety. Was his wife going mad? Then he felt an acute fear, and a chill passed over him as the image from his dreams flashed into his mind, of the midwife and the monster. He shuddered, swallowed, his mouth dry.

'What do you mean?'

Kate looked at him, hesitated. 'I — I'm not sure.'

Simon felt another shiver of fear.

'Please — try and explain.'

'Its voice seems to be saying, "What about me?" I keep thinking about it. Over and over again, until I think I'll go crazy. The voice only stops if I concentrate on it, so in the end — I do. It's the only way I can get any peace.' She was crying again. 'It's trying to fight its way in even now!'

Simon was trying to think what to say next, to try and get her to talk more about it, when Kate pulled away from him, her hand to her mouth, her eyes wide.

118

'What is it?'

'Feel sick.' Kate rushed into the bathroom. Simon could hear her retching, the tap running, the medicine cabinet door opening. He was only half-listening, his mind racing, trying to work out the next move. He thought he should go to her, make sure she was all right, but he had to *think*.

She was gone some time. When she came back into the bedroom, Simon was no nearer knowing what to do. He kept coming back to the same question: who is the best psychiatrist around here? She looked more in control when she climbed into bed. She lay down, and gave him a weak smile.

'Are you all right now, love?'

'Yes, fine. I'm tired, that's all.'

Perhaps it would be better to let her sleep, and talk again in the morning, Simon told himself.

'All right, love.' He pulled the duvet up around her neck.''Night, then.'

''Night, love.' She shifted a little to get more comfortable. They lay there for a few minutes in the dark, side by side. Kate, drifting into sleep, murmured something he couldn't make out.

'What did you say, love?'

She didn't open her eyes, but she spoke quite clearly.

'All right, if that's what you want. We'll have apple green instead of white in the nursery after all.'

13

The following day was a difficult one for Simon. Most of the staff knew at least something about what had been going on; knew of his suspension, were aware of the publicity surrounding the death of his friend, and were now meeting him again for the first time. There were a number of awkward silences, strange looks and whispered comments, but they diminished as the day went on and Simon became less uncomfortable. He was pleased to be with patients again, though those he might have known in the wards had long gone home, and he would not know any of Jeremy Greenwell's anyway.

It appeared that his 'secondment' to his new firm was unofficial, there being some problem over the contracts with the District Health Authority. This was hardly surprising, as it was a very unusual procedure. As a temporary arrangement the two Senior Registrars had swopped jobs. Simon knew, but was not particularly friendly with, the Senior Reg on Greenwell's unit. He was an aggressively ambitious man, and Simon thought, a little cynically, that he had probably agreed to this unusual arrangement because to show co-operation and flexibility would stand him in good stead when he came up for a consultant's job.

There was a ward round in the morning, and a busy outpatient clinic in the afternoon. Simon was relieved there were no terminations to be considered. They stopped for a cup of tea halfway through the afternoon, and he found himself alone with Greenwell in his office.

'How are you finding it, Simon?' the Consultant enquired.

'All a bit strange at first. Different staff, different system — and feeling a bit self-conscious after all the recent publicity.'

'That's understandable, I'm sure. Hasn't affected your confidence, though, I trust?'

'No, I'm sure it hasn't.' Simon was able to answer truthfully. He hadn't really thought about losing his confidence, and he had certainly felt at ease with his clinical judgement, if not with his fellow clinicians. 'And I'd like to thank you for suggesting this arrangement.'

'Not at all. Best thing all round, I'd say.'

'I was very sorry Mr D'Arcy took it as he did. I liked working with him. I thought we were getting on well.'

'Yes, I think you were. In fact, whenever he spoke of you before all this business blew up, he was always most complimentary.'

'So why d'you think he's so antagonistic now?'

'Not sure.' Greenwell looked at Simon over his cup, and took a sip. 'Think it shook him up a bit. I don't want to be ungenerous, but I think he thought if the balloon was going to go up, some of the mud might stick — if you'll pardon me mixing my metaphors.'

Simon was surprised at one consultant being so candid about another. 'Don't you have the same fears?'

'Me? Heavens, no. It all happened while you were working with D'Arcy, not with yours truly. Besides — ' Greenwell smiled, and assumed an innocent air — 'I'm not so worried about my private practice.'

Simon wasn't sure what to say. Greenwell seemed to sense his discomfiture, and changed the subject.

'How's your wife? Kate, isn't it? Bit early yet, I suppose.'

Simon felt embarrassed when he realised that Greenwell didn't know she was pregnant. He hadn't thought much about ante-natal care, it was still so early in the pregnancy; but he should, if only out of courtesy, let the consultant involved know his efforts had been so rapidly rewarded. The gynaecologist caught the expression on the younger man's face.

'Nothing wrong, I hope?'

Simon remembered last night, but thought he'd keep it to himself for a while. 'Look, I'm awfully sorry — but what with everything else, I forgot to tell you.'

'Tell me what? Come on, out with it, man.'

'Well — ' Simon met his eyes and tried a broad grin. 'She's pregnant.'

'You're joking! That's a bit quick, what?'

'Confirmed on two pregnancy tests. It must have been a day or two after her op.'

Greenwell smiled crookedly. 'Didn't waste much time, then, eh? Still, well done, congratulations.'

'Thank you, sir. Thank you very much.'

'Please, it's Jeremy. So, when are you going to bring her in to see me? I take it you'd like me to follow it through, so to speak?'

Simon was genuinely grateful. 'Oh, yes please. If you would.'

'Glad to. Bring her up tomorrow, after the list, and we'll do a scan on her, shall we?'

Simon's stomach lurched, and he felt himself go pale.

'A scan — so soon? But — she's only . . .'

'You feeling all right, old boy?'

'Yes, sorry, I'm OK.' He felt a fool, reacting like that. Why should he be worried about Kate having a scan? All because of a dream? Or

121

because of what he thought he had seen inside Gemma Randall . . .

Greenwell was talking, and Simon tried to concentrate.

'Let's see now, her last period was what, ten days before her investigations; that was three weeks ago, so now — ah yes, nearly five weeks by dates. I suppose it *is* a bit soon. We'll fix it for when she's about twelve.'

Simon felt a wave of relief that made him go weak. He nodded his agreement, afraid his voice would sound too shaky. Christ, what's the matter with you? he chastised himself.

'You sure you're all right? Did you skip lunch or something?'

'I'm fine, really,' Simon protested as he rose to leave. 'I'd better get back to work.'

'Yes, back to the madding crowd, I suppose. I may have to go off a bit early. You all right to finish up if I do?'

'Yes, of course, sir — Jeremy. Glad to.'

'Righto. See you in theatre tomorrow, then. I usually come in about 9.30. I'd appreciate it if you could make a start at nine.'

'Shouldn't I wait for you? I'm supposed to be under supervision.'

'No, no.' Greenwell was dismissive. 'Not for the simple stuff. First one's a piece of cake. Won't take you twenty minutes.'

'Well, if you're sure it'll be all right. What is it?'

'Girlie's twelve weeks pregnant. Had rubella. It's a termination.'

* * *

Simon rushed into his office and sat down. Bloody hell, it couldn't be true. A TOP! He'd thought it would be impossible for him to have to do any on Greenwell's firm, but of course when he thought about it, it wasn't. Greenwell wouldn't have anything to do with 'convenience' terminations, but this was a different matter. CRS, or congenital rubella syndrome, occurred in some form in well over half of all babies whose mothers suffered German measles in early pregnancy. It didn't happen so much these days, thanks to the vaccination programme, but even ardent anti-abortionists seldom argued against termination in such a case. The baby could be born deaf, blind, have heart defects or mental retardation and a damaged bone marrow. Simon could see that Greenwell would not feel it necessary to turn such a case over to another consultant — even though he might ask one of his juniors to carry out the actual procedure.

His first reaction was to refuse. He was not meant to be operating alone anyway. But he could understand Greenwell's attitude. He knew Simon could do the procedure blindfold, almost — it would be like supervising an experienced orthopaedic surgeon while he did a bunion. Simon concluded there was no alternative. If he couldn't do it now, when would he? He'd fallen off the horse, and he knew the best thing was to get straight back on. Even so, it was ten minutes before he was ready to call in the next patient.

He felt mentally and physically exhausted by the time he got home at 6.30. At least he wasn't covering the junior house officer for emergencies that night. He wondered what sort of reception he'd get. The old Kate would have been looking out for him, welcomed him with a kiss, asked him how it went, had something ready to eat. The new Kate would be sitting in the lounge surrounded by things relating to babies, and would pay him scant attention.

In fact, she wasn't there at all. He looked through the house, calling her. He looked upstairs, and stopped when he went into the spare bedroom which was to be the nursery. The wallpaper was partly stripped from the walls, hanging in shreds and making untidy piles on the floor. In the middle of the room was the ever-increasing number of boxes of baby clothes, a baby-bouncer, sterilising equipment, a cot mattress, a parasol, and other smaller items she was accumulating. Simon was already getting concerned about the amount of money she was spending, and doubtless she was now out spending more. Except that the shops had closed over an hour ago — or had they? There was a new cash and carry about three miles away that opened late.

Feeling somewhat neglected and irritated, Simon made himself some tea and a sandwich. He pulled the evening paper out of the letterbox, flopped down on the sofa, and after a few minutes was asleep.

He woke an hour later to the sound of someone going upstairs. 'Kate? Is that you?'

She called out, 'Hello, Simon. I'll be down in a minute.'

At least she sounded bright enough. Rubbing his tired eyes, Simon went out into the hall, where he found two very large plastic carrier bags. One, he was relieved to see, contained food. The other, predictably, was full of baby clothes. He heard the tap running upstairs, the clink of a glass, the medicine cabinet door opening. For some reason he recalled lying in bed last night, when Kate had gone out to the bathroom. The same sequence of sounds. Some instinct told him to go and see what she was doing — or rather, if he was honest with himself, what she was taking.

The running water hid the sound of his approach. Kate was just going to drink from the glass tooth-mug, unmistakably about to take a tablet.

'What are you doing, love?' he asked from the doorway.

Kate whirled round, looking guilty. She forced a smile.

'Nothing, why?' Trying to be casual, she dropped whatever was in her other hand into the basin, and slipped something into a box of tampons in the medicine cabinet. She started to wash her face with a flannel. Simon stayed where he was.

Kate looked up from the basin and said, 'Gosh, that new place is so busy. I'm whacked out.'

'What were you taking then?'

'Taking?' She tried unsuccessfully to look innocent.

'When I came in, you were about to swallow a pill.' Simon was getting angry — angry at her attempts to cover up, angry because he was so strongly opposed to any medication that might jeopardise a developing foetus, especially his.

Sensing his mood, and realising she had been caught out, Kate said dismissively, 'Oh, that, it was just an aspirin. I got a headache in that place. So crowded.'

She finished wiping her face, and reached for the towel. As she began to dry herself, Simon stepped forward and took the box of tampons from the cabinet. Kate saw him and tried to grab the box.

'No!' she cried out, but too late.

Simon held up a bottle and stared at it.

'What in God's name is this?' He turned to her, shaking the bottle in front of her, shouting now. 'D'you know what this is?'

'It's none of your business.'

'What? For God's sake, of course it is! Now come on — tell me!'

'It's — it's something I was given in the hospital.'

'Given? In God's name what reason could anyone in the hospital have for giving you this stuff?' He waved the bottle at her aggressively.

'He said it was important. It was to help implantation of the embryo.' She looked at Simon with a mixture of defiance and triumph. 'Anyway, it worked, didn't it?'

Simon could barely comprehend what he was hearing.

'But Jesus Christ!' He was almost speechless. He looked at the label again, scarcely able to believe what he was seeing. 'This is azathioprine! It's an immunosuppressant! I should think it's more likely to *prevent* implantation than help it!' He felt tears of rage. 'And God knows what it'll do to foetal development.'

'Rubbish! Don't you try to frighten me!'

'I'm not trying to frighten you, Kate. Don't you know what this stuff *is?*'

'I — I've never heard of it.'

'And you're still taking it? Even though you're pregnant?'

Kate looked away. 'He — I was told I had to keep taking it until the second trimester, otherwise any foetus implanted under its influence might abort.'

'Bullshit!' The bottle shook in his hand. It was from the hospital pharmacy. 'Why the hell didn't you tell me about this stuff?'

Kate wiped her mouth with her hand, and adopted a defiant stance. 'I knew you'd try to stop me taking it if you knew.'

124

'Too damn bloody right I would!'

'But he said I needed it. He said you wouldn't agree with it, but it was vital I took it.'

'I can't believe this!' Simon was almost weeping. 'And who's "he"? Who's the stupid bastard who told you to take this crap?' He was waving the bottle in front of her, his fist clenched, threatening. 'Come on! Who was it?'

'I'd better not say. He asked me not to say.' Her eyes showed her failing determination to face Simon down. She backed off a step, and sat down on the lid of the toilet. She deliberately looked away.

Simon lost all control. Almost incoherently, he shouted, '*TELL ME!*'

Kate jumped at the explosive sound in the small room. She lifted her face defiantly, and then her resistance broke. She started to cry.

Simon knelt beside her. His head was spinning, he felt as if he might faint. God! What was his wife doing to herself?

'Kate! Kate, try to understand.' He was stroking her, trying to calm her, reassure her. 'I'm upset because — because taking this drug is just plain crazy. I'm frightened of what it could do to the baby — and to you.'

Kate looked a little afraid. 'But you're so angry with me.'

'I can't pretend I'm pleased you hid them from me, didn't trust me.'

She pushed her hair back from her face, roughly wiped away some tears, then reached out and took his hand. 'I do trust you. Really.'

'Then tell me,' he said, as gently as he could, 'who told you to take these tablets?'

'No, please.' She shook her head.

'Come on.' He tried hard to keep his voice calm and even. 'I must know.'

She looked down, sniffed loudly, almost whispered.

'It was Gwyn. Gwyn Reece.'

Simon just couldn't accept it. He could not believe that Gwyn, his friend, whom he trusted, and whose attempts to help had cost him his life, would have prescribed such a potentially dangerous drug to his wife. It made no sense to give it to her to try and encourage pregnancy, but to tell her to continue to take it *after* she was pregnant . . .

Going downstairs, he poured himself a stiff gin and tonic, and made Kate a coffee. He tried to push away his fears of what the treatment might have done to their baby. There was nothing he could do about that immediately and he wanted to try and find out all he could about how she had come to be taking the azathioprine.

'Are you *quite* sure it was Gwyn who gave you the tablets?' he asked her again.

'Well, yes, as sure as I can be.'

'When was it?'

'Directly after I came round from the anaesthetic, I think. I can't remember it all that clearly, I was a bit fuzzy still — but I know he repeatedly impressed upon me how important it was.'

'Do you remember seeing Gwyn before the operation? Can you remember talking to him when he was getting ready to anaesthetise you?'

Kate looked at Simon, puzzled. 'No — no, I can't. In fact, I remember being disappointed because the anaesthetist *wasn't* Gwyn.'

'So at least that wasn't a lie, I suppose,' Simon said, almost to himself.

'What wasn't?'

'I met Gwyn soon after you had been for your tubal insufflation. He said he hadn't put you under. And yet he was there afterwards?'

'I — I just don't understand this at all.'

'You and me both. Look, if it wasn't Gwyn, who *did* give you your anaesthetic?'

'Nobody I knew. She seemed to know me, though — but then I suppose she would.'

'Hmm. That's not much help.'

'Simon, tell me something — and I want you to be honest.'

Simon's heart sank. For some reason he thought she was going to ask him about Pauline. 'I'll try,' he said.

'Tell me all about this drug. What might it do — have done? I want to know.'

Simon thought for a moment. There was no point in hiding anything from her. 'Azathioprine is an immunosuppressant — that is to say it suppresses the immune system so that it doesn't react so strongly. It's mostly used in the field of organ transplantation, where it helps the host accept the donor organ, prevent rejection. It's also used in some fairly rare illnesses called the auto-immune diseases, where a person virtually tries to reject one of his own organs.'

'So what might it do to me, or — or the baby?'

'It stops the body producing adequate lymphocytes — the most important cells for combating disease. It also suppresses other defence-mechanism cells, and the bone marrow. So you would be more liable to infection, from viruses and bacteria, and you might become anaemic, or bruise and bleed easily. In theory, I should imagine the same things could happen to the baby.'

'Can it cause — ' Kate hesitated, summoning up the courage to express her dread — 'malformations?'

'To be honest, I'm not sure. It's hardly ever used in pregnancy. I'm sure you'd try and avoid it at all costs if you could. I don't think much is known — I'd have to look it up.'

'But you think it *could*? You can't be certain?'

126

He looked at her directly, and took her hand. 'No, love, I can't be certain.'

Simon thought she would break down again then, but with a great effort of control she threw her head back, sniffed, and swallowed hard. She spoke very quietly.

'Why do you think anybody would want to give it to me?'

'I haven't the faintest idea.' Simon stood up, and paced in front of her, running his fingers through his hair. 'It just doesn't make any sense at all.'

'Would anyone be wanting to — well, to kill me?'

Simon stared at her, amazed at the suggestion.

'Whatever makes you ask that?'

'Well, someone has been trying to get rid of people associated with the hospital around here.'

Simon thought for a moment. 'I can't imagine it's anything like that. If you had enough medical knowledge to have access to drugs like that, you'd choose something much more lethal than azathioprine. And you're forgetting it was Gwyn who gave it to you.'

'But supposing I'm wrong? Suppose it was someone with less medical knowledge. They might have stolen it, or found it, and then looked it up. They might have thought it sounded dangerous, and used it, not knowing it wouldn't be fatal.'

Simon felt himself clutching at a straw. 'You aren't absolutely *positive* that it was Gwyn who gave you the tablets, then?'

Kate was thoughtful. 'I'm sorry, love. I know I was drowsy with the anaesthetic, half asleep, wondering what was going on — but I can picture him there now, his red hair, speaking softly, insistently even, and pressing the bottle into my hand.' She sighed, and nodded her head sadly. 'Yes, I'm sure it was him.'

The glimmer of hope dashed, Simon started probing again.

'It's so strange. I've never heard of anyone giving a patient their own treatment in hospital — let alone just as they're recovering from an anaesthetic. You've worked in hospitals enough. Didn't you think it was odd?'

'I do now! In fact the more we talk about it, the more preposterous it seems. It's almost as if . . .'

'As if what?' Simon stopped his pacing and sat down by her.

'Well, I've been believing so unquestioningly in what I was told about the tablets — to take them regularly, how important it was, and, most difficult of all, not to tell you. All things that are quite alien to me, and yet I did them slavishly.'

Despite everything, Simon laughed. 'As if you'd been brain-washed, you mean?'

'No, I'm serious. Don't you see? It does seem like that. As if I was — hypnotised, or something. So that I'd do it without question.'

Simon thought it was perhaps not so impossible after all. A patient would be vulnerable, just recovering from the anaesthetic: a bit of extra pentothal if you had any, and your victim would be very susceptible to strongly reinforced suggestions . . .

Kate interrupted his thoughts. She suddenly sat up straight on the sofa, her eyes alight. 'Look — look at me!'

Simon gave her a fond smile. 'Yes, love, I'm looking.'

'Well, don't you see a difference?' She jumped up and did a quick turn.

Simon looked, and slowly began to realise what Kate was getting at. When was she last this animated, this talkative, this rational? And she hadn't mentioned baby paraphernalia once since she came in earlier in the evening.

'You certainly look a bit more alive than you have been. I haven't had a proper conversation like this with you for weeks.'

'And I *feel* different, too. And I know why!'

'Well, come on!'

'I've been out since this morning — and I forgot to take the tablets with me. It's been nagging at me all the time, but I kept telling myself I'd take one as soon as I got home. I'm meant to take — that is, I was told to take — three a day. And you've just made me miss another dose.' She looked really excited. 'Don't you see, the effect is already wearing off. My compulsion to take them, not to talk to you about it, is wearing off!'

'I can see what you're getting at, love, but the effects of azathioprine come on gradually, and wouldn't be gone in a few hours. Besides, I'm sure it doesn't cause any neurological effects that might change your mental state.'

'Oh.' Kate was disappointed only momentarily, as another idea occurred to her. 'Suppose the tablets don't only contain azathioprine?'

'That may not be such a silly suggestion.' He reached in his pocket for the bottle. 'I thought there was something about them.' He shook one out, turned it over. 'Yes, look, there are no markings on them. That's very unusual. There's normally the maker's name on one side, and some symbol or identifying mark on the other.'

'How can we find out?'

'I've no idea. An analytical chemist, I suppose.'

'Simon, you must find out!'

'I could ask Pauline. She might know how the police get drugs identified.'

Kate lost some of her new vitality. 'Oh, her. You've been seeing a lot of her lately.'

'Only trying to work out what I can do about Gwyn's . . .' He tailed off. He felt somewhat differently about Gwyn now. 'Anyway, I didn't

128

think you'd noticed.'

'Oh, I'd noticed all right. But — it's funny — I couldn't seem to make myself care about it. Could drugs make you like that — not caring, changing your personality like that?'

'Yes, I'm sure there are some that could. Now look, I've got some things to find out about. Like whether anyone has had azathioprine from the hospital pharmacy recently. Were you given any tablets on the ward?'

'I was given something else — three times a day, like those. I kept the ones Gwyn gave me and didn't start taking them until I got home.'

'Right, it should be easy enough to check the drug record charts and see who wrote you up for it. Then I'd like to know who really *did* give you your anaesthetic.'

The change for the better in his wife, the adrenaline flowing at the thought of getting something done, made him temporarily set aside thoughts about the dangers of the drugs and the possibility that the baby might have been affected. He got up purposefully, pulling Kate to her feet.

'You're not going right now, are you?' she asked anxiously.

'Not to the hospital.' He led her towards the stairs. 'Just now I want to find out if stopping those tablets has resulted in any other improvements!'

14

When Simon woke up the next morning, the Friday before the Spring Bank Holiday weekend, he was almost afraid to waken Kate lying beside him, in case the previous night's change in her had been just a dream. But as soon as she opened her eyes he could see the old Kate was back. It was the boost he needed for the coming day, to see him through his first termination of pregnancy since the Gemma Randall incident.

On more than one occasion during the last few weeks he had determined that he would never perform another abortion operation. He still was unsure of his attitude to the procedure. He had argued with himself that he had helped a lot of women from the depths of despair, and saved a lot of unwanted babies from a life of misery. But was he a fit person to judge whether a life of misery was better than no life at all? It was a question that was impossible to answer. Of one thing he felt certain: if you asked the baby, it would surely opt for life at any price. Then there were the risks to the mother, and the damage done to poor Gemma was evidence enough of that. But Simon was also a scientist, and told himself that one disaster did not mean a principle should be abandoned. Terminations were generally very safe procedures. He had never even considered it as having any significant risk before. But now . . .

All these thoughts had been going through his mind as he drove to the hospital, and had continued while he prepared for surgery. The scrub nurse could see he was preoccupied, and made no attempt to strike up a conversation. Even knowing the little about the situation that she did, she could well understand his quiet mood.

Simon finished scrubbing, and took a deep breath as he turned for the nurse to help him into his gown. This was a routine procedure, he told himself; if he didn't do it, someone else would, and this particular one was for a very good reason. In future he would have more time to consider his attitude to terminations for lesser causes. He felt tense, and tried to boost his own confidence. He looked at his hands as he pulled on the surgical gloves, and was relieved to see they were not shaking. The anaesthetist, John Matthews, was not someone Simon knew well, but he was certain he was a friend of Gwyn's. He was glad he didn't mention him.

The patient was already anaesthetised, and towelled up in the lithotomy position. It was 9.05. As a nurse pulled up his seat for him, the theatre door opened, and he heard his name called.

'Mr Robinson!'

He turned. Jeremy Greenwell had his head round the door.

'Came in a bit early. Thought I'd let you know I was about.'

Simon smiled at him, although Greenwell couldn't see it because of his mask. 'Right, thanks.' He felt a moment's relief, as he was unhappy about not properly following the rules of his reinstatement regarding supervision. He appreciated the Consultant's gentle way of letting him know he was there. The feeling was soon swept away, however, as he asked for the swabs, and the memories of that last awful time came flooding back. He felt slightly nauseated, and he must have looked pale, because the nurse asked him if he was all right, and had to mop perspiration off his brow.

Simon had a strong feeling of *déjà vu*. Wasn't this how it had all started before? And were not feelings of *déjà vu* often associated with an imminent epileptic attack? He made a conscious effort to control his rapid breathing, told himself to try and relax, reminded himself he *didn't have* epilepsy.

The anaesthetist was getting impatient. 'Shall we begin, Simon? I didn't give her much alcuronium.' He was obviously concerned that the muscle relaxant would wear off if he didn't get a move-on. He could always give some more, but then it would have to be reversed, and cause more delay.

Simon looked up, almost surprised that it wasn't Gwyn at the other end of the table.

'Sorry, John.' He made a start.

He soon opened up the cervix enough to insert the spoon-shaped curette and thus start scraping out the uterine contents. He held his breath, half-expecting the strange shock-like feeling to rush up his arm again, for the nightmare to begin once more.

It didn't.

Afterwards, he couldn't wait to get back into the surgeons' room for a cup of coffee from the vending machine. His mouth was dry, and he was uncomfortably wet with sweat, but he was a happier man than he had been twenty minutes ago. Greenwell was there, changing for the first major operation which was scheduled for 9.30, and at which Simon would be assisting.

'How did it go?'

'Oh, no problems, thanks. I can't pretend I wasn't a bit nervous about it, though, after, well . . .'

'Knew you'd be all right. Every confidence. Now, down that coffee, and we'll go and have a look at this damn great ovarian mass. Should be pretty interesting.' He headed for the door. There was

131

no one else in the room, so Simon thought he'd ask now.

'Er, Jeremy — ' he was still a little uncomfortable with his temporary boss's Christian name — 'could I have a word with you at the end of the list, if you've got a moment?'

Greenwell looked at him sharply. 'What's up? No more cock-ups, I hope?'

'No, nothing like that,' Simon said hastily. 'I'd like to have a confidential word about Kate — my wife.'

Greenwell looked relieved. It was obvious to Simon that any more problems with his work would not be well tolerated. 'Oh, I see. Yes, yes, of course, old chap. Now, let's get cracking on this belly. There's about half a mile of fat to get through, if I remember rightly . . .'

* * *

Greenwell eased himself down behind his desk and looked benignly at Simon. 'Now, then — about your good lady. What's the problem?'

Simon told him, starting with Kate's changed behaviour and ending with his discovery of the tablets which Kate was certain had been given to her by Gwyn Reece. Greenwell's expression became increasingly serious as he listened, barely interrupting except to mutter 'Good God!' when Simon gave the name of the drug, and 'I don't believe it!' when Gwyn's name was mentioned.

'This is very serious. Very serious indeed,' he said when Simon had finished. 'I just can't believe anyone would give a drug like that on such a pretext. And as for it being young Reece . . .' He shook his head, as if unable to accept these bizarre events. 'You're quite sure that's what the tablets were?'

Simon reached into the pocket of his white coat.

'Here. Have a look.'

Greenwell looked carefully at the label, then opened the bottle and tipped a few of the pills into his hand. 'Looks like the real thing. No maker's mark on the tablets, though.'

'Yes, I wondered about that, too. I thought I'd try and get them analysed.'

Greenwell looked up sharply, then became thoughtful. 'Hmm. Could be just as well. Don't want to be panicking about some sugar pills, do we?'

'It's not just that. Kate's changed behaviour — I don't see how that could be due to the azathioprine, do you?'

'Not familiar with that as a side effect, no. But I don't know much about the stuff, to be honest.'

'Well, I know it probably sounds silly, but — ' Simon hesitated. It seemed such a far-fetched idea . . . 'perhaps the tablets were made up specially, and contained something else — something deliberately

132

put there to make Kate less critical, more compliant to suggestion.'

Greenwell gave a short, humourless laugh. 'That does sound pretty way-out, but this whole business is almost unbelievable, so I suppose we must consider every possibility.'

Simon took the tablets back and returned them to his pocket. 'What do you think we should do now?'

'I must see her, of course. As soon as possible. We'd better get her along tomorrow morning, get some blood from her, perhaps a bone marrow aspirate as well.'

'That's very good of you, Jeremy. Are you sure? It's Saturday tomorrow.'

Greenwell waved dismissively. 'No problem.'

'I — I really appreciate it.' It was a relief to have someone else taking responsibility.

'One more thing. As I've said, this whole business is very strange. Very strange. I think we'd better keep it to ourselves, for now at any rate. Until we know a bit more about what's going on.'

Simon readily agreed. He didn't want any crazy stories going round the hospital, and he didn't want anyone alerted before he had a chance to make a few investigations of his own. He left to start the afternoon session in theatre in a much better frame of mind.

The list finished earlier than expected. They had two big cases scheduled, but the second was cancelled because the anaesthetist found the patient's blood pressure very high. There was a rather angry scene, because the woman had not had a pre-anaesthetic check which would have discovered the problem earlier. Now it was too late to rearrange the list, or get anyone else in from the waiting list at short notice. Greenwell was not pleased, said so in no uncertain terms, and left.

Simon decided on the spur of the moment to visit Gemma Randall. He had thought before about going to see her, but didn't think he would have time with two theatre sessions to get through. He had been concerned about D'Arcy as well. He didn't want to be accused of interfering, but she was on a medical ward now, and no longer under D'Arcy's care. He didn't think the physicians would be very sensitive about a gynaecologist seeing one of their patients informally. He checked with the new gynae house surgeon, Dr Susan Parker, that there were no problems on the post op ward, and told her where he could be found if he was needed.

The Sister on Med 3, where Gemma now had a bed, was very pleasant, much to Simon's surprise. She looked like a real old dragon, and was chewing off a student nurse when he went into her office. She seemed to know who he was, and to be almost expecting him.

'There's someone with her at the moment, Mr Robinson, but I should think he'll be going soon. He's been there nearly an hour.'

'How is she getting along?' He was almost afraid to ask.

'Well, her mobility is improving a little. She can't walk at all, but the physios are getting her up every day; she can take some weight on her right leg, and can make some leg movements when she's supported. The arm's not coming along so well, though. She can't use it for support, so she won't be able to use crutches or a frame. Looks like the wheelchair for her, I'm afraid.'

'And what about her speech?'

'No progress there, I'm sorry to say. But her writing's getting better.' She smiled at him. 'That's how I know about you.'

Simon's heart sank. What did she know about him? The Sister saw his alarmed expression.

'Don't worry, it's all good. Gemma often asks about you. If you hadn't shown up soon, I was under orders to ask you to come and see her!'

As he went into the ward, he saw a tall young man bending over her wheelchair, giving her a kiss on the cheek. For a moment Simon felt a pang of disappointment. He recognised at once how selfish that emotion was. This lass needed all the attention and support she could get, and if that was her boyfriend visiting her, well, he should be pleased. He waited until the good-looking visitor had left, then approached Gemma. He could see the happy expression fading as her guest departed from view, but then her face lit up again as she saw Simon. He could tell she was really pleased to see him, and he felt a warmth as he basked in her happiness. She reached up and took his hand, pulling him into the seat beside her chair. She was bubbling with enthusiasm, almost hugging herself with joy. Simon felt suddenly saddened that she could not express herself in words. It must be so frustrating for her, but she didn't show it. She just sat there, beaming at him, giving little soundless giggles.

'You look well.' She did, too. Lively, alert, attractive even, her lopsided face now barely noticeable, giving her grin an impish quality. 'Do you feel as good as you look?'

Gemma nodded vigorously.

'What's it like here?'

Gemma held up the thumb and forefinger of her left hand, making a circular shape, meaning 'OK.'

'No speech yet, though?' Simon didn't know what made him ask such a question, but he could not pretend that she did not have this profound disability, and somehow didn't think Gemma would want to gloss over it either.

Her eyes saddened momentarily, then brightened as she reached for her pad and pencil. She wrote quite quickly with her left hand now, he noticed.

Writing's getting better

'Simon laughed. 'It certainly is.'

He felt awkward for a moment, unsure what to say, but trying to think of questions that would not tax her writing, and could be answered with a nod or shake of the head. To fill the pause he asked the first question that came into his mind.

'Who was your handsome visitor?'

Her eyes twinkled, and she wrote again, handing him the paper with a smile:

My secret lover

Simon was completely at a loss. He opened his mouth, closed it again, then looking away said fatuously, 'That's nice.'

He felt himself blushing, then realised that Gemma was convulsed in silent laughter. In other circumstances he might have felt annoyed that he was being made fun of, the butt of a joke he could not share, but he could only marvel at her high spirits in the face of her continuing disability. He found himself laughing with her, not really knowing why. He was about to ask her what they were laughing at when the Ward Sister hurried up to him. 'I'm sorry to interrupt, but Dr Parker has just rung to say she's worried about someone from this afternoon's list, and could you go up?'

Simon stood up and saw the look of consternation on Gemma's face. She was writing hurriedly as Sister finished speaking.

'OK. Tell her I'm coming, would you?' He turned back to Gemma. 'I'm sorry, I've got to go. I'll be back soon.'

She smiled and nodded vigorously in reply. As he turned, she grabbed the sleeve of his coat and gave him a folded piece of paper. He took it, waved, and hurried out of the ward. As he went past Sister's office, she came out and walked with him to the end of the corridor. 'You were certainly cheering up that brave young lass. Whatever were you giggling about?'

Simon laughed. 'This may sound daft, but I don't know! I didn't have time to find out.'

The fearsome-looking but kindly nurse was clearly amused. She stopped at the end of the corridor, and as Simon hurried towards the lifts she called after him, 'You're welcome back, any time.'

He just had time to call his thanks before he turned the corner. There's one old dragon whose bark is worse than her bite, he thought. He reached out and jabbed the lift button, and noticed he was still carrying Gemma's note. He opened it and read:

135

He was only my brother, silly.

He was laughing quietly to himself as he went up in the lift. Her brother! But why did she tease him about it? The tone of her note almost suggested that she thought he might be feeling jealous of this visitor. And if he were honest, in a way he was — and she had noticed. He was responsible for her present predicament, and he wanted to be the number one person in the drive to return her to normality or, failing that, to help her rehabilitate as best she could. But to be jealous of anyone else who wanted to help — that would be unworthy.

His thoughts were interrupted as the lift doors opened and he saw the young doctor waiting anxiously for him.

'It's Mrs Wallingford. I can't rouse her. She's the one who had the hysterectomy this afternoon.'

'Anything to find on examination?' he asked as they hurried down the corridor to the ward.

'No. Blood pressure's OK, pulse and respiration are normal.'

'Any neurological signs?'

The girl looked at him, her worried frown deeper. 'You mean, like, er — ?'

'Well, pupils, reflexes?'

'Gosh, sorry, I didn't look. I — '

'All right, don't worry.' They were through the curtains and at the bedside now. Simon sat down on the edge of the bed, picking up the patient's wrist as he did so. The woman looked all right: good colour, regular, even breathing, pulse was fine. He took out his pen-light, lifted each eye in turn and shone the light in them. The pupils were not unduly dilated, and reacted rapidly to the light.

'What have you done to try and rouse her?'

The fledgling surgeon looked uncertain. 'Well, I, er, gave her a shake — and called her name a few times.'

Simon reached forward and pressed firmly under the woman's eyebrow, stimulating the sensitive infra-orbital nerve. The woman screwed up her face, moaned gently, and moved her position in the bed. Simon repeated the manoeuvre, and this time the patient opened her eyes, and looked confusedly about her. Her eyes focused on Simon.

'Oh, hello, doctor,' she said thickly. Her lips and tongue were dry, and she tried unsuccessfully to moisten them. Simon held the plastic tumbler of water from her bedside cabinet to her lips with one hand, supporting her head with the other. The woman took a sip and lay back.

'Thanks.'

'How are you feeling?'

She thought about it for a moment, her head still not clear.

'Still sleepy. Tummy's a bit sore.' She paused, licked her lips again. 'Can I have some more water?'

Simon gave her another sip, then she lay back and closed her eyes. He stood up, and turned to the house surgeon, who was flushed with embarrassment.

'I think she'll be OK,' said Simon, trying hard not to sound sarcastic.

Following him out through the curtains, Dr Parker stammered, 'I'm — I'm ever so sorry, Mr Robinson, I thought — I mean I didn't — '

Simon could remember his own first days on a busy ward, suddenly a doctor instead of a medical student. All that theoretical knowledge seemed of very little help. He recalled feeling lost, having to ask constantly for advice, often feeling foolish for having done so. But it soon changed, confidence grew. He always said that he learned more in his first few weeks as a houseman than he did in all his previous training. It was not really true, of course, but he certainly learned things you can't teach in a lecture theatre, or at the bedside after the crisis has past, however long you spent there.

He stopped and turned to the girl, put his hand on her arm.

'Look, don't worry about it. She was just in a deep post-anaesthetic sleep, but you weren't to know. And you've just learnt another trick, so it's not been a waste of my time or yours.'

The girl — for that's all she seemed, although she must have been about 24, looked pathetically grateful.

'Thanks, Mr Robinson. And I'm sorry if I seemed to panic.'

'It's Simon. And I'd rather you called me or the Junior Registrar ten times for something like this, especially if you're going to learn from it, than be afraid to call and make some dreadful mistake.'

Offering more thanks, the young doctor went back to her ward round. Simon popped his head into the office.

'Mrs Wallingford's OK. Just a bit deep after her anaesthetic.'

The Sister tutted. 'I thought she was all right, but Doctor Parker insisted I call you.'

'Don't worry about it. She'll get better.'

He hoped the Sister would support the new girl. Over-critical and unsupportive senior nursing staff could make an inexperienced doctor's life a misery, destroying her confidence. He remembered his own first ward sister, Sister Bennett. He'd thought her a bit of a tyrant at first, but they had soon built up a good relationship and she had become his right arm. She had years of experience on which she could draw, and he was not too proud to ask. They had made a good team.

It all seemed a lifetime away, and the problems he had coped with

137

then faded into insignificance compared to those he faced now. He glanced at his watch. Five o'clock. Pauline would probably still be at her office. He'd ring her now and ask her if she knew anything about analytical laboratories.

He got out of the lift and walked to his own office, and called her from there. Afterwards, as he put the phone down, his mind still on the tablets, he absently put his hand in his pocket to take them out and look at them again.

He reached for them, stopped, checked and double-checked. They were no longer there.

15

'What do you mean, stolen?' Kate was visibly upset by this latest turn of events. Without the tablets, the reality of what had been happening to her was threatened, and she desperately wanted some explanation for the whole frightening business. Now the one tangible link with her recent strange state of mind was gone.

'I'm sure it was stolen. The bottle was in my pocket when I went back to theatre after seeing Greenwell at lunchtime. It wasn't there afterwards. My white coat was hanging up in the doctors' changing room all afternoon. It must have been taken then.'

'But who would want to take it?'

'Well, obviously someone who didn't want me to have them as evidence.'

'Or didn't want you to find out what was really in them.'

'But Greenwell was the only one I mentioned analysis to.' Simon was quiet for a moment. 'No, I just can't imagine it was him. Why would he be concerned about my analysing the tablets? He was all in favour.'

'Yes, you're right.' Kate looked really down. 'So who, then? And why?'

Simon had no idea. He had asked Pauline the same questions, after he had gone back to check in theatre, looked around the whole suite, and retraced his steps through the wards. He had even looked in on Gemma and Mrs Wallingford to see if the bottle had fallen out of his pocket while he was with them.

He had been over the whole story of Kate with Pauline — her behaviour, and the suspect but now missing tablets. She had asked him if he thought he might have been overheard talking to Greenwell about them. He could not think of any opportunity. The finger seemed to point to Greenwell, but Simon couldn't bring himself to accept the possibility. He trusted the Consultant — he had to trust him: the man was going to take care of his wife and child. No, he did not think Greenwell could be involved in anything so bizarre, so sinister.

When he and Kate finally gave up the struggle to make some sense out of it all, it was gone midnight. They went up to bed together, each silent with their thoughts, and slept in the reassuring comfort of each other's arms.

The next morning Simon woke to find Kate still sleeping beside him. He looked at her fondly, watching her peaceful expression, the steady rise and fall of her chest. He reached out a hand and gently cupped her breast. She stirred slightly, and he felt the nipple responding.

As he moved closer to her, the phone rang. It was Greenwell. He must have heard the sleepiness in Simon's voice. 'Sorry to disturb you, old chap.' He sounded wide awake, almost jolly.

'No, it's all right, really.' He looked at the clock. Seven-thirty. 'I was just about to get up anyway,' he lied.

'Good. Right. Look, I've got rather a lot on this morning. Don't think I'll have time to get in to the hospital.'

'Oh, I see.' Simon couldn't hide his disappointment. He wanted to get Kate checked out as soon as possible.

'It's all right. D'you think you could bring your wife out to see me in my rooms? I'll be here until about 12.30, I should think. Whenever it suits you.'

'Yes, yes of course, that's fine.' He glanced at Kate, now fully awake and listening. She leaned towards him, mouthing, 'Who is it?' He waved her away. 'Thanks very much, er, Jeremy. Would any particular time be better for you?'

There was a pause, a rustling of paper. He was scanning his private appointments list for the morning. 'Well, if you're flexible, let's say — 11.15, shall we?'

Simon put the phone down. 'We've been invited to the Harley Street of Bournemouth,' he said, smiling. 'But we've nearly four hours yet. Now where was I?' He rolled over onto Kate, but she pushed him away, laughing.

'No, Simon, not now! Mr Greenwell will find the evidence!'

They drove away in silence from Greenwell's 'rooms' — actually part of his own house converted for the purpose of seeing private patients. The clean yellow gravel crunched under the tyres as they passed along the small avenue of conifers lining the drive, which was some 150 yards long. The house was invisible from the road, and although Simon had expected it to be something special, he was surprised at just how wealthy Greenwell appeared to be. He knew that NHS consultants in many specialities more than doubled their income from private work, but even so . . .The marble staircase in the huge hall, the paintings and antiques, the magnificent indoor pool, all spelt more than just average opulence.

Simon felt no envy. His career was getting back on the rails, his own dream of becoming a consultant was once more a tangible prospect, and, once achieved, that status unlocked many other sources of income, including the private practice that Simon hoped to develop for himself.

Kate seemed to read his thoughts. 'Quite a place, wasn't it?'

'It soitenly was, Stanley!' Simon mimicked Oliver Hardy. He looked quickly across at Kate, then back to the road. 'One of these days — '

Kate patted his thigh. 'Dreamer! Still, you never know, I suppose.'

'How was it?' He nodded in the direction of the house, now invisible as he turned onto the main road.

'Fine. He was very pleasant, very gentle. It's a bit of a surprise, the size of the uterus, though, isn't it? I thought there was something wrong at first, especially when he did the bimanual again.'

'About twelve weeks, he thought. I don't see how that can be possible. I mean, even if it were, well — '

'Go on, say it! Twins, you mean.' She giggled. 'I'm not sure how I'd feel about that.'

'I don't know what other explanation there is. Even if you'd got your dates wrong, or kept menstruating while you were pregnant, I don't see how a pregnancy could have survived your tubal insufflation.'

'Well, we'll soon know.'

Simon felt a slight icy grip around his heart. A scan. Kate was to have a scan on Tuesday, as soon as the Bank Holiday was over. 'Yes,' he said softly, 'we'll soon know.'

He dropped Kate at home and then went in to the hospital. He'd told Dr Parker he would look in sometime on Saturday to see if there were any problems. The Junior Registrar was off for the Bank Holiday weekend, so it was up to Simon to provide the back-up to the new house officer. Anyway, he had the blood samples Greenwell had taken from Kate to take to the lab. He hoped he wouldn't have any difficulty persuading the duty laboratory technician to process them. He or she was only really meant to be available for emergencies at the weekend, and could refuse what was in reality a routine procedure. Still, for one of the hospital's own doctors . . .

Simon went into the now familiar corridor of the main laboratory building, past poor Janice Marshall's office, on to the duty technician's room. There was no one there. That either meant she — he now knew it was Jennifer Dorset who was on duty — was not in the building, or was already working in the lab. He heard a centrifuge spinning in Haematology, and knew with some relief that she was at work.

She was a pleasant girl, who treated Simon's request to have the samples processed sympathetically. Not at all like some of the older men, who could be quite bolshie and inflexible about out-of-hours work, always quoting the rules, trying to minimise the actual work done and maximise the overtime. He left the samples with her, and went back into the corridor.

141

At the far end he caught a glimpse of a familiar figure: white coat, red hair, brisk stride. The outside door opened and closed, the bright light flooding in momentarily, leaving only a brief silhouette.

The hairs on Simon's neck bristled, and he felt suddenly cold. Surely — for God's sake — that was Gwyn!

* * *

'I know it's impossible — but I really thought I saw him.' Simon felt another shiver go through him as he recalled the incident to Kate. She looked at him worriedly. He was on his second gin and tonic since he came in, and it was barely past midday. He took another long drink.

'Don't have any more, love. Suppose that young houseman calls you back in?'

He put the drink down. 'Yes, you're right. I'd forgotten. But it was so — so bloody frightening.'

'I can see it was!' Kate was sympathising, not mocking. 'Didn't you try and chase after him — or it, or whatever?'

'Not immediately. I was — sort of frozen for a few moments; then I ran down the corridor and out into the car park, but there was no one there. Completely deserted.'

Kate rubbed her arms. 'It does sound rather spooky. But I'm sure your mind must have been playing tricks. Much as I'd like to believe in ghosts, I can only think you imagined you saw Gwyn, or it was someone a bit like him, who triggered off the illusion.'

Simon went over to his wife and gave her a hug. 'I'm sure you're right. Either that or I'm going round the bend.'

'Don't say that, it's not funny.'

'Sorry. By the way, the Duty Lab Tech is going to process your blood tests. She'll do the haemoglobin, white count, platelets and film now, and set up the ESR, and spin and separate the rest and leave it in the fridge until Tuesday.'

Kate prepared a salad lunch, and as it was a beautiful warm day, they sat in the garden to eat it. Simon rocked gently on the swing seat, feeling the warmth of the sun gradually relaxing him. He closed his eyes, and tried to think of more pleasant things. The sun made him remember past holidays. They both liked to go somewhere hot — the Mediterranean usually. Not somewhere flash, or crowded, or even full of architectural splendour — just somewhere where they could be by themselves, do as they pleased and, best of all, be away from the damned, demanding telephone. Right on cue, it rang.

Kate went back into the kitchen and answered it. She called out to him.

'It's for you, love. Someone called Miss Dorset.'

Simon felt weak. The Lab Technician! Why was she ringing? What was wrong?

142

'Hello, Jennifer.' He tried to sound calm.

'I'm sorry to ring you at home, sir, but those blood samples — '

'Yes, what's the problem?'

'Well, you did say they were your wife's, so I thought — ' She stopped again. Simon felt himself getting increasingly anxious and impatient.

'Yes, yes, you're right to call me. Have you got some results?'

'Well, yes. The haemoglobin's a bit low — nine point three.'

Christ, more than a bit, thought Simon. Not dangerously low, however. 'Anything else?'

'I'll check them again if you like, because it's all very odd.'

'What is? Come on, girl, tell me what you've got.'

Simon heard her take a deep breath, as if summoning strength. 'The white count's way down, only thirteen hundred polys, and even fewer lymphocytes. But the platelets are only sixty thousand. I mean, I'm not the pathologist, I know, sir, but it's as if there's a severe bone marrow depression.'

A feeling of fear and nausea swept over Simon. He gripped the phone very hard, till his hand shook.

'Sir, are you there?'

'Yes, sorry, Jennifer.' He could not disguise the tremor in his voice. 'Thanks for letting me know so promptly.' He put down the phone, and was aware that Kate was watching him, the colour draining from her face.

'Simon! What is it? What's wrong?'

He steadied himself with his hand against the wall. 'There's no doubt about it. We don't need an analysis. That stuff you were taking. It was definitely azathioprine.'

16

Simon was desperate to get in touch with Kenneth Leighton, the Consultant Haematologist. He was the one person who could best tell him whether the state of Kate's blood warranted any emergency treatment. As Kate was no longer taking the drug, he hoped that her bone marrow would recover and the problem would solve itself, but it was a long time since he had done any general medicine, let alone haematology.

Kate insisted she didn't want to make any fuss, certainly not go into hospital.

'I'm fine,' she proclaimed. 'Look at me. I'm not dizzy, I'm not short of breath — and I haven't got any bruises.' Her nursing knowledge was good enough for her to recall some of the possible signs of severe bone marrow depression.

Despite his anxiety, Simon felt proud of his wife's stoical attitude, but he knew he could not rely on how she felt.

'It's not just that, love. You're at risk of infection — even a common cold could be disastrous. And your platelets are dangerously low. I don't know if you're at risk of a sudden severe bleed. If you had one, and it happened in the placenta, that would be the end of the baby. And if it happened in your brain, that would be the end of you.'

He was being deliberately blunt, trying to impress on her the potential seriousness of the situation. He picked up the phone and began to dial the Haematologist's number.

'That's why I need to know just how great the risks are.'

He listened to the ringing tone for some time, then put the phone down again.

'Damn! No reply.'

'Well, it is the Bank Holiday weekend. I expect most of the laboratory staff are away. Why don't you ask one of the physicians? They'll probably have a good idea whether we need to do anything.'

Simon was gratified that Kate had at least accepted the need to seek some advice.

'I think we'll have the same problem. There'll only be the housemen on over the weekend. They won't know any more about it than me.' He thought a moment. 'There must be a duty pathologist, though. Perhaps he'll know where Dr Leighton is.'

He dialled the hospital, and asked for the Duty Lab Technician.

144

'Hello, Jennifer. It's Mr Robinson again.'

'Oh, yes, sir. I've just been checking those blood results. They've all come out about the same.'

'Oh, thank you, that was very good of you. I'm obviously a bit worried about this. D'you know who the Duty Pathologist is this weekend?'

'Yes, of course, sir. It's Dr Ravensbourne.'

Simon thought he must be hearing things. Ravensbourne! The missing histologist who did the report on Gemma Randall!

'Who did you say?'

The voice on the other end of the line repeated the name.

'Simon! What's the matter?' Kate saw her husband stiffen, his eyes widen in surprise.

For the second time that morning Jennifer Dorset was puzzled by a long silence from the doctor.

'Mr Robinson? Are you still there?'

Kate moved closer. 'Simon, whatever — ?' He waved at her to be silent, then swallowed hard before speaking into the phone. 'Er, sorry, Jennifer. When did Dr Ravensbourne come back?'

'Yesterday, I think. It was supposed to be Dr Ironside on this weekend, but when he heard Gillian — Dr Ravensbourne was back, he put her on the duty instead.'

'Have you seen her?'

'No. No, I haven't. She called me to say she was at home, and was going to try and catch up on some sleep. She was very tired after her travelling.'

'How long ago was that?'

A pause. 'It must have been about . . . 9.30 this morning.'

Simon glanced at his watch. It was now 2.15. Long enough for her to have had a rest. 'Thanks. Have you got her home number there?'

The girl left the phone for a moment, then came back and gave Simon a Bournemouth number.

'Thanks, Jennifer. You've been very helpful.'

'That's OK, sir . . .' She hesitated. 'Mr Robinson?'

'Yes?'

'I hope your wife's going to be all right.'

'Well, thank you. So do I.'

He didn't bother to replace the hand-set, but just pressed the button to get a dialling tone and started to key in the number he had been given. As he did so, Kate's curiosity could bear it no longer.

'For heaven's sake! What's going on?'

Simon was listening to the ringing tone. Putting his hand over the mouthpiece, he said, 'Gillian Ravensbourne is back! I've got to talk to her about Gemma Randall's report.'

'And what about my blood tests?'

'Well, of course, I'll — '

145

A sleepy voice came on the line, gave the number.

'Dr Ravensbourne?'

'That's me.'

'Look, I'm terribly sorry to trouble you, but — this is Mr Robinson, Senior Registrar in Obstetrics.'

The voice sounded suddenly more awake, but still had a silky, almost husky quality. 'Oh, yes. Simon, isn't it? What can I do for you?'

'Ah, well — look, I hope I didn't wake you or anything, and I understand you've only just got back from abroad, but — well, there are a couple of things I'd like to discuss with you.'

'Who said I'd been abroad?' The voice was suddenly harder.

'The Duty Lab Tech said you were tired from travelling, so I just assumed . . .'

The voice came back more relaxed. 'It doesn't matter, anyway. What did you want to discuss?'

'Actually, I'd much rather see you, if I could.' There was no response from the other end of the phone. 'Would you mind?'

'No, sure, that's OK. But I'm not planning to come in to the hospital today unless I get called.'

'Of course. May I . . .? Well, I'd like to see you at home — now, if that's all right.' He assumed she lived somewhere nearby, so he'd still be available if Dr Parker needed him.

She seemed somewhat reluctant. 'Well, I suppose that'd be all right. Everything's a bit of a mess here, I'm afraid. I only got back yesterday, and old Ironside's put me straight on duty, so — '

She was obviously hedging, and normally Simon would have taken the hint, but he was determined to see her, and as soon as possible.

'Yes, I understand. But I really would like to talk to you this afternoon.'

There was a sigh of acceptance. 'Do you know where I live?'

'No, sorry.'

'It's number 11, Marlborough Court. That's just off the top of Knyveton Road.'

'Yes, I think I know where that is. I'll be with you in fifteen minutes. Is that OK?'

The only reply was the dialling tone. Kate could see her husband was fired up, and knew it had as much to do with this opportunity to find out more about the Randall girl's missing report as about her own predicament.

'Don't forget to ask about me,' she said teasingly, following Simon as he prepared to leave.

'Of course not, love.' He grabbed his car keys from a row of hooks in the kitchen. 'I'll be at this number if the hospital want me.' He handed Kate a piece of paper. 'See you later.'

Driving through the outskirts of Bournemouth, Simon's mouth was dry and his stomach felt tight. How should he best approach this situation? Would Ravensbourne be hostile to questions about Gemma Randall? Old Ironside had warned him and Gwyn off the report, so surely he would have spoken to Ravensbourne as well? In fact Simon had formed the opinion that Ironside had in effect sent Ravensbourne away to prevent her being questioned. He would soon know.

He turned into a small cul-de-sac with a notice stating 'MARL-BOROUGH COURT — *Residents Only*. He decided that he would ask the pathologist's professional advice about the blood tests first, as the main reason for his visit, and then try and inquire more casually about the missing report.

Marlborough Court was quite a place. Simon had rather expected a nondescript block of flats, but this was clearly quite exclusive. A large area of tinted glass enclosed an elegant foyer, with leather seats and potted plants. There was a desk that looked as if it were for a commissionaire, but was currently unoccupied. Double glass doors gave access to the foyer at one end of the outside wall, and on the adjacent neatly pointed brickwork was a panel of buttons with names by them, and a speaker grille. He followed the instructions and pressed the call button.

'Yes, whose there?' The voice was scratchy and distorted by the little loudspeaker, but was still recognisable as Gillian Ravensbourne's. Simon announced himself, and after a moment there was a buzz and a click. He pushed the glass door open, entered, and heard it lock behind him as he walked over to the lift.

An up-market apartment building, no doubt about that, thought Simon. Nice pictures, elaborate light fittings, marble tiles in the entrance giving way to carpet with a soft, thick pile. Dr Ravensbourne's flat was on the first floor, and as he approached the door marked No. 11, written in a delicate gold script, it opened. An attractive red-head looked out. He recognised her from their previous brief meetings around the hospital. She waited for him to come closer, then held the door wide.

He walked through a small hall which still found space for an escritoire on which stood an ivory figurine, into a large, light room decorated tastefully in Wedgwood blue and white. Simon was impressed by the high quality of the furniture and fittings, but it was obvious that the pathologist's preparations for his arrival had been minimal. The apartment was untidy, with a pile of partly opened mail on the floor, and discarded clothes adorning the two armchairs. A small suitcase lay open on the sofa.

Gillian Ravensbourne herself was no better prepared to see visitors

147

than her accommodation, making Simon feel a little uncomfortable about bothering her. She was wearing slippers, and wore no make-up. Her short hair was tousled, but she was blessed with that soft, naturally wavy hair that falls more or less into place with a shake of the head. She was dressed in a rather crumpled silk blouse and jeans, and wore an expensive-looking cardigan, but that too looked as if it had only just come out of a suitcase.

She went to clear a chair for him. As she bent over to remove the discarded clothing and a hospital white coat, she brushed her untidy hair away from her eyes and sighed. Simon thought she seemed somehow distracted.

'Sorry about the mess,' she said as he sat down.

'I'm sorry to disturb you so soon after your return.'

She pushed some more wayward hair away from her cheek.

'Would you like some coffee?'

Simon hesitated. 'If it's no trouble.'

'Won't be a minute.' Simon watched her leave the room, and through the door caught a glimpse of a brightly-lit kitchen, furnished with units that were a silvery grey with pastel pink borders.

She called from the sink as she filled the jug-kettle.

'Are you on duty as well this weekend, then?'

'Yes, 'fraid so.' Simon raised his voice a little. 'Greenwell's away for the weekend, and so is the Junior Reg.'

'Greenwell?' She sounded alarmed. 'I thought you were on D'Arcy's firm.'

'Yes, yes I was — but haven't you heard about my, er, troubles, then?'

'Troubles? No, what troubles? I've been away, don't forget.'

And only got back last night. Simon realised it could mean she knew nothing of his suspension, or even Gwyn's death.

'I think I'd better — '

'Just a minute. Can't hear.' The kettle was nearly boiling, making noisy squeaks and bubbles. Simon heard the chink of mugs, water pouring, a spoon stirring, and then she came back into the room with the drinks. She gave one to Simon, before sitting in the chair opposite. She held her mug with both hands, settled back in her chair, crossed her legs, and looked at him over the rim and through the steam.

'Come on, then. What's this all about?' She took a sip.

'Ah, well, first — ' he began slowly, cautiously drinking a little coffee to disguise his uncertainty. 'I'd like your professional opinion about something.'

'Oh?' Gillian Ravensbourne looked interested, sat a little more forward.

'Yes. About some haematology results.' He wanted an honest

opinion, and knew how difficult it was to be clinically objective when close friends or colleagues were involved. So he did not mention Kate's name as he related the story of a woman who had been receiving azathioprine whilst pregnant. At the mention of the drug, Ravensbourne nearly spilt her coffee.

'What the hell was a pregnant woman doing taking that?'

Simon said he didn't know, thought it had been a dispensing error. Then he went on to explain the altered blood picture that suggested bone marrow depression.

'How serious do you think these results are?' he asked when he had finished. 'And do you think we should take any action immediately?'

'Well, now.' She leaned forward. 'I'm not a clinical haematologist, you know. Wouldn't you be better off asking Kenneth Leighton, or one of the physicians?'

'I've already tried Leighton. There's no reply. He's probably away for the weekend as well. Seems as if most of the senior staff are missing,' he added with a wry smile.

'I'm not sure I can tell you what to do about it, but I can tell you the significance of the results.'

'That would be a help.'

'First, the white count. Well down, but probably enough polys and lymphs to cope. So I think the risk of an overwhelming infection is small.'

'That's a relief.' Simon licked his lips anxiously.

'The platelets are the main worry. The method of counting them has a wide margin of error. If she's really got sixty to a hundred thousand, that should be OK — I take it the drug has now been withdrawn?'

'Yes, a couple of days ago.'

'Really? Well, there should be quite rapid recovery of platelet numbers. The trouble is, her true count could be as low as thirty-five thousand, in which case there is a real danger of some bleeding. I don't know the risk of a placental bleed — it's such an unusual situation in pregnancy but the adrenals are most at risk, I should think.'

Simon hadn't thought of that. It was basic stuff, really. In many conditions associated with low platelet counts, bleeding occurred into the little steroid hormone-producing glands sitting on top of the kidneys. Their destruction produced a syndrome of rapid onset shock with low blood pressure and electrolyte disturbances.

'You think she should have steroids?'

She smiled at him. 'Now look, I said I'm not a clinician. But steroids would help the marrow recover, push up the platelets — and afford some protection if there was an adrenal bleed.'

Simon wasn't sure. Steroids in pregnancy were also something of an unknown quantity to him. He could imagine them causing all sorts of problems for the foetus. On the other hand, he could not afford to take any risks with Kate's life. They could always try for another baby, sad though it would be to lose this one after all the waiting. He realised it was not a decision he could objectively take himself. He must hand the whole thing over to someone else. But who? Greenwell was the obvious choice, but he had said he would be away, and hadn't said where. However, he should have left a number with the hospital switchboard, as it was his firm that was on for the weekend. He'd call him when he got back, tell him everything he'd found out about Kate's tests, and then it would be up to him.

Inwardly relieved at having decided on a course of action, he turned his mind to the matter of the report. He looked back at Ravensbourne, and grinned sheepishly as he realised she had been watching him intently as he gazed into the distance, deep in his thoughts.

'You're obviously worried about this case.'

'Yes, yes I am.'

'What are you going to do about it?'

'I think I'll try and get hold of Greenwell and dump it all in his lap.'

She looked relieved. 'Good idea. That's what the consultants are for, after all.' She paused. 'I don't want to rush you, but you implied that there were two things you wanted to talk about.'

'Yes. Yes, there are.' He looked up at her face. Her eyes were a very pale light brown, he noticed, and they were searching his face intently.

'Well, aren't you going to tell me?'

Simon was afraid of what her reaction might be. 'I wanted to talk to you about a histology report.'

'Oh. Another professional problem. Right.' She looked tired, rubbed her face with her hands. Simon took the hint.

'I'll try and be brief. I want to ask you about a histology report you did on a foetus. It was just before you went away. The patient's name was Gemma Randall.'

He watched her closely to see if there was any significant reaction to the mention of the name. Her eyes opened wider for a split second — or was it his imagination?

'Randall. Is there any special reason why I should remember that particular patient?' She looked directly at Simon, and her expression seemed one of studied disinterest.

Simon felt suddenly irritated. 'You bet there is. For one thing, the girl had a rough time with a TOP and nearly died, and for another the bloody report seems to have vanished.'

'It's not that unusual for a report to be mislaid. What's got you all screwed up about this one?' She seemed agitated, somehow.

150

'I'll tell you what's got me all screwed up. When I went to get the report, your boss, Ironside, passed instructions not to let anyone see it. Then Janice Marshall — remember her, the Path Lab secretary?' He couldn't conceal the sarcasm in his voice. 'She was killed. You'll have heard all about that. And I'm sure it was something to do with the report.'

Ravensbourne seemed about to make some sort of protest, but Simon cut her off.

'Hang on a minute. I haven't finished yet.' He stood up, took a few paces and turned.

'After that, Gwyn Reece and I tried to find the computer records. They'd been erased. We also tried to find you, but hey presto, you'd disappeared, too.'

'Don't be stupid. I went on holiday.'

'One that nobody seemed to know you were going to take. And no one knew where you'd gone, either.'

Ravensbourne was looking flushed. 'I don't have to tell anybody where I am when I go away.'

'No, you don't. But it seemed mighty convenient. With Janice gone and the computer tampered with, you were the only one who could say what was found on those sections.'

'This is crazy! Why should I remember any one set of histology slides rather than another. Why didn't you get someone else to look at them, anyway?'

'Because they went missing too — together with the original specimen.' Simon was getting desperate. 'You've got to remember!'

'Some hope! D'you know how many I look at in a week?'

'Jesus Christ—' Simon realised he was shouting, and started again, trying to control his voice. 'Listen, woman, you *must* remember this one! Someone tampered with the lab computer to erase it, and when Gwyn found a way to unlock the information, someone killed him!'

That really struck home. She stared at him, hands grasping the arms of her chair, shock draining colour from her face. 'You're lying!' She almost screamed at him.

'D'you think I'd lie about a thing like that? He was my best friend, for God's sake!'

She looked at him a moment longer, then buried her face in her hands, sobbing uncontrollably, and crying, 'Gwyn, Gwyn, oh, Gwyn,' over and over.

Even through his anger Simon sensed that this was no charade. He wasn't sure what to do. This wasn't working out at all as he had planned.

He sat on the arm of her chair and put a hand on her shaking shoulder. 'I'm sorry. I didn't realise Gwyn meant anything to you.'

Gillian Ravensbourne made a big effort to control herself. 'He was

151

just — just a friend. A good friend.' She reached for a box of tissues near her on the floor, wiped her nose, and turned to look up at Simon with red eyes.

'What — what happened to him?'

'He was working on the computer in the Path Lab. He'd got the back-up file containing Gemma's report — '

'B-back-up file? What's that?'

'When some computer programs store a document, they may automatically make a back-up of it. You can't access it unless you know how. Gwyn had found out. While he was doing it, someone came and chopped open his skull with a fire-axe.'

She shuddered, then seemed suddenly more composed.

'Did — did he tell you what he'd found?'

'Not all of it. There was nothing left on the computer. But — surely you *must* remember something about it? Didn't Ironside mention it to you?'

Ravensbourne shook her head.

'Dammit, it was hardly routine. There was something about radiation damage to the foetus!'

The pathologist stood up, eyes wide, turned to him, and then crumpled to the floor.

Simon realised she must have fainted. Her obvious shock at Gwyn's death, combined with standing up suddenly, had been too much.

He knelt beside her. It didn't seem too bad. She was pale, but not particularly sweaty, and her pulse, which he would have expected to be weak and thready, was strong enough, although a little fast. He straightened her out, pulled her blouse down where it had ridden up as she fell, and waited for her to regain consciousness.

After less than thirty seconds, her eyes fluttered open. She lifted her head, looking puzzled.

'What am I doing down here?' she asked weakly.

'You fainted, that's all.'

She struggled to sit up. 'Me? Fainted? I don't think I've ever — I haven't done that since I was at school.'

Simon helped her back to her chair. She flopped back and closed her eyes.

'D'you feel OK now?'

She opened her eyes again and smiled faintly at him.

'Yes, I'll be all right.'

Simon got up. 'Look, if you're sure, I think I'd better go. We can carry on this conversation another time, when you're feeling better.'

'No, please — it's all right. There's no need. Just — just get me some water, Simon, would you?'

He went to the kitchen, and returned as quickly as he could. She was standing in front of a mirror, wiping her eyes and trying to push her hair into some sort of shape. She took the glass from him, drank, and then looked directly at him with an earnest expression.

'Simon — you must believe me. I don't remember anything at all about this Gemma Randall's histology report. And as for seeing radiation damage in a foetus — well, my God, I'd remember *that*, now wouldn't I?'

Simon felt a desperate, bitter disappointment. A couple of hours ago he had thought the return of this woman would go a long way to solving the mystery behind Gwyn's senseless murder. Now he was no farther on.

Gillian Ravensbourne seemed to read the sadness and frustration on his face. Simon looked up as she moved closer to him, and touched the side of his face very gently with her fingers.

'I'm sorry. I really am.'

Simon turned and left the apartment without a word.

17

Simon drove home, bitterly disappointed. What the bloody hell was he going to do now? Was there any point in trying to do *anything*? He drove his car into the garage, and sat there for some minutes, brooding, feeling completely drained. A shadow passed the window, and Kate opened the passenger door and got in beside him.

'I heard you come back. What are you doing out here?'

'Feeling fed up.'

'Oh, love. What's happened now?'

'It's what's not happened. I had a chat with Ravensbourne about Gemma Randall. Absolutely zilch.'

Kate felt hurt, but tried not to show it. She knew how upset Simon was about his friend's death, although it surprised her that he was still so concerned now he knew about Gwyn and the tablets. At times he seemed so preoccupied with it. Even in her recent drugged state, when she had seemed incapable of caring about anything but the baby, she had been aware of his concern about Gwyn. She had hoped, however, that her husband's first thoughts would have been about her own predicament. She put her hand on his arm, and tried to raise the subject discreetly.

'I'm sorry, love.' She gave a sympathetic squeeze. 'Did you — did you get the chance to ask about the blood tests?'

Simon turned to her, immediately aware of his thoughtlessness, concern in his eyes.

'Oh, Christ, Kate, I'm sorry, I should have — '

She cut him off, upset by his further distress. 'It's all right, honestly. Just tell me what she said.'

It was quite dark in the garage, but Kate thought his eyes looked moist. 'Sorry,' he muttered again, and told her what the pathologist had said — essentially that the blood should soon recover, but that there was a risk of bleeding.

'So what do you think?' Kate looked at her husband anxiously.

'I think I should try and track down Greenwell. I want him to make the decision. I hope it'll be no steroids, but I don't want the responsibility when it's yours and the baby's lives that are on the line.'

She leaned forward and kissed him gently on the cheek.

'Are you going to ring him now?'

Simon got out of the car, his energies partly restored.

'I'll do it straight away.'

It didn't take long to locate Jeremy Greenwell. The hospital switchboard gave him a number in Lyndhurst, some twenty miles away in the New Forest, which turned out to be that of Greenwell's brother. The phone was answered by the brother's wife. Simon explained who he was, and was reluctantly given the information that Greenwell was playing golf with her husband. Simon established that he would be back in about two hours, and asked if she could give him a message to call when he returned.

Kate was exasperated.

'How can he be on call to back you up, from a golf course in Basingstoke?'

'I suppose he knows his Senior Registrar is on, who should be able to cope with most things.'

'But if something serious went wrong in theatre? And you're not even supposed to be working on your own at the moment!'

'I think a lot of consultants regard being "on call" fairly loosely,' said Simon with a wry grin.

'You mean they rely on their juniors and their colleagues to bail them out if they get caught on the hop.'

Simon wasn't certain where he stood on this issue. Naturally he looked forward to the time when he would be a consultant, released from the strict rota of duty which now tied him to the hospital. But would he go so far afield, and be so far from a phone, as Greenfield now was, when he was supposed to be providing the back-up?

Kate broke into his thoughts. 'I suppose we'll just have to wait, then.'

They went and sat in the lounge, Simon absently turning on the TV as he passed. He flicked through the channels — motor racing, horse racing, American football, and a very ancient film in black and white. He turned it off, using the remote control.

'So — ' Kate tried to sound cheerful — 'what was this Ravensbourne woman like? Tall and tanned and young and lovely from her holiday?'

Simon realised he had not asked the pathologist much about her holiday. He had meant to ask her more, but had been near to losing his temper because she couldn't tell him anything about Gemma's report and treated it so dismissively.

'Funny you should say that. We hardly talked about her holiday at all. She seemed very defensive about it. And no, she didn't look tanned.'

Kate looked puzzled. 'She obviously didn't go anywhere hot, then.'

'Didn't look like it. And she didn't know about Gwyn's death.'

'She didn't *know*?'

'It came as a complete shock. She was really upset about it.'

Kate reached out and touched his hand gently. 'And you still are, too.'

They sat in sympathetic silence, then Simon spoke.

'Kate?'

'Yes, love?'

'It's good to have you back to normal.'

'Likewise,' she said.

'What d'you mean?'

'When you came in you were all depressed again. Now you're more normal, too.'

They kissed, and went upstairs.

Jeremy Greenwell rang about two hours later. They were were still in bed, Kate asleep, but Simon was awake and going over the meeting with Gillian Ravensbourne.

Greenwell wasn't too pleased at first, grumbling gently about how something always turned up just when he was beginning to relax.

He was sympathetic and concerned, however, when Simon told him the reason for troubling him. As Simon had half-expected, even Greenwell wasn't certain of the best way to handle Kate's haemato logical abnormalities. He was not at all keen on using steroids. He asked if Kate was otherwise well, whether she had any bruises, any blood when she passed water, obviously worrying about the platelet count. In the end he made up his mind.

'I think on balance we should wait and see what the trend is. I know it's Bank Holiday on Monday and all that, but I think we should get some more blood then and see what the platelet count is doing. Any sign of bruising or bleeding, of course, and I want to know straight away. But it should all gradually right itself now the causative agent has been stopped, and we should avoid any other drugs this early in pregnancy if we can.'

Simon and Kate were both content with that, for differing reasons: Kate because it meant no pills and no hospital, and Simon because it seemed entirely reasonable, and was not his personal decision.

* * *

The next day was Sunday. Simon was still on call, and as much to give himself something to do as to help Susan Parker, the new house surgeon, he went in to the hospital in the morning and did a ward round. They were on take, responsible for any emergency admissions. Unusually, there had been only one, a woman with a miscarriage brought in during the night. She had not been bleeding badly, and Dr Parker had correctly felt it was all right to wait. They

156

discussed the case afterwards, and decided that as she was still bleeding slightly, and her womb felt bulky, it was unlikely that the miscarriage had been complete. This meant that the uterus was not properly empty and the job would need to be completed with a D & C. Dr Parker would arrange for her to be included on the Tuesday morning list if things had not resolved themselves by then.

Mrs Wallingford, who had caused all the concern two days before, was now sitting up, chatting animatedly with her neighbour in the next bed. The house surgeon gave a sheepish grin when Simon commented on how well she looked. That's more than can be said for you, he thought, glancing at the young doctor. She had been up twice in the night, once to admit the patient with the miscarriage, and again later to re-insert a drip that had come out of the vein and was running into the tissues. Her tiredness, and the stress of her new responsibilities, were showing on her face. He hoped she would find it easier soon. Some juniors couldn't take the strain: he had heard of one who had committed suicide.

Simon thought this one would be all right: she still had her sense of humour.

He left the ward at about noon, as the staff were starting to serve the patients with their lunch. He was on his way to the lift when he thought again of Gemma Randall and his interrupted visit of the previous Friday. He headed for Med 3.

Gemma was in a day-room at the end of the ward, having her meal with the other patients who were not bed-bound. When she saw him, she abandoned her place immediately, wheeling herself away from the table one-handed and coming to the door.

'I didn't mean to interrupt your meal. I'll come back later,' said Simon, starting to withdraw. Gemma shook her head vigorously, rubbed her stomach and blew out her cheeks, indicating she was full. He was impressed with how well she manipulated her wheelchair, especially with only one good arm, and said so. She responded by crouching down in the seat, squinting her eyes, and swaying from side to side, her left hand grasping an imaginary steering-wheel, as if she were driving a racing car. He laughed aloud, and this drew the attention of several of the patients who were still eating. They stopped to stare at him, knives and forks hovering in mid-air.

'If you're sure you've had enough to eat, let's go back to your room, shall we?'

Gemma's reply was to rush past him and lead the way to the small ward which contained four beds. Simon was pleased to see the other occupants were not present. Gemma settled herself in her wheel-chair, note-pad and pencil at the ready, whilst Simon sat on the edge of her bed.

Gemma looked up at him, eyes sparkling, blonde hair shining, her open face slightly flushed so that her few fading freckles were barely visible. She was certainly an attractive girl, Simon realised. She was scribbling busily.

What shall we talk about?

Simon thought for a moment, looking around the room. 'I know.' He gave her an innocent smile. 'We'll talk about your brother.'

He knew Gemma would find that amusing, after her previous leg-pull about her visitor. When her silent mirth had ceased, she wrote for some time before handing over the paper.

Jonathan. He's 24. Doing his articles to be a solicitor. In Manchester, Came in specially to see me. He's very nice.

Simon looked up when he read the final sentence:

But not as nice as you!

'You're blushing!' he said, feeling slightly warm himself. She wrote quickly:

Don't mind me!.

They looked at each other, smiling. Simon was not sure what to say next. This wasn't his normal doctor-patient situation, where he could rely on his professional position to open, direct, and close interviews. The silence drew out, began to get awkward. He was clearing his throat to make some banal comment when Gemma started writing again.

Do you come here often?

They laughed together at the corny line. Simon responded to her mood. 'Now I suppose I should say, "Have you read any good books lately?" '

Gemma giggled, then wrote:

As a matter of fact, I have.

158

'Well, come on, then. What was it? *War and Peace*? *The Beano Annual*?'

Instead of replying with another message, she reached into her bedside locker and handed Simon a thin volume. She watched him intently as he read the title: *Recent Advances in the In-utero Detection of Foetal Abnormalities.*

Simon looked at her. 'You've been reading this?' She nodded. 'Whatever for?'

Gemma was writing, and as she did so Simon developed an unpleasant feeling of unease in the pit of his stomach. He realised that he was not sure if Gemma knew that his story of the abnormality of microcephaly in her own pregnancy was a fabrication.

I wanted to try and find out

'Try and find out what?'

What you might have seen

So she knows I didn't see microcephaly, thought Simon. He pushed his hands through his hair. He felt weak, sick. She knew. He'd have to tell her the truth. There was no other way he could justify his course of action to this trusting girl, this innocent victim.

'You know then.'

It was a statement, not a question. He looked at her, expecting to see anger, or at least resentment. He saw only sadness. She wrote:

I know it wasn't micro-cephaly

'They told you?'

Gemma nodded, wrote again:

Please tell me. What did you really see?

How did she find out? He felt a sudden chill. How could she know there was anything other than what he had told her?

'Why are you so certain there *was* anything else?'

Gemma wrote for some time.

Mr. D'Arcy told me there was no micro-cephaly. But I just know you wouldn't do an abortion on me so quickly

159

for no reason And if telling me I had a baby with micro-cephaly was a better alternative than the truth then GOD please <u>what is the truth?</u>

How perceptive she is, thought Simon. She'd realised that he had avoided telling her what was really wrong, and had chosen an horrendous abnormality as being more acceptable. What could he say?

'I don't know how to explain this, I really don't. I haven't told this to anyone else, except my wife and my lawyer.'

Gemma stared at him, wide-eyed.

'I saw something on your scan that I couldn't explain. The baby looked — looked like some sort of — ' He hesitated, then continued quietly, head bowed. ' — like something that wasn't wholly human.' He heard her gasp, but did not look up. He waited some moments, gathering his thoughts, knowing he could not stop now.

'The foetus was bigger than I expected from the dates, and incredibly detailed. I could even make out facial features. I've never seen anything like it before.'

He glanced up at her. She had not moved a muscle since he started talking.

'You think I'm crazy — gone round the bend.'

He felt her touch his hand, and when he looked she was shaking her head slowly from side to side, compassion in her eyes.

'It's why I haven't told anybody. They'd think I'd flipped.' He took a slow, deep breath, and let it out again. 'I saw an evil face. I swear it knew I was looking at it. It — it grinned at me.'

Gemma was watching him, mouth hanging open, breathing shallow and fast. She nodded frantically, urging him to keep going.

'I forgot to photograph it. Afterwards — afterwards I could only think of getting rid of it as soon as possible. I didn't see how I could convince anyone of what I'd seen.'

Gemma put her hand over her mouth as if to suppress a cry. Simon looked at the floor. Gemma wrote, and pushed another note into his hand.

Why didn't you wait for someone else to do another scan? To see if they saw the same thing?

'To make sure I wasn't imagining things, you mean?' He managed a weak smile. 'I've asked myself that a few times, I can tell you. I was so *certain* of what I'd seen. I'm sure that if someone else had done a

160

scan, and said it was normal, I wouldn't have believed them anyway. I can't really explain it any better. It seems so irrational, so unscientific, now. It just —' He shrugged his shoulders, searching for the words. 'It just got to me. And now . . .' He put his hand over his eyes, massaged his forehead. 'And now, look at you. God, I'm so sorry.' He shook his head, trying to ward off his despair.

I'm sorry too. But it's not your fault. I shouldn't have got pregnant.

He looked at her, trying to stay in control. What quality is it that makes some people react to personal tragedy like this, he thought, when the world seems full of idiots who are so ready to moan about imagined ills, let alone minor real ones? Gemma picked up his hand and stroked it soothingly. *She* was consoling *him*! He almost laughed aloud as he realised what was happening, prompting her to give him a warm smile. I wonder if her boyfriend realises how lucky he is, he thought.

'Has your boyfriend been in to see you?' he asked. Gemma's face fell, her mouth hardened. She shook her head, just once.

Simon was surprised. 'What, not at all?'

Another negative shake of the head. Simon felt his anger rising. 'You mean he's left you to face all this on your own?'

This time an affirmative nod.

'The rotten bastard!'

Gemma looked down, and Simon saw a small tear roll down her cheek. He reached over and lifted her chin. He wanted to comfort her, give her some hope, make her know she was not alone.

'Don't worry, Gemma. I won't desert you.'

She reached up and took his hand, laying it against her cheek, and forced a smile through her tears.

At that moment the Ward Sister came to the door. It was not the same one who had welcomed Simon so warmly three days ago. The nurse stood for a moment taking in the little tableau, then, with a small gesture of disapproval, came farther into the room.

'I think you should leave now, doctor. Miss Randall is due for her physiotherapy.'

'Yes, of course, Sister.' He drew his hand away slowly. 'I've been trying to cheer her up, but I haven't had a very successful time, I'm afraid.'

'So I see,' she replied tartly.

Gemma wiped her eyes and made a determined attempt to look happy. She tugged at his sleeve to detain him a moment longer as she

161

wrote quickly. Simon took the note, and read it aloud for Sister's benefit.

'"Please come back soon." I'll certainly try,' he said to Gemma, nodded at the nurse as he passed, and left the ward.

Simon drove home to find Kate humming to herself in the kitchen, a substantial lunch almost ready. He went up to her as she stood at the sink washing the pans, put his arms around her waist and gave her a kiss on the neck.

She tried to look up at him. 'You seem in a good mood.'

'Just pleased to see you back to normal.'

'Right,' she said, easing away from him, 'if you give me a bit of room, I'll serve lunch.' Simon moved to the kitchen table, sat down, and watched.

Kate busied herself getting out warm plates, putting a joint of meat out for carving, straining vegetables. She looked up through a small cloud of steam.

'I'd like to go back to work when my blood tests are OK — I feel so good I'm sure they soon will be.'

'There's no need to rush it. No need to go back at all, if you don't want to.'

'I know, but I'll go mad if I just sit around here.'

She handed Simon the carving knife so that he could start cutting up the joint. 'By the way, Pauline Jamieson phoned. She wants to come and see you. Today.'

'What did you say?'

'I said I thought it'd be all right, so long as you weren't called in to the hospital suddenly. She's coming round about three, unless you ring her before.'

Simon and Kate were sitting watching television when Pauline arrived at about 3.15. Simon thought she looked tired, and told her so as they went to sit in the lounge.

'I had a late night in town — only got back this morning. I had to meet a QC in chambers on Saturday. Sir John Charlesworth, no less.'

Simon smiled. 'I should obviously be impressed, but I'm afraid I'm not aware of his importance.'

Pauline spoke with exaggerated pomposity. 'Sir John Charlesworth, QC is one of the finest divorce lawyers in the land.' She laughed. 'Seriously, he's a top man — he's acted for the best.'

'And taken a generous cut of the proceeds to boot, I've no doubt.'

'He's well-heeled, all right. Chauffeur-driven Roller — the works.'

Kate joined them, bringing three cups of tea from the kitchen. 'Sounds as if helping the rich and famous to get divorced pays well.'

Pauline laughed again. 'It certainly does!'

'Don't tell me you're working on a divorce case of some famous personality,' said Simon.

'No, nothing like that. Someone who keeps a very low profile, in fact, even though he has pots of money. But that's confidential, of course, and *not* why I'm here.'

'Of course, m'Lud,' Simon mocked. 'My lips are sealed. So just why *are* you here?'

'While I was waiting for the Great Man to arrive, I was "entertained" by one of his juniors. We were making small talk, and it transpired he was in Bournemouth last year, advising a local solicitor on a case. To put it in simple terms, it concerned a red-haired Welsh doctor who was taking out an injunction to prevent a wronged husband from duffing him up for having it off with his wife.'

Simon sat up. 'Good grief! Gwyn! You told me something about that when the police were thinking Gwyn's death was a "crime of passion".' He grinned. 'You said that theory was bullshit!'

'Spot on. Small world, isn't it?'

'But we already knew about that bit of his past.' He frowned, and looked at her intently. 'I can tell by the look on your face that you're holding back the juicy bit. So let's have it!'

Pauline looked conspiratorially from Simon to Kate.

'All right. Here's the interesting part.' She paused, savouring the moment. 'The man who was making all the threats, the man with whose wife Gwyn was having the affair, was called Ravensbourne. And his wife worked as a pathologist at the Princess Marina Hospital, Bournemouth.'

There was a long silence as her words sank in. Then suddenly they were all talking at once as they tried to unravel the implications of her news. They had argued over the problem for some time before Simon attempted to summarise.

'Let's look at what we've got. One: Gwyn and Ravensbourne were lovers until about a year ago — that's about eight months before I came here.'

'And he kept pretty quiet about it,' put in Kate.

'Right. So point two: he didn't say anything about their relationship even when it seemed that Ravensbourne was the one who might hold the key to the missing report. Now why? I find that pretty difficult to understand.'

'Perhaps it was out of a sense of loyalty,' suggested Pauline.

'Or maybe she had some sort of hold over him.' That was Kate.

'There must have been some reason he didn't mention it to me,' said Simon. 'I'd only known him a few months, but I thought we were really good friends.'

Pauline agreed. 'I should say that was an understatement. It looks as though he got himself killed trying to help you out. You can't have a much better friend than that.'

Kate bit her lower lip as an unpleasant thought occurred to her. 'You don't think their affair was still going on — that Gwyn was protecting her in some way?'

'If that was the case, it would have been a contemptuous deceit.' There was no doubting the feeling in Simon's words, and he looked worried. He had still not come to terms with Kate's assertion that Gwyn had given her the azathioprine, was afraid that his faith in his friend was indeed misplaced . . . 'I just can't believe that of him.'

'There's one way to find out,' said Pauline determinedly.

'And what's that?' Simon frowned.

'Go and ask her.'

'Christ, I couldn't do that!'

'Why not?'

'I don't think I'd have the nerve. And what about point three?' he went on. 'Did Ravensbourne's disappearance on holiday have anything to do with Gwyn? Did she know he was looking into the matter of the report? She left the morning we went to see Janice Marshall and found it had been deleted from the computer.'

'If she did,' said Kate, 'it would mean there must still have been some contact between her and Gwyn.'

'I don't like to support this line of argument, but . . .'

'But what, Simon?' Pauline looked at him, eyebrows raised.

'Well, it would explain why she was so devastated when I told her about Gwyn being killed. She went to pieces for a while, and then fainted. Would she have done that if he was just an old flame?'

'Yes, I see what you mean.' Pauline was thoughtful. 'Look, I don't suppose she was *pretending* to be grief-stricken?'

'It looked pretty convincing to me. Although she *did* seem to recover quickly.' He hesitated. 'What makes you ask?'

'You said she didn't look tanned, and was evasive about her holiday. If she hadn't left the country, it would be surprising if she didn't already know about Gwyn. After all, it made the national papers, *and* got on "News at Ten".'

'But what's the significance of her behaviour if she *did* know about Gwyn?'

Pauline sighed. 'I just don't know. I really don't.'

The phone rang, and Simon went into the hall to answer it. When he returned, Kate and Pauline were lost in thought, still trying to make some sense of this latest development.

'I'm going to have to leave you two thinkers to carry on. There's a woman in the labour ward who's having trouble in the second stage. Sounds like a forceps, and Dr Parker sounds distinctly nervous.'

It was one thing after another for the rest of the day. Simon and the young doctor ended up spending a lot of time in theatre. The possible forceps turned out to need a Caesarean section, the woman who had come in with the miscarriage started to bleed again, so had to have her D & C straight away, and a girl was admitted with what sounded like an ectopic pregnancy, so it was back to theatre again. In fact it turned out to be an inflamed appendix, but it still took some time.

It was after 10.30 when Simon at last let himself in at his front door again. The house was in darkness, and Kate was asleep in bed. He kissed her gently as he slipped in beside her, and she murmured something unintelligible and cuddled up to him.

Thinking about Gwyn again kept him awake for some time, but eventually he drifted off, his last thought a hope that he wouldn't have to get up in the night.

18

Simon was not disturbed in the night, but a call came from Dr Parker as he was eating his breakfast. It was another obstetric problem, another hold-up in the second stage of labour. The new house officer clearly lacked confidence, and as he burned his mouth gulping some hot coffee he hoped she would improve soon. When a new junior doctor arrived on the firm, it always put the call rate up for the registrars. He tried to be understanding, to remember that he had once been in the same situation. He left the house chewing on some toast and putting his coat on at the same time.

'See you later,' he mumbled at Kate through his mouthful, gave her a marmalade-laden kiss on the cheek, and rushed out to the car.

He'd gone about half a mile when he realised that his hurried departure had made him forget something important. It was Bank Holiday Monday, and today he was meant to take another blood sample from Kate, as Greenwell had suggested. He cursed under his breath, then gave a sigh of resignation. He would have to go back later. He didn't think this mother and baby would wait while he returned home.

He was wrong about that: by the time he reached the ward, he found the baby safely delivered, with Dr Parker sewing up the mother's perineum. Simon waited until she had finished repairing the episiotomy, then went with her to the ward office while she wrote up the notes.

One of the midwives came in and offered them coffee.

'Yes please,' said Simon. 'I only had one mouthful of my last cup.' He wasn't trying to get a dig at his junior, but she took it personally.

'I'm so sorry, Mr Rob — er — Simon. I've really wasted your time, haven't I?'

He thought she had, but he wanted to listen to the whole story, and not condemn her without a hearing. After all, he had told her not to hesitate to call if she was worried.

'Tell me about it, and then I'll decide.' He smiled to show he wasn't annoyed with her.

'The midwife called me because she was so long pushing, and the perineum just wasn't stretching. It was her second baby, and the first had been delivered without an episiotomy, so we both thought this one should be. But when the baby's heart rate began to get a bit irregular, we thought we should do one anyway.'

'Who did it?'

'The midwife. But it didn't seem to make any difference. The mother was getting tired and not pushing so well. That's when I called you.'

'So how did she push it out? Did you give mother some spinach, or what?'

Dr Parker relaxed a little and gave a smile. 'No, not exactly. I examined her and thought that the episiotomy was a bit small. I remember being told recently that if you decide to do a cut, make it a good one, no messing. So I enlarged it quite a lot — keeping away from the anal sphincter, of course — and the baby came out on the next push as easy as pie.' She looked sheepishly down at the floor.

'Well done.'

Susan Parker looked up in surprise. 'Well done? But I called you in for nothing.'

'As it turns out. But you exercised your judgement and you were right. That deserves congratulations.' He continued before she could reply. 'Tell me, why were you so reluctant about cutting her in the first place?'

'Well . . .' she looked uncomfortable, glancing around and avoiding Simon's eye. 'There's so much talk of unnecessary episiotomies and sections these days. I always try to deliver without cutting if I can. I — I don't want the reputation of being scissor-happy — nor do the midwives.'

It was more or less the reply Simon had expected. 'And where does all this pressure towards less intervention come from?'

'How do you mean?'

'Well, is the advice to stay your hand coming from your professional teachers?'

'Well, not really. But there always seems to be something in the papers . . .'

'So you make your professional judgements on the basis of what you see or hear in the media?'

She began to see where this was leading. 'No, of course not, but —' she faltered.

'But you want to conform to the popular conception of good practice.'

'You make it sound as if I'm letting my decisions be clouded by popular opinion.'

'That's exactly what I'm saying, and it's a mistake too many doctors are making these days.' The coffee arrived, and he took a sip before continuing. 'You must have faith in your own judgement and stick to it. What I often do is imagine myself justifying my actions in a particular case to my colleagues, or to some independent professional inquiry — not to the newspapers! If you can do that, *even if your decision turns out to be wrong* — ' he emphasised the words deliberately — 'then you have exercised your professional skills correctly and to the best of your ability. No one can ask more than that.'

The young doctor grinned at Simon. 'So tell me, after all that — did I waste your time with that incident this morning?'

Simon looked at her sternly.

'Yes.' He saw the girl's expression falter, and smiled.

'Only kidding. It's a bit like last time, with the Wallingford woman. There was no clinical need for my presence, but a lesson's been learnt. That's what this stage of your career is all about. And if I get called unnecessarily, I have to grin and bear it.'

'Until you become a consultant!' She laughed.

'Things *should* get better then, I agree.' He got up from his chair. 'Any other problems?'

'No, all quiet on the Western Front. Thank goodness, after last evening.'

Simon was at the door. 'Right. I'm going back home now, but I'll be back in less than an hour, so if you want me then, I'll be around the hospital somewhere.'

'I should be OK.' She looked directly at him. 'And — thanks.'

Simon waved dismissively, and set off for the car park and home.

He took the blood from Kate himself: he didn't see the point in involving someone else for such a simple task, and Kate certainly preferred it that way. He was back in the hospital thirty-five minutes later, and rang the Duty Laboratory Technician. He was pleased that it was still Jennifer Dorset, who had done the previous tests, because it would save another round of explanations. As before, she was quite amenable to doing it. Even so, Simon emphasised that it was Greenwell's decision, not his own. He didn't want the girl to think he was making unjustified use of her at a Bank Holiday weekend.

The tests would take about an hour, so he decided he would fill in time by going to the hospital pharmacy. He wanted to see if there were any records of Kate's damaging prescription. The pharmacy was only open for an hour that morning, and he arrived just as it was about to close. He vaguely knew the woman on duty, and thought she was a friendly sort. He went up to the counter from which staff and patients collected their medicines, and leaned on it.

'Nearly finished?' he asked.

'Just about, doctor,' she said. 'Anything I can do before I shut up shop?' She paused as she was about to lower a steel grille to secure the counter area.

'I don't need anything dispensed, but I do need some information, if you can help me.'

'I'll try, of course, doctor.'

Simon had prepared his explanation. 'I'm trying to track down a prescription that was issued about three weeks back. It was given to a patient in the Gynae Ward, but it now looks as though there may have been a mistake. Not by the pharmacy,' he added quickly, in case her co-operation might be hindered by a desire to protect herself or her colleagues, 'but by the doctor. It's nothing serious, but if perhaps you could check for me?'

'Of course, doctor. When was the prescription issued?'

The day Kate had had her investigations was 7th May. Simon told the pharmacist the date, and she went to the department's computer and called up the data for that day. 'What was the patient's name?'

This is where it could get tricky, thought Simon.

'It was my wife. Mrs Kate Robinson.'

The woman hesitated, and looked across at him from the monitor screen.

'Oh, I see.' Her tone made Simon think she might change her mind about co-operating, but she just shrugged her shoulders and typed in the details. After a pause, she said, 'Nothing here for anyone of that name.'

Simon wasn't really surprised. He hadn't thought it would be that easy. 'Can you access the prescriptions by drug rather than by patient's name?'

'Sure. What was it for?'

'Azathioprine.' He held his breath.

She gave him a long look. 'We don't dispense much of that. Is Mrs Robinson — ?' She stopped, and Simon knew what she was thinking. Azathioprine was an unusual drug all right, and wasn't associated with trivial illnesses. It might mean this doctor's wife was quite ill, so she didn't want to pry or risk upsetting him.

'Just a moment,' she said, busying herself at the keyboard. 'No, none dispensed that day.'

Simon had one more suggestion. 'Does it take long to go back over the last few weeks to see when the last prescriptions for a drug were issued?'

The woman smiled. 'If it was paracetamol or penicillin, something common like that, it would take forever. But not for something like azathioprine. Hold on.' She addressed herself to the computer again.

'Since the first of April there've only been five prescriptions. You'd better come and look.'

Simon went into the pharmacy through a door set in the wall to the left of the counter. The pharmacist stood back from the screen so that he could look at the list. Glowing in green text was a list headed 'Azathioprine — April'. Below this heading was a table of figures. There were six columns in the table, the headings indicating the date they were dispensed, the number of tablets issued, the number of tablets remaining in stock, the initials of the prescribing doctor, and a code for the dispenser. The last column was headed 'Pt. or Dept'.

There were five entries on the register, listed in chronological order. Simon was interested in the column headed 'prescribing doctor'. The fourth entry made his heart jump. He read the whole line. It showed that 90 azathioprine tablets had been dispensed on 26th April. The prescribing doctor's initials were given as 'G.R'.

'So it *was* Gwyn Reece.' Simon spoke aloud without realising it.

'Sorry, doctor?'

'Oh, nothing.' Simon had been secretly hoping that Gwyn's involvement in giving Kate the drug would turn out to be some sort of mistake, but here was irrefutable evidence. He was upset by this discovery, and it showed.

'Is everything all right, doctor?' The pharmacist looked genuinely concerned.

'I'm OK,' Simon said, denying the obvious. He made an effort to sound relaxed about it. 'Tell me, from this entry, can you find out for whom the drugs were dispensed on this occasion?' He pointed to the entry that had caused his anguish.

The woman was relieved to be asked a question she could answer almost automatically. 'Certainly, doctor. If it's given to an individual patient, we can cross-reference it by looking at the entry for that day. All the prescriptions filled will be entered, and we can locate the individual patient or patients who were prescribed the drug that day. If there were more than one for the same drug, we can narrow it down further from the doctor and dispenser.'

'And in this case?' Simon nodded at the screen.

'In this case,' the pharmacist continued authoritatively, 'there is no individual patient.' She pointed at the last column, which on this entry contained a letter 'T'. 'This tells me the prescription in question was issued for use in theatre.' She paused, furrowed her brow. 'Though what the devil they'd be doing with azathioprine in theatre, I can't imagine.'

'Neither can I,' said Simon, his fears confirmed. He headed for the door. 'Look, you've been very helpful, and I'm sorry if I've delayed you getting off for your lunch.'

The woman warmed to the flattery and the concern for her welfare. 'That's OK, doctor, pleased to be of assistance.' After Simon had gone, she thought about the reasons for his interest. Why should this unusual drug be needed in the operating theatre? As a rule, the only drugs used there were injectables, for the anaesthetists. Her stomach grumbled, and she looked at her watch. Satiating her hunger took over as the focus of her thoughts. She prepared to leave, and did not consider the matter again.

Simon headed for the **Records Department**. At weekends the key could be drawn by certain personnel from the hospital Reception, upon proving identity and signing a book. Such access to records was often necessary when patients with complex past histories were admitted out of hours. Usually it was a member of the ward staff who was sent to find them, but Simon had been shown the procedure when he arrived. He'd had no reason to use it until now.

He let himself into the enormous store-room where the records were kept, and noted his entry in the book kept there for the purpose. When he left he would have to make a similar notation, and add the details of any records he was taking out. He had no intention of actually removing any notes, but would just enter NF — meaning the file he was looking for was not found.

It did not take him long to locate Kate's records. He half-expected them to be missing, but there they were, correctly filed. The quickest way to find a record was to use the patient's hospital number, and Simon had taken the precaution of writing Kate's down before he left home. He sat down at a small desk, and began to go carefully through the notes.

First he looked at the cardex — the nurses' record of the patient's stay in hospital. It was written in the standard *ersatz* shorthand the nurses soon learned to adopt, varying from hospital to hospital, but generally all very similar. The same phrases occurred again and again, however many notes you looked at.

The cardex stated that Kate had been admitted on 6th May to the Gynae Ward c/o (under the care of) Jeremy Greenwell. She had been s/b (seen by) the anaesthetist in the early evening. Simon cursed silently as the name was not recorded. She'd had a GN (good night) nil sed (no sedation). She had had her pre med at 0830 and WTT (went to theatre) at 0930. Then followed the legend 'DNRTW' and a signature. After a little thought Simon decided that must mean 'did not return to ward'. As if to confirm this, the record continued in a different hand and a different-coloured ink, which stated: Pt transferred to PW (private wing) from T (theatre) at 1100. She was C&0 (conscious and orientated) after 30 minutes, and was s/b JG (seen by Jeremy Greenwell) soon afterwards. She was e & d (eating and drinking) normally by the evening, and was FFD mane (fit for discharge home the next morning). She left the ward at 1015, 'Pt has own TTOs'.

That was the abbreviation he had been looking for. 'TTO' meant 'treatment (or tablets) to take out' — that is, any drugs that the patient was to remain on after discharge home. So the ward knew she was to take tablets, but what were they, and who had prescribed them?

He turned to the medical notes. Unusually for in-patient notes,

171

which were normally written up by the houseman, they had been written up by Greenwell himself. Presumably, as this was a colleague's wife, the Consultant had thought he should do them. The problem was, they were succinct to the point of being valueless — and almost illegible. There was still no mention of the anaesthetist's name. At the end, however, he could make out 'R$_x$ Fe succ. i tds'.

That was Greenwell's prescription for an iron tablet, ferrous succinate, often given after Gynae procedures where the patient was at risk of anaemia. He looked at the drug record card, and there it was again: ferrous succinate. It had been dispensed as directed on the ward. A final note on the chart repeated the statement 'Pt has own TTOs'. It was just as Kate had said: she had been given the correct prescription in hospital, but had taken the tablets Gwyn had given her when she left.

That was very unusual. Normal practice was that the patient couldn't take so much as a Smartie without it being given by a nurse, and certainly patients weren't allowed to take their own medication from a supply they held themselves. Invariably, they were relieved of all tablets when they went into hospital, and it was a universal moan that they never got them back.

In this case, Simon supposed the staff had thought that, as it was only an iron preparation, it was all right if she used her own supply when she went home. After all, she was a doctor's wife. It still bothered him, though. He didn't think the staff would take this course of action unless specifically instructed. But by whom? Greenwell had prescribed ferrous succinate — but in her 'own' bottle Kate had the azathioprine.

If it *was* just azathioprine. Kate's tablets did not have the maker's name, he recalled, and the pharmacy records showed that the azathioprine had been taken from there more than a week earlier. Plenty of time for them to be reconstituted with another ingredient.

It came back to the same question: why? What the hell was Gwyn up to? What the bloody hell did he think he was doing?

Simon's researches had left him feeling bitterly disappointed. They confirmed Gwyn's culpability in prescribing the azathioprine, but he was no nearer finding out who had anaesthetised her. It looked to him now as if it had probably been Gwyn all along, and he had denied it to distance himself from the administration of the harmful drug.

Simon banged his forehead with his hand, as an obvious solution struck him. All this ferreting about! All he had to do was introduce the topic of anaesthetists into a conversation with Greenwell about Kate, and casually ask him who had administered to her. Even now, he didn't want to condemn Gwyn publicly until he was one hundred per cent sure of his facts. He locked the Records Department, returned the key, and went to the Path Lab.

172

Jennifer Dorset was expecting him. 'I was just about to bleep you with the results,' she said as he came in.

'You look pretty pleased. Is it good news?'

'Yes, I think it is. Haemoglobin's about the same — you wouldn't expect that to change in a couple of days. But the white count's up over three hundred to nearly two thousand.'

'And the platelets?'

'Over a hundred thousand. They were only sixty thousand before. It certainly looks as if the bone marrow is recovering, sir.'

'Yes it does.' Impulsively he took her hand and gave it a squeeze. 'Thanks, Jennifer,' he said, and rushed out, leaving the girl with a warm glow of pleasure. She rarely saw the personal consequences of her laboratory results; it was all so impersonal — just a lot of figures relating to patient numbers. They didn't even have names any more. If she found kidney failure, leukaemia, barbiturate poisoning, she could only imagine the underlying human tragedy. And when a test improved — a child pronounced clear of meningitis, a transplanted kidney found to be working well — she could never share in the joyful news of recovery. For her to see directly the heartening effect her skills could have gave her a great boost. She thought about it for a long time.

Meanwhile, Simon was rushing to the car park. He couldn't wait to tell her. His wife was going to be all right!

19

The following morning Simon woke with a feeling of almost overwhelming anxiety. He lay there for a few moments, waiting for his pulse rate to settle and the feeling of slight nausea to pass. He must have had his old nightmare. He breathed deeply a few times, then turned slightly to look at his wife. Immediately he felt anxious again, and realised why. It was Tuesday today, when Kate was to have her scan.

Why do you have this irrational fear of a simple investigation, you idiot? he rebuked himself. But he knew why. Ever since Kate had become pregnant he had been dreading seeing her scan. He was afraid he would see again what he had seen with Gemma Randall.

This would be different, though, he reassured himself. It would be done by the technician, and probably Greenwell would be there, too. Other people. If it was abnormal there would be other witnesses, and he wouldn't have to wonder if his brain or his eyes were playing him tricks. He relaxed a little at the thought.

'Come in, Simon, come in Mrs Robinson!' Jeremy Greenwell sounded almost hearty as he invited them into his consulting room. They were in the Obstetric Out-patients' department at the hospital. It was mid-morning, and Greenwell had ushered them in during his busy out-patient session. Kate felt guilty walking right past the hordes of ladies who were waiting, most of them seemingly in very advanced pregnancy. She felt as if all eyes were on her, that someone would suddenly shout out, 'Hey! You've only just got here! Get to the back of the queue!' She was not onc to exploit or abuse privilege, and her embarrassment was heightened by the gratitude she felt at not having to wait her turn out there with masses of strangers.

Her relief at seeing the door to the consulting room close behind her, shutting out the crowded scene, was fleeting, when faced with the prospect of what was to come. She knew Simon was keyed up about the scan, and she was pretty nervous herself. Most of all she was afraid that the drug she had been tricked into taking might have caused some harm to the baby. She looked around the room, taking in the examination couch, the nurse standing almost to attention to one side of it, the pile of folders on the desk.

'So how are we feeling?' A few seconds passed before Kate, lost in

174

her thoughts, realised that Greenwell's remark was addressed to her.

'Oh, fine, thanks. Just a little nervous.'

'No need to be, no need at all. Piece of cake. Simon told me about the improving blood picture. Good news, eh?'

'Yes.' She tried to raise a smile, to seem enthusiastic. 'I'm sorry to hold up your clinic like this.' She gestured towards the door. 'There seem to be so many people waiting.'

'Don't worry yourself. They'll be all right. Now then, hop up on here, would you?' He patted the couch. She felt like a circus animal that had been trained to jump up onto a stand and perform. Dutifully she clambered up, and the nurse pulled up her dress and pulled down her tights and pants before she had a chance to prepare herself. She felt exposed and vulnerable, which she told herself was silly; there were only her husband, Greenwell and the nurse present. But it was a big room, and she felt open to all of it. Besides, someone might come in . . . She wanted to ask the nurse to pull the curtains across but was afraid that would sound prudish — she, a nurse herself, embarrassed at showing a bit of her stomach in front of these medical people.

Greenwell prodded her abdomen expertly, pushing down above her pubis. Her bladder was quite full, as she'd been told to come that way for the scan. She was afraid she was going to wet herself.

'Right, let's have these right off, shall we?' He nodded to Kate and then to the nurse, who stepped forward and removed Kate's tights and pants completely. Kate waited for a blanket to be provided to cover her, but none was forthcoming. When doing nursing herself, she had always tried to be aware how embarrassed some people could be, and never assumed that patients were comfortable in accepting exposure and examination. Now on the receiving end, she was surprised to find not everyone was so considerate.

'Tray,' Greenwell commanded.

The nurse wheeled over a trolley on which there was a steel dish laid up for vaginal examinations. Kate tried to catch the nurse's eye, and looked at her pleadingly. The nurse frowned for a moment, then followed Kate's glance to the curtains. She reached for them, and as she pulled them across, said tactfully to Greenwell, 'Shall I pull the curtains round for you, Mr Greenwell?' He looked up absently as he pulled on a glove. 'What? Yes, oh, all right.' Simon, equally tactfully, withdrew to the other side.

The Consultant approached Kate. 'Legs apart, dear.' He held out his hand to the nurse, who was already waiting to squeeze some lubricant jelly onto the glove. With barely a moment's hesitation, his fingers were inside her, the other hand once more pressing on her bladder. It was quite uncomfortable, and she winced and bit her lower lip. The nurse saw her reaction, and came and held her hand.

'Just relax, Mrs Robinson,' she said soothingly.

Kate was disappointed, lying there as Greenwell rummaged about inside her. He had not been at all like this when she had seen him at his rooms on Saturday. She was even surprised he felt it necessary to do another vaginal examination. She knew he was busy this morning — that would explain him appearing rushed — but his whole manner seemed more abrupt. Could it be that he had one manner for his private clinic and another for the hospital? She had heard of consultants being like that, but had not seen it for herself. The fact that she was certain Simon would never be like that was some consolation.

Greenwell was talking again. 'Confirms what I thought. Don't understand it.' He swished the curtain back with one movement and strode over to his desk, leaving Kate to pull on her underwear without privacy. She was sticky between her legs where the lubricant jelly had been, and began to ask the nurse for a tissue to wipe it away, then changed her mind. She realised she would have to wipe herself in full view of those in the room. It seemed such a personal act, and to perform it standing there, naked from the waist down, even in front of medical staff, seemed so undignified that she couldn't do it.

'It's all right, it doesn't matter,' she said, and the nurse, who had paused in putting a new paper towel on the examination couch, carried on with clearing up. Kate scrambled hastily into her pants and tights, and went to sit in the chair Greenwell indicated as he glanced up from the notes. He finished writing and looked from Simon to his wife.

'Better get that scan done right now, I think. Definitely large for dates.' He completed a form and handed it to Kate, but spoke to Simon. 'Take her along to the technician, would you, Simon? Tell her to call me when she's got a decent picture.'

Kate and Simon arrived outside the small side-room which housed the ultrasound scanning equipment. There were two other women waiting, sitting on steel-framed chairs. There were no other seats, so they stood, exchanging glances but not talking, for several minutes. The two women seemed to know each other, and were discussing the merits of their respective doctors.

'Oh, mine's *ever* so nice,' said one, 'but 'ee's got such cold 'ands.'

'Well, at least you sees yours. I ain't seen mine but once this pregnancy, and that was when the midwife couldn't get no blood.'

''Snot right, that,' the other woman nodded sagely. 'You oughter see yer doctor reg'lar, like, I reckon.'

Careful to be sure they were unobserved, Kate and Simon exchanged a smile of gentle amusement. The door to the side-room opened, and a young girl, no more than eighteen, and her husband (or boyfriend, perhaps? wondered Kate) came out. The technician looked out of the door, and was about to speak to the woman seated nearest to her, when she saw Simon.

'Oh, hello, Dr Robinson.' She came farther out of the room and smiled at Kate. 'This is Mrs Robinson, is it?'

'Yes, hello, Jane. My wife has just seen Mr Greenwell, and he wants her to have a scan.'

'You'd better come in, then.' She turned to the two waiting women. 'Won't be long.'

Kate saw a belligerent scowl pass over the face of the woman who was next in line. She hesitated.

'No, it's all right, these ladies were here first.'

The first woman gave a satisfied nod and began to rise, but her friend restrained her with a hand on her arm. 'Go on, Maureen, let the doctor's missus go first. 'Ee must be busy, an' all. We've got plenty o' time.' The first woman scowled again, but her generous companion was not to be swayed. She looked up at Kate. 'You go on, luv.' She nodded towards the door, where the technician was waiting. When Kate hesitated again, she waved her arm in the direction of the scanning room. 'Go on, now. We don't mind, honest.'

'Well if you're sure.' Kate made a point of looking at the patient whose position she had usurped. 'That's very kind. Thank you very much.' She was rewarded with a grudging smile and a brief nod, and rushed into the little room, guilt unassuaged.

'Now then, Mrs Robinson, how full is your bladder?'

The little scene outside had made her temporarily forget that she was bursting to go. 'Nearly at the leg-crossing stage.'

'That's good. Now, let's get you up on here, shall we?' She helped Kate up onto the examination couch. 'I expect you know all about this.'

'No, I don't really. Just assume total ignorance, and go through everything as if I were an ordinary patient.' That phrase says a lot, thought Kate. A doctor's wife is never an 'ordinary patient', and it's not always an advantage. They often get many unnecessary investigations. And people assume they know everything, and as a result don't bother to explain what's going on.

'All right, then. My name's Jane Forsyth.'

'Hello, Jane.'

'First we want to expose your tummy.' The technician put a sheet over Kate's legs and lower abdomen, then helped her pull up her dress and lower her tights and pants. More concern for my modesty here, thought Kate, relaxing a little.

'Now this is quite a painless procedure,' she continued, 'and doesn't do any harm whatsoever to you or the baby.' She picked up the ultrasound probe. 'I'm just going to move this device here over your — ' The technician stopped as there was a knock on the door,

177

and one of the nurses from the Obstetric Out-patients put her head round it.

'I'm sorry to interrupt, Mr Robinson, but Sister says could you possibly come back to the Out-patients? There's only you and Mr Greenwell this morning, and hardly anyone's been seen yet. There'll be a riot if we don't try and catch up.'

'Oh, hell. I wanted to see this.' Simon looked at Kate questioningly.

'Go on, love, I'll be fine here with Jane.'

Simon went out reluctantly with a sigh, following the nurse back to the crowded Out-patient Department. It took a real effort for him to concentrate on the first patient, and he found it difficult to sympathise when she wasted the first few minutes of the consultation complaining about the delay.

Doctors, mused Simon as she rambled on, are not permitted problems of their own. Their own anxieties and concerns always have to be subjugated to the problems of the patient, however trivial by comparison. The woman went on and on about the impossibility of getting her shopping done for her husband's lunch when she was kept waiting like this, and meanwhile all he could think of was Kate and the scan. With a great effort and with no display of sympathy, he said, 'Let's not waste any more time on complaining, shall we, or we'll be later than ever.'

The woman was somewhat taken aback. 'Well, if *you* won't listen, I shall write a letter.'

'Please do,' Simon told her, feeling certain she wouldn't bother, and beginning to feel a little guilty since it was he who had contributed to the delay by seeing Greenwell with Kate. The woman began to tell Simon about her problems and he was soon immersed in the stream of patients; for a time he was able to forget about what was going on at the other end of the department.

He got through six patients in the next half-hour, which helped reduce the back-log. When one was under a lot of pressure the patients seemed able to sense it, and many were succinct with their problems and didn't ask many questions, not wishing to take up too much time. It was not a good way to practise medicine, where the patient felt unable to relax and talk, but it happened all too often and was one aspect of National Health Service work that Simon did not enjoy. In a way he could see how someone like Greenwell could behave so differently in one environment, where time was not too vital, compared to another where, through weight of numbers, it was of the essence.

He glanced at his watch and saw that Kate must have long since finished her scan. He saw one more patient, but couldn't concentrate. He went over to Greenwell's office, and walked in as a patient came out.

'Sorry to interrupt, Jeremy. I was wondering if you'd heard anything about the scan?'

'Oh yes, come in, come in.'

Simon closed the door behind him, mouth dry. The nurse busied herself tidying the couch and examination trolley.

'Young Jane gave me a buzz and I nipped round to have a look. Think you were a bit tied up at the time.' It sounded a lame excuse. Another five minutes' delay in the clinic while he dashed along to see his baby for himself wouldn't have made much difference.

'Bit of a mystery. Baby in there is a good twelve weeks, maybe a bit more. Don't understand it at all. When we blew through the jolly old tubes she must've been what, six or seven weeks already. *And* we had a good rake round inside the uterus — or so I thought. Don't recall thinking it was bulky then. Don't know how I could've missed it.'

From some sense of professional loyalty, Simon felt he had to come to the Consultant's defence.

'It's happened before. After all, the last thing you were expecting was to find a pregnancy there.'

Greenwell looked pleased.

'Good of you to say so. Anyway, fact is, we've got a twelve- or thirteen-week-old foetus in there.'

'Does it look — ah . . .?'

'Normal?' Greenwell finished for him. 'Yes, looks fine. Fine. Strong foetal heart. Placenta well up out of the way. Matching pairs of everything that we could see.'

'It doesn't look as if your attempted D & C or the azathioprine have done the baby any harm, then?' Simon could hardly believe it.

'No, none at all that I can tell. Must be a tough little beggar, eh?'

There was a knock, and the clinic Sister came in.

'Excuse me, Mr Greenwell, but Mr Robinson's wife is waiting for him in the patients' canteen.'

'Oh, thanks.' Simon went towards the door. 'I'll just see her off, then come and help finish the clinic.'

'Righto. We'll talk about it some more later. Wheel the next one in, Sister.'

As Simon left the department, the Sister followed him anxiously. 'Don't be long, Mr Robinson, please. We've still got some patients who've been waiting over an hour.'

'Two minutes,' he called back to her, already hurrying down the corridor.

Kate saw him coming and met him at the entrance to the canteen. She was smiling broadly. 'Twelve weeks! Isn't that amazing! And it's all right! Old Greenwell said everything was all right!'

Simon gave his wife a squeeze. 'I don't understand how you're so

179

far on. But so long as everything's OK.'

'Oh, love.' Kate looked at him with moist eyes. 'I'm so relieved. This weekend has been hell, what with the tablets and my blood and everything.' She patted her stomach. 'Thank God it's normal.'

They were walking down the corridor now, towards the car park.

'Did you see it?' Simon asked.

'See what?'

'The baby. On the ultrasound.'

'Oh. No.' She looked disappointed. 'I thought I would, though.'

'So would I. It's normal practice, usually. Said to help maternal bonding.'

'Oh. I would have liked that.'

Simon felt a twinge of anxiety. 'Never mind. We'll look at the pictures.'

'I — I don't think there *were* any pictures.'

'No pictures? Why not? Didn't Jane take any?'

'She wasn't there. Jeremy sent her off to do something. He said he didn't know how to work the camera.'

Kate hadn't seen the scan, nor had the technician, and there were no pictures. Simon felt a knot of fear in his stomach. What the hell was going on?

* * *

The pressure of work from the waiting patients absorbed Simon's attention for the time being, but he still had a nagging doubt. Damn! Why hadn't he insisted on staying? But the Out-patient Sister was right: there would have been a riot if at least one of them had not turned up and seen some patients.

He tried to keep an eye open for Greenwell leaving the clinic. He knew the Consultant was in the habit of clearing off as soon as he thought the remaining work could be finished in a reasonable time by his juniors. He might easily miss his departure if he was closeted with a patient for more than a few minutes. He told a nurse he wanted to catch his boss when he left, so that she could alert him if necessary.

Sure enough, when there were four patients left to see, all simple reviews, Greenwell left his office. The nurse put her head round Simon's door.

'Mr Greenwell's just leaving, sir.'

Simon excused himself from the woman he was talking to, and went out into the waiting area. He was just in time to see Greenwell disappearing into the corridor, making great haste. Simon almost sprinted after him, and had still not caught up the Consultant when he went through the door to the staff car park.

'Jeremy!' he called out as the door closed. He felt sure the other

180

must have heard him, but when he reached the door he saw Greenwell still striding purposefully on. Simon increased speed and called again. The Consultant stopped and turned, and Simon thought he saw a fleeting expression of annoyance pass across his face.

'Oh, Simon, it's you,' he said, in what seemed to Simon to be feigned surprise.

'Sorry to chase after you like this, Jeremy.' Simon was somewhat breathless after his haste. 'I just wanted a word about Kate's scan.'

'Yes, of course. Was going to have a word with you, but Sister said you were tied up with a problem patient.'

Rubbish, thought Simon, you're trying to avoid me.

'Was everything really all right?'

'Everything was absolutely fine, old chap. Thing is, as I said to your wife, foetal measurements confirm she's about twelve weeks, which really is a bit of a mystery. However, it's not unknown to miss an early pregnancy like this, and the main thing is, all's well.'

Simon thought he'd try to be a little crafty. 'Were there any photos? I'd like to see them as I couldn't be there.'

'Awfully sorry, old chap, but young Jane had to go off and I didn't know how to work the blasted camera.'

Jane had to go off? But Kate had said Greenwell sent her away. He didn't know why he phrased the next question as he did, but for whatever reason, he asked, 'Did Kate enjoy seeing the baby on the scan?'

'Seeing the baby?' He reflected for a moment. 'Funny thing . . . she didn't want to see it.' He shrugged, and smiled charmingly. 'Ah, well, each to their own. Now, awfully sorry, Simon, but I really must dash. We'll talk about it again later. When I've got more time.'

You lying devil, thought Simon, as he kept up the cordial exchange by apologising for delaying the Consultant. He turned and rushed back to the remaining patients he had abandoned in the clinic.

* * *

Simon felt washed out when he finally got home that evening. At least he wasn't on call, that was the Junior Registrar's lot for the next two nights, so he was looking forward to relaxing. He was going to find it difficult, however, with thoughts of the morning's events still going round in his head.

After their evening meal, he and Kate went through everything that had happened that morning, with Simon trying to coax things along conversationally. He did not want to alarm Kate and get her thinking that there might be something wrong after all, but he wanted to double-check a couple of points. There was no doubt about it, however: Greenwell *had* sent the scan technician out on an errand,

and Kate had *not* said she didn't want to see the TV image of the baby for herself.

Despite his attempt to sound casual, Kate sensed her husband's anxiety.

'You don't think there's anything wrong, do you?'

'No, love. I spoke to Greenwell afterwards, and he assured me that everything was just fine.' At least that much is true, anyway, thought Simon, but even as he spoke he was recalling his dream. He shuddered involuntarily.

'Are you all right?'

'Yes, love, just tired. Let's go to bed.'

Kate was a long time in the bathroom, and Simon wanted to empty his bladder before he got into bed and got too warm and comfortable. Whatever's she doing? he wondered. He put his head round the door, and saw Kate putting something that looked like a bottle of tablets into the medicine cabinet.

He positioned himself before the lavatory.

'Need a leak, sorry.' Kate, naked to the waist, was applying some talcum powder. 'What was that you were putting in the cabinet?' He tried to sound casual.

'Oh, just iron and vitamin pills Jeremy Greenwell gave me.'

Simon's stream stopped itself in mid-flow. 'Pills? You didn't tell me?' He tried to keep alarm out of his voice.

'He said it was time I started on iron and folic acid.' She saw Simon's expression and laughed gently. 'It's all right, I'm not that daft. He explained what they were. You know I'll need them now, especially as I'm already a bit anaemic.'

Of course. Routine treatment, Simon reassured himself. Mustn't get paranoid. Nearly all pregnant mums had them. Good idea. In fact with her level of haemoglobin, they were important. He relaxed, and finished urinating. Kate went out, but after washing his hands Simon could not stop himself from opening the cabinet and examining the bottle.

'Fepregfol', he read, then thought, God, the names they give these drugs. It was a branded combination of iron and folic acid often dispensed by the hospital pharmacy, and well known to him. He tipped some out, and instantly recognised the familiar green and pink capsules, the name and manufacturer stamped on them. He breathed a sigh of relief. Perhaps I'm getting too uptight about all this, he thought.

As he was dropping the capsules back into the bottle, Kate came back for a box of tissues, now completely naked. Simon looked a bit guilty, and Kate grinned at him.

'Checking up on my medication, then?'

'Well, you can't blame me for making sure.'

She took his hand. 'Of course not, darling. I checked them in "MIMS" myself before I took one. I was going to get you to double-check anyway — just hadn't got round to it. Now — ' Her other hand reached down. 'Come to bed and let's ignore our trials and tribulations for a bit.'

And they did. Kate was her old self, and despite his tiredness and anxiety, Simon found he forgot their troubles as they enjoyed each other's bodies more than they had in a long time.

Simon considered it best that Kate shouldn't go back to work just yet, although she was keen to do so. Her anaemia would take as long as a month to recover fully, so there seemed no point in taking chances. He managed to persuade her to be patient, and she went to see her GP who was quite happy to sign her off for a while. A student midwife was able to help out on the district temporarily, and Simon was pleased to have Kate around and able to relax. Everything settled back to a normal routine, and life seemed full of promise again.

Only two weeks passed before Simon began to notice that his wife's personality was once again taking a turn for the worse.

20

At first he thought he was just being over-anxious. He realised he was tuned in to every little change in Kate's behaviour, and asked her how she felt so frequently she must have got fed up with it. Her most recent blood test showed further improvement all round and there seemed no danger now from that source. But towards the end of the week he thought she seemed a little more withdrawn. Up until then she had been taking a renewed interest in the house, in his work, in preparing varied meals for them both — as well as showing impatience to get back to work.

Just over a fortnight after the Bank Holiday weekend, Simon was supposed to have a day off. Conscientious as always, he went in to the hospital in the morning anyway, to see someone who had undergone major pelvic surgery the day before. When he got back, he suggested to Kate that they should go out for a pub lunch and one of their 'wishful thinking' walks by Poole Quay, admiring the boats. They had not been there for weeks.

Although it was by now 11.30, Kate was still wearing only her bathrobe, looking rather unkempt as she sat, watching television. She didn't want to go. 'Can't be bothered,' she said. She told him she'd get something quick for him, she wasn't hungry. He decided to busy himself in the garden, but by 2.20, when he went back into the house, feeling desperate for something to eat, Kate was still stretched out on the sofa, TV on.

His hunger was making him tetchy, and he was about to make an unkind remark about his wife neglecting him, when he realised he should consider that she might be unwell. He turned the sound down on the TV to get her attention.

'Are you all right, love?'

'What?' She looked up rather absently.

He sat on the edge of the sofa beside her. 'I was just wondering if you're feeling OK? You've hardly moved from there today.'

'Yes, I'm fine. Honestly.'

'I was getting pretty peckish. Any chance of a bite?' He tried to make the suggestion as gentle as possible.

'Oh, Simon.' She looked up at him. 'I'm sorry.' She sat herself up wearily, and Simon felt bad about cajoling her into activity if she really didn't feel up to it.

He gently pushed her back. 'No, you stay there. I'll get something for us. What do you fancy?'

'I don't think I want anything. I'm still not — ' She paused, and winced with pain. Holding her stomach for a moment, she waited until the discomfort passed, before continuing as though nothing had happened — 'hungry, thanks, love.'

Simon was alarmed, but tried not to show it.

'What was that? Did you have some pain?'

'No, nothing really. Just another twinge.'

'Just a twinge of what?'

'Sort of little flutterings and poking.' She didn't seem at all concerned, or even interested.

'How long have you been feeling this?'

She looked around the room slowly before focusing on Simon. 'A couple of days.'

'Here. Let me look.' He encouraged her to lie flat, and opened her bath-robe. He hadn't looked at her stomach with a professional eye for a while, and was surprised to notice the gentle swelling now evident. She would be nearly fifteen weeks now according to the scan. There shouldn't be much visible yet, but this swelling looked more like an eighteen-week size at least. He gently placed his hand on the bump. It felt like a uterus all right. But how could it have grown this much so quickly?

He pressed gently around Kate's lower abdomen, watching her face as he did so. She seemed quite unconcerned. As he knelt beside her, hand resting on her stomach, he thought he felt something move under his hand. He concentrated his senses on the hand, letting it rest motionless. After a moment there was another small movement, then another. At the third one, which was more pronounced, Kate winced again.

'Did you feel that?' Simon asked her with concern and wonder.

'Yes.'

'Is that what you've been feeling the last couple of days?'

'Yes.'

Simon withdrew his hand and rubbed his eyes. This was incredible! It shouldn't be possible to feel the baby move yet! It was almost inconceivable at fifteen weeks. And even if this *was* an eighteen-week foetus, as the size suggested, it would still be very unusual in a first pregnancy, especially movements as strong as he had just felt.

'It — it feels like foetal movements,' he said, almost with an expression of awe.

'Yes, I know. It is.' She seemed certain.

'It can't be. You're only fifteen weeks!'

'Doesn't matter. It is. I know.' Still dispassionate, Simon noted. Where's the excitement, the wonder, that this moment should bring

185

to a mother? Why is she so — unemotional?

The scientist in him started to try and analyse the situation. What possible explanation could there be? Large for dates early on usually meant twins. But the ultrasound hadn't shown that. Or had it? He only had Greenwell's word for it, and he wasn't too impressed with the Consultant's honesty lately. If it *were* twins, why would he try and hide it from him? And from Kate? It was often a bit of a shock for a couple to find they were going to have to cope with two new babies at once, but it was normally a joyful occasion, nevertheless. It wasn't as if they already had half-a-dozen children. Once the thought of twins entered his mind, he could not dismiss it. He didn't stop to consider that even twins wouldn't explain foetal movements at this stage. He told himself it just might account for Greenwell's secretiveness about the scan. He had to know the answer. At once.

He covered Kate's abdomen, and stood up. 'You lie there quietly. I'm just going back to the hospital for a while,' he told her. 'I won't be long.' She did not reply. She was looking at the silent, flickering image on the television.

Simon drove to the hospital, put on his white coat, and went straight to the Obstetric Out-patient Department where two portable ultrasonic heart monitors were kept. Strictly speaking, they were not meant to be removed from the hospital. He picked one up and went out with it. There was no reason why anyone should challenge him, except that he was supposed to be off duty. The machine was in a plastic case about the size of a small briefcase. Simon was relieved when he got into his car, put the machine down on the seat beside him, and set off for home.

As he drove back he tried to think of any other possibilities that might explain Kate's large uterus. He dismissed the thought that it might not be a uterus at all, but some other pelvic organ, such as an enlarged ovary. Ovarian cysts could become very big rapidly, but never this quickly in his experience. Besides, Kate's swelling was definitely in the mid-line. An ovary would be to one side.

Hydatidiform mole was a rare condition that could present this way. This was a proliferation of small cysts in the pregnant uterus that caused it to increase rapidly in size. But in such cases the foetus invariably died and was absorbed, and there would certainly be no movements. Then there was hydramnios, a condition where there was an excess of the amniotic fluid surrounding the baby. It could cause over-large uterine swelling in later pregnancy, but he had never heard of a case before about twenty weeks.

What else? He probed his mind, prepared to entertain any possibility. Pelvic inflammatory disease? No, there had never been any evidence of that. Endometriosis? That could cause a pelvic mass sometimes, but it didn't fit. Drugs? Some were known to cause proliferation of the endometrium with enlargement of the uterus, but not to this degree, not in pregnancy. All Kate was taking were the iron and folic acid capsules.

He had no intention of getting caught out as he had before. He kept secretly checking the bathroom cabinet, making sure Kate wasn't trying to hide anything. She only had the Fepregfol, of that he was sure. She'd got that from Greenwell personally — he'd casually checked on it in a conversation with the Consultant. There couldn't be any room for doubt. Still . . . perhaps he'd take one of the capsules even so, just to double-check, just in case.

Simon was nearly home. He had virtually dismissed all his alternatives. Surely, it could only be twins. He turned into the drive. It had to be twins. Having convinced himself, he began to feel a little excited at the prospect.

Kate was as he had left her. She hadn't even turned the sound back up on the television. He knelt beside her once more.

'I want to look at your tummy again, love,' he told her, exposing her abdomen.

'Why?'

'I've brought the foetal heart monitor so we can listen to the baby's heart.' He thought she would be pleased.

'Oh. The sound's gone on the TV.'

'No, it hasn't. I turned it down. I'll put it up again in a minute.'

He took the electronic gadget out of its box. It was about the size of a pocket transistor radio, and had a cylindrical probe about four inches long attached to it by a thick, coiled wire. He took a tube of electrode jelly from the case, and put a generous dollop on the end of the probe. He then switched the machine on and placed the probe on the left side of Kate's belly.

By carefully adjusting the direction in which he pointed the probe, he hoped to pick up the baby's heartbeat. The device emitted high-frequency sound waves, well over the range of human hearing. When these sound waves met an object, they were reflected back to the probe. If the object they were reflected from was moving, the sound waves were out of phase when they got back to the probe. The device could detect this change of phase and, via a tiny loudspeaker, turn them into an audible sound.

At first there was just a high-pitched hissing noise. As Simon slowly moved the probe, he heard a slow, rhythmic 'shushing' sound. That was turbulence from the blood flowing through large blood vessels in Kate's pelvis. He moved the probe a little more, but heard nothing else.

He moved it then to the right side of her abdomen, and almost immediately he picked up the soft and rapid 'per-thump-per-thump-

187

per-thump' of a baby's heart.

'There it is!' Simon was overjoyed to hear for the first time the sound of his son or daughter's heart beating strongly. 'Kate! Listen!' He had heard this sound many times before, but always it had been someone else's baby. Not this time!

Kate peered down at her bump, looked at the machine, then at Simon. She nodded. 'Foetal heart. Sounds OK. Better stop now.'

'OK! Is that all you can say? It sounds wonderful!'

'I've heard lots of foetal hearts. So have you.'

'But this one — this one is ours, Kate. Aren't you excited?'

Kate looked at him in puzzlement. 'Not particularly.'

Simon felt so wounded, so deflated. He felt as if he could weep with frustration.

'Kate. Love. Why? What's wrong?'

She looked at him again, this time her expression and tone suggesting annoyance. 'What do you expect me to do? Do a triple somersault and sing, "Oh, what a beautiful morning"?'

Simon laughed then, expecting Kate to crease up as well. She'd been leading him on! She was pulling his leg!

But she wasn't. She looked at him, her face clouding with anger. 'Why are you laughing at me?'

'I'm not laughing at you, love. Kate, please.' He was feeling so confused he didn't even know what he was pleading for.

'And you must turn that thing off now.' She tried to brush the probe away.

'No!' Simon almost shouted. He tried to sound calmer. 'No, love, not yet. I want to check that there aren't two heartbeats.'

More annoyance. 'There's only one in there, you know. You're wasting your time.'

'Let me try, Kate. Please?'

She didn't reply, just shrugged her shoulders and turned to look at the still silent television.

Simon took that as acceptance, and continued to move the probe around gently from area to area. If there were twins, there should be a point where he could hear both the babies' hearts at once. But however hard he tried, there was only one.

He was about to stop when Kate, who up to that point had been ignoring all this, suddenly grabbed the ultrasound monitor. Her movement was so swift that Simon could not prevent her snatching it out of his grasp. Before he could take it back, she threw the device across the room.

Simon jumped to his feet. 'For God's sake, Kate, what did you do that for?'

'The baby didn't like it.'

'What on earth do you mean?'

188

'I told you. It didn't like it before, either.' She turned to Simon, jaw clenched so hard her face was trembling slightly. Barely opening her mouth, her features twisted in a grotesque snarl, she hissed at him, 'I won't tell you again. The baby didn't like it.'

Simon was alarmed at this dramatic change. From being apparently totally uninterested in what was going on, her manner was now almost ferocious. He spoke gently.

'What do you mean, love? What doesn't the baby like?'

'The noise, of course. The noise! How would you like a high-pitched scream pointed at your ears all the time?'

'Kate, I don't understand. What makes you think the baby doesn't like it?'

There was a look of almost pitying condescension on her face. 'Because she told me, stupid man!'

Simon looked at his wife in total incomprehension. Was she having him on? He'd never known her play practical jokes before. But if she wasn't playing games with him, she must be going out of her mind! His heart sank. They were right back where they had been three weeks ago.

'The — the baby told you it didn't like the noise from the ultrasound?'

'Yes! How many more times?' Her eyes were narrowed in impatient anger.

'But, darling, you know the ultrasound is well above the range of human hearing. Even dogs can't hear it.'

'I know that! What do you thing I am? Daft or something? But a foetus isn't a dog, and it can hear it!'

Simon walked slowly round the room and picked up the heart monitor. The battery compartment had sprung open and the battery had fallen out. He switched the machine off, and replaced the battery. It appeared undamaged. He walked back round to Kate, knelt beside her, and, doing his best to conceal the movement, switched the machine on again.

Kate swung round, her eyes wide, a look approaching hate directed at Simon. She screamed at him.

'I SAID TURN THE FUCKING THING OFF!'

Simon reeled back, shocked not only that she had detected him turning on the ultrasound, but also by the force of her anger, and by her language. He had never heard any but the mildest swear-words from her before. He stood there stunned, not moving. Kate started to rise from the sofa, something menacing about the way she began to move forward.

'Your hurting it! Turn it *OFF!*'

Simon stepped back, almost tripped as he fumbled for the switch, and turned the device off. Immediately Kate began to relax. He

189

watched her warily as she sank back onto the sofa.

'Kate — ' He had to stop and make some saliva come into his mouth, it was so dry. 'Kate, how could you tell — ?'

She smiled at him, but it was a sly smile. 'As I said. She told me.'

'You know it's a girl?'

This time a look of scorn. 'Of course I know it's a girl.'

'And it — ' Simon swallowed before he could continue. 'And it talks to you?'

Anger crossed Kate's face. 'Don't look at me like that. I'm not crazy, you know. Now leave me alone. We want some rest and peace and quiet.'

Simon suppressed a shudder as he felt a chill pass over him. Kate had as good as admitted she was hearing voices, and seemed to think Simon should accept that without question.

Depression? A psychosis of some sort? Mental problems were known to be associated with pregnancy, but this early? This suddenly? And with someone as stable as his Kate? It seemed impossible, and yet . . .

She was looking at him intently. He almost felt she could read his thoughts. 'All right, love. I'll leave you to have a rest. You just take it easy.'

'I don't need to "take it easy",' she sneered, mimicking the last three words. 'And you don't have to humour me. Just leave us alone.'

'Us'. 'We'. Twice in a few seconds she had referred to the baby as if it were already an entity, as if she really were in communication, in partnership, with it. Simon needed time to gather his thoughts, and he didn't want to antagonise Kate any more.

'I'll take the ultrasound back to the hospital, out of your way, then it won't bother you.' That would also give him a chance to think about this, look up some books, maybe even get in touch with Greenwell about this latest development. Kate did not appear to hear him. She was once more studying the silent images flickering on the TV screen.

He went for his white coat and his car keys, felt the need to empty his bladder and went up to the bathroom. As he stood there before the medicine cabinet he considered the capsules again, took one out and looked at it thoughtfully, decided to keep it.

He looked into the lounge on his way out.

''Bye then, love.' She did not acknowledge his departure, and Simon left, worry and despair once more weighing on his shoulders as they had done so often these last weeks.

As he drove away from the house, Kate listened to the sound of the departing car. Apparently satisfied that he had gone, she stood up and went to the kitchen. She spoke aloud.

'Yes, I know. It's all right.'

She paused, then started looking in one of the drawers.

'No, no. I won't let him hurt you again.'

She found what she was looking for, then went upstairs to the bedroom. She looked around the room, then nodded to herself with a satisfied smile. Walking over to the bed, she lifted the mattress on her side and slipped under it the eight-inch long, razor-sharp boning knife.

21

It was nearly five o'clock as Simon entered the hospital for the third time that day. He went straight to the Obstetric Out-patient Department to return the foetal heart monitor. He was about to replace it in its storage cupboard when he was spotted by the Sister in charge of the clinic. She was one of the older nurses in the department, and was well known to be very protective of the equipment in her charge. However she was always well disposed to Simon, and he didn't anticipate that she would make a fuss.

'So *that's* where the other ultrasound had got to. I was just about to send out a search party!'

'I'm sorry. All present and correct now.'

'I thought you weren't coming in today, Mr Robinson?'

'No, well, there were a couple of things I wanted to follow up . . .'

He was saved from more explanation by the appearance of his old boss, D'Arcy, from the Consultant's office. Hoping things had cooled down a bit, Simon thought he would try and be friendly.

'Good afternoon, Roger.'

His attempt at pleasantry went unrewarded.

'What the devil are you doing here?'

'I was just returning the foetal heart monitor.'

'Well put the thing down and get out.'

Simon felt himself colouring at being spoken to this way in front of the nurse. She appeared embarrassed too, and made a pretence of busying herself tidying an instrument trolley which already looked immaculately laid out.

'I'm sorry.' Simon found himself apologising. 'I had no intention of causing any friction.'

'And a damn good job you've made of it!' responded D'Arcy sarcastically, then turned abruptly and left.

Now Simon felt he had to apologise to the Sister.

'Sorry about that.'

'Most unlike Mr D'Arcy. Mind you, he's been a bit grumpy lately. Perhaps he's got something on his mind.'

Simon bit his lower lip with the sheer frustration and injustice of it all. Excuses were being made for D'Arcy, when it was Simon whose life was being plagued by one crisis after another, and now Kate's mental state seemed to be threatened. He only gradually became aware that the Sister was still talking to him.

'Mr Robinson?' She looked anxiously at him.

'Sorry, what was that?'

'I was only thanking you for returning the equipment. Are you all right?'

Simon felt he couldn't risk saying much. An offer of sympathy right now and he might break down completely.

'Fine, thank you,' he managed, before turning away and hurrying out, head down.

The Sister watched him go, shaking her head gently.

'Some of these young doctors work themselves too hard,' she murmured, and went back to checking the equipment.

Simon arrived at his own office, took off his white coat, and picked up the phone. He drummed his fingers impatiently on his cluttered desk, waiting for the hospital switchboard to answer. This should be a fairly quiet time. What was the hold-up? Eventually the ringing tone stopped.

'Switchboard,' a bored voice announced.

Simon was tempted to make some comment about the delay in answering, but knew it would only waste more time.

'This is Mr Robinson. Could you find Mr Greenwell for me, please?' There was no response, just a click as he was put on hold. An acknowledgement that his request was to be complied with would have been nice, he thought. He waited several minutes. At one point the girl came back on the line to ask him what he was holding for. He was about to give up when she returned.

'He's not in the hospital, sir. At any rate, he's not answering his bleep. I tried his home number, too. His wife said she wasn't expecting him home until late. Couldn't tell me where he is, either.'

The girl had been surprisingly thorough. Simon thanked her, but before he could finish there was another click and he was talking to the dialling tone. That annoyed him, not because of the discourtesy but because he wanted her to try and locate someone else. Unable to face going through the whole rigmarole again, he decided to go down to the Path Lab and see for himself.

As he walked down the main corridor of the laboratory, it was obvious that there was a general exodus. It was nearly 5.30 now, and everyone except the duty staff was going home. He passed the office where Janice Marshall used to work, and where Gwyn had met his death. Her replacement, an older, less glamorous girl, was sitting in front of the monitor, entering details of the last reports of the day. Simon suppressed a smile. Poor old Gwyn wouldn't have wasted his time chatting *her* up, he thought.

It struck Simon then how incongruous it was that he still thought of Gwyn with affection. Everything that he had learnt since his friend's death suggested that he was a womaniser, a breaker of marriages, and had deliberately poisoned Kate. And yet he had not learnt to hate him or despise his memory. As he thought about it, he realised it could only be that he had not fully accepted that Gwyn was indeed the villain he appeared. He was still clinging to the hope that there was some other explanation, however unlikely. Perhaps it was because he'd liked Gwyn so strongly, trusted him so much, that he was reluctant to admit he had made so severe an error of judgement.

'Can I help you, Robinson?' A gruff voice startled him out of his contemplation.

Simon did not expect to see Ironside, the Senior Pathologist, still around. He was well known for early departures, usually to his small but lucrative private laboratory.

'Oh, hello, Walter. Actually, I was looking for Dr Ravensbourne.' He was not really sure why he felt it important to see her. He was going to ask her if she knew whether azathioprine could have any effects on mental stability. And perhaps then take the opportunity to bring up the question of Gemma Randall's report again. He would feel happier seeing her again in the hospital, rather than in her apartment.

'Left about an hour ago. What d'you want her for?'

Simon was caught rather unprepared for this particular interrogation. 'I — um — just wanted to ask her about some possible drug reactions.'

'Well, you're out of luck.' Ironside began to put on the coat he was carrying. 'If I were you, I'd keep out of her way.' And with that piece of most unexpected and gratuitous advice, the pathologist left.

The library was Simon's next port of call. He was getting worried about the time. He was not sure how long he should leave Kate alone in her present state. So far he had been gone an hour, and had achieved nothing. He had little experience of true mental illness in pregnancy: it was not that common a problem. He had, of course, dealt with many women who were depressed or anxious during their pregnancies, and helped them through 'the blues' after the baby was born. However, if they had a severe post-natal depression that lasted more than a week or so, they were no longer considered obstetric cases but psychiatric ones, and he didn't see them again. The same applied to puerperal psychosis, where the unfortunate woman had a true schizophrenic-like madness. He had only come across one case in his career, and she had become so disturbed she had to be compulsorily detained in a mental hospital within days of giving birth.

It was about this condition that he now sought more information. He knew that the affliction could cause auditory hallucinations, the classic 'hearing voices' of schizophrenic illness. Was this what Kate was experiencing? He arrived at the library on the first floor, found several reference books, and sat down in a secluded alcove to read.

194

An hour and a half later he had learnt only one thing for certain. Puerperal psychosis was just that: it only occurred in the puerperium, that is in the few days or weeks immediately *following* birth, not beforehand, and certainly not in earlier stages of pregnancy. If such symptoms occurred then, it should be considered like any other psychotic episode. There were even those authorities who made no distinction at all between such an illness occurring in relation to childbirth or at other times. In their view they were all to be considered variations of schizophrenia. It did not make comforting reading. Was this the explanation of Kate's current behaviour? A couple of weeks ago she had been fine, and had got over the depressing effects of the azathioprine poisoning. Now, within the course of a few days, she appeared to be developing a severe mental breakdown. Simon struggled with his thoughts for a while, then, unseen in his alcove, he put his head on his arms and wept silently.

*　*　*

Slowly he became aware that he was not alone. He made an effort to control himself, and listened. Someone was talking nearby; he could not clearly make out what was being said, but there were two voices, male and female. He tried to make himself presentable in case he was seen, wiping his eyes and smoothing his hair. Presumably the two speakers were doctors, because he could make out the occasional word of medical jargon. They were talking in little above a whisper and, despite himself, this heightened Simon's curiosity. He found himself straining to listen, and almost jumped when the woman's voice suddenly became almost a shout.

'I don't care! I'm going to look now!'

He could hear the male voice urging her to keep quiet.

There seemed something familiar about it. But the female voice he knew beyond doubt. It was Gillian Ravensbourne.

A few brief, hissed exchanges followed, full of suppressed anger but still unintelligible, then silence. He heard the library door open and close, and, after a moment's hesitation, made up his mind to see where the pathologist was going, and maybe take the chance to talk to her. He hurried along between the rows of bookcases housing weighty tomes and vast collections of medical journals, barely glancing at a man sitting at a table near the door, his elbows on it and his face resting in the hands which covered his face. Simon was out in the corridor and about to follow the retreating figure in its white coat when the realisation struck him that he knew who the man in the library was. It was surely Jeremy Greenwell. He stopped, about to go back and make certain, when he experienced a strong feeling of recollection. As the white-coated figure of Gillian Ravensbourne, short ginger hair bobbing, hurried down the corridor, he tried to think where he had seen the same image before. As she disappeared round the corner, he knew! It was when he was in the Path Lab, and thought he had seen Gwyn!

He forgot about the figure of Greenwell in the library as he set off in pursuit. Racing down the corridor, he turned into the large hallway that housed the lifts, just as the doors were closing. He watched the floor numbers light up one by one, stopping on the fourth. He punched the buttons of the next lift, which was waiting on the floor below, urging it to hurry.

By the time he stepped out on the fourth floor, there was no sign of Ravensbourne. He went to the private wing, which occupied most of the floor, and looked into the Sister's office. The nurse looked up from a cardex she was writing. It was the pleasant woman who had been on the ward when Kate had her tubal insufflation. She smiled as she recognised Simon.

'Hello, Mr Robinson. What can I do for you?'

'I was looking for Dr Ravensbourne, actually. Have you seen her around?'

'Goodness me, no. She never comes in here.' She laughed as if there were some private joke, but her laughter faded as she saw Simon looking puzzled, not sharing her amusement.

'I'm sorry, doctor, but she's so "anti" private medicine, you'd never catch her doing anything with these patients. She went on at me once, jumped down my throat when I said something about working up here. Told me I was being a traitor, and letting my profession down. Well! And I mean, we were only standing there queuing for something to eat in the canteen.' She shook her head as she recalled the experience. 'I thought she'd gone off her rocker. Talk about blowing your top. I'm afraid I can't get that worked up about things.'

Simon hoped she would keep talking, interested in what else she might say about the pathologist, but the Sister stopped suddenly, as if aware she was idly gossiping instead of being professional.

'Sorry. I didn't mean to go on.' She paused. 'She does come up to the fourth floor, though, doctor. I'm sure I've seen her in the theatre, despite her going on about private facilities; and she often goes into the MFRF.'

Simon absorbed this information with interest. 'Thank you, Sister. Sorry to disturb you.'

'Oh, no problem.' She seemed reluctant to end the conversation. 'It's pretty quiet up here. I'll make you a cup of tea if you like.'

'That's very kind, but no thanks. Some other time.' He closed the door to the office and went back to the lift area. To his left were the two small operating theatres, used occasionally for minor private surgery. He went and pushed one of the double doors open. The rooms were in complete darkness.

Opposite the operating theatre was another set of double doors, above which a discreet sign announced: **'Meadowmead Foundation Research Facility'**.

Simon had toured this complex when he first came to the hospital. It was a sad story, he was told by the Unit General Manager, as he was shown round the impressive suite of rooms.

Being near Bournemouth University Medical School, the Princess Marina Hospital often had students visiting, sometimes for short periods, but also there were regular secondments to various specialities. Because of this, it had been thought appropriate that some sort of research facility be established at the hospital. It would provide kudos for the staff, more prestige for the hospital, and better training opportunities. When the new private wing was added, a large non-profit-making charitable trust, the Meadowmead Foundation, whose largesse was directed at the world of medicine, had put up the money to build and equip the Research Facility. It was intended to be used particularly for research into genetically related diseases, one of the new and exciting fields, and the unit contained two high-resolution light microscopes, an electron microscope, and equipment for chromosome analysis, amongst other high-technology gadgetry.

The problems had begun when it came to running the facility. It really needed several permanent members of staff, from a Senior Lecturer specialising in such research, to laboratory technicians expert in the use of the sophisticated equipment. The equipment itself was expensive to maintain and run. Where was the money to come from? Inconceivably, such problems had not been ironed out before the project went ahead, but everyone had assumed the money would be forthcoming from everyone else.

The Foundation thought it had done enough, but offered to pay half the staff and running costs if the hospital would do the same. The Regional Health Authority refused to come up with more money, and so did central Government. The only way the Facility could be funded was if some other service was curtailed, and that was politically unacceptable.

The hospital had tried to raise some money locally, but attempts to generate interest and publicity were not successful. Media attention was focused instead on an alternative appeal to provide the hospital with a body scanner, and there was no enthusiasm in the public's heart for this rather esoteric project.

The facility and its equipment had therefore lain fallow, being used only rarely for small projects that were of particular interest to individual doctors, mainly industrious senior registrars out to enhance their prospects of a good consultant post with a learned paper or two in the journals.

Simon stood contemplating the entrance to the Facility as he recalled this example of administrative penny-pinching and planning incompetence, and as his eyes roved over the impressive hardwood doors, he noticed that a light shone under them. Was Ravensbourne in there now? He stepped forward and gave them a push. They did not move. He pushed harder, but it was clear that the entrance was locked.

He knocked on the door loudly. Almost immediately the glimmer of light coming under the door disappeared. He knocked again, and called out.

'Gillian! It's me, Simon!'

Silence. He stood there very still, listening intently for some sound, some indication that whoever was in there might think he had gone away and come to the door. There was nothing. Ten minutes passed, then twelve, then fifteen. Simon gave up. Was it coincidence that the light had gone out when he knocked? Could it have been shining through a window from another part of the building?

He decided that he must get back to Kate, and returned to the lift, glancing hopefully over his shoulder as he did so. He continued to watch the entrance to the Research Facility even as the lift doors closed on him. It remained dark and unmoving.

On the way down, he changed his mind about leaving immediately, and just in time punched the first floor button. He went back into the library. No sign of Greenwell, if indeed that was who he had seen. He went on and took down the second volume of the *Medical Directory*. He knew, or thought he knew, something about Ravensbourne's background, but not much. The directory contained details about every registered medical practitioner in the British Isles, and might give some additional information. However, it would not tell an enquirer more than the individual doctor wanted you to know, as the entries were submitted and vetted by the doctors themselves.

The entry on Gillian Ravensbourne was brief. It told him she had trained at St Bartholomew's Hospital, which he already knew. She had gained her MRCPath, her specialist qualification in pathology, only four years after qualifying. She had worked for two years in the Marlenstein Clinic in New Jersey, USA. Simon whistled under his breath. That was a pretty prestigious place. She had written a paper on genetic engineering for the *New England Journal of Medicine*. After that, no more important posts or learned publications were listed.

Simon read the entry through again, then closed the volume. As he was putting it back on the shelf, he hesitated. Something was niggling at the back of his mind. He took the book down again and once more located the Ravensbourne entry. He read from the beginning.

Ravensbourne, Gillian Michelle.
Qualified St Barts. 1978 — MB, BS.
MRCPath (London) 1982.
FFA 1984.

He stopped, his mouth going dry. That was it! That was what had subconsciously registered when he read the entry before. Gillian Ravensbourne was also qualified as an anaesthetist.

An avalanche of possibilities tumbled into his mind. He sat down at a nearby table, and tried to make some order out of the chaos.

It was the fleeting image of the white coat and the red hair disappearing down the corridor that had first tripped a memory circuit in his subconscious. It was then he had realised that he had not seen a reincarnation of Gwyn in the Path Lab, but a flesh and blood Ravensbourne. What was she doing in the Lab that morning? She'd told him later on the phone that she had no plans to go into the Laboratory — and yet she had already been back in there the moment she returned from her 'holiday'.

He had been fooled then into thinking Ravensbourne was Gwyn. Perhaps Kate had made the same mistake as well — he had never established who had anaesthetised Kate when she had her tubal insufflation. Gwyn had denied doing it, but Kate was certain it was he who had been there when she came round, and had given her the tablets that proved to be azathioprine. But in her drugged, half-asleep state, could she have mistaken one red-head in a white coat, whispering instructions softly into her ear, for another?

Simon hesitated, reconsidered. Come on, you're going too fast, he told himself. Gwyn issued that drug. You saw where he'd signed for the medicine in the pharmacy. Surely that means he was implicated somewhere along the line? No, wait a minute — he didn't *sign* for it. He put his initials — G.R. — Gwyn Reece. But that could equally well be Gillian Ravensbourne!

Simon felt excitement beginning to build up inside him. He left the library almost at the trot, not sure yet where he was going, and headed downstairs, two at a time. He had a desperate urge to talk all this through with someone, to try and make some sense of it. Someone he could trust. There was no point in trying to talk to Kate about it in her present mental state. Pauline was the only one. He glanced at his watch. Nearly eight o'clock. Surely she'll be at home now. He was going past the public phones in the waiting area. He dived into the first one and took out a phonecard. He knew Pauline's home number off by heart, dialled it, could hear it ringing. Please be at home, he urged. Someone came into the booth next to his as the ringing continued. He turned his back and hunched over the phone to conserve his privacy. The ringing tone stopped as the phone the other end was picked up.

199

'Pauline? Pauline, it's Simon.'

There was a slight pause, then a rather plummy male voice answered.

'I'm sorry, who is it wishes to speak to her?'

'Damn!' Simon swore softly to himself. She's got someone there with her! He should leave her alone, talk to her tomorrow. But he couldn't do that. He needed to talk to her — now!

The voice at the other end enquired, with a touch of annoyance, 'Hello? Are you still there?'

'Yes, sorry. Tell Miss Jamieson it's Mr Robinson.'

He held his breath as he heard the voice, now muffled by a hand over the mouthpiece, saying, 'There's some chap here, says he's a Mr Robinson, wants to talk to you. Shall I say you're out?'

He was relieved to hear Pauline's voice rebuff the suggestion. 'No you won't, Marcus. Let me speak to him.'

Simon heard a succession of noises as the phone was handed over, then footsteps and a door closing. Pauline was taking the phone somewhere else.

'Simon?'

'Yes, hello, Pauline.'

'Sorry about the delay. I was just taking the phone through to the bedroom.'

'Look, *I'm* sorry if I've interrupted anything — '

'No, don't be ridiculous. Saved me, more like. What's the problem?'

'It's about some things I've found out — about Gillian Ravensbourne. In the *Medical Directory*. She's also an anaesthetist. And I also think she signed for the azathioprine. You remember her? She's the pathologist who — '

'Yes, I remember — I found out about her and Gwyn, didn't I?'

'Sorry, of course you did. And Kate — I'm worried about her mental state. And there's this place, the Meadowmead Foundation Research Facility, here in the hospital, it's — '

'Whoa, hold it there a minute. You sound really worked up. Slow down.'

'Sorry.'

'And stop saying sorry. You'd better come round here and talk about it.'

'Yes. Thanks. I was hoping you wouldn't mind if I did just that, but what about —?'

'Don't worry about old Marcus, I'll soon get rid of him. How soon can you be here?'

'Ten minutes, I should think, if that's not too soon. No, wait, I really ought to check up on Kate first.'

'What's the matter with her? Not a problem with the baby?'

'No, not exactly, she . . .' Simon's voice faltered as he faced putting Kate's strange behaviour into words.

'Tell me, Simon, please.'

'She thinks the baby is talking to her.'

'Oh, Christ!' Pauline said the words almost under her breath. There was a silence before she spoke again, more assertively. 'Simon, you'd better make sure she's all right. I'll excuse myself easily enough with Marcus — he's only one of my partners who dropped me off in the hope of a free supper. If you think you're going to be very long, you can call me again from home. I'll be waiting.'

'Thanks, Pauline. You're a pal. See you later.'

Simon hung up, then paused, still gripping the receiver. Coming to a decision, he picked it up again and dialled his home. He was beginning to think Kate wasn't going to answer, when the ringing tone was finally interrupted. He listened. There was only silence, but he could sense someone's presence the other end.

'Kate? Kate, are you there?'

Still nothing. 'Kate, it's Simon, love. Are you all right?'

A long pause, then, 'Simon? What do you want?' There was more than an edge of suspicion in her voice.

'I'm sorry I've been so long. I just wanted to make sure you're all right.'

'You needn't have worried. We're fine.' Her voice changed, became slightly sing-song. 'Aren't we, little one? Everything is just lovely, isn't it?'

Simon closed his eyes. God, she still thinks she's talking to the baby. He swallowed, tried to sound quite natural.

'Love, I think I'd better come home straight away.'

He could hear some murmuring, as though a muttered conversation was going on, then Kate's voice, very firm:

'No!'

Simon ignored this rejection. 'I won't be long.' More silence. 'All right, love?'

He jumped, almost dropping the phone, as Kate's voice screeched out at him: 'I said *NOOOO!* You keep away! Keep away from us!'

Softer sounds then came from the phone — soothing, mothering tones. A chill went through Simon. It was as if she were actually nursing the child.

'Listen, Kate, what's the matter? Why don't you want me to come?'

Kate laughed then, an uneven, off-key sound, increasing Simon's already mounting fears for his wife's sanity. When the laughter had died down, he heard her voice again. It sounded quite different, almost as if another person were talking. She spoke abruptly, clipping the sounds and hesitating between each word. '*We* don't want you!

201

We don't need you. *We* want you — ' a longer pause, then a long, high-pitched screech that he could barely understand: *'GONNNE!'*

There was a clatter, and Simon realised she must have dropped the phone. He waited for her to pick it up again. He thought he heard movement, then sounds of a faint conversation, cut off abruptly.

Simon slowly replaced the receiver, feeling sweaty and nauseated. He took a deep breath, trying to control his trembling.

Sitting on their bed at home, Kate was trembling too, but with suppressed mirth. Smiling, she held her stomach with one hand, and patted the mattress beside her with the other.

It was a full minute before Simon felt sufficiently in control to leave. He took his phonecard, and hurried out. He barely noticed the woman in the next booth, red hair covered by a silk square, secreting the stethoscope she had been keeping pressed up against the plexiglass partition.

22

To Simon's surprise, the house was in darkness when he pulled up outside. He'd driven much too fast on the way over from the hospital, and was sweating from the stress of the drive as well as from the anxiety of what he was going to do about Kate. He had thought about calling their own GP, but he had never even met him, and didn't want to involve him, not yet. Anyway, it somehow seemed like an admission of defeat, to call in someone else at this stage. He still clung to the hope that this was a temporary aberration, and would resolve when some simple explanation could be found.

He put his key in the door and turned it, opening the door slowly. He thought he heard the sound of someone on the stairs. Reaching over to his right, he felt for the light switch. His hands encountered something unpleasantly sticky. Damn! Where is it? Why aren't there any lights on? He withdrew his hand, feeling the texture of the substance on his fingers. Tentatively he drew his hand near his face, and sniffed. He jerked his hand away and his head back as the odour reached his nostrils. What in God's name! He nearly cried out. It smelt like — like faeces!

He reached again for the elusive light switch, and this time he found it. It took a moment for him to adjust to the light, and as he looked around his jaw dropped in horror. The place was a mess — the hall stand tipped over, a rug in folds on the floor, pictures askew. And the walls! They were streaked with brownish stains, some showing smears of a hand-print. He looked towards the light switch he had searched for in the dark. There was more there. He knew it could only be excrement.

Simon clenched his teeth, tears stinging his eyes. Kate! Now he knew she must really have gone mad. Such degrading acts could accompany complete breakdown of the personality. There could be no other explanation for this. He went towards the stairs, and stopped, rigid, as he looked at the white goatskin rug that lay on the hall floor. Spattered across it in an irregular line was a trail of dark red marks. They were bloodstains, he knew beyond doubt.

'Kate! Kate!' He shouted her name, the intonation sounding like an anguished wail. Almost sobbing now, he began to climb the stairs, still calling. He reached the bedroom door, pushed it open, this time finding the light switch immediately. The room was empty, and quite tidy — except for one corner of the bed, where the duvet was pulled back, the pillow was on the floor, and the corner of the mattress was slightly raised, propped up against the headboard. He stood, his back to the door, the open doorway behind him and to his left. He was breathing rapidly now with anxiety, looking about the room for signs of movement.

'KA — ' Shock choked off his shout as, with a guttural cry, Kate, his lovely, intelligent, gentle wife, leaped into the room and crouched before him. He could barely believe the apparition that presented itself. Kate swayed slightly, hands clenched by her sides, dressed only in knickers and a filthy, loose-fitting T-shirt. The lower part of the T-shirt was soaked in blood, and rivulets of red flowed down over her lower abdomen and on down her legs. Simon could see bloody footprints on the carpet, and even as she moved her feet, squaring herself up to him, a small pool of blood was forming round her toes. Her face was a grimace of rage, faecal material smearing the ashen skin. Her breath hissed in and out through her clenched teeth, her breasts heaving with the effort of each noisy respiration. Her eyes, wide, showing the whites all round, darted from side to side, to Simon's face and away again.

Simon held out his hands and took a step towards her, a mixture of pity and agony in his heart. Kate's hands flashed into view, and she brought them together above her head. They were grasping the handle of the boning knife, gripping it with such ferocity that her arms shook.

Simon tried to speak, but his mouth was too dry. He backed up against the door, open against the wall, desperately trying to get some saliva into his mouth. Kate glanced from her husband to the doorway, and uttered a low growl. Simon's eyes travelled from his wife's face, then to her blood-streaked lower body. He managed at last to force his voice to function.

'God, Kate, what have you done to yourself?'

'Done?' Her voice was low, guttural. 'Done?'

'The blood — you're bleeding — let me get you to the hospital.'

'Blood? Bleeding?'

He took a step forward again, but retreated as Kate made a threatening gesture with the knife, still held aloft in a rigid grip. He spoke again, softly.

'Your stomach. What happened?'

Kate looked slowly down, and Simon thought about rushing to overpower her, but her head jerked up quickly as if she sensed his intentions. She was smiling, a twisted, cold grin.

'She wanted to come. I was trying to let her out.'

Simon felt a wave of nausea as he realised what she was saying. She had been trying to get the baby out from her womb!

'God! What are you trying to do? Kate . . .' His voice broke, but with an effort he controlled it. 'Kate, let me help you.' He was whispering, desperately pleading.

She raised her hands a little higher, eyes narrowed.

'We want you gone!'

Simon was near to panic, trying to think what he could say, what he could do, to win her round and at the same time reduce the danger he was in. He closed his eyes for a second, breathing deeply, trying to gather his thoughts. He somehow sensed a movement, and opened his eyes again just in time to see the knife blade flashing down towards him.

Instinctively he raised his left arm to shield himself from the blow, and at the same time tried to throw himself to the right. He barely noticed a jag of pain in his left hand, a fraction of a second before he was thrown back against the door with a thump that knocked half the breath out of him. He saw Kate staggering backwards away from him, hands working feverishly in front of her. They were bloodstained, but empty. She no longer had the knife!

Feeling a surge of hope, Simon tried to move towards her, but could not. He became aware simultaneously of an ache in the left side of his chest, and the fact that he was held against the door. He looked down to the source of this new pain, and his eyes flew wide in shock as he saw the handle of the blade protruding through his coat just beneath his shoulder. His left hand was going numb, and blood was dripping from his fingers. He reached with his right hand and felt around the knife. It appeared to have been deflected under his upraised arm, and had penetrated the flesh of the side of his chest and his armpit, driven with such force that he was pinned to the door.

The realisation of this injury brought on a further wave of weakness. He thought he would pass out. He grasped the handle of the knife with his right hand, and tried to pull it out. Sticky blood spoiled his grip, and his hand slipped off. The movement produced a searing pain down his now useless left arm, and he slipped into a faint. The weight of his body achieved what his right hand could not. As he slumped forward, the knife could not support him and it pulled out of the wood. He slithered to the floor, distantly hearing Kate's coarse laughter through his blackness and pain.

Simon was not sure what was happening to him. He seemed to be moving around, first this way then that. Someone was helping him onto a chair. Help? Someone was helping him! He felt further movement, and there was more pain from his left shoulder and arm as it was twisted behind him, a tugging on both his wrists.

Things were beginning to swim back into focus, though only slowly. He was being kept forcibly upright, and the blood and oxygen were having trouble getting through to his brain. He was bathed in sweat, beads of it all over his face, his shirt sticking to him, and he retched with the intense feelings of fear and nausea.

Some clearing of his vision began at last. Kate stood before him, a few feet away. Blood was still trickling down her legs, though less rapidly now; thin, bright rivulets coursing between wide, darker, drying streams. She was panting, both with exertion and the beginnings of the effects of loss of blood. Simon soon found the reason for her physical efforts. He tried to get up from the chair he was sitting on, but his hands appeared to be tied behind his back, and more struggling suggested they were also tied to the chair itself.

He looked frantically round, trying to see behind him. He was restricted by the wooden arms of the chair. It was an old carver that was kept in the bedroom for him to throw his clothes on when he couldn't be bothered to put them away. He could see the thin electric flex that had been used to effect his immobilisation, trailing away to a bedside lamp which now lay on the floor near him, its shade crumpled and bloody. Looking down and to his left, he groaned softly as he saw the handle of the knife still protruding from his shoulder.

Each attempt to heave himself free from the crude ties was rewarded with a sickening pain and another wave of faintness. He tried to summon some strength, licked his lips frantically to moisten them.

'Kate.' The effort of saying his wife's name caused him to pause and take several panting breaths. 'Kate. Please. Let me go.'

Kate shook her head slowly, with the sort of sad smile a mother gives a toddler about to get into more mischief.

'Oh, no, my darling Simon. I couldn't do that.'

'Kate, *please*. Why?'

She assumed a sort of grotesque coyness and, like a petulant child, said, 'Because.'

'Kate . . .' Simon paused again, his head swimming. 'Kate, you've hurt me.'

She grinned with pleasure. 'Yes, I know.'

'And you're hurt, too.'

She glanced downwards, a look of concern passing over her face. As if rejecting what she saw, she looked back at Simon, jaw jutting stubbornly. 'I'm all right. *She* needs help.'

Simon puzzled about that for a moment, his brain still woolly, then remembered. She was referring to the baby. Was there a chance of a way out?

'Can I do anything to help her?'

'Depends.' That awful coyness again.

She was playing with him, and he could sense her instability.

'Depends on what? What can I do?' He tried to sound eager, yet sincere.

Kate moved for the first time since their conversation began. She walked a few steps one way then the other, swinging her arms exaggeratedly; stopped, and glanced at Simon, looking worried.

'I forgot to get any eggs this morning.'

He stared at her. 'Eggs?'

'Don't try and change the subject.' Now she was darkly angry. 'Are you going to help her or not?'

Simon realised that her mind was struggling with the loss of logical reasoning. This sort of grasshopper thinking was yet another feature of psychotic illness.

'Of course I'll help her. Just tell me what you want me to do.'

'I've told you already.' She spoke with sudden aggression, moving closer and almost spitting the words into his face.

He tried to stay calm, sound soothing. 'I know, but tell me again, just to make sure I understand.'

'Fool! Don't you listen? She wants to get out.'

It dawned then on Simon what she was getting at. She wanted him to do a Caesarean section on her — what was it now? — eighteen-week-old foetus. His mind revolted at the idea, and he couldn't stop himself.

'Kate, I can't. It'll die!'

He expected her to react with rage at this refusal, but instead she looked at the ceiling and said, 'In that case don't forget to wash the car this afternoon.'

Her mind was jumping again, snatching at passing glimpses of normality. In other circumstances he might have found it amusing in a strange way, but in his present predicament it was only chilling.

He tried to get her back on track, his revulsion at even contemplating her request dissolving into the vestige of a plan to escape this nightmare.

He was finding it difficult to think clearly: his shoulder and arm were coming increasingly to life again and the pain from the still-present knife was interfering with his thoughts. Blood was still trickling down under his arm, although it did not seem to be excessive. It was painful to breathe deeply, but he did not think his lung had been punctured. Whether he would be strong enough to overpower Kate if he got free, he wasn't sure. But he had no choice: he had to try.

'Listen, love. I've got an idea.' He was choosing his words carefully, knowing how suspicious and paranoid she would be. 'I'll do what you want, get the baby out.'

'Good.' She took a pace forward. 'Now.'

Simon shook his head, the gesture meaning that she must wait.

'Not here. I can't do it here.'

Kate's response was threatening. She took another step towards

Simon, teeth clenched. 'Yes! Here! Right here. You'll do it here. Now!'

'You want the best for her, don't you?'

'Oh yes.' Kate nodded her agreement. Her face softened a moment, the look any mother proud of her baby might give. 'She's already told me.'

'Well, things can go wrong at home. I'll need proper instruments, I might need to resuscitate the baby, intubate it. We might need to give it oxygen, suck out its lungs. It would be much better for her in hospital.' And if I get you there, we'll get this mess sorted out, he thought, almost afraid to hope.

Kate appeared to consider it. 'Well . . .' She turned almost completely away from him, then swung abruptly back. 'No! You're trying to trick me.'

She moved even closer, standing over him now, nostrils flaring as her chest heaved.

'No, I'm not, I promise — '

'*LIAR!*' She screamed at him, slapped him, clawed at his face, pulled at his hair. 'Liar! Liar! Liar!' She kept chanting the word, each shout accompanied by a blow or a raking hand. Simon realised he was losing consciousness again under this onslaught. When he first heard the other voice he thought he was hallucinating.

But Kate heard the sound too, and stopped at once, her hand, raised ready for a blow, pausing in mid-air.

'That's right, Kate,' the voice said soothingly, 'don't do it any more.'

Simon was on the point of passing out again completely. His vision was reduced to a grey central area surrounded by blackness. In the grey fog he could see Kate's face, held to one side, listening, eyes looking past his head towards the open doorway. She backed slowly away, just two small paces, then stopped.

'Good girl,' the voice said, 'leave him alone. Good girl.'

The voice was soft, persuasive. Simon was trying to place it, knew it was familiar, but it wouldn't register. He was suddenly overwhelmed by such a strong feeling of relief that it threatened to drain away his last hold on consciousness.

'Thank God you've come!' He managed to sob out the words, barely above a whisper. 'Help me, please.'

He was rewarded with a reassuring hand on his uninjured shoulder. Kate seemed to respond to this gesture, eyes narrowing, and moved close again. 'No!' The voice sounded authoritative, then gentle. 'No, Kate. Please.'

Kate stopped, but this time did not retreat.

The voice spoke almost into Simon's ear. 'I'm sorry, this will hurt. Hold on.' An arm came over his left shoulder and gripped the knife.

His field of vision was still narrow, still grey; he could only make out the shape of the hand as it held the knife handle, then with one swift tug pulled the blade free.

Simon was surprised it did not hurt him more. In fact there was very little pain, but he felt a fresh trickle of blood down his arm. He moaned softly, and a hand began gently to stroke his hair. He was beginning to feel himself reviving as hope and salvation worked their tonic effects.

'Thank you, thank you,' he whispered.

'It's all right, it'll soon be over.'

Kate was still watching intently, eyes flicking over the scene, her tongue constantly licking her lips, but she had edged a few paces farther back.

'Let me look. Are your hands tied?' He felt the cord being tugged, and he tensed his arms, pulling them apart to make the bonds tighter and easier to cut.

The hand that was still stroking his hair suddenly gripped it tightly, and jerked his head back. He caught a glimpse of a face, and then saw the knife. It went out of his field of vision, and he had a second's confusion, followed by sickening realisation as he felt a searing, burning sensation in his neck, caused by the knife being drawn swiftly and forcibly across his tautly stretched throat.

The hand holding his hair let go, and Simon's head lolled to one side. The chair tipped as he slumped over, and he lay on the floor, looking up at the two faces that grew dimmer as his life began to drain away into the bedroom carpet.

23

Pauline had done a great deal of thinking since the previous evening. She was surprised at first that she had such difficulty keeping emotionally detached from the situation. She had assumed that she regarded this case like any other part of her work — but the more she thought about it the more she realised it was no ordinary case, and Simon no ordinary client. She wanted, now more than ever, to get to the facts of the matter, and she was determined as she set out that morning that her journey should represent the first step to a solution.

She was driving to the hospital, trying to work out how best to approach Gemma Randall. Breaking the news to her about Simon was of course the first and most important priority. Perhaps she had better leave other matters until later. She had a pretty good idea that the girl would be shattered by what she had to tell her, and that to try and discuss anything else might be unwise or even impossible.

She found herself coming to the same conclusion she had reached in so many other situations in her working life, in a profession where unpredictability was the nature of the game. She would have to play it by ear.

She had telephoned the ward earlier, to make sure it would be all right for her to visit at this time of the morning. After she had made her explanations, the pleasant Ward Sister she spoke to had assured her it would be no problem, especially as the other beds in Gemma's room were currently unoccupied. On her arrival Pauline found the Sister in her office.

After the usual pleasantries, the blue and white uniformed nurse stood up. 'I'll take you along myself. You will be kind, won't you? You'll find her in quite a state.'

'Oh! Does she know, then?' Pauline hadn't considered that possibility.

'Yes, she does.' She was leading the way down a yellow and green corridor. 'It's been on the radio, and before that on the local television news.'

Stupid that she hadn't thought of that. Somehow she had considered Gemma's being in hospital as isolating her from the outside world, from where word gets through only slowly.

'She likes Mr Robinson a lot. He's been very kind to her, given her a lot of encouragement.'

'Yes. Yes, I know.'

'Here we are.' The nurse stopped outside a door with a glass panel set in the upper half. She peered through it into the room. 'Gemma's on the bed, but I don't think she's asleep.' She opened the door for Pauline and stood to one side. 'I'll leave you to introduce yourself.'

Pauline went in, and heard the door close gently behind her. Gemma was lying curled up with her back to the room, and did not seem aware of her visitor.

'Hello?' It was more of a question than a greeting. 'Gemma Randall?'

Gemma sniffed, and curled up smaller.

'I'm sorry to bother you like this.'

A pale hand came into view and made a gesture that suggested, 'Go away.'

Pauline moved over to the bed and sat on the edge. Slowly she reached out and gently touched the girl's shoulder. There was no response, but Pauline was at least grateful she did not pull away.

'I'm Pauline Jamieson. I'm a solicitor.' She felt Gemma's muscles tighten under her hand. 'I've been working with Simon Robinson. Professionally, but also as a friend.'

She was not prepared for what happened next. Gemma rolled over and struggled to sit up, awkwardly but urgently, showing her red eyes and tear-stained face for the first time. She looked at Pauline for a moment, unselfconsciously using her good left hand to wipe her nose and eyes. Then her mouth turned down in despair and she fell against Pauline, her face buried in her shoulder, sobbing helplessly.

It was not quite the greeting Pauline had expected. She sat quite still for a moment, then slowly began to stroke the long, blonde hair, gently pat the shuddering back. Gradually the sobbing subsided, and eventually Gemma pulled away. Immediately her blotched face showed a look of concern, and she touched Pauline's jacket.

Pauline looked down to where Gemma was pointing. The lapel of her pale grey pin-stripe suit was now mottled with dark tears-stains and smears of mucus.

Pauline smiled at her. 'Don't worry, it'll clean all right.'

Typical of a woman that in such distress she could still show concern for spoilt finery! 'Here.' She produced a small linen handkerchief.

Gemma shook her head in refusal and reached across to the bedside cabinet for some tissues, clumsily pulling one free one-handed, noisily blowing her nose, wiping her eyes. She tried to mouth a word. It was obviously 'sorry'.

'No problem. Honestly.'

More composed now, Gemma reached for her pen and paper, then settled herself sitting cross-legged on the bed, using her left hand to pull her right leg up into position. She began to write awkwardly but quite rapidly, still having to use her left hand. Her right hand was turned upward and was slightly clawed. Pauline noted a little movement in the thumb and first finger, but the arm itself would not move unaided. To hold her pad of paper, Gemma used her left hand to place her right in her lap, then carefully put the pad in position where her feeble grip could exert some pressure to hold it steady. Pauline waited, then read the long note that was eventually handed to her.

> It's just that — it was when you said you were a friend of Sim Dr. Robinson's. You're the first person I've met who was a friend of his. I felt you were like some sort of connection with him, I suppose.

'He told me how concerned he was about you. I knew he would want me to come and see you. I didn't realise you'd already heard . . .'

Gemma almost managed a smile, and wrote again.

> Could hardly miss it.

'I was hoping to ask you some questions, if it's not too difficult for you.'

> Anything if it will help.

'Well, to start with, I'd —' Pauline stopped as Gemma held up her hand and then wrote some more.

> First tell me what you think happened

Pauline had been anticipating that question, and as she had gone over the events so often in her own mind, she did not have any difficulty summarising last night's horrors.

'Simon rang me from the hospital at about 9.30. He said he'd found out something he wanted to talk to me about, and that he was worried about Kate — that's his wife.'

Gemma nodded her head, indicating she knew.

'It sounded as if she was — well, acting strangely. He went to check

212

up on her before he came round to see me. I told him to ring if he was going to be long. Of course, he never arrived.'

Pauline thought Gemma was going to cry again, and paused. Her own throat was getting dry, and she indicated the jug of water by the bed.

'May I?'

Gemma nodded, and handed her a glass.

'Thanks.' Pauline poured some water, took a sip, then returned to her story.

'After about half an hour, I rang Simon's home. All I got was an unobtainable signal. I found later the phone had been smashed. So —'
She paused, took a deep breath. 'I got in my car and drove round there. I could see the flames as soon as I turned into the street. All the services were there — police, ambulance, and the firemen of course. I had a job getting anywhere near the house, I had to lay it on a bit about being Simon's solicitor. They were just bringing him out when I got there.'

She had to stop a moment then, eyes cast down at the bed. She looked up as she felt Gemma's hand on hers, and saw tear-brimmed eyes trying to transmit sympathy. After a few moments the hand was withdrawn to write.

How did the fire start?

'The fire was upstairs, and it was really raging. I managed to talk to one of the firemen later, when they'd got it under control. He said he was certain it was started with petrol or paraffin, to have got so fierce that quickly.'

Gemma started to write, then stopped, pressing the back of her hand to her lips, waiting until the urge to cry again had passed before continuing.

Who cut Simon's Throat?

'Well, it looks as though it must have been Kate. She was next to Simon. They were both lying in the hall, near the front door.'

What about the other body?

'They didn't find that until much later. It was in the bedroom where the fire started. Burnt beyond recognition. They haven't identified it yet.'

Is Mrs. Robinson still alive?

'I presume so. She was when they got her to the hospital, and there was nothing more about her on the last Radio Solent news.'

Gemma looked out of the window, fighting for control, breathing deeply. Christ, thought Pauline, this girl's had a rough deal. The termination, the horrendous disability, then Simon, her white knight on his charger, a victim of a terrible assault. She's got guts, and I like her.

She forced a smile. 'He'll be all right, you'll see.'

Gemma looked up sharply, then wrote.

Have you seen him?

'No. No visitors allowed. He's in the Intensive Care Unit.'

How can you survive having you're throat cut?

'I don't know. But they were resuscitating him even before they got him in the ambulance — drips up and everything — he was still just breathing. He's tough. He'll make it, you wait and see.' Pauline hoped her optimism was not so transparent that Gemma would see her doubts.

You're just saying that.

'I believe it. *You've* got to believe it.'

Gemma looked so desolate, forlorn. On impulse, Pauline made a decision.

'Look, I gather you're due to come out of hospital soon?' She'd learnt this from her earlier phone call to the ward.

Gemma nodded.

'Any idea where you're going to go?'

A shake of the head.

'They must have some idea, surely?'

Gemma wrote.

Convalescent home, I suppose. Must be near here for my physio.

'Come and stay with me.' Pauline decided there was no point in beating about the bush.

214

Gemma looked at her sharply, eyes wide. She tried to smile, shook her head slowly.

'Don't you want to?'

Gemma reached for her pad.

It's not that. I couldn't impose

'It's no imposition. I'd enjoy the company. Besides, I have an ulterior motive. You can help me.'

Don't be daft!

'No, really. I want to talk to you more. A lot more. I think you can help me find out what the hell has been going on here.'

I do want to help you if I can.

'Then come and stay.'

Another shake of the head.

'Don't you like me?'

I don't know you. But you're really kind

'So what's the problem?'

I'd be too much trouble

'No, you won't. I can get some help in if you need it. Give it a try. If we don't get along, we can call it off, no hard feelings. What d'you say?'

Pauline thought she might be winning. At least there was no shake of the head this time.

'Come on. Please.'

Gemma looked at her, her eyes scrutinising Pauline's face, as if checking closely for any sign of insincerity.

If you're REALLY sure.

She'd only just met this girl, but Pauline was genuinely delighted. She leaned forward and gave her a little hug.

215

'That's great! I'll get things organised straight away.'

Thanks

'None needed. Now then, as we'll have lots more time to talk, I'd better go now, and start my interrogation later.' She smiled to make sure Gemma knew she was joking. Standing up, she smoothed her skirt and checked her jacket. The lapel was almost dry.

'Look, it won't even have to go to the cleaners!'

Gemma gave a short, silent laugh, which turned almost instantly to tears. Pauline moved closer again, put a hand on her shoulder.

'What is it? Is there something else?'

Gemma reached for her pad, started to write unsteadily, her hand shaking. She gave up, threw her pen aside and dropped the pad.

Pauline picked it up.

Do you really think

She held the girl close to her, feeling the trembling of the thin body, and finding she was having to fight down her own emotions.

'I don't know, Gemma. We just have to wait.'

24

Sitting in her wheelchair in front of the open first floor window, Gemma looked out over the small garden. It was good to be so near to the outside world again. In hospital, however nice the staff or pleasant the surroundings, you were somehow separated from everything, some invisible curtain shielding you from normal contact with reality — and especially with nature. Looking out of a high double-glazed window at distant trees growing the other side of a sea of concrete car parking was not the same as this. Here there were two large silver birch trees towering above her, their still-new leaves glittering in the afternoon sunlight of early June. She soaked up the warmth, her skin hungry for the invigorating rays.

Gemma had not seen much of Pauline since she had moved in two days ago. Her benefactor was a busy woman, and was involved at this moment in a particularly awkward divorce case. The night Gemma had arrived, Pauline had had to go to a meeting with her partners, and last night she had been with a barrister working on the case. By tonight, however, the hearing should be over, she promised to be free, and they were going to talk.

I'm pretty lucky really, thought Gemma, looking about her and then down, savouring the joy of being free from hospital routine. Pauline seems really nice, and it's a superb place here. She looked around the room, uncluttered and simply furnished with bright modern pieces. 'Easy-clean surfaces and no bric-a-brac for minimum-effort tidiness,' Pauline had told her.

It was a town house, a narrow three-storey terrace in Richborough Road, a wide, quiet street with a tree-lined pavement. The properties were quite old, but had been tastefully modernised. Gemma was confined to the first floor, and it had been quite a struggle to get up there. But here she had a small bedroom, and the TV room was on this floor which served as her day-room, and a bathroom and lavatory.

Pauline had been very thoughtful towards her new guest. Gemma had wanted to try and be independent, without any imported help. Pauline knew that she could easily be away for hours at a time, and might not be able to get back for meals. Accordingly she had provided a low table in the TV room, on which stood an electric kettle, a toaster, mugs and cutlery, tea and coffee. Next to this was an insulated cabinet containing butter, milk, bread, cheese and various spreads. There was also a laden bowl of fresh fruit.

Gemma could therefore make herself hot drinks, and try her hand, literally, at preparing some simple food. She had already attempted this over the last two days, and despite the difficulties, enjoyed it immensely. After so many weeks of not being allowed to do anything for herself, she was happy to face the challenge of such simple tasks as spreading toast and pouring tea. With her still unpractised left hand she had to be extremely careful when it came to handling boiling water, but she felt reasonably confident, and it was a minor triumph when she tasted the first 'cuppa' she had made herself in ages.

Some things she had found even more of a challenge. Going to the lavatory, for instance. Her right leg had been showing some signs of recovery for several weeks, but was worse than unreliable when it came to bearing her weight, and she could not really give herself any useful support with her right arm.

In the hospital there was plenty of room beside the lavatory for her to park her wheelchair, which was designed so that one arm would come off. It was then a fairly simple matter to slide herself over from one seat to the other, and even then there was a nurse in attendance.

Here there was no one. She and Pauline had experimented first to see whether she could cope with the task alone. If she failed this test, then her stay at Pauline's would perhaps be brief indeed. The entrance to the lavatory was narrow, but she could park her wheelchair directly facing it. If her walking frame was already inside the small room, she could haul herself up, and there was just room for her to execute a turn. All she had to do then was to sit down. The most difficult part was adjusting her clothing and cleaning herself afterwards, but she was getting used to coping with such minor indignities. Gemma was only too grateful that it had not proved an insurmountable problem — she could stay!

Then there was the telephone. Essential, of course, if she needed help. Pauline had given Gemma her cherished unlisted number which would put her straight through to a phone on her desk. If Pauline was not there, Gemma was to ring her secretary, Janet. The problem with this was, of course, that of communication. It was no good holding up one of her messages to the phone, Pauline had pointed out. So they had agreed on a sort of crude Morse code, a series of rapid taps if it was an emergency, slower ones if she needed help but not urgently. The office wasn't far away from the house — it was only ten minutes, if the traffic wasn't too heavy.

On Gemma's behalf, Pauline had called her brother Jonathan in Manchester, and had a long chat about recent events and her change of circumstances, afterwards passing on Jonathan's news as best she could recall. Then she had tried to call Gemma's parents. Their house was near Folkestone in Kent. Gemma had indicated that she didn't really think they'd be there, but it was worth a try. Their first love was their antiques business, and they specialised in Moorish *objets d'art*. They were probably in Spain, where they had been when Jonathan had at last caught up with them to tell them about Gemma's illness. Apparently, once they had ascertained that their daughter was not going to die, they had decided to continue their current expedition.

'We'll see her when she's well,' they'd said. 'She'll appreciate it more then.' Her mother never could stand it when her children were unwell, and she hadn't changed. Gemma wasn't really sorry. They had ceased to have a really close relationship years ago.

Gemma pushed these unhappy thoughts from her mind. There was too much to be miserable about here, right now, without getting more depressed about a relationship she had given up for lost a long time ago. Thoughts of Simon were always circling the edge of her consciousness, like wolves around a fire, ready to rush in if the flame of her resistance died. Gemma was resolved that she would not spend these days of rehabilitation and recuperation dwelling on events over which she had no control. She lifted her head up, closed her eyes, and turned her face to the sun. Even through her closed lids there was a patch of brightness. The area of pinkish light danced around, and as she watched, it began to look more and more like a familiar face. She tried to deny the face more detail, but the image of her doctor friend became all too clear. His eyes were closed, and she was convinced it was the mask of death. The grief that was released was almost a physical thing, making Gemma cry out, her body shaking with a succession of heartbroken sobs.

* * *

Pauline arrived home earlier than she had thought she would. It was only four-thirty. The court session had finished in the morning unexpectedly, and by keeping going almost non-stop the rest of the day she had got herself up to date with all her important business.

She let herself into the house, full of anticipation of a long talk with Gemma. A remarkable girl, she thought, determined to overcome her disability. And not a shred of resentment against the world, fate, God, or, even more remarkably, Simon.

'Gemma!' She called out as she took off her jacket and threw it over an armchair. As she walked past the foot of the stairs to the cloakroom, she called up again.

'Gemma! I'm home!' She wasn't expecting a reply, of course, but the stillness in the house made her uneasy. Ignoring the calls from her bladder, she went quickly up the stairs. Gemma's wheelchair had its back to the door, facing the open window. At first the chair seemed empty, but as Pauline approached she could see the long, blonde hair hanging down from her head, which was slumped forward onto her chest.

Pauline had a surge of fear, and rushed forward, grabbed Gemma's shoulders and jerked her head up.

'Gemma! What's the matter? Are you all right?' She was shaking the girl hard, but stopped abruptly when she noticed the eyes open sleepily.

Gemma saw Pauline, then looked about her, bewildered.

Pauline felt suddenly foolish. 'Oh. Sorry. I didn't realise you were asleep. I thought, well . . .' She ended with a feeble laugh.

Gemma looked at her in puzzlement, then reached for her ever-present writing pad.

You thought I'd snuffed it, didn't you?

'No, really, I — ' Pauline didn't know when she'd last felt so embarrassed.

Yes you did! Look at you. You're as white as a sheet

Gemma's incredulity was turning to amusement. She wrote again.

You thought I'd O.D.'d or something, didn't you?

Pauline saw Gemma's smile, and sat down opposite her. 'Yes, all right, I did think something like that. I'm sorry.'

It's alright. I'm not offended. Oh ye of little faith! But if I ever feel like doing anything like that, I'll leave a message on the front door so you don't come and shake me out of a snooze like that again!

Pauline leaned forward and gave her good hand a squeeze.

'Fair enough.' She looked more closely at Gemma's face, her eyes. 'Have you been crying?' Her tone was accusing.

Gemma nodded, her smile fading.

Yes. 'fraid so. Guilty as charged.

'Simon?'

Gemma nodded.

'You mustn't give up on him.'

Gemma looked at Pauline expectantly, waiting for her to continue.

'They still won't let me see him. Mr Benham — he's the consultant surgeon, remember? — is not very communicative. He won't talk to me. I don't think he trusts me to keep my mouth shut. The police have asked that no details be released to the press.' She looked at Gemma and tried a smile, to soften the impact of her words. 'He's still deeply unconscious.'

Gemma bit her lower lip and looked down.

Pauline didn't want to give her false hope. If Simon died, they would both need to be prepared for it.

'I can't pretend it's not touch and go. But listen — I asked Sister to tell us immediately if Simon recovers consciousness, and she promised she would. Now I'm sure she wouldn't say that if she thought it would never happen!'

Gemma reached out and touched Pauline's hand. The solicitor returned the grip for a moment, then stood up.

'Look, I'm breaking my neck for a pee, as we genteel lady lawyers say. I'll be back in a minute with some tea, and we'll talk some more.'

Ten minutes later she had changed into trousers and a comfortable sweater, and they settled down with mugs of tea. Pauline was working round to asking some of the questions that had been begging an answer for the past few days.

'Gemma, enquiring about your medical history is really none of my business. But there are some things I want to know. Do you mind?'

Gemma did not mind, and indicated by shaking her head.

'Righto. Here we go, then. Have you ever had a termination of pregnancy before?'

Gemma shook her head again, then with a smile made a sign crossing her heart to emphasise that she was telling the truth.

'Have you had any gynaecological operations before?'

Gemma nodded her affirmation, and Pauline sat forward eagerly.

'When? When was it?'

Gemma had her note-pad ready.

Earlier this year

'How recently?'

Gemma thought for a moment.

221

Three or four months ago

'What was it?'

A D and C

'Why did you have it done?'

I was having heavy periods, and they weren't very regular. Once I flooded in a lecture, and I had to leave. It was so embarrassing.

'Didn't they try you on the pill?'

No. I don't like pills. And Mr. Greenwell said a D and C would be better.

'Greenwell! You mean he did the operation?'
Gemma could not mistake the anxiety in Pauline's voice.

Yes. He was very nice to me. Is that bad?

'I don't know, yet. Think, Gemma, when exactly did you have the D & C?'
Gemma looked down, frowning.

Have you got a diary?

Pauline went to her handbag, and produced one. She gave it to Gemma, but she could not manipulate the tiny pages with one hand. Pauline reached over and found the page with the calendar for the year, and held it open while Gemma studied it. After a while, she pushed the diary away and reached for her note-pad again. She wrote for some time.

It must have been about 2 months before I had my T.O.P. – I think I might have got pregnant the first time my boy-friend and I made love after the D and C. I thought I was safe. And we used a sheath, but he got a bit frantic, and it came off.

'Did Greenwell do the operation himself?'

Yes, I think so.

'You said he was very nice to you. What do you particularly remember that makes you say that?'

Well I suppose it was just that he was charming - and he let me stay in the private ward after the operation.

Pauline was getting more and more interested in Gemma's replies, but impatient, too, with the slow method of communication. 'Tell me about that.'

When I recovered from the ~~anaesthetic~~ gas, I was in a private room. I was worried at first, cos I thought I might have to pay. But Mr. Greenwell came to see me himself, and said that there were no beds on the gynae ward so I was put in the Private Wing. I was only to be in 2 days and he said he'd fix it for me to stay there till I left. I was rather flattered.

I bet you were, thought Pauline. And I bet I know the answer to the next question.

'Who gave you your anaesthetic?'

I don't know. But she had red hair.

Gemma could see that Pauline was getting excited about something, and was desperate to be told. She wanted to ask what she found so interesting, but was frustrated by her limited ability to communicate.

She watched every move as her new friend walked up and down, lost in thought, and tried to be patient, hoping she would soon be included in her ruminations.

Pauline stopped, frowning in concentration, and pointed at Gemma. As she opened her mouth to speak, the telephone rang.

'Damn!' said Pauline, and went to answer it. Gemma beat her hand on the arm of the wheelchair in frustration, which was exacerbated by being able to hear only one side of the ensuing conversation.

'Yes, this is Pauline Jamieson.'

Pause. Pauline's face changed abruptly to deep concern.

'Oh. Oh dear, I'm sorry.'

Another silence. 'Thank you for telling me.' Pause again.

'Yes, yes, I think perhaps I will.' She listened for a few moments.

'Are they? Well, in that case, I think I'll come straight away.'

She replaced the receiver slowly. Gemma watched her fearfully, eyes wide, hand to her open mouth. Pauline realised what she was thinking.

'No, it's not Simon. It's Kate.' She looked down at her hands, massaging one with the other. 'She's just died.'

Gemma put her hand to her mouth, as if to stifle the cry that could not be heard.

'Her parents are there. I rather feel that I ought to go in and see them.'

Gemma nodded her head slowly in agreement. A tear began a meandering journey down her cheek, and she wiped it away. Pauline went over to her, stroked her hair. 'Poor Gemma.'

Gemma breathed deeply a few times, then reached for her pad.

No. Poor Simon.

* * *

Pauline was shown into a visitor's waiting room, just opposite the Intensive Care Unit, where a large woman and a stocky balding man, both in their early sixties, sat with their heads bowed, holding hands. Kate's parents. They looked up and separated almost guiltily as Pauline entered, as if it was bad form to show your emotions to strangers.

'Mr and Mrs Howard?'

'We are, yes,' said the man stiffly, making an attempt to rise. It was only a half-hearted gesture, but somehow Pauline was touched by the vestigial bid at courtesy.

'I'm Pauline Jamieson. May I talk to you for a moment?'

They both looked somewhat surprised at the request. It was not that they weren't expecting to be questioned, but that they were being given a choice. Pauline detected their reaction. These were unsophisticated people in a strange and stressful situation, and would be easily manipulated. She did not want to be found guilty of that.

'You don't have to talk to me. It's just that I think it may help us both.'

'It's all right, of course. Sit you down, lass.' As he relaxed a little there was a trace of a northern accent. Mr Howard indicated a chair.

When she was settled, Pauline looked from one to the other. 'I know it's easy to use words, but I really mean this. I'm very sorry about your daughter.'

'Thank you, thank you.' Mr Howard drew himself up, to help stay in control. His wife took out a handkerchief and gently wiped her eyes, then said very softly, 'Yes, thank you, Miss Jamieson.'

'I knew Kate quite well, you know.'

'Yes, so we understand.'

'And Simon, of course. I was acting for him, as his solicitor, through all his recent problems.'

'Yes. Poor Simon. What a business.' Mr Howard looked at his wife, as if for confirmation that he had said the right thing.

Mrs Howard nodded. 'It's all such a terrible mess. We don't know whether we're coming or going. Young Simon, fighting for his life, and now our Kate . . . dead . . .' She smothered a sob in her handkerchief.

'We don't know what to do about it, you see.' Mr Howard made a self-conscious attempt to comfort his wife, patting her arm.

There was obviously some new development that Pauline didn't know about.

'I'm sorry, Mr Howard. To do about what?'

'Why, the baby, of course.'

Pauline was so astounded she nearly shouted.

'The — the baby?'

'Yes, Kate's baby, dammit.' The stress was causing his façade to crack.

Pauline looked from one to the other. 'I'm so sorry, but I don't understand.'

Mrs Howard blew her nose, then spoke to the floor, shaking her head as she did so. 'When they realised Kate was — going to die, they took the baby out — you know, with an operation, a Caesar something — '

'Caesarean section?'

She nodded. 'They said it was as much a last-ditch attempt to save Kate as the baby.'

'But the baby was only, good God, fifteen weeks at the most, according to the last scan!'

'That's what we thought. In fact up till now we thought she was much less than that. But the hospital reckons when she came in she was well over twenty weeks. They didn't think there was any hope for it, anyway — but you should see it. It's on a ventilator, but they said it's showing all its reflexes and things.'

Pauline was trying hard to assimilate all this. 'You mean you've actually seen the baby? It's still *alive?*'

'Yes.' The man closed his eyes and sighed deeply. 'I think they thought it might help us to see it. You know, the hope that life may go on, that sort of thing.'

'But let me tell you something.' His wife looked at Pauline, frowning sternly. 'I'm no expert, but that ain't like no premature baby that I've ever seen.'

* * *

As soon as she could, Pauline excused herself and went to the Sister's office on the ICU. She introduced herself, then asked the nurse if she could tell her anything about Kate's baby.

'No, I'm afraid I can't. You're not a relative, are you?'

'Well, no, but I have been closely involved with the Robinson family.'

'I'm sorry, but I can't disclose any information except to the relatives.'

Pauline turned to leave, but paused when she got to the door. She knew Kate's parents were only a few yards away. Should she involve them, ask their permission? How would she explain this interest?

'Where is the baby now?'

'I presume it went to the Prem Baby Unit. But they won't tell you anything, either.'

'Thank you, Sister. By the way, everyone keeps calling the baby "it". I suppose you're allowed to tell me what sex it is?'

'Female,' she said bluntly, and closed the office door.

A girl. Pauline shivered. Why should that make me feel spooky? she wondered. She hesitated outside the room where Kate's parents were still waiting, decided against bothering them again, and went in search of the Premature Baby Unit.

'I'm Sister McArthur. Can I help you?'

Pauline turned quickly, feeling as if she'd been caught in the act of doing something improper. She was standing in the corridor outside the Post Natal Ward, looking through the window that ran the length of the wall, and into the room in which there were a number of cots containing tiny babies. There were two incubators as well, one of them occupied, and she was wondering if that might be Kate's baby. There were no mothers in there, and she had just been thinking about dashing in for a quick peep.

226

'I — I'm sorry. I was looking for the Premature Baby Unit.'

'Well, that's not it.' Sister McArthur was tall, thin as a rake, and had thick lenses in her spectacles. She looked through them now with disapproval. 'That's the nursery. The Prem Unit is down there.' She pointed to closed double doors at the end of the corridor.

'Oh. I see. It's just that I saw the incubator in there and . . .'

'That baby's not really a prem. It's a bit irritable, that's all. It's only using it to sleep in really.'

'Oh.' Pauline thought she might as well give up, and turned to go.

'And you are . . .?' the nurse enquired.

'Miss Jamieson. Pauline Jamieson. I'm a solicitor, and — '

'And you are Mr Robinson's friend.' Pauline looked startled, but the grey eyes behind the thick glass were friendly. She smiled. 'Come into the office a moment.'

Sister McArthur turned and led the way, and Pauline, intrigued, followed.

'Sit down, please.' When Pauline was settled facing the desk, the Sister continued. 'Let me explain. I've been hoping I might get a chance to meet you.'

'Really? I'm amazed you even know who I am.'

'Ah well, Mr Robinson and I have worked together a lot. He took a special interest in the prems he delivered. Often used to come down here. I like him. We'd often have a coffee and a chat.'

'I see.'

'He's had a lot of problems lately, as of course you will know only too well. He'd mentioned there was this nice lady lawyer who was, ah, very supportive — I think was the phrase he used.'

Pauline found herself blushing slightly. 'That was very nice of him.'

'I never heard him speak ill of anyone.' She paused, head bent, shaking it slowly. 'Dreadful business. Dreadful business.'

'You said you wanted to meet me. To ask about something?' Her mind was going ahead, preparing the way for some questions if the opportunity arose.

'No. I didn't have any special questions, I just hoped to see you.' She gave a short laugh. 'See if you measured up!'

'I hope I'm not found wanting.'

'No, indeed. Mr Robinson's assessment is as good as usual.' She shook her head. 'Such a nice man.'

'You obviously value his judgement.'

'Absolutely. When you've seen as many doctors come and go as I have you soon know the ones who've got it.'

'Got it?'

'Yes. You know: sympathy; understanding; confidence. Takes the time to talk *to* the patients, not talk *down* to them. That's my sort of doctor.'

227

Simon had obviously made a more than favourable impression here, thought Pauline. She drew the courage to try for some information.

'You know his wife died this evening?'

'Yes, I heard. Poor thing. Mr Robinson spoke so fondly of her.' She clicked her tongue several times. 'It's all so strange. Her injuries. That baby.'

'I've just been talking to Kate's — Mrs Robinson's parents. They told me the baby was delivered by Caesarean section. And that it's still alive.'

Sister McArthur looked up sharply, and Pauline thought she'd gone too far too soon. However, her expression was one of shrewd recognition rather than anger. 'So that's why you're looking for the Prem Baby Unit?'

'It's not really any of my business. I know you're not meant to talk about it to anyone who isn't a relative.'

'Well, yes.' Her brow furrowed, then her face cleared. 'But you're sort of a legal representative, aren't you?' The Sister was obviously looking for a way to bend the rules.

'Yes, I suppose I am.' Pauline's conscience gave her a small dig, but she ignored it.

'So what do you want to know?'

'How can it be possible for this baby to survive when it's so immature?'

'You tell me! It's incredible, and I use the word in it's literal sense. I just cannot believe that the infant is only twenty-four weeks.'

'Twenty-four? Who said Mrs Robinson was that much on in her pregnancy?'

'That's what it said in the notes. "Twenty-four to twenty-six-week size foetus." She weighs about 800 grams — that's about one pound twelve ounces.'

'But — but by dates she was only twelve weeks — though the scan said fifteen.'

Sister McArthur shook her head firmly. 'I really don't understand it. She must have got her dates wrong.'

'The scan can't be mistaken, surely.'

'Well, *something's* wrong. I haven't had a chance to look at the infant very closely, but it looks too well, too active, to be so premature.'

'What would you expect if the baby was very premature?'

'Well, it'd be flat — that is to say no reflexes to speak of, except the very primitive ones. Muscle tone poor — feeble movement. Wouldn't make much noise. Wouldn't open its eyes. Even with the brief look I got I could see the little blighter breaking all those rules.'

'How do you explain that?'

'Can't. Poor little bugger should be dead, no hope. But it isn't.'

'You mean apart from being so tiny, it's almost as if it were a normal infant — born at the usual time?'

'Yes, except for the lungs. They aren't ready to breathe air at this stage, and often they need help with breathing. This one's no exception as far as that goes. It needs ventilating — it has a tracheostomy.'

'A hole in its throat?'

'That's right.'

Well, here goes, thought Pauline. 'I don't suppose — ' She was interrupted by the phone. Sister listened for a moment, then looked at Pauline in surprise. 'Yes, she's here now. Just a moment.' The nurse put her hand over the mouthpiece. 'It's for you.' She added conspiratorially, 'It's the police.'

'Miss Jamieson?' She recognised the voice of one of the desk sergeants from the station.

'Yes, speaking.' Before the man had a chance to continue, she added, 'How did you track me down here?'

'Hah! Bit of a long story. Someone answered the phone at your place, but didn't speak — we could hear noises, though. Our chap thought it was a bit funny, sent a car round. Found a rather frightened young lady — Miss Randall, as I recall. Handicapped girl. She, er, can't talk, I understand. She wrote down who she was, where she thought you were.'

'However did you get in? She's on the first floor.'

The officer gave an embarrassed cough. 'In the circumstances, Miss . . .'

'I hope you didn't do any damage.'

'Goodness me, no. We have our more subtle methods, as you well know . . .'

Pauline smiled at the air of discomfiture coming down the phone. 'No wonder she was frightened, hearing someone gaining access to the house like that.'

'Yes. Cheery lass, though, Soon brightened up by all accounts.'

'What did you want me for, Sergeant?'

'Oh yes, of course. Sorry. Would you — could you call into the Station on your way home? Something's turned up we feel we should let you know about. It concerns a client of yours, in a roundabout way.'

'A client?'

'Can you come round, Miss?'

'Yes, yes of course. Give me ten minutes.'

'Righto. No great rush.'

Pauline replaced the phone carefully. It must be something to do with Simon, she thought.

Sister McArthur was looking at her with concern.

'Everything all right?'

'What? Oh, yes, sorry.' Pauline stood up. 'Look, I really ought to go and see exactly what all this is about. Can we talk again?'

Sister smiled. 'Be glad to.'

'This isn't so desperately urgent that I couldn't spare a minute to see Kate's baby — if you'll let me?'

'Well I would, but I can't.'

Pauline was disappointed. 'Orders from on high?'

'No, it's not that. The baby isn't here.'

'Not here? But this is the Premature Baby Unit, isn't it?'

'It is. But this little specimen is having special treatment. A little unit all of its own, I believe.'

'Where's that?'

'Well, I don't understand why, but it's up in that Research Facility next to the private wing.'

25

Pauline inspected her front door carefully for signs of damage but could find none. The lock worked perfectly, and she let herself in, calling out to Gemma as she did so.

It was not dark yet, but the hall and stairway were gloomy, and she switched the lights on as she went. Gemma was waiting in her wheelchair at the top of the stairs, looking anxious, and held her good arm out to Pauline as soon as she saw her. Pauline went quickly up to her, leaned over and gave her a hug.

'Are you all right? I've heard all about it. The policemen at the station said you were very brave.'

Gemma had been busy, a note prepared.

The Police rang. I couldn't answer. They came round. I could hear someone trying to get in. I was scared to death.

'I bet you were. Poor Gemma. I'm sorry.' Gemma reached for her pad.

I'm alright now.

Pauline looked around, and saw the remains of their tea, still where she had left them when she'd dashed off to the hospital.

'Have you had anything to eat?'

In reply Gemma held up a banana skin and then a cup.

'Oh dear. You must be starving. I'll get something.'

Gemma grinned and nodded eagerly. Pauline was moving away, but Gemma grabbed her sleeve, and wrote whilst she waited.

I'll survive another 5 minutes. What happened at the hospital? And the Police station?

'It'll take more than five minutes. Are you sure you don't want to eat first?'

231

Gemma indicated she did not.

Pauline sat down facing the wheelchair, and related the events at the hospital. Gemma looked amazed, then worried, at the news that Kate's baby was still alive, and by all accounts doing well.

Pauline then went on to describe what she had been told by the police.

'They'd got the results of the autopsy on the badly burnt body they found upstairs at Simon's house. And they've identified it. The details will have to be released to the press soon, and they wanted me to know first, as I'm representing Simon's interests.'

Pauline paused, and Gemma made rapid winding movements with her left hand, urging her friend to continue.

'Patience, patience!' Pauline smiled at her, and decided to tease her a bit. 'Are you sure you don't want me to get something to eat first? I'm starving.'

Gemma assumed a mock grim expression, and scrawled hurriedly.

You're mean! Get on with it!

'All right, all right! Now — ' Her mood changed abruptly as she recalled the sombre details she had been given. 'It's not very nice, I'm afraid. The cause of death appears to be knife wounds. Lots of them. There were no cuts to see on the skin, because there was hardly any skin left — all burnt off.' She made an expression of distaste. 'But the tissues showed extensive damage. She was subjected to "a frenzied attack", was how they put it. They're not sure if she was dead when she was burnt, it happened so quickly afterwards, but the knife wounds would have killed her if the fire hadn't. A major artery in the chest was pierced.'

Pauline stopped because Gemma was writing.

She? You said "she". Who was it?

'The most certain way to identify a badly burnt or decomposed body is by dental records. That's what they did in this case. The body is that of Gillian Ravensbourne. We were going to talk about her earlier, before I got the phone call about Kate. She's a pathologist at the hospital. But she's also a qualified anaesthetist. And she's got red hair.'

Gemma gaped, and looked at Pauline with wide eyes.

'Yes, it would seem to be the same person who gave you your anaesthetic when you had your D & C. And I think she also anaesthetised Kate when she had a gynae operation recently — and

232

gave her some dangerous treatment that I think had something to do with her going out of her mind.'

Gemma looked down, confusion and consternation on her face as she tried to assimilate this new knowledge.

A thought occurred to Pauline, and she leaned forward, speaking urgently. 'I want you to think hard, Gemma. When you had your D & C, did the red-haired woman give you any pills to take afterwards?'

Gemma looked away, almost guiltily.

'She did, didn't she?'

Gemma nodded, her mouth turning down with distress.

'What happened? Did you take them?'

Gemma wrote a note.

> She gave a bottle of pills to me just after I came round from the gas. I didn't take them. I didn't know what they were for. She said they were important. But I don't like pills.

'Did you tell Simon about them?'

> No. I thought he would be cross with me for not taking them.

'Christ. If only you knew . . . Why are you so against taking pills?'

> Cos my best friend at school had an aunt who was a Thalidomide victim. I asked my doctor about the pills — he said there was nothing in the hospital letter about them. So I didn't take them. I feel so bad about it, now.

'Why? Why do you feel bad about it?'

> Because I think that if I had taken them it might have prevented my baby from being abnormal. Then Simon wouldn't have been so keen to do my termination, and got into so much trouble. And I might not have ended up like this.

Pauline could hardly believe it. 'You mean you hold yourself responsible for all this —' she indicated the last note — 'because you didn't take the tablets Ravensbourne gave you?'

Gemma looked up, eyes full of tears, misery creasing her face, and gave a slow affirmative nod.

'Oh, Gemma.' Pauline picked up both her hands, gave them an affectionate squeeze. 'Gemma, I think not taking the pills may have saved your sanity — or even your life.'

Once again Gemma was looking bewildered and surprised. Pauline continued. 'I don't understand it yet, but I think this Ravensbourne woman gave Kate some pills when she was coming round from her anaesthetic, and told her to be sure to take them. They contained a drug which affected her blood, made her very anaemic, and seemed to change her personality too. I'll bet anything you were given the same ones, and that they'd have done the same to you.'

Gemma brushed the tears from her eyes before they could fall, and wrote one word.

Why?

'Gemma, that's the trouble. I have no idea. But I'm sure there must be some link between you, Kate, your missing histology report, Gwyn Reece's murder, and what happened at Simon's house. The Ravensbourne woman is linked with them all. And there's one other piece of news I haven't told you.'

Gemma sniffed loudly, and Pauline reached for her box of tissues and gave her one. Gemma blew her nose, then tucked the tissue up her sleeve. She leaned forward, nodding her head quickly to encourage Pauline to carry on.

'I haven't told you an extraordinary thing that happened after they identified Gillian Ravensbourne's dental impressions — that's what they do, take impressions and try and match them with known records. It's a bit like looking for a needle in a haystack, unless you have some knowledge of who the victim might be, or if you're sorting out bodies, say after a plane crash. In this case, one of the forensic people thought he recognised something about the teeth. To do with missing teeth and an overbite, I think they said. This technician thought it was impossible, but checked anyway, and he was right. He had seen the impression of Ravensbourne's teeth before, quite recently. They came from another murder victim. Her name was Janice Marshall. There were teeth-marks on her breasts. Gillian Ravensbourne's teeth-marks.'

* * *

Pauline and Gamma sat talking in their unusual fashion for a long time that night. By the time they had finished, Gemma had covered the floor around them with discarded messages. They went over the whole story, from the first moments they had known Simon — what he had told Pauline, and what Pauline herself knew. Gemma was quick and intelligent, and put forward several possible theories as they tried to make some sense out of what information they had. There were huge gaps in their knowledge, which only speculation could fill, and in the end they gave up, tired and exhausted.

Pauline helped Gemma into bed, a now familiar routine even after only three nights. She tucked the girl in, patted her head, and headed for the door. Gemma banged on the headboard to attract attention, and gestured to Pauline to bring her writing pad.

I don't know how to thank you.

'Don't be silly. What for? I've hardly done anything yet.'

Apart from letting me be here, you've relieved me of a terrible worry.

'That you were somehow responsible for all those things because you didn't take the pills?'

Yes. Silly, wasn't I?

'No. Just sensitive and caring.' She gazed down at Gemma's face, little-girlish as it looked over the top of the covers. One day I'll have to have a daughter, she thought. 'Now, stop worrying. We both need some sleep. See you in the morning.' She blew her a kiss and put out the light.

It was some time before Pauline was able to follow her own advice and get to sleep, and when the alarm woke her at seven, she felt as if it were only minutes later. Her head was aching slightly, and her eyes were sore. She dragged herself from the bed, checked on Gemma, helped her onto the lavatory, and ran a bath. Half an hour later, refreshed to some degree, they were having breakfast. Pauline brought hers upstairs, so that neither of them would have to eat alone, and they sat by the occasional table in the TV room that served as Gemma's lounge. They took their time, still mulling over the mystery surrounding Gillian Ravensbourne.

It was nearly 8.30 when the phone rang. It was the Sister from the hospital, and by the time Pauline put the receiver down everything else was forgotten. They left their coffee unfinished, toast half-eaten, as Pauline struggled to get Gemma into a coat, then with dangerous haste got her down the stairs. She left her car, engine running, outside the house, while she half-carried Gemma to it, then went back and put the folded wheelchair in the boot.

The drive to the hospital was a little reckless, she admitted later, but neither of them noticed at the time. Frustration set in as they neared the city centre, both of them fuming at the slow-moving traffic. At last they arrived at the Princess Marina Hospital, and Pauline parked in a space marked 'DOCTOR ONLY'. The wheelchair was hauled out, Gemma man-handled into it, and Pauline, sweating and dishevelled, pushed it to the main lifts.

The wait appeared interminable. The doors were slow to open, slow to close. The lift seemed to think about it for ages before it started to move. It stopped at every floor. At last they got out on the fourth, and Pauline turned the chair into the private wing.

Sister must have heard the wheels squeaking on the floor, and came out of the office to meet them.

'My word, that was quick.'

Pauline was breathless, and could only manage to say, 'Which one?'

The Sister took them to a large side room. 'In there. And don't be long.'

They went in, and stopped transfixed as the door was softly closed behind them. They looked around at the cardiac monitor, the bottles of blood and saline, the drip tubes, and then the apparently sleeping recipient of all this technology. Both girls were near to tears, when the eyes opened, and despite the weakness, the pain, and the nasogastric tube, Simon managed a smile.

26

In her heart of hearts, Pauline had feared that Simon would not pull through. When she had last seen him, being taken off to hospital, he had still been bleeding profusely — faster, it seemed, than the substitute plasma could be run in. She had tried to be optimistic for Gemma's sake, but found it hard to believe anyone could survive such injuries. It seemed scarcely possible that she should now be standing here at his bedside. Gemma was trying to control her tears, and Pauline too had a lump in her throat as she searched for something to say, not even knowing if Simon was aware that Kate was dead, or that he had a daughter upstairs clinging to life despite incredible prematurity.

Pauline looked at his neck, which was covered with gauze dressings held in place with special surgical tape. What hideous scars they covered she could not imagine. What do you say to someone in this situation, whose wife has tried to kill him in an insane frenzy?

Simon solved the problem by speaking first. It was not easy for him. He had a tracheostomy, a hole made in the main breathing tube, which had been used to ventilate his lungs when he was in a state of severe collapse. An opening in the dressings on his neck indicated the presence of the aperture. The ventilator was now disconnected, but the hole was still present in case it was needed again, and because there was still a lot of swelling in the damaged tissues around his larynx. This had the effect of narrowing the airway, and made breathing in the normal way difficult.

In order to speak, Simon had to cover the hole in his throat, so forcing air to be diverted through his larynx, enabling him to use his vocal cords. With the hole open, no sound could be produced, as air then went straight into the trachea. His left hand came up to his neck, and his fingers covered the hole. Immediately his breathing became audible, a rasping sound coming from his throat with each breath.

'Hello, girls.' His voice was thin and croaky, but the words were easily discernible. He took his hand away, easing his breathing. He could only manage a few words at a time.

Pauline sat on a chair by the bed, and rested her hand on his right arm, which was bandaged heavily and had a drip running into it.

'Hello, Simon.'

Even in the haste of their departure, Gemma had remembered to bring along her notebook. She held it up for Simon to see. It announced, as large as she could get it on the A4 page:

Simon raised his right hand just off the bed in greeting, and mouthed 'hi' in reply.

Pauline swallowed. 'Looking at you like this, it seems a stupid question, but how are you feeling?'

Covering his tracheostomy again, Simon, with a hint of humour, replied:

'As well as can be expected.'

'Are you in pain?'

'Remarkably little. It's great . . .' He paused for breath. '. . . to see you two. Thanks for coming.'

'When did you — come round?'

'Late last night. I'm told . . .' Another pause, another rasping intake of air. '. . . it's been four days.'

'Yes.' Pauline looked away, and then back. 'Have you heard . . .?' She could tell without continuing that he had. He bit his lower lip hard for a long moment.

'Yes. Early this . . . morning they told . . . me.'

Pauline moved her hand down to enclose his.

'I'm so sorry, Simon.'

He closed his eyes, taking two deep breaths through his tracheostomy before covering the hole again.

'She saved my . . . life, you know.'

Pauline wasn't sure how to react to that. Before she could stop herself, she said, 'But I thought — '

Simon looked directly at her. 'That she had . . . done this to me?'

Pauline looked down, then glanced across at Gemma, who was almost opposite her on the other side of the bed, eyes moist and very wide.

'Yes.'

'It was . . .' He paused, took an unobstructed breath. '. . . Gillian Ravensbourne who was . . . responsible for all this.'

'Ravensbourne!' She looked across again at Gemma, but her eyes were fixed on Simon. 'You — you know she was found dead at the house?'

Simon nodded.

'I'm sorry, Simon, but I must know what happened. Can you tell us?'

He nodded again. 'Yes, I'll . . . tell you. I want you . . . to help me

238

find . . . out what's been happening . . . to Kate.' He took his hand away from the tracheostomy, needing several breaths to recover from the effort of the long speech.

'Of course I will.'

Gemma patted the bed with her left hand to gain attention, then raised it in the air.

Pauline took the hint. 'I mean, we will. Gemma wants to help, too.'

Simon turned to her. 'Thanks, Gemma. I . . . really appreci-ate . . . that.' He looked her over with renewed professional interest. 'How are you . . . doing? You look . . . fine.'

Gemma wrote as fast as she could.

I'm OK. I'm staying with Pauline.

Simon turned his attention back to Pauline.

'That's very good . . . of you.'

'Not at all. Gemma's no trouble, and she's going to be a great help to me.'

'I see. The solicitor . . . and the student. Interesting . . . combina-tion to . . . do a bit of . . . sleuthing.'

Pauline smiled, not wanting to change the mood. However, at any moment the nursing staff might ask them to leave; she knew she had to press on.

'Can you help us, then? Tell us what happened?'

Simon also was aware that this visit was likely to be curtailed at any moment.

'Have to be . . . brief. Dragon lady may . . . return . . . any time now.'

As if on cue, the Sister opened the door. 'Sorry, ladies, it's time to go.'

Pauline cursed under her breath, and stood up. Simon raised his hand in protest, his voice as urgent as he could make it.

'Please. Very . . . important. Just another . . . minute.'

The Sister looked round at the trio and their pleading expressions. 'All right. One minute more, then I'll be back.' She left, not waiting for thanks.

Simon looked at both women in turn.

'Listen. Think this is . . . how it was, though . . . bit hazy about detail. Was barely . . . conscious much of the time.' He paused, panting.

'Go on,' Pauline urged, with a glance at the door.

'I thought Kate . . . was going to . . . kill me. She . . . wanted me to . . . take out . . . remove, like a Caesarian . . . her — our — baby. She said it was . . . ready. That it wanted to . . . come out.

239

Kept . . . talking to it.' He was forced to stop again, breathing deeply through the open tracheostomy.

'Cut me . . . under here.' He gestured in the direction of his left shoulder. 'Tied me to . . . a chair. Then Ravensbourne . . . came in. Didn't know who it . . . was at first. Thought she . . . was going to . . . rescue me. But . . .' Another pause for air. 'But she cut . . . my throat. Thought I was . . . going to die. Me . . . I was lying on the . . . floor. Could see Kate . . . she went . . . wild . . . attacked Ravens . . . bourne. Couldn't see properly . . . think she must have cut . . . her up a bit.'

Christ, that's an understatement, according to the post-mortem, thought Pauline, and Gemma looked across, clearly thinking the same thing.

Simon was struggling with his breathing now, in his haste to get the story told.

'Anyway, don't know . . . how, but Kate got . . . me loose and . . . dragged me down . . . down the stairs . . . Passed out for . . . a bit then. Next thing, Kate . . . trying to drag me . . . to front door. Funny thing . . . she smelt of . . . petrol. Must have set . . . fire to . . . to our . . .'

He stopped then, partly because of his need for more air, and also because he was fighting to keep control.

Pauline stood up, bent over him, touched his face, then drew back quickly as the door opened. This time it was Martin Benham, the surgeon, with Sister anxiously fluttering behind him. He was tall, with a face excessively lined for his 48 years, and an almost permanent lugubrious expression. He could see the distress on Simon's face, and sounded angry.

'Sister tells me you've already had an extension. Time to leave, ladies.'

Pauline didn't want to antagonise the man. She would need his co-operation.

'Yes, of course. We'll go.' She looked down at the pale figure in the bed. 'We'll be back soon, Simon.' She walked round the bed and stood behind the wheelchair, pausing before she turned it round whilst Gemma held up her book, which simply said:

Bye

''Bye, Gemma. Bye . . . Pauline. Thanks for . . . calling.'

Mr Benham stood aside for them to leave, and was virtually ushering them out when Simon spoke again.

'Martin. Please . . . talk to them. Help them any way you can. I'd like you to . . . tell them anything they . . . want to know.'

240

Benham frowned, glanced at the two women, then looked resigned.

'All right, Simon, if that's what you want.' He turned to Pauline. 'If you'd like to wait in Sister's office, I shan't be long here.'

True to his word, after only five minutes, he came to speak to them. He seemed a little embarrassed.

'I thought you were upsetting him in there. I, er — didn't mean to sound so gruff. Seems to have bucked him no end, however. Unfortunate fellow. "What's the point of living?" he said to me earlier . . . didn't mention it this time.'

His rare attempt at an apology effected, he sat back in his chair and observed the two women closely.

'I just called in to see Simon on my way to theatre.' He looked deliberately at his watch. 'I've got a couple of minutes. What do you want to know?'

'That's very kind of you.' Pauline leaned forward earnestly. 'Look, we're not just being curious. I'm his solicitor, and we want to try and help.'

'Yes, yes.' He waved his right hand dismissively. 'I understand all that.' He was impatient to get to the point. Gemma pushed a note into Pauline's hand. She read it, then looked up.

'Yes, of course. First, is he going to be all right?'

'Should be, now. It was touch and go, and the shock and blood loss have caused some problem with kidney function. I thought he might need dialysis. We think he's out of the wood, though.'

Gemma held her hands up, the good one clutching and supporting the other, as if in prayer, her eyes alight.

'Will he be able to get rid of that hole thing in his neck soon?'

'The tracheostomy? Yes, in a few days, if the oedema, the swelling, goes down.'

Benham waited impatiently for the next question as Pauline paused for a moment. 'How did he survive? Having your throat cut like that, and by someone who should know all about the way to do the most damage? It sounds impossible.'

'People survive having their throats cut more often than you might think. Combination of luck and circumstance, usually. If you have your carotid artery chopped, or the trachea cut right through, well, it's Goodnight Vienna, no matter what. But usually it's not done in a cool, collected fashion, and I'm sure that the lady that did this — we know now it was Dr Ravensbourne — was not thinking anatomically when she took a slice at her victim.'

'Just how much damage was done?'

'Lucky for Simon, she cut too low. Damaged the cricoid cartilage, but not irreparably, plus some of the sternomastoid muscles. Much of the bleeding came from the external jugular vein, a relatively small

241

blood-vessel compared to the internal jugular, and from the thyroid gland tissue. She just nicked the left carotid artery, which gave a pretty spectacular blood loss, but sustainable in terms of blood volume for twenty minutes or so. It could have been enough to convince her she'd done a good job, seeing the spurt of arterial blood, even though it was only a thin stream, and so didn't cut again. Or she was prevented by the intervention of Mrs Robinson, poor soul.'

'You know about that, too?'

'Yes, indeed. Just what the bloody hell is going on here? Do you know?'

'No, not yet. But we're working on it.'

'It's a job for the police, surely?'

'Yes, of course. They've been very helpful so far, and I'll do all I can to help them. They haven't told me not to interfere, or anything like that, so we — ' she nodded to include Gemma — 'are trying to find out what we can. Have they — the police — seen Simon yet?'

'No. Perhaps tomorrow, if he's up to it.' Benham stood up. 'Now, if you'll excuse me, I really must go.'

'Thanks very much for your time. We're very grateful.' Pauline hesitated. 'When can we see him again?'

The surgeon made an attempt to look benignly at them. 'Wait till this afternoon. I'll tell Sister, leave it to her discretion. If you don't overdo it, I'm sure visits from two attractive ladies will do him more good than harm.'

With this uncharacteristic attempt at gallantry, he left, rushing down the corridor at high speed, white coat flapping behind him.

Pauline began to push Gemma to the ward exit, when they heard Sister call.

'Miss Jamieson! One moment, please.'

Pauline stopped and waited, as the Sister bustled up to them. 'I've just spoken to Mr Benham. You must be very privileged! Would you like to ring this afternoon? See how he is? I expect Mr Robinson could cope with another visit soon.'

'Thank you, Sister.'

'One more thing. A message — from Mr Robinson. Sounds a bit mysterious. He said to look in his white coat. Search the pockets, he said. I think that's right.'

Pauline frowned, 'What for?'

The nurse looked puzzled. 'He didn't say. I presumed you'd know.'

'You couldn't just pop back and ask him?'

'No, I'm sorry. He's just going off to sleep. I don't want to disturb him again.' She looked adamant.

Gemma and Pauline looked at each other. 'Where might his white coat be?'

'In Gynae Out-patients, somewhere, I should think. Probably in his office.'

'Thank you, Sister. We'll go there straight away.'

'Have you no idea what you're looking for?'

'None at all, Sister. Look, you couldn't ring down and tell them we have permission, could you?'

'I'll do it now.' She shook her head. 'Anything that might help the poor man.'

The Out-patient Department was crowded, and Pauline didn't attempt to push Gemma through the rows of chairs, leaving her in the corridor outside. As she looked around the throng, feeling a little lost, one of the staff nurses came up to her and asked if she could help.

'I'm Miss Jamieson. I'm looking for Sister,'

'Oh, you'll be wanting Mr Robinson's white coat, won't you? Sister Rhodes rang to say you were coming. Just a moment.'

She dodged her way through the general bustle, returning after only a few moments with a coat which she held up.

'This is it. Look, there's his name-tag. It was out for laundry, but there's still some of his things in the pockets.'

Pauline took it. 'Thanks very much. I'll bring it back.'

'Oh.' The nurse looked doubtful. 'I'm sure I shouldn't let you take it away.'

Pauline chanced her arm. 'No, it's OK, I've got permission.' Without giving the girl the opportunity to argue, she turned and left hurriedly. The staff nurse started to protest, then shrugged her shoulders. She had too much to do to waste time on a hospital white coat.

Pauline got Gemma back in the car, having put the wheelchair in the boot. They sat in the front together, Gemma watching intently as Pauline went through each of the pockets in turn. In the top left breast pocket was a hospital bleeper with Simon's name on it in embossed sticky tape. In the left lower pocket was a diary and some odd pieces of paper, and in the right a stethoscope and an elastic tourniquet for taking blood. Pauline looked at the things in her lap.

'That's all there is, Gemma.'

They sat and looked at the articles. Gemma picked up the diary, and held it up inquiringly. Pauline took it, went through the pages. It was a day to a page one. There was not much in it. Dates of clinical meetings, ward rounds, occasional scribbled notes about patients.

'Nothing exciting there,' she said, putting it down again. She sighed and looked out of the window. 'Perhaps someone has been here before us.'

Gemma held the coat in her lap, stroking the material absently. Suddenly she poked Pauline, pointing to the top pocket, then rolled the seam at the bottom of the pocket between her finger and thumb.

Pauline took the coat, and felt where Gemma had indicated. Her hand wouldn't go right into the narrow pocket, it was only designed to hold the bleeper. She held the pocket upside down and pulled at the material. Gemma held her good hand underneath. After a moment's shaking and working at the base, something fell out into Gemma's hand. It was a small green and pink capsule.

27

As soon as they got back to the house, Pauline made a phone call. When Simon had told her about his suspicions of the first tablets Kate had taken, she had made some inquiries about getting them analysed. Although they had disappeared before he could do anything about it, she knew who to approach now to find out what was in the two-coloured capsule.

The chemist was about twenty-five miles away, outside Southampton. Pauline announced to Gemma that she was going to take the capsule to the laboratory herself, and the younger woman insisted on going too. Pauline called her secretary and told her to put everything on 'hold' for the day, and the two of them set out soon after eleven o'clock.

* * *

On the fourth floor of the hospital, Simon was trying to use the tiny headphones that relayed the radio broadcasts. He just caught the end of the eleven o'clock news on Radio Four, and decided he would try and listen to the current affairs programme that followed; it might stop his mind from going over and over all the questions he had been asking himself since he regained consciousness, questions to which there seemed to be no answers that would give him any comfort.

He lay there with his eyes closed. The sound of the radio in his ears masked the footsteps of his latest visitor coming into the room. The touch was so delicate that the tubing gave no perceptible tug when the drip was turned off, nor did it move when a needle was pushed into the rubber section designed to be used for adding drugs to the intravenous fluid. The injected liquid passed silently into the saline solution within the tube; then, when the drip was running again, it began to work its way slowly into Simon's bloodstream. The needle was carefully withdrawn and the empty syringe slipped into a pocket.

The visitor turned to leave, but some sense — of not being alone, or perhaps the slight draught from the movement — caused Simon to open his eyes. All he saw was a white-coated back disappearing through the door. He thought he recognised the person, and wanted to call out.

He had a brief monent of puzzlement as he found he could not move his hand to close the tracheostomy hole to speak. He began to feel as if he were suffocating, but he could not draw a breath. He tried to raise his arm, reach for the bell-push, but he could not. He was possessed by a rush of terror, but tried to push it away. What was going on? He was conscious, but completely paralysed. He could not even breathe.

Confused and frightened, he thought for a moment that he must be having a nightmare — yet everything seemed so real. He tried in vain to turn his head; he could not even move his eyes. His lids drooped half over them, obscuring his vision. What the hell was happening? Was this a hysterical paralysis? His mind made a tremendous effort to cajole his unwilling muscles to do something. Anything. Breathe, move, scream. He wanted to do all these things, but could not.

By now thirty seconds had passed, and the feeling of suffocation was becoming overwhelming. He lay, completely helpless, the knowledge that he was paralysed screaming at him from his already oxygen-starved brain. In another thirty seconds or so he knew he would lose consciousness, and another ninety seconds after that his brain would suffer irreparable damage. At any time in the next minute or so after that, he would be dead.

His mind tried to summon an anguished shriek for the help that must surely be somewhere within earshot. Wasn't that a nursing trolley going past his door? The tiny muscles in his inner ear, which acted as dampers to protect the cochlea from excessive noise, were paralysed too, and so all sound was enhanced, almost painful. Yet there was no way he could attract attention. He thought he was going insane, with the desire to breathe so strong, and the need to call out so overpowering. Gradually consciousness began to fade. The fight for life between the different biochemical factions in his cytoplasm was joined in ernest, with the large dose of paralysing drug in his veins rapidly gaining the upper hand.

It was the Ward Sister Simon had heard, taking the drugs trolley to another patient farther down the corridor. She glanced into his room, through the window set in the door, as she went past. All seemed well. Or was it? She went to the door of the next room, and opened it to push the trolley inside. Something nagged at her. Something she had seen in Mr Robinson's room was not quite right. Something about his posture seemed wrong. She could not put her finger on it, but it was bothering her. She went back and looked through the window again. Her patient lay there, eyes half-closed, jaw slack, not moving. He could have been asleep, but her years of experience told her it was not the attitude of someone in natural sleep. She hurried in, saw his increasingly dusky colour, the lack of respiratory movements,

246

rang the emergency bell, and started mouth-to-mouth resusitation.

Simon's life was probably saved by a combination of the Sister's presence of mind and his tracheostomy. The anaesthetist on emergency stand-by was there in less than a minute, and although he had no idea why Simon had stopped breathing, he was able to reconnect him to the ventilator instantly, and add extra oxygen which was piped to all the rooms.

His colour was soon restored, his pulse, which was beginning to falter, grew steady again, and his blood pressure returned to normal. Although his attendants were not aware of it, he also regained consciousness, and could take in all the activity around him. It was an agonising situation, because he was still paralysed and could not let the doctors and nurses know that he was aware of what was going on. He could hear their voices, unnaturally loud, discussing his condition and trying to explain it. They were completely baffled. Pulmonary embolism, stroke, sub-arachnoid haemorrhage, were all suggested. A cardiac monitor was brought in. Simon was relieved to hear that the electro-cardiographic tracing was normal.

Meanwhile he was increasingly sensitive to the fact that he was lying there naked. As is usual in an emergency, the bed had been stripped and the patient undressed, making every area of the body visible and accessible. But now the crisis was over, at least as far as Simon was concerned, he wanted to be covered up. He wasn't prudish, but it made him feel uncomfortably vulnerable. However, he could not accuse those around him of being guilty of insensitivity, as they did not know he was awake.

His concern about his nakedness turned to alarm as he heard the doctors — there were now three present, a senior anaesthetist, a consultant physician, and Martin Benham, his surgeon — discussing what to do next. They still had no idea what had caused their patient to stop breathing. The physician wanted to do a lumbar puncture, and the others agreed. This procedure involved inserting a needle into the centre of the lower back, penetrating through a gap between the vertebral spines into the space that surrounds the spinal cord, to draw off some of the cerebrospinal fluid. It would help to confirm or eliminate some form of catastrophic stroke or brain haemorrhage as being the cause of his cessation of breathing. Simon did not want anyone sticking needles into his back, but was powerless to complain.

It was now about ten minutes from the onset of the paralysis, and another ten passed while the aseptic trolley with its sterile equipment was prepared. With the help of two nurses, Simon was rolled over onto his side and curled up into a ball to make it easier to insert the needle into his spine. He heard the nurse ask if the anaesthetist would like any local anaesthetic, customary on a conscious patient. 'No need to bother,' he replied.

The paralysing drug that Simon had been given was beginning to wear off at last, and as the needle was pushed into his back the searing pain made his muscles contract involuntarily, but feebly. The movement of his chest was enough to enable him to emit a feeble groan.

'Thank God, a response at last,' said the anaesthetist, carrying on with the procedure. Simon, realising his muscle power was returning, tried desperately to keep still. He didn't want any sudden movement to cause the needle to be plunged into his spinal column. He forced himself to bear the pain.

'Clear fluid,' the anaesthetist reported after about half a minute. 'It's not a brain haemorrhage, anyway.'

He was rolled once more onto his back, and once the paralysing chemical began to lose its effect, he rapidly regained full use of his limbs; within another ten minutes he was talking fairly normally and could breathe without the assistance of the ventilator.

All three consultants and the Sister returned to his bedside, amazed at his recovery. The doctors plied Simon with questions. He described how he had seen someone leaving the room, and then found himself paralysed. He could only guess that he had been given a curare-like drug, such as was used in anaesthetics, to have brought on these effects so quickly.

'It sounds incredible,' said Martin Benham. 'Are you suggesting that someone came in here and deliberately tried to kill you with an injection of curare?'

'What other . . . explanation is there?'

'I just don't know.' Benham scratched his head. 'Well, come on. Who do you think it was?'

Simon looked puzzled. 'I'm really not sure.' The others exchanged glances, undecided whether even to accept the possibility of attempted murder under their noses.

At the back of the group, Simon's earlier visitor stood, unnoticed. Upon hearing Simon's uncertainty as to who his assailant might be, the white-coated figure smiled, turned, and left silently.

Sister Rhodes, who was in charge of Simon's ward, insisted that the police be called, despite the scepticism of the other staff. She had been badly frightened by the incident, was only too aware that her patient had nearly died under her nose. So a member of the CID came and talked to Simon, and a young constable was posted outside the door.

While the room was full of hospital staff, Simon had been deliberately vague about the identity of his assailant. Very astutely, considering he was still suffering the aftermath of his brush with death, he realised that if he were to make known his suspicions, and

248

they were correct, the word would get round and might allow the guilty party time to cover his tracks. If he were wrong, to accuse someone publicly, a respected member of staff . . .

He was not so reticent, however, when he spoke confidentially to Detective Superintendent Barnes. Simon had his suspicions, and he voiced them.

* * *

Pauline and Gemma postponed their visit to Simon until the following day.

'Good God, man, can't I leave you alone for five minutes?'

Pauline's jovial greeting was mostly an effort to try and mask her concern about the attempt on his life.

'Sorry.' Simon played the game, made a face like a chastised schoolboy. 'I didn't mean to get into trouble.' His speech was a lot better, with further lessening of the swelling in his damaged throat.

Gemma wheeled herself near the left side of the bed and took Simon's hand. She bit her lip, then wrote:

You were nearly dead. It's not funny.

Simon looked tenderly at the girl in the wheelchair.

'No, I know it isn't. It's just a way of trying to deal with the horror of being the target of two attempts at murder in less than a week.'

Pauline looked at Gemma. 'And I hadn't told — we now know for certain it *was* an attempt to kill Simon. Urine samples showed traces of a curare-like drug that would have caused the paralysis.'

Still looking troubled, Gemma was about to write again when Simon spoke.

'But what about the analysis of the capsule?' He sat himself a little more upright. 'Isn't that what you've come to tell me about?'

'Well, now, since you ask.' Pauline made herself comfortable on the edge of the bed, opposite Gemma, holding some notes written in long-hand.

'The chemist who did the analysis was a bit cagey about committing himself. He said it was a very small sample to deal with, and he'd like to check it again.'

Simon smiled. 'A true scientist!'

'He also said he wouldn't have been able to confirm anything at all if we hadn't suggested what sort of substances we expected were present. Apparently it was quite easy to confirm one of the drugs as azathioprine.'

Gemma was writing.

But they were proper capsules. I remember Simon saying he'd checked up on them.

'Yes, but only by looking at them,' said Simon. 'I couldn't tell what was in them. They looked like the real thing — Fepregfol — iron and folic acid. I should have been more suspicious! Bloody hell! It's quite easy to open most drug capsules — you only have to try it. They're made in two halves, often not sealed together, that you can slide apart. It would be simple, if tedious and time-consuming, to change the contents.'

But those capsules were given to your wife by Mr. Greenwell, weren't they?

Simon looked at Pauline, then at Gemma. 'They were indeed.'
There was a short silence, before Pauline continued.
'The other drug — '
'So I was right. There was something else in them!'
'All right, clever clogs. Yes, there was. But it was a bit of luck that the chemist found it and was able to identify it on such a small sample.'
'Because of the clues we gave him?'
'Yes. He looked first for broad groups of drugs, that he could screen for with one test because they share identifiable common chemical radicals. He was just guessing, really, but he looked for groups of drugs that can cause thought disorders or psychotic reactions as side effects. And at the second attempt — bingo!'
'Well, come on. What was it, for Christ's sake?'
'Look, don't get too excited. Although he's pretty sure what the drugs were, it just doesn't make sense.'
'Ye Gods, Pauline! Just tell me, will you?'
'There were actually *two* other drugs, similar ones, found in proprietary treatments for Parkinson's disease.'
'Parkinson's? Which ones were they?'
Pauline looked down at a piece of paper she held in her hand, and read slowly. 'Carbidopa and Levodopa.'
'Carbi — !' Simon shook his head slowly. 'You're right. It doesn't make sense. Why on earth would anyone want to give a drug that's used for helping the shakes in old people to a young woman in pregnancy?'
'That's what the chemist said. He looked it up for me, because he didn't know much about them.'

'I must confess I don't know much about their side effects either. What did his book say?'

Pauline consulted her notes again. 'This particular combination of drugs works by increasing the amount of a chemical called dopamine in the brain. Dopamine is thought to be deficient in people suffering from Parkinson's disease, in which they develop a persistent and disabling tremor, and muscle weakness. If you have too much of it, on the other hand, you can get muscle twitching and spasm.'

'Yes, I remember that.' Simon looked puzzled. 'But Kate didn't have anything like that.'

'The chemist said something about the muscle spasm side effect being usually — ' she looked down at her notes — 'dose related. You only get it if too much is taken. He said there was only a small amount in Kate's capsules. Not enough to cause muscle spasm.'

'So what about her strange behaviour?'

'That's when he got excited. You *can* get behaviour disturbances as a side effect — sometimes serious ones.' She went back to her notes. 'Some patients exhibit psychosis, delusions and hallucinations, sometimes at small dose levels. They appear to be idiosyncratic reactions.'

Gemma immediately wrote furiously.

What does that mean?

Simon turned to her. 'It means it's an unpredictable side effect: some people won't get it however much they take, others will get it on a small dose.'

Pauline nodded. 'That would fit with Kate's case, wouldn't it? It would mean she was particularly sensitive to the possible mental effects of the drug.'

'Yes, it would fit exactly. She did seem to be getting psychotic, detached from reality. And she was certainly deluded — and hallucinating about the baby talking to her. But what I just don't understand — '

He rubbed his eyes with his hand, pinched the bridge of his nose, and the women realised he was trying to control his emotions, to think in a detached way about the death of his wife. There was a silence, charged with understanding and sympathy. Eventually he looked up, in control but clearly no nearer a solution.

'What I don't understand, is why anyone would want to give a mixture of that stuff and azathioprine to a pregnant woman.'

'Oh, Simon!' Pauline's expression was a mixture of exasperation and disappointment. 'I was relying on you to have an answer. You must have *some* idea.'

251

Simon looked from Pauline to Gemma, then nodded slightly, as if coming to an agreement with himself.

'I'll tell you the truth, girls.'

They leaned forward expectantly.

'I haven't got a bloody clue.'

28

There were no major developments over the next seven days, except that Simon got rapidly stronger. After two days, he had another blood transfusion, as his haemoglobin was still low, and that helped his physical recovery. The swelling in his throat resolved, and he was thankful to have his endotracheal tube removed and his trachcostomy closed. He could now talk normally, albeit with a slightly husky voice.

It was now two weeks since the events which had shattered his life, and despite the tonic effect of his visits from Pauline and Gemma, he had moments of utter despair. He had been put on a mild sedative, and it was no surprise to him when one afternoon he received an unsolicited visit from Piers Christiansen.

Christiansen was a Consultant Psychiatrist. He was a nice enough fellow whom Simon knew slightly from his visits to the Gynae wards to see the occasional patient with post-natal depression.

Simon found himself rather irritated by the intrusion. He had been sitting in a chair by the window, reading. Putting down his book, he watched the Consultant settle himself on the edge of the bed. He was a tall, lanky man in his mid forties, with thin black hair that he always had well greased down. Simon was not fooled by the quasi-social nature of the visit, and after a few minutes of tentative probing by the psychiatrist, he asked bluntly:

'Who sent you?'

Christiansen gave an embarrassed smile. 'Your old boss, Roger D'Arcy, asked me if I'd pop in and have a chat. Actually, they're all pretty worried about your, well, your low spirits.'

Despite his annoyance, Simon had to smile at the use of the medical euphemism for depression. 'Surely it would be abnormal if I *wasn't* in "low spirits" in the circumstances?'

'Well, yes, of course,' the psychiatrist agreed. 'But the trauma you've been through, physical and mental, is hardly within the sphere of normal human experience. Two attempts on your own life, the death of your wife, the recent, ah, difficulties you have had with your job.' He paused to study Simon's reaction, saw none. 'Then there was your involvement in the death of the Marshall girl, being a suspect and beaten up by her boyfriend, not to mention the murder of your best friend, and the burning down of your home.'

Simon felt himself getting angry. 'I'm only too well aware that I've been dragged through the shit. I don't need anyone to issue me with a catalogue of it all!'

'But it's important to talk about these things. The staff tell me you don't mention any of these troubles to them.'

'Get it all off my chest? Don't bottle it all up? Let it come to the surface? Any other hoary old counselling clichés I've missed out? Is that what you mean?' Simon turned away, clenching his jaw.

Christiansen was unperturbed. 'It's all right,' he soothed. 'I don't mind if you get angry with me. That's a good thing if — '

'For Christ's sake, Piers. I don't need that sort of condescending crap.'

This time the psychiatrist could not disguise his hurt.

'Look, old chap, I'm only trying to help. It's all too easy to make the assumption that because you're a doctor you can cope with everything life throws at you. And one's fellow professionals are just as bad. They don't like to get involved in another doctor's personal troubles. Perhaps it makes them uncomfortable, wondering how they'd manage in the same situation.'

He stood up, turned away for a moment, then back, his voice rising.

'It's not easy for me either, you know, trying to help a colleague, especially knowing the scepticism with which many of you regard my speciality.' He stopped abruptly, realising he had gone too far, been unprofessional. 'Look, I'm sorry, that was inexcusable. I'm supposed to be helping you, not getting rid of my own frustrations.'

Simon's astonishment at this outburst changed to something akin to amusement, and he could not stop himself saying, with a hint of sarcasm, 'It's all right, Piers. It's important to talk about these things.'

Christiansen's knuckles whitened as they clenched at his sides, and Simon immediately regretted scoring such an easy point.

'Sorry, Piers. That was unfair. I know you're trying to help, and helping another doctor is probably the worst thing out.' He tried his best to sound grateful. 'Look, I really appreciate your efforts. I just don't think I need psychiatric help. Of course I get depressed. Yes, I cry a bit. Of course I wish my wife were alive. But I'm not going to throw myself out of the window or take an overdose, if that's what's worrying everybody.'

Christiansen's resentment was fading. 'Glad to hear it,' he said gruffly. 'That's something positive I can write in the notes, anyway.'

In a moment of revelation so strong it made Simon's heart rise in hope, he smiled gently at the psychiatrist. 'And you can also write down that I've got my own counsellors, and they're doing me a lot of good.'

Christiansen looked up sharply in surprise. 'And who might they be?' he asked suspiciously, as if half-afraid this would be another put-down.

'You don't know them, but they're regular visitors. Pauline Jamieson and Gemma Randall.'

'Professionals?'

Simon smiled again. 'No, just friends. Very good friends.'

'Hmph! So you really don't think I can offer you anything?'

'No, not really, Piers. But thanks for trying. I know just what you mean about it not being easy trying to treat a colleague. I honestly appreciate your efforts.'

The psychiatrist stood up. 'All right, then. I suppose we might as well leave it there. If there's anything else . . .'

'Yes of course. I'll give you a call.'

Christiansen reached the door, turned as he grasped the handle. 'I nearly forgot to ask. How's the baby?'

Simon turned abruptly and stared out of the window, and the psychiatrist could see his jaw muscles working against the clenched teeth, knew he'd hit the target he'd been aiming at all through the interview. There was a long silence, until Christiansen prompted gently, 'Simon?'

Simon turned to him, his expression dark. 'I don't know. You know damn well I don't know. And don't ask me why I haven't been to see her. I don't know the answer to that either.'

'I think you ought to go and see her. She's an amazing child, Simon. I really mean that. Amazing.'

Simon was looking out of the window again, thoughts racing. Everyone kept using that same adjective. *Amazing.* And they had all been trying to persuade him to see his daughter, even Pauline and Gemma. He honestly didn't know what was stopping him. He knew it was irrational, knew this little human being was his flesh-and-blood link with Kate, should be a prize to cherish in the middle of all the mayhem and destruction. But in some strange way that he could not explain, he felt no bond with the child, no attraction strong enough to pull him out of his room and across the hallway that separated them. The emptiness he felt when he thought about the baby distressed him perhaps more than anything else, knowing how unnatural it was. Even now, distressed as he was, he knew that Christiansen had won a clever strategic battle.

The psychiatrist took no comfort from his victory, just felt genuine compassion for the man across the room struggling to keep his composure. 'Think about it, Simon, please. Go and see her.'

Simon bowed his head, then looked up again and stared out of the window.

'All right, Piers. I'll think about it.'

Dr Christiansen didn't hear. He had already closed the door softly behind him, knowing his objective had been achieved.

* * *

Simon didn't sleep well that night, despite the administration of the almost compulsory 'sleeping tablet'. He kept waking up, sweating, mouth dry, temporarily disorientated, then knowing he had been thinking, or dreaming, about seeing his daughter. Why should this be such a trial to him? He lay awake between bouts of fitful sleep, worrying, wondering again and again why he felt as he did, why he was somehow *afraid* to go and see his child.

The conflict, the indecision, was driving him mad. Even with the support he received from Pauline and Gemma, he knew he was getting more depressed, and equally he sensed that the main obstacle in his path to recovery was the baby. God! He hadn't even given the poor child a name! The nurses called her Angelica, because she was so good, so amazing — that word again . . . He'd heard them talking in the corridor outside his room, wondering why he hadn't been to see her, making him feel guilty . . .

Guilt was part of his problem. He could see that. He knew it was ridiculous, irrational . . . Nevertheless he could not avoid holding the child in some way responsible for Kate's death. It was almost as if he believed the unborn infant *had* been influencing her, telling her it wanted to come out, making Kate inflict those horrific injuries on herself, urging her to ask Simon to cut into his wife's belly and release it. Unreasonable, illogical, but the thoughts were there and they would not go away.

If he did go and see the baby, what was he afraid of?

That he would try and harm it? That others would see his hostility, sense his thoughts? He was certainly afraid that he would not be able to act out the role of loving father, to show rejoicing at this being in whose persona his wife lived on. And that was the crux of it. The real source of his fear. Going to see the child would be like a circus, of which he would be the major freak attraction. It would entail exposing his confused and fragile emotions to an avid and curious audience of fellow professionals, all agog to see how this strange man, apparently rejecting a child that should be doubly precious, would react when he set eyes upon his offspring for the first time. They would be ready to pounce on every sound, every movement, the slightest nuance to be interpreted, chewed over, spat out, redigested later. It would be like the *paparazzi* pawing over a juicy Royal scandal, their senses inflamed by the lust to gorge themselves on others' personal tragedies until —

Simon turned over, burying his head in the pillow. Moments later

256

he felt a hand resting gently on his shoulder, and the soothing voice of the Night Sister asking if there was anything she could do. Simon turned his head and looked up at her in the dim light.

'Yes, there is.' In that moment he made up his mind. He could not keep going through this torment night after night. He would go and see the baby. But only on his terms.

After breakfast the next morning he asked if he might see Sister McArthur, the sympathetic nurse on the Prem Baby Unit. She sat her spare middle-aged frame on his bedside chair whilst he told her in simple terms about the position he found himself in.

'One question,' she said when he had finished. 'Why me?'

'Because I don't know how I'm going to react. I'm *afraid* of how I'm going to react. And I don't want to go through this experience with a horde of curious strangers looking on.'

'That explains why you don't want an audience. I understand that perfectly, I have every sympathy with how you feel about that. But it still doesn't explain, why me? Why not the sister who's been in charge of your daughter ever since she went to the Research Facility? She knows all there is to know about your amazing little offspring.'

Simon sighed. 'I don't know her from Adam. I know you well enough to think you'll be matter-of-fact and supportive, but not so well that I'll feel a personal involvement.' He shook his head. 'I'm not making myself very clear, am I?'

Sister McArthur smiled at him. 'Not very. But I don't mind. You're obviously very confused about your feelings.' She patted his leg through the covers. 'I'll come with you, with pleasure, if you think it'll help.'

Simon took her hand briefly. 'Thanks. Why do you think the baby is on the fourth floor and not in your Prem Baby Unit?'

'I'm not sure. It was Mr Greenwell's idea, although I'd understood Mr D'Arcy was really in charge of the case. Something about there being some facilities in there we don't have. First I've heard of that.'

'Me too.' There was a long silence.

'Come on. Let's make some sort of decision on this. When do you want to go?'

'Right now, if that's possible. Before I start to think too much about it again and change my mind.'

Sister McArthur stood up and straightened her uniform skirt. 'I'll go and see what I can do.'

'Sister?' Simon sounded tentative.

'Yes, doctor?'

'I'm sorry to be making all this fuss about one visit to my own child.'

'Don't worry about it. The circumstances are hardly normal.'

'And what about the baby? Is that normal? No one has said it isn't, but they all use the same word when they talk about her.'

The nurse looked puzzled. 'What word is that?'

'You used it yourself just now. Amazing.'

She looked thoughtful. 'Yes, you're right. I did.'

'So? What's so phenomenal about her? It could mean so many things. Amazing something so deformed could still live? Amazing the way it's not having prem fits? Amazing how its lungs collapse when they turn the ventilator off?'

McArthur shook her head. 'No. None of those things. Nothing so negative. All positive. Amazing how fast she's growing. Amazing how she responds to her nurses. The sounds she makes. The way she follows you with her eyes. The way she smiles.'

Simon looked astounded. 'Smiles?' He sounded incredulous, then derisive. 'Smiles? Don't be ridiculous! Babies that premature can't possibly smile — or show any response — or open their eyes, let alone look around. The staff up there must be fantasising.'

'Well, that's what they're saying, and you must agree that "amazing" would fit the bill if any of it's true.'

'"Unbelievable" would be more like it. Have you yourself seen any of this?'

She took off her thick spectacles and gave them a quick wipe, giving herself a moment to consider. 'No, I must admit I haven't. But all the nurses are talking about it.'

'And you believe them?'

'Why shouldn't I? But I can't be sure.' She opened the door, turned back to him. 'I think it's time we found out for ourselves.'

Together they set out across the hallway of the fourth floor. He waited in the large area between the private wing and the double doors to the Meadowmead Foundation Research Facility, while the thin, lanky form of the nurse went inside. He felt a stranger, out of place, standing there in a dressing-gown and slippers instead of his white coat. Such a simple symbol of authority in hospitals, he thought, the white coat. Without his, he had some insight into how patients must feel in this unfamiliar environment – vulnerable and exposed.

After a minute or so a nursing sister, a staff nurse, and two third-year student nurses came out of the Research Facility. They gave Simon some curious and rather resentful glances as they crossed the hallway, before going into the staff room on the private wing side. Simon waited until the door closed behind them, then went to the double doors. He was about to enter when he heard a raised and angry voice. He recognised it immediately. It was Jeremy Greenwell.

'I don't care!' he was saying. 'I'm not leaving that man alone in here with that baby. Do I make myself clear, Sister?'

'But, sir, he won't be alone. That's why I'm here.'

258

'Ha! What difference do you think that'll make?'

Sister McArthur was using her most persuasive tone. 'But Mr D'Arcy agreed, and so did Mr Benham. And Dr Christiansen thought it was a very good idea.'

'Bloody psychiatrists. What the hell do they know about premature babies?'

'It's Mr Robinson they are concerned about, sir.'

'The man ought to be locked up. That's what he needs.'

'Shall I get the District General Manager's office on the phone, sir? I know the doctors did clear this with Mr Featherstone.'

'You — you impertinent — ' Greenwell was shouting now, and Simon heard his footsteps just in time to step back from the door and avoid being slammed in the face by it. Greenwell stormed out without seeing Simon, who was hidden by the open door, and went down the emergency stairs, too impatient to wait for the lift.

Simon was still standing there, ashen-faced, when Sister McArthur came looking for him. She was as flushed as Simon was pale.

She tried to sound calm and composed. 'It's all right. You can come in now.'

'I — I'm really sorry. I shouldn't have got you into this.'

'That's as maybe,' she said briskly, 'but we're here now and we might as well get on with it before his Lordship comes back.' She smoothed her skirt, patted her flat bosom, and, lifting her chin in a mixture of pride and defiance, ushered Simon through the doors and closed them firmly behind her.

'The baby's in here.' She indicated a half-panelled glass door. Simon went up to it and looked into the small room. All he could see was the perspex dome and associated attachments of the most complex-looking incubator he had ever seen. He opened the door, but Sister held his arm.

'We must gown up first, Mr Robinson.'

By the door were two stainless steel dispensers attached to the wall, and from these they each took a mask and a paper cap. On a small glass-topped trolley nearby were packs containing surgical gowns, and these they donned too, helping each other tie them at the back.

They returned to the door, and after the briefest hesitation Simon went inside, Sister McArthur at his shoulder. He went up to the incubator, his eyes sweeping over the assortment of tubes, pipes, oxygen delivery systems, humidity controllers, dials, gauges, and two oscilloscopes, before finally resting on the naked object that was the focus of all this technology.

He drew in his breath sharply, and looked up at Sister McArthur standing beside him. Although he could only see her eyes above the mask, he could tell she was registering surprise. Simon looked back at his daughter, and the adjective 'amazing' at once leaped to mind. He had expected to see an incredibly thin, wizened creature, which is what very premature babies usually look like. Yet here was this infant, well-covered, pink, a fuzz of blonde hair — strange, he thought, neither he nor Kate was blonde — moving actively as it lay on its back, its little arms waving in the air in front of its face, and — yes, the eyes *were* open, seeming to watch the tiny hands moving before them.

There were two electrodes attached to the baby's chest, and a ventilator tube was attached to its neck, the machine that was assisting the breathing wheezing and whirring gently at the side of the incubator. There was also a thin naso-gastric tube taped to one side of the face and bending its way into the left nostril.

Simon had seen worse-looking specimens at full term. The only thing that belied the baby's prematurity was its size. It was certainly tiny, but surely more like 30 weeks than 24, which is what Sister McArthur told him was the child's equivalent birth weight.

The nurse broke the silence. 'I can hardly believe it's the same one. It seems to have grown six weeks' worth in a fortnight.'

Simon froze, the hairs on his neck bristling. The baby seemed to hear the voice, turned her head towards them, and the deep blue eyes set in the disproportionately large head looked from one to the other of the faces peering in through the perspex.

A hand gripped his arm so fiercely it made him jump, but he didn't turn away. He heard Sister McArthur's voice, hoarse with tension.

'Did you see that? Or did I just imagine that she heard me?'

'It has to be impossible.' Simon found himself whispering his reply. 'It must have been a coincidence.' The hand eased its grip, and the nurse moved slowly away from Simon. The baby's eyes seemed as if they were going to follow the movement, but then flicked back to Simon, staring at him, unblinking.

Sister McArthur continued to move round the incubator until she was on the opposite side. She looked across at Simon, then back at the tiny human form. She cleared her throat gently, then spoke loudly and clearly.

'Hello, Angelica.'

There was no mistaking the sudden turn of the head towards the sound, this time accompanied by a scrawny hand reaching out in the direction from which it came.

Simon and the nurse looked at each other, astounded, trying to grasp what they were witnessing. Simon shook his head and turned away.

'This is crazy. Am I having some sort of nightmare?'

'Not unless we're both having one.'

Simon turned back to the nurse. 'But a *full term* baby can't do that.'

'We were warned this was no ordinary baby.'

Simon rubbed his eyes wearily, then looked up, anxiety creasing his face. 'This isn't how it's meant to be. All I'm doing is assessing the child's development. Why aren't I — ?' He rubbed his face with his hand again.

Sister McArthur came round to him, put her hand gently on his arm. 'Come on, tell me. Why aren't you what?'

Simon looked at her, his expression almost desperate. 'I knew I'd be like this.'

'Like what?' A trace of exasperation.

'I ought to be going "ooh" and "aah", feeling proud, feeling love, feeling protective — or at least emotional in some way.' He looked at the incubator, then back to Sister McArthur. 'But I'm not. All I feel is — ' He paused, swallowed.

'Go on, say it.'

'All I feel is a kind of detached professional curiosity, and — and a sort of fear. When I saw her turn and look at us, I didn't feel wonder and joy — I felt fear.' He was shaking, his voice rising. 'I must be some sort of weirdo. What's wrong with me?'

'There's nothing wrong with you. I felt it too — a sort of — anxiety. It's so unnatural for a prem to be so active. One *should* be thinking of it as something good, and yet it seems — well — wrong.'

Simon regarded her steadily. 'Good try, Sister.'

'Look, I'm not trying to humour you. I usually get all maternal and broody myself, and — ' She saw Simon's eyebrows go up. 'Don't laugh, I'm not that old. But I do feel protective of all the little waifs, as I call them, in the Prem Unit.' She glanced at the incubator. The baby seemed to be watching them, as if listening intently to their conversation. 'But this one so far just gives me the creeps.'

Simon looked at the floor. 'Yes. I see.'

Sister McArthur touched his arm again. 'I'm sorry. I shouldn't have said that about your daughter.'

There was a silence, broken only by the gently rhythmic hum of the ventilator.

'It's all right. That's part of the trouble. I don't *feel* as if she's my daughter.'

'You — er — haven't any reason to doubt that she *is* your daughter, have you?' That would explain a lot, thought the nurse.

Simon looked directly at her. 'No. No reason whatsoever. I almost wish there were. It would make everything a lot easier.'

At that moment the baby gave a cry, and began moving its arms and legs in an unco-ordinated fashion that seemed to convey frustration. Simon and Sister McArthur watched with increasing astonishment as the hand actions became more purposeful, making grasping movements in the air in front of her face. The miniature appendages appeared to be trying to grab something close in front,

261

which on one attempt seemed to result in a poke in its own eye. The movements stopped for a moment, then began again, more slowly, carefully. One tiny hand found the naso-gastric tube taped to the side of her face, and made a small fist around it. The other hand came across and gripped the tube in the same fashion.

The two observers were now totally absorbed in this activity, mesmerised by a display of hand-eye co-ordination that should be completely impossible. And there was more to come.

Gently at first, but then more strongly, the baby made a series of tugging movements on the tube. Now, as she repeated the action, she turned her head away from the tube, to get more purchase on the tape attaching it to the side of her face. Simon and Sister McArthur exchanged a rapid questioning glance as they both realised what this remarkable little creature was trying to do.

Slowly the tape began to detach from the skin of the face, pulling the delicate flesh of the cheek out of shape.

Two more tugs, and the tape was free, and the tube with it. Almost without hesitation, the baby began pulling on the tube, let go with both hands, grasped again, pulled, repeating the action until within a few moments the end of the thin tube slipped out of her nose. She held the end of the tube in front of her face, looking at it, following it as it waved about in front of her eyes. With a deliberate action, she placed the tube in her mouth, and began to suck on it vigorously. After three attempts to suck some nourishment through the tubing with no success, she let it go, began to let out a series of plaintive cries, and went red in the face.

Simon was trembling, and when he turned to speak to Sister McArthur he could see she was pale and had beads of perspiration on her face above her mask.

'Good God! Did that really happen?'

The nurse blinked the sweat from her eyes. 'That baby knew its food came from the naso-gastric tube! It knew! So it took it out and tried to suck milk through it!' The baby was still crying, red-faced, waving its arms and kicking its legs in frustration.

'Hadn't we better give it something?' asked Simon.

'Well, I don't know.' The nurse went round the incubator to the trolley which held the case notes and input and output charts, looked through them.

'She's on hourly feeds.' She picked up a small plastic container. 'This is the formula, here.'

Her finger ran down one of the charts. 'She should have been fed a quarter of an hour ago. They must have just been going to feed her when we turned up.'

'I suppose we'd better call the others back.' Simon turned towards the door.'

262

'No, wait. I want to try and feed her. I've never seen anything like this in my life. Do you mind?'

'No, go ahead. But there's not much point in putting the tube back if she can just pull it out again, is there?'

'No, I agree.' She reached onto the lower shelf of the trolley. 'They've got some sterile feeder bottles here. I'm going to try that.'

McArthur picked up a small polycarbonate feeding bottle with tiny teat attached, sealed in a clear cellophane wrapper. Setting it down on another clean trolley, she went to a sink and thoroughly washed her hands, drying them on a disposable sterile towel. Returning to the feeder, she removed the wrapper and expertly twisted off the teat, poured some of the formula in, then replaced the teat.

There are various ways of gaining access to an incubator, all designed to avoid having to open the lid and so avoid sudden changes in temperature and humidity, and prevent the access of contaminants and bacteria. On this machine there were two apertures in the side, one for each hand, each covered by a flexible rubber diaphragm. By inserting a hand between the overlapping layers of the diaphragm, an arm could reach inside, the soft rubber forming a seal around it.

Sister McArthur soon had both hands inside the incubator, one holding the feeder bottle. She had anticipated that even this remarkable infant might not manage to get the hang of using a teat, but she was wrong. Within moments the baby was sucking vigorously and swallowing down the formula.

Simon looked on from the other side of the incubator. 'That is just incredible. No trouble at all.'

Sister McArthur thought the baby was taking the feed too fast, and withdrew the teat. Immediately the infant tried to grab the bottle held near it.

The Sister spoke soothingly to the child, her anxieties about this unusual little mite temporarily forgotten. 'Not too fast, my tiny waif. Take it easy.'

The baby turned towards her, listening.

'That's right. Just a little rest.' She stroked the side of the baby's face gently with the back of her first finger. 'Is it nice, then?'

The infant looked from the bottle, then back to Sister McArthur. Slowly, unmistakably, it gave her a broad smile.

The nurse almost dropped the feeder, eyes wide in astonishment. 'Well, well. So you *can* smile!'

Simon found himself wanting to laugh. 'So it bloody well can! God, she *is* amazing!' The baby's grin was infectious, seeming to remove any sinister connotations about her precocity. Sister McArthur was laughing now, too. The baby's grin faded, then came again as the bottle was moved within reach. The tiny hands guided the teat into her mouth.

'Come on, why don't you try?' Sister nodded at the feeding bottle.

Simon barely hesitated. 'All right, I will.' He went to the sink and scrubbed, then, when Sister McArthur withdrew her arms, he took the bottle and inserted his own hands into the incubator. He carefully manipulated the teat until it was near the baby's mouth, and once again the tiny hands guided the teat home. She began to suck contentedly, and Simon was aware of a feeling of tenderness rising in him. He spoke gently, his mouth near the perspex.

'Hello, little one.' The baby stopped sucking, listening. Simon looked up at Sister, could tell from her eyes that she was smiling at him. He smiled in response, then turned back to the still attentive baby. 'Hello,' he soothed again. 'This is your father speaking.'

The baby turned its head to one side so that the teat came out of its mouth. Simon moved the feeder away a little to see his daughter's face more clearly, waiting expectantly for the smile he was sure would follow.

The baby's mouth slowly began to change. But not into a smile. There was a sound almost like a snarl, and the face contorted into an expression that to Simon conveyed only one emotion: malevolence. He felt a shudder shake him as his head swam. He knew he had seen that expression before. In his dreams. And on Gemma Randall's scan.

29

'Are you sure you didn't imagine it?'

Pauline sat in the chair by Simon's bed, Gemma in her wheelchair the other side.

'Quite sure. Ask Sister McArthur. She saw it, too.'

'I already have. She says she *thinks* she saw it, but it didn't really have a chance to register because you passed out on her.'

'I passed out because of the shock,' Simon said, sounding defensive.

'Your surgeon says it was because you tried to do too much too soon.'

'Rubbish! It's been two weeks. I ought to be leaving hospital.'

'I don't think they'll be too keen on that.'

'Why not?'

'Well, for one thing, you've nowhere to go. What's left of your house is quite uninhabitable.'

Gemma wrote a message:

Can't Simon come and stay with us?

'Well, I don't know about that.' Pauline thought for a moment, then laughed. 'I suppose I could always put a sign up. "Jamieson Convalescent Home!"'

'Don't even think about it. I couldn't impose on you any more than I have already.'

Gemma finished writing again and handed the message to Pauline.

I know it's not for me to say, but there is a spare bedroom.

'Yes, that's true. We do have room.'

Simon looked embarrassed. 'No, really, I couldn't.'

'Don't you fancy our company, then?' said Pauline with mock hurt.

Simon reddened. 'No. Of course it's not that.'

'What, then?'

'I — don't know. It just doesn't seem right. I'd be taking advantage.'

265

Please, Simon!!

Pauline held up her hands. 'Whoa, hold it. I tell you what — we'll both think about it. I can't see any reason why you can't stay, at least for a bit when you come out of hospital. But we'll have a few days to consider the idea, so — we'll wait and see, OK?'

'OK.'

O. K.

'Now, to go back to what we were talking about. Apart from the funny look you say she gave you, why do you think Angelica is so far advanced in her development?' They had all seemed to slip naturally into calling the baby by that name.

'I just don't know. The whole sequence of events is so extraordinary. If anything, what with the drugs and prematurity, I'd have thought some sort of retarded development was likely. But it's as though everything has been accelerated, right from the moment of conception — and we don't even know for sure when that was.' Simon looked down at the floor, the implied intimacy of that statement causing him momentary discomfiture with the two women. He took a deep breath, then continued.

'Yes, it *is* as though everything has speeded up. When the foetus should have been only six weeks, the scan said twelve. A couple of weeks later it appeared to be a sixteen-week size, and then when the baby was delivered it was a twenty-two to twenty-four week birthweight equivalent. And now, a fortnight after birth, it's like a thirty-week prem in size, but behaving like a two- or three-month-old baby born at full term.'

Are they doing tests on her?

'Yes, so I'm told.' Simon managed to smile at Gemma. 'Apparently she's caused quite a stir. They're checking growth hormone levels, thyroid function, anything that might have an effect on growth and development. So far, it seems there's nothing abnormal.'

Pauline felt she had to ask. 'When are you going to see Angelica again?'

Simon looked uncomfortable. 'I, um — ' He avoided their eyes, looked out of the window at the darkening sky. 'Right now, I'm not sure that I want to.'

* * *

The next week saw Simon's wounds continuing to heal well, and physically he became much stronger. His mental state still gave some cause for concern, partly because the excursion to his daughter had rather back-fired. Instead of removing guilt and forging a bond, it had introduced new anxieties and further feelings of culpability.

Thanks largely to Pauline and Gemma, however, the doctors and nursing staff noted that he was calmer and seemed to be sleeping better. It was clear to everyone, including Simon himself, that it was time to consider his discharge from hospital.

Following a discusson with his surgeon, Martin Benham, and the psychiatrist, Piers Christiansen, it was Pauline who was given the task of broaching the subject.

'They're planning to throw you out,' she announced when she came to visit him on his twentieth day in hospital.

Simon wasn't sure if she was joking. 'What? Straight out on the street?'

She suppressed a smile. 'That is rather up to you.'

'Meaning?'

'Meaning that it depends on whether you want to take up my kind offer of accommodation at the Jamieson Retreat for Homeless Invalids, or not.'

'You're serious about that, aren't you?'

'Yes. Gemma and I talked it over, and — '

'Where is Gemma?' Simon was so used to them visiting together, it felt strange without her.

'She's having some extra physiotherapy. There's been just a flicker of movement in her right hand, and she wants to work on it. It was a toss-up, though, between that and coming to see you.'

'That's terrific — about her hand, I mean. What about the leg?'

'That's just the same. Now, don't try and change the subject. Gemma and I are both happy with the idea. So — are you coming or not?'

Simon stood up and walked to the window, absently exercised his injured arm.

'It seems such an imposition. You may well joke about it, but thanks to me you've already got one handicapped person to worry about.'

'What do you mean, thanks to you?'

'I'm responsible for the state she's in.'

'Now don't let's go down that road again. And *you're* not handicapped.'

'Maybe not physically, but I'll be a liability just the same.' He sat wearily on the bed.

'For Christ's sake, Simon, stop putting yourself down. You ought to know me by now — I wouldn't be asking you just to be an altruist. I *want* you to come.'

'I don't deserve it.'

'Bullshit!'

Simon looked up at her in surprise, then gave her a weak smile.

'Such language for a lady in the legal profession.'

'I'm not practising law now. And stop being such a pious drip.'

He looked hurt. 'Honestly Pauline. I just want — '

'Do you want to come to stay at my place or not?'

'I really think I'm — '

'Yes or no, Simon.'

He sensed the hardness in her tone, knew the exasperation was born of a genuine desire to help him. He knew he was vacillating, but every decision seemed so hard, lately.

'Pauline, I — '

'Yes or no?'

He looked away, took a deep breath, let it out slowly.

'Yes. Please.'

'Thank God for that! Jesus, that was hard work.' She sounded angry, but when Simon looked up at her she was grinning with pleasure.

'You're a strange woman, Miss Jamieson.'

'And you're a bloody funny bloke, Dr Robinson — sorry, *Mr* Robinson. Come on. Chuck your things in a bag and let's go.'

'Hadn't we better clear it with Martin Benham? And what about the discharge procedure?'

Pauline reached in her bag and waved a brown envelope.

'All done. Cleared from the Almighty down.'

'You cunning devil. What if I'd said no?'

'I would have torn the papers up into a hundred pieces under your nose, thrown them out the window, and you would have followed.'

He looked up at the heavens. 'Oh Lord, what have I let myself in for?'

'If you don't get moving, it'll be another week before you find out!' She went to the door, opened it. 'We, sir, are leaving.'

'I'm sorry to contradict you, madam,' said a male voice from the corridor, 'but for the moment I would like Mr Robinson to stay where he is.'

The owner of the voice stepped into the room. It was Detective Superintendent Barnes.

Simon's cheerful mood vanished in an instant, and, white-faced, he sat back on the bed. Pauline looked from the police officer to Simon and back again.

'What's going on?'

'I'd like to have a word with Mr Robinson, Miss Jamieson. If you don't mind.'

'What's happened now? Why can't I leave?' Simon looked at Pauline for support.

'You can't detain him, you know. And if you wish to talk to him, as his legal representative I must insist on being present.'

'I'm sorry, doctor, Miss Jamieson, I haven't presented this very well.' He put the black attaché case he was carrying on the bed. 'I'm not here for anything to your client's detriment.'

'What are you here for, then?' Pauline was getting angry.

'Please, give me a chance. And don't be so hostile.'

'Mr Robinson is about to leave hospital after three weeks recovering from serious injuries, and you walk in saying he can't go. That isn't exactly designed to make us feel happy.'

The detective looked distinctly uncomfortable.

'I've said I'm sorry.' He took out his handkerchief and dabbed perspiration from his upper lip. 'Can I start again? What I've come for is your help.'

'You want our help!' Pauline raised her hands in perplexity, then let them drop to her sides. 'Funny way of going about it.'

Simon could see Barnes' discomfort, and recalled the sympathetic hearing he had been given after the curare poisoning incident. He'd liked him then, and was anxious to try and get back on the right footing.

'It's OK, Pauline. I think we should hear what the Superintendent has to say.'

'Thank you, doctor. This may take a little while, and that's why I hoped you might delay your departure from the hospital for a bit. More informal than the station, I'm sure you'd agree.' He managed a smile. 'Shall we all sit down?'

Simon and Pauline sat on the bed, and Barnes sat in the room's only chair, facing them, placing his briefcase on the floor and opening it. He took out a sheaf of papers, put them on his lap, and rested his hands on top.

'First of all, I should tell you that early this morning we arrested a Consultant in Obstetrics and Gynaecology from this hospital — Mr Jeremy Greenwell.'

Pauline looked at him in astonishment, but Simon merely nodded, as if he were expecting it.

'Did he confess to being the one to give me the curare overdose?'

'No, doctor, as yet he has not confessed to anything.'

It was Simon's turn to look surprised. 'Why did you arrest him, then?'

'He was caught breaking and entering a property in Bournemouth. The property belonged to Miss Gillian Ravensbourne, now deceased.'

'He broke into Ravensbourne's flat? Whatever for?'

'We have reason to believe he was looking for these documents —' He patted the papers in his lap — 'which were found in his possession at the time of his arrest.'

'How did you manage to catch him?' asked Pauline. 'Did you have a tip-off?'

'No, Miss, we have had the property under discreet surveillance, following the unusual circumstances of Dr Ravensbourne's death.' He was observed slipping through the main entrance, behind another visitor and we followed him upstairs.'

'And you saw Greenwell break in, looking for those?' Simon pointed at the documents.

'These, and some tapes which we have not yet had the chance to transcribe fully.'

Simon shook his head. 'What the bloody hell did he think he was doing?'

'He looked for, and found, a floor safe. Our men had previously searched the place, but it was hidden under a bedroom carpet.'

'And what,' asked Pauline, sitting up on the bed and drawing her knees under her, 'is so important about this stuff?' She pointed at the documents.

'That,' replied Barnes smiling, 'is where we hope Mr Robinson can help us.'

'Why, what's in them?' Simon leaned forward, full of interest.

'A lot of medical jargon and terminology that doesn't mean much to us, I'm afraid.'

Pauline was puzzled. 'Just a minute. Shouldn't this be a matter for your police surgeon?'

'He's on leave. We showed it to the chap who stands in when the official doctor is away. He's an elderly fellow, retired, just does it to help out now and again. He took one look at it and said it was too technical for him. But he did say parts of it concerned gynaecology and foetuses — so we thought of you.'

'Is this strictly regular? Bringing such important evidence for us to see?'

'We don't know that it is important evidence yet. I'm not asking you officially as an expert witness or anything, especially after the curare business, but I'd very much like a brief run-down on what you think all this medical mumbo-jumbo is about. Off the record.' He looked earnestly at Simon. 'I'm really asking you a personal favour. Unofficially.'

'Simon turned to Pauline. 'You're my solicitor. What do you think?'

'I can't see any harm in it.' She grinned. 'Besides, I'm too damn curious.'

'So am I.' He held out his hand. 'Let's have a look.'

Simon read for nearly twenty minutes. He was quickly absorbed, and did not say much, restricting his communications to an occasional expletive, whistles, and sucking through his teeth, which only served to inflame the curiosity of his two onlookers. At one point he swore under his breath, slammed the papers down, and muttered, 'The bastard!' before resuming his reading. Eventually he reached the last page, when he became more upset. He put the papers down slowly, his hands trembling, then covered his face. His voice was quiet, but harsh with anger, shaking with emotion.

'The lousy, conniving, heartless, murdering bastards.'

His body shook, but no sound came. Pauline got up, moved in front of him, and put a hand on each shoulder. Simon leaned towards her, and she took him in her arms, his face against her breasts. She stroked his hair, and when he seemed to have become calmer, spoke softly.

'Can you tell us about it now?'

Simon did not lift his head. His voice was muffled, but intelligible.

'I'll tell you one thing. That baby up there — it's not mine. Or Kate's.'

30

It took some time for Simon to compose himself, the Superintendent discreetly keeping in the background. Although he and Pauline were desperate to hear more, they agreed to Simon's request to go to Pauline's home first. He wanted to get away from the hospital, he told them, and to have time to work out how best to present what he had learnt.

Forty minutes later, refreshed with tea and toast, they were sitting in Pauline's comfortable sitting-room. Gemma was back from her physio, in her wheelchair. Pauline was on the sofa, and Simon and Superintendent Barnes were each in an easy chair. Barnes now had a small tape recorder, which he'd collected from the police station on his way across town.

'Christ, where to begin?' said Simon when they were all settled. He looked at the policeman. 'I'm sure there's a lot more I would need to know to explain the whole story, but I'll give you a simplified run-down of what's been going on as best I can, from all this.' He held up Ravensbourne's papers, then put them across his knees.

'Just do the best you can, doctor — and don't worry about the tape,' Barnes assured him, reaching down to switch it on. 'I've no intention of using this in evidence, it's just so I can go over it afterwards, saves me slowing you down by taking notes.'

Simon started to talk, and he and his audience formed a small circle of intense concentration.

'Gillian Ravensbourne worked for a time in the States, I found that out the night — the night it all happened. She worked in a very specialised unit, where they were doing research into genetic engineering. She wrote a paper about it that was published in a high-powered medical journal, so she must have been something of an expert in her field. It was there she learned about manipulating genes and chromosomes, and basically that's what she — and Greenwell — have been doing in the Research Facility on the fourth floor.'

'Do you mind if we interrupt?' Pauline sounded apologetic.

'No, of course not.'

'Well, what's the difference between a gene and a chromosome?'

'Oh, yes, sorry. If I say anything you don't understand, for heaven's sake say so.' Simon looked up, trying to fashion his answer.

'Chromosomes are long chains of complex molecules that carry all the information necessary to programme the activity of body cells. They are found in a mass in the nucleus of a cell, except when the cell divides, when they separate out into long, thin strands — they are actually spirals which can be seen under a high-power light microscope. The information they carry is amazing, both in its quantity and its complexity. Everything from what type of cell that particular one will become, and what particular function it will carry out, to more general characteristics of the whole being, such as how tall it will grow, what colour eyes, hair, and so on.'

'Yes, I think I've heard about chromosomes, but what about genes?'

Simon smiled at Pauline. 'OK, I'm coming to that. Each strand of the complex spiral of the chromosomes is divided up into a huge number of tiny segments. Each segment is identifiable, but now you need an electron microscope. And each segment carries one or more sets of specific instructions. The sequence of genes on a chromosome is a bit like a computer program, designed to carry out a complex series of instructions. Let's take colour of eyes, for example. When fertilisation takes place between a sperm and an ovum, that starts off the process of making a new human being. The two lots of genes are combined.' He took a sip of his mug of tea.

'You mean they get all mixed up?' Barnes was anxious to see where all this was leading, but wanted to be sure he understood.

'Not at random. Let's try a simplified example. If there's a gene, or instruction if you like, for brown eyes in one parent's chromosomes, and one for blue eyes in the other, the blue eyes are usually a weaker signal, suppressed by the gene for brown eyes. The child will probably have brown eyes. Sometimes it doesn't work properly. I have seen people with one brown eye and one blue, or mixed colours in the same eye. But generally it works pretty well. The same system can work for colour of skin, size of feet, size of brain, intelligence. Are you with me?'

'Near enough,' said Pauline, and Gemma nodded her understanding.

'Superintendent?'

'Yes, I think I've got it — and I have an inkling already where you're going.'

'All right. Now we come to genetic engineering. This is increasingly an area of advanced research, some of which is now actually put into use, in the world of animals used for food production — and the same principles are applied in the plant world. Let's take another simplified example. Say you want to improve the growth rate and ultimate size of a steer, for beef. If you can make it grow bigger more quickly, it'll be worth more, and you realise your profit sooner. It is possible to identify the genes in the animal's chromosomes that are responsible for growth rate and size. It is even possible to detach those genes, and insert them into another cell. If that cell is fertilised and grows into another animal, it will incorporate those sought-after characteristics. You would get a breed of "super cow".'

'Has that actually been done?' asked Pauline.

''Yes, though not yet with very dramatic or widely available results. But I don't think it'll be that long before you could have fast-growing four-legged chickens, if you wanted, so you could sell more drumsticks!'

The others laughed at the image this conjured up.

'And it's certainly been done in the plant world, with strains of super fast-growing disease-resistant rice, and in bacteriology, where scientists can make bacteria produce specific valuable chemicals, or even vaccines. One readily available vaccine for Hepatitis B is produced by genetic engineering already.'

'It sounds like pure science fiction to me,' said the Superintendent.

'A few years ago it would have been. But not now.'

Gemma, who had been quiet and thoughtful, was writing. She held up her message.

And Ravensbourne has been Experimenting doing this with humans?

There was a silence. Simon licked his lips, swallowed, and looked around the three faces.

'Yes.'

Pauline made a sharp intake of breath.

'That — that baby in the incubator — is it the result of one of her experiments?'

Simon looked at the carpet for a moment before facing her. He spoke softly.

'It looks like it, yes.'

Barnes paled momentarily. 'For God's sake! How the hell can that be? I mean — you and Mrs Robinson were — that is, you must have known . . .' He looked helplessly at the others. 'I'm sorry. But you know what I'm trying to say.'

'Yes, I do, and I'm sure I know how it was done. But first . . .' He held the papers up and tapped them. ' . . . we've got to go into a bit more background. It looks as though when she was in the States, Ravensbourne mastered the techniques required to identify and extract genes. She was working with animals — chimpanzees mostly — but the principles are exactly the same. When I was in hospital I tried to find out a lot more about what she did there. I got copies of some journals, and read the papers. What generated all the interest was that she had identified the human gene — or rather genes, it was a

274

closely related group — that were responsible for intelligence. One of her co-workers then isolated the gene responsible for growth rate. Soon after that, she came back to the UK.' Simon's brow furrowed. 'I did find out one other thing from her paper in the journal. In the little personal profile about the author, it mentioned she had married while in North America.'

'And must have brought her husband back over here. Gwyn Reece was in trouble with the husband, remember?' said Pauline. 'Was he working with her on this genetic engineering stuff?'

'I don't think so.' Simon indicated the documents. 'It seems quite clear from these that she was working with Jeremy Greenwell.'

'Greenwell!' Pauline frowned. 'I suppose that's not a great surprise, now. Except that Greenwell is a Catholic. How could he let himself get involved with this? Did she have some sort of hold over him?'

Barnes looked uncomfortable, and coughed. 'I, ah, think I can help there. This is off the record, of course, but one thing we did learn from the papers in the Ravensbourne woman's flat was that there is indeed a strong connection between them. To be precise, they are — were — father and daughter.' He sat back while this new information sank in.

'Ravensbourne was Greenwell's daughter?' Simon's surprise was quickly suppressed as he considered the implications. 'He must be very cool, or very callous. He's been coming into the hospital as usual, not showing any distress about his daughter's death or saying a word about his personal tragedy.'

'From what we've heard already, I should think he would want to keep their association quiet at all costs,' Pauline suggested.

Simon nodded in agreement. 'I've told you this already, Superintendent, but now I'm even more certain: it was Greenwell who tried to poison me with curare — and there's a further motive from what you've just said. I survived, his daughter didn't. He probably wanted to even the score.'

Gemma held up a question:

But what exactly did ~~she~~ they do?

'I'm coming to that, Gemma. You've all heard of test-tube babies?' Simon looked round and they all nodded. 'In the simplest terms, this is where an egg is taken from an ovary, mixed with spermatozoa to fertilise it, and then placed in the mother's womb, where with luck it will implant and develop as a normal pregnancy. The name "test-tube baby" is really very misleading. It rather suggests the foetus grows into some recognisable form before it's put back in the mother, whereas it is simply a tiny spherical clump of cells that have divided a few times, and it all happens within hours of fertilisation. It's possible to let the fertilised ovum go on dividing, and such embryo research is carried out on "spare" eggs. But it's not permitted to allow the embryo to grow beyond the fourteen-day stage — even that has been disputed — and then the embryo must be destroyed, not implanted.'

'Is it possible to check if anyone keeps embryos for longer?' asked Pauline.

'No. There's no effective policing system. In a large laboratory you couldn't get away with it anyway. Too many people involved. But if just two people were working together . . .'

'Like Ravensbourne and Greenwell . . .'

'Exactly. Ravensbourne had all the facilities she needed to manipulate the genes, and the knowledge to do it. Her father could get hold of eggs and spermatozoa from patients under the guise of perfectly legitimate investigations. They were then producing embryos and keeping them for four weeks or more — and they were no ordinary embryos, either.'

Simon's mouth was dry. He took another sip of his tea, which by now was almost cold. He hardly noticed.

'What Ravensbourne was doing was selecting the segments of chromosomes responsible for both intelligence and growth rate, then injecting them with an instrument called a micropipette into egg cells so they had a double or triple dose, and then fertilising them. She found that as a result of the extra genes, the growth rate was incredibly fast, and that brain tissue development was well ahead of what was expected. So she started looking around for women to implant them in.'

'It seems obvious that Kate was "selected". And Gemma, too?' Pauline said.

Simon nodded.

'You're not suggesting that they *agreed* to this?'

Gemma started to shake her head wildly, banging her good hand repeatedly on the arm of her wheelchair as she did so.

'No, no, of course not.' Simon got up and crossed to Gemma, kneeling beside her. 'It's all right, Gemma, don't worry. No one is suggesting you knew anything about what was going on. I'll explain it all to you, and then you'll see.'

Gemma quickly became calmer, and Simon gave her a tissue so she could wipe her eyes.

'All right now?'

She nodded, gave him a weak smile.

Simon resumed his seat. 'Ravensbourne and Greenwell both knew they would never get consent for such a programme from anyone.'

276

Barnes spoke for the first time in a while. 'Who has the authority to give permission for things like test-tube babies?'

'The General Medical Council lays down guidelines. Then each district has a Local Ethical Committee to consider any research programme that involves patients. Ravensbourne's scheme would have been thrown out without discussion. So they decided to do their "research" opportunistically. If Greenwell had a patient coming in for something minor, like Gemma's cervical polyp — '

'Or Kate's investigations for infertility.' Pauline's interest was growing in intensity, and she could hardly contain her impatience.

'That's right — then they would schedule the patient for the private wing theatre under some pretext, like not wanting to hold up the main theatre at the end of a long list. Greenwell and Ravensbourne would do the procedure up there, out of the way of prying eyes, and at the end of it, implant an embryo that was growing away next door in the Research Facility — a little deviousness would be all that was needed to hoodwink the assisting nursing staff. That's why Ravensbourne's qualification as an anaesthetist was so important. She could safely and officially give the anaesthetic, so no other doctor was involved.'

'What about following them up to see what happened? They wouldn't want to lose track, after all that hard work.'

'Yes, I wondered about that. It would have to be on a pot luck basis. Gemma, they thought, would be around in Bournemouth and would keep coming back to the ante-natal clinic, and Kate — well, of course she was right under their noses.'

Were there any others?

'It looks like it. The notes here are very sketchy and abbreviated, but it looks as though there were two before you, and they both had spontaneous abortions. That's why they started to use drug treatment, I think.'

'I was going to ask you about the drugs,' said Pauline, 'but how come they didn't anticipate the obvious fact that Gemma, a single student, would ask for a termination?'

'They did. Greenwell was the consultant in charge of her case, and reinforced that by doing a follow-up after her cervical polyp was dealt with.'

Gemma nodded her agreement.

'Then it would be simple for him to issue instructions that any further referrals would be to him. But that went wrong. I was doing Mr D'Arcy's Abortion Pool clinic, if you remember, when he was away — and Gemma was put on as an extra by the sister because she

277

thought a mistake had been made. She knew Greenwell didn't do abortions. If *he* had seen Gemma, as intended, he would have refused a termination and tried to dissuade her from seeing anyone else, then overseen the pregnancy. As it was, I saw her, and from then on . . .' Simon looked at Gemma sadly, gave a big sigh, and bent his head.

The others waited in silence, not knowing what to say. He looked up.

'From then on, everything went wrong. Gemma's handicap, the search for the report leading to Janice being murdered, then Gwyn's death — '

'It's no good trying to catalogue the disasters that followed — and certainly not as if you were to blame for them.' Pauline felt her heart go out to Simon, and picked up his hand, gave it an encouraging squeeze. 'So come on — tell us about the drugs. Why were Gemma and Kate given them?'

The Superintendent raised his eyebrows. 'Miss Randall was given drugs as well?'

Before Simon could speak, Pauline explained.

'Yes. After her cervical polyp operation, when presumably an embryo was implanted, Gemma was given some tablets by Ravensbourne as soon as she came round from the anaesthetic — just as Kate was. But she didn't take them — she has a hang-up about pills.' She looked at Simon. 'You said you had no idea why the drugs were given. Do you know now?'

'Yes, I'm pretty sure,' Simon continued. 'Kate's tablets contained azathioprine and carbi- and levodopa — and I'm sure Gemma's did as well.'

'What was this — ' Barnes struggled over the unfamiliar word — 'azathioprine — supposed to do?' He was leaning forward in his chair now, eager to hear more.

'It's a drug used in transplant surgery. It suppresses the body's reaction to foreign tissue, and stops the rejection process. It was needed to make sure the embryo wasn't rejected.'

'But you didn't say anything about that being used in test-tube babies,' Pauline pointed out.

'No, that's because it isn't necessary. When the fertilised egg is in such a primitive stage of development, it hasn't any foreign characteristics to cause rejection. It's accepted as it is. But the embryos that Greenwell was using were much more advanced, and could have been rejected. Hence the need for azathioprine.'

'But it was that other stuff the analyst found that made Kate behave so strangely, wasn't it?' asked Pauline.

'The carbidopa and levodopa. Yes, it was. As we discussed before, Kate was very sensitive to one of the side effects on the brain. From these notes it looks as if Ravensbourne had found that the speeded-up growth of the brain tissue was inhibited by the fact that it used up all the available dopamine — a chemical essential for brain metabolism. There wasn't enough to keep the high growth rate going. This combination of drugs increased the amount of dopamine available, and so the rapid growth of brain tissue could be maintained.'

'This fast rate of growth — it would explain why there was so much confusion about how far on Kate was in her pregnancy — why it seemed to go in leaps and bounds?' Pauline raised her eyebrows expectantly.

'Yes, it would. And don't forget the embryo was already at least a month old when it was put in. That in itself was a remarkable achievement, getting such a mature embryo to implant.'

Pauline nodded her understanding. 'But I thought drugs in early pregnancy were dangerous, and could cause malformations — like thalidomide.'

'In principle you're right, but in practice very few drugs are associated with major defects. It depends on so many factors — whether they cross the placenta, the stage of pregnancy, when they are given. They were playing a dangerous game, and were prepared to take chances. Angelica seems to have suffered no physical deformities. It remains to be seen what's happened to her brain.'

'OK,' said Barnes, 'I think I understand all that. But what was it all about? What were Greenwell and Ravensbourne trying to achieve, messing about with double doses of genes?'

'We get a good idea from some notes in this lot — ' Simon waved the sheaf of papers — 'where Ravensbourne has been trying to justify their objectives. She points out that man's development from the baby to adulthood is terribly slow. Consider: a new-born calf can walk within minutes of birth, feed itself without any help from mother almost as quickly, can communicate adequately from the word go. A bird can be completely independent of its parents within a few weeks of hatching. But man is completely helpless at birth, and remains totally dependent on the parents for several years — less in primitive societies, but longer and longer the more civilised we become.

'Ravensbourne felt a lot of time is wasted in human development. Our brains are truly remarkable — their capacity is always under-utilised. Suppose you could get a child to talk, or at least comprehend, almost from birth, walk at six weeks, acquire skills and become independent in terms of food and hygiene by six months, comprehend danger, and by a year be teaching itself to read and write . . . Imagine a baby of less than twelve months, two and a half feet tall, walking, talking, feeding itself, dressing, not needing nappies — and learning, learning all the time.' Simon looked round, eyes shining with excitement.

'Hold on a minute!' Pauline held up her hand. 'You sound as if you're on her side.'

'Christ, Pauline, how can you say that?' He looked hurt.

Pauline reached out to him. 'I'm sorry, I didn't mean it like that. But you look so fired up about it.'

'That's because, as a scientist, I can see the fascination of the concept. It would revolutionise motherhood, for a start. It's true that even such an advanced and rapidly developing infant would still need supervision — but not in the totally dependent way that babies do now. Most benefits, however, would come from the increase in human knowledge — especially in the fields of scientific advance, but perhaps in other areas too, even politics. The human brain is at its most receptive and functioning at its peak in the early teens. If intellectual maturity could be reached *before* the teenage years, just think how well equipped these young people would be, with all their acquired knowledge and experience. Innovation, wisdom even, to be used throughout their lives — not just from when society currently looks upon people as being "mature" — when they are forty or even fifty.'

Does that baby mean she's been successful?

Simon looked at Gemma. 'In a way, I suppose it does, although we have no way of knowing what effects are yet to come — in intellectual capacity, physical development, or even psychologically.'

Pauline frowned. 'You mean the baby could be brilliant but crazy.'

'That's one way of putting it.' Immediately in his mind he pictured the creature he had seen on Gemma's ultrasound — the first contact he had had with this terrible business.

Is that baby yours — legally, I mean?

'Gemma! What sort of question is that?'

'It's all right, Pauline. It's a question that has to be faced. To be honest, I'm not sure what the legal position is. Genetically, it's got nothing to do with either Kate or me. We'll probably never know the true parental origins of the egg or the sperm — anyway, the chromosomes were tampered with. As to whether I'm, well, responsible for it, I don't know. Do you, Pauline?'

'I've absolutely no idea. I've never even dreamt of a problem like this before — and I don't suppose anyone else has, either.'

Do you want it?

Pauline and Barnes looked at Gemma in astonishment.

Simon gave a tired smile. 'My, you're into the direct questions, aren't you? But you're right, I've got to start facing these matters sometime, so I might as well start now.' He tipped his head back and rubbed the back of his neck. 'But to be honest, Gemma, that's one I'm going to have to think about.' He put his elbows on his knees, and put his face in his hands.

Superintendent Barnes coughed. 'Look, doctor, I think you've done enough for one day.'

Pauline gave him a grateful look. 'Yes, I agree.'

'So may I make a suggestion?' the policeman continued. 'I'll go home and digest all this, and do some work on the tapes as well. Then I'd very much like to talk again — in a day or so.'

Simon straightened up. 'Sure. I'll be glad to help.'

We still don't know about Dr. Reece's death — or that poor Marshall girl.

'We're working on that, Miss,' said the Superintendent. 'And of course after what Mr Robinson has just told us, I think we can bring a little pressure to bear on Mr Greenwell. Perhaps he can shed some light on the matter.' He gave a mirthless smile.

Pauline stood up, and Barnes followed her cue.

'Er, just one more question before I go. That business of you, er, collapsing at Miss Randall's operation.' He looked awkward. 'Could that have been anything to do with the embryo having been tampered with, so to speak?'

Gemma looked from the policeman to Simon, eyes wide. Pauline saw Simon react, wanted to protect him from this.

'That's something that's been bothering me, too, Superintendent, but I don't think — '

Simon held up a hand. 'No, it's OK, really. It's a very astute question, and I can only guess at an answer. I honestly believe that the foetus implanted inside Gemma was able in some extraordinary way to perceive me as a threat.' He shuddered. 'I think it somehow knew that when I did the scan. Don't ask me how, but I think that's why I saw what I did.' The others were transfixed. 'And when I tried to abort it — ' He paused for a deep breath. Pauline felt her skin prickle. ' — my reaction was so like an epileptic fit that I think the thing may have been capable of releasing some sort of electrical discharge that gave me a seizure.'

281

They were all silent for a moment, absorbing this.

'Good God,' said Pauline at last. Like some sort of defence mechanism, you mean?'

'Yes. Sounds, crazy, doesn't it?'

The Superintendent put a hand on his arm. 'Not after all we've heard, doctor. Not crazy at all.'

Pauline decided to end it there, and led Barnes towards the door.

'You'll keep us posted, won't you, Superintendent?'

'Of course, Miss Jamieson.' He went to the door. 'It may have to be off the record, but you'll be the first to know anything new. All of you deserve at least that much.' He closed the door gently, leaving the three of them to their thoughts.

* * *

On the fourth floor of the hospital, the nurse tending the incubator was cleaning out the tracheostomy tube which connected the baby to the ventilator. They were instructed to do this every four hours, and to leave the tube out until there were signs of respiratory distress, then replace it. This would help them assess progress, and give an idea when the ventilator could be dispensed with. So far, despite the rapid growth and improvements in all other areas, after a few minutes the breathing became laboured, and the tube had to be replaced.

The nurse had only just taken the tube out. The infant made some gurgling sounds, coughed, and then made a strange noise. The nurse thought something was wrong, and prepared to re-insert the tube. The baby repeated the noise, which had a strange familiarity. She spoke, quite naturally, to the baby, as the nurses did to all the prems, as if they could understand.

'What do you want, little one?'

Again the strangely familiar sounds. The nurse canted her head, listened carefully, then went weak with shock, the hairs on her scalp rising, as the baby made the noise again. Because now she recognised that this was no ordinary noise. She watched the tiny lips move as she heard the words:

'An-gel-ic-ka want feed.'

31

The next three days saw Pauline, Simon and Gemma trying to organise themselves in Pauline's town house. There was minimal disruption as far as accommodation went, with Gemma still in her first floor bedroom, and Simon on the second floor, where Pauline's bedroom also was. The kitchen/dining room and lounge were on the ground floor, so there was plenty of space, albeit on a small scale in the narrow terrace.

It was the bathroom that caused all the problems. There was only one, and Simon saw immediately that he would stand no chance against the demands of two women. The first morning he had already made two abortive attempts to gain access, and was sitting in Gemma's day room, smiling with resigned amusement. He heard Pauline turn on the shower, and for a brief moment found himself wondering how she would look, naked, lathering her body under the streaming water. A poignant memory jolted him, and he thought of Kate, spending so long in the bathroom, making him cross. He wished it could be her in there now, the old, carefree, normal Kate. He wouldn't care how long she took. Lost in his thoughts, he jumped when a hand touched his.

He'd forgotten that Gemma was by the window in her wheelchair, and hadn't heard her push herself silently over to him. She looked at him sadly, and held out her message pad.

Painful memories?

Simon nodded, turning his face away.

Gemma stroked his hand. He didn't pull away, but after a moment she drew hers away to write again.

Kate?

'Yes, Kate,' he managed, trying to keep his voice steady.

This time it was Gemma's turn to look away. She didn't know what to do, how to help, couldn't use comforting words. They sat there in awkward silence until Pauline came out in a bathrobe, rubbing her hair in a towel, to see their glum faces.

'Well, you two look as if you're having a good time. Have I kept you waiting that long?'

Simon stood up, and he and Gemma glanced at each other before he went into the bathroom. Pauline noticed the exchange, then shrugged her shoulders and went up to dry her hair.

For the most part, the atmosphere in the house was one of slightly forced jollity. Simon was not yet strong, but more able than Gemma, and helped all he could. Pauline was clearly the boss, however, and was also the most active. She was in and out for food and toiletries, and also had to fit in trips to her office to deal with essential problems. Her partners, thankfully, were being very understanding about her newly acquired commitments, and in any event had very little cause to complain. She rarely took her full entitlement of holidays, and was one of the most conscientious and hardworking of her firm. She had started out that way from the very beginning, determined that no one would ever have grounds to say she was not pulling her weight — especially as she knew when she first arrived that there was some resistance to having a female partner.

After three days, they were in some sort of routine, and the arrangement seemed to be working out well. They were laughing about a cartoon on the front page of the *Telegraph* when the phone rang. It was Superintendent Barnes, asking if he could come round to see them straight away.

Within ten minutes of his arrival the four of them were seated once more as they had been three days earlier. This time, however, it was the CID officer, not Simon, who was centre stage.

'We've learnt a great dealt,' he began, 'thanks to your interpretation of Ravensbourne's papers, doctor. We were able to put on a show to Greenwell of knowing a lot more than we did about his involvement. The tapes helped a lot, too. Some of them were conversations between Ravensbourne and Greenwell, made apparently without his knowledge. He was pretty upset about that. It seemed she didn't fully trust her father, but they prove his complicity conclusively. As a result, he has been, shall we say, considerably more forthcoming than he might have otherwise.'

'There's a couple of things that puzzle me before you go any further,' said Pauline. 'One is why he and Ravensbourne kept their relationship so quiet.'

'I can only speculate about that. I think it was because they didn't want it obvious that they were so close. That would raise the suspicion that they were up to something, so to speak. It just helped them keep a lower profile, attract less attention.'

'Yes, I can see that, I suppose. But how come Greenwell didn't

284

have a key to the flat? He could have let himself in, then he wouldn't have been guilty of breaking and entering. It might have made it much more difficult for you initially if he could claim authorised access.'

'That's a good point,' conceded Barnes. 'But the fact remains he didn't. I think, as I said before, that his daughter didn't fully trust him. Or perhaps she was so ambitious, or maybe "greedy" would be a better word, to make the most of her discoveries that she didn't trust anyone — even her father. Greenwell admitted that he only knew the location of the safe — and its combination — because he had covertly watched his daughter using it.'

Simon shifted his position as he pondered.

'What exactly *were* Ravensbourne's ambitions?' he asked 'She was hardly likely to get much of a professional accolade as a result of such clandestine, not to say illegal, research. Universal condemnation would have been more likely.'

'That's what we were wondering, too. Surely she wasn't going to all this trouble, and destroying half-a-dozen people's lives on the way, just for the satisfaction of knowing her research theories could be put into practice.' Barnes leaned forward, resting his elbows on his knees. 'I'm afraid the answer, as is so often the case in human deceit and tragedy, is money.'

Gemma moved her chair a little closer, and Pauline sat up very straight. It was Simon, however, who asked the question.

'How can something as esoteric and unethical as this earn anyone money?'

'You can sell anything if you can find a market and someone with enough money to buy. There are people and places in the world well known for putting making money above all else — and where ethical considerations are of no consequence.'

Pauline sat back. 'The United States, for example?'

'Right on the button, as our transatlantic cousins would say. While Ravensbourne was there she obviously got infected with the wealth ethos, someone planted an idea, and she was away. After that, nothing was going to stop her making her fortune.'

Gemma scribbled.

Please, what was the idea that would make her so much money?

Barnes nodded at Gemma. 'Imagine you say to someone with unlimited funds and who was unscrupulous enough not to care about minor details like other people's lives, "I can provide you with a dozen potential Einsteins, who'll come on stream in ten or twelve years' time. They'll be young, malleable, do whatever you say." '

He looked around the three of them before continuing.

'The potential is enormous. You could use them for scientific invention, politics, military strategy. You could sell such an incredibly valuable commodity to other power-hungry individuals and organisations — even to other countries. I don't suppose the Russians or the Libyans would say "no" to an under-the-counter deal to sell them a few captive geniuses.'

There was a silence while they all digested this concept, broken eventually by Simon.

'When you said a fortune, you weren't kidding?'

Barnes nodded. 'Millions — perhaps hundreds of millions of dollars.'

'And she obviously had contacts with someone willing to do a deal, once she had proved she could deliver the goods?' asked Pauline.

'She certainly had. Everything was virtually set up. In fact, she went to the States to finalise matters when she suddenly disappeared, after the Marshall girl's death. Her passport told us that, and we've had the New Jersey Police, and the FBI no less, tracing her movements their end. It looks as though she's been doing business with an organisation over there that runs abortion clinics and small private hospitals, as well as being in pharmaceuticals.'

'A perfect combination,' observed Simon. 'A ready supply of female patients, the facilities, and the medicines.'

'That's right.'

Why didn't she carry on over there?

'Exactly what we wondered. We spoke to the Marlenstein Clinic where she worked. It seems that although she was one of their brightest rising stars, she was eventually asked to leave because of persistent irregularities in the way she conducted her research. When pressed, they implied that she was keeping embryos longer than Federal Law allowed. Her work permit was withdrawn.'

'Superintendent — ' Pauline frowned with concentration — 'earlier you said that Ravensbourne had destroyed half-a-dozen people's lives. I've been trying to work that out.'

'That's easy, Miss Jamieson. There's Miss Randall here, Janice Marshall, Dr Gwyn Reece, Mrs Robinson, her baby, and the doctor here. I make that six.'

Gemma gave a gasp, and Pauline's eyes were wide, her expression one of disbelief.

'You have proof that Ravensbourne killed Janice Marshall *and* Gwyn Reece?'

'Not that would stand up in a court of law — not yet, anyway. But I think we'll end up with enough evidence.'

Simon shook his head sadly. 'And all for the possibility of making some money.'

'Not entirely, doctor. Ravensbourne had a bank account in New Jersey. It had eight hundred and fifty thousand dollars in it. More than just a possibility, don't you think?'

'Presumably the killing of Miss Marshall had something to do with the missing pathology report about Gemma's termination?' Pauline looked anxiously at Gemma, but she didn't seem unduly distressed.

'It would seem so. She probably knew Janice Marshall had a photographic memory, and would be able to recall the report. When Mr Robinson started asking about it, she got nervous.'

'I'm getting a bit confused here,' said Pauline. 'Didn't Ravensbourne make the report in the first place? Why didn't she just ditch the specimens, and not put anything down on paper? It would never have been seen by anyone. Then once the samples had been "lost", no one could check.'

'I've wondered about that, too.' Simon gave Pauline an approving nod. 'I think it was because she didn't immediately recognise that specimen as being from one of her "experiments". After all, she wasn't expecting it, and she would examine large numbers of slides every day. She probably didn't pay much attention to the names. It must have been later, when she thought about the abnormal report, that she realised what she'd done, and tried to obliterate all trace of it. She got rid of Janice, destroyed the slides, and wiped the record from the computer — or so she thought.'

Barnes consulted his notes. 'I've got a question here about the report. When you were interviewed after Dr Reece's death, you told us that he said the report mentioned radiation damage. How does that tie in?'

'I think she'd simply made an error of interpretation. What she was seeing were strange-looking cell nuclei — the sort of thing that *could* be caused by irradiation, but in fact was caused by messing about with the chromosomes. When that thought hit her, she checked up on the names, realised what she'd done and poor Janice paid the price.'

But Janice Marshall was raped, wasn't She? How could that be Gillian Ravensbourne?

'Exactly so, Miss. It was very clever. Very clever indeed. It was

287

made to look like rape, so that we'd never even consider a woman as a suspect. It was the sheer chance of having to identify Dr Ravensbourne's body from the dental impression that put us on to it — you remember that the teeth-marks on Miss Marshall's breasts matched Ravensbourne's?'

Pauline nodded. How could she forget a bizarre fact like that?

'But what about the other forensic evidence? Didn't they find sperms in the vagina?' asked Simon.

'Yes, they did. Ravensbourne had to be there, no doubt about that, so we assumed she had an accomplice. Then some bright spark suggested it was easy enough for a pathologist to get sperm samples — they would be brought in for analysis all the time.' Barnes allowed himself a smug smile. 'We checked up with the Lab for the day of the murder. Only one seminal fluid sample was brought in that day. We traced the chap, and he had a cast-iron abili. He was driving a train into Waterloo Station at the time Miss Marshall was killed. He agreed to supply us with a sample, and the DNA profiling showed it was his sperm that was inside the dead girl. Ravensbourne must have put it there — easy enough for a doctor.'

Pauline's face registered her disgust. 'Whatever possessed her to make bite marks on the poor girl's breasts?'

Barnes considered. 'To make it look authentic, I suppose. She knew rape victims are often bitten in the frenzy of the act, so to speak, and for the same reason — authenticity, that is — she did some damage around the vaginal area, too.'

Simon closed his eyes for a moment. 'She must have been mad.'

'Quite likely, doctor. But cunning with it.'

What about Dr Reece? You obviously think she killed him too?

'As far as we can tell. She makes a reference to his death on the tape. She sort of worked around to the subject when she was talking to her father — as if she was making sure she had a record showing he was involved. But she didn't go as far as spelling it out for us.'

'Just a minute!' Simon sat forward. 'You said Ravensbourne was in America then.'

'I said she went to America, yes. But her passport shows she left New York the day before Dr Reece was killed. She must have come straight back to her flat.'

Simon looked puzzled. 'How did she know Gwyn was in the Lab that night?'

'I think he told her himself.'

'I — I'd find that very hard to believe.'

288

'Well, sir, I think it's something along these lines.' The Superintendent glanced at his notes. 'You remember, doctor, again from one of our interviews, that you were suspicious of the Senior Pathologist, Dr Ironside.'

'Well, yes, but — '

'It's all right, sir, I'm not criticising. It seems that he is, shall we say, an awkward customer, and his obstructive attitude to you was no more than his usual cussedness. However, it was enough for you and Dr Reece at the time to be wary of him. In fact, when we questioned him about being obstructive concerning the report, he denied it vehemently. If he's telling the truth, and frankly there's no reason to disbelieve him, what probably happened was that Ravensbourne simply told Janice Marshall it was Ironside who was being obstructive — when of course it was really her.'

He paused, licked his lips, then looked at Pauline. 'Er, sorry, Miss Jamieson, but I'm getting a trifle dry. I couldn't have a drink of water, could I?'

She grinned at him. 'I can take a hint. I'll put the kettle on.' Barnes waited until she came back before he continued.

'As I was saying, Dr Ironside's hostility made Dr Reece think of Ravensbourne as a potential ally, despite her disappearance. I gather he and Ravensbourne had an affair at one time?' He raised a quizzical eyebrow at Pauline.

'Yes, that seems to be true, Superintendent.'

'Well, I reckon he called her from the Lab when he made his discovery about the report, about the same time as he called you, Mr Robinson.'

Simon was sceptical. 'Whyever would he call her just then?'

'I expect he'd called several times since she left so suddenly, to see if she was back, and what with him being excited about finding out how to access the back-up files in the computer, he thought he'd try her again — and bingo! — there she was. I can imagine her pleading ignorance, but if he read out what he'd found in the computer — well, she had to make her mind up, fast. She did — and got there before you, Mr Robinson. Dr Reece would have been a sitting duck, in front of the computer with her behind him, not suspecting any threat. She would have surgical gloves handy, so there'd be no finger-prints. She picked up the fire-axe — and that was that.'

Simon massaged his eyes with his fingers, distressed at the recollection. 'She must have been in the building when I found Gwyn, to put that cryptic message on the screen — and take it off again. I wonder why she did that.'

'And why she didn't attack you,' added Pauline.

'Attacking Mr Robinson would have been too risky. If she failed to catch him completely by surprise, only wounded him, she'd be in

trouble. She was too canny to chance that. As for the message — '
Barnes took a deep breath and blew out his cheeks — 'who knows?
Trying to scare you off, I suppose. Or perhaps a crack in her façade.'

'A hint of her losing control — a psychosis developing?'

'Something like that. But you're the doctor.' Barnes smiled at
Simon to show he was not being sarcastic. 'In any event, she was sane
enough to know she had to lie low for a while — probably out of town
somewhere — so that everyone would think she was still away on
holiday. Then, when she thought the dust had settled, she returned to
her flat and announced her presence to Dr Ironside, who put her
straight back on the rota.'

'But — ' Simon paused, remembering. 'When I told her about
Gwyn's death, she fainted with shock.'

From the open kitchen door came the sound of the kettle boiling,
then the click as it switched itself off. No one took any notice.

'I'd say that was a very good acting performance, sir — which it
must have been, you being a doctor yourself.'

Simon looked remorseful. 'Well, it certainly fooled me.'

Pauline reached out and touched his arm. 'You can't blame
yourself for being taken in.'

'But if I'd been more suspicious then — '

'Don't be silly,' Pauline interrupted him. 'Anyway, she was
obviously suspicious of you, and kept a close eye on you from then
on. Otherwise she wouldn't have followed you that night in the
hospital. Remember. you said later, when you thought about it, that
it was she who was listening when you were in the phone booth.'

'Yes,' Simon agreed. 'I don't know how I could have failed to
recognise her at the time. I'd been reading about her only minutes
before. I reckon that was how she found out I was going to see Kate.
It was my last thought before I passed out, looking up at her and
Kate . . .' He made an effort at control. 'Kate saved my life,
attacking her like that.'

There was silence for a while. Then Barnes made to get up. 'I think
we've covered everything, doctor — '

'No, it's all right, really.' Simon looked up and squared his
shoulders. Gemma handed him a piece of paper, and as he took it he
could see tears in her eyes.

Her love for you was stronger than her madness.

Simon tried to give Gemma a grateful smile, but failed. He got up,
went over to her, and gave her a gentle kiss on the cheek instead.
Without saying anything or looking at anyone, he left the house, and
went for a long, long walk.

32

It felt quite strange walking down the corridor from the Gynae Ward, wearing a white coat for the first time in six weeks. Simon had been in the hospital since 8.30 that morning, briefing himself on the in-patients. He had expected to feel awkward and out of place, and to be the object of too much attention. He needn't have worried. He had received a comfortingly warm welcome, but hardly one curious glance. Everyone seemed quite open and natural towards him. He thought it must be because he was being treated just as the other problems that occur in hospital were treated. That is to say, the staff focused their attention on it until it was resolved, one way or the other. Then, when the patient left hospital, alive or dead, you forgot about that problem and concentrated on the next one. When you did that with twenty or thirty situations simultaneously, you soon got used to it. It was no good dwelling on past events — you had no time for that, with new problems replacing the old all the time.

He was made very much aware of this constantly changing environment when he went into the ward. There was not one patient still there from when he was last working. Although the problems were familiar enough, with a completely new collection of patients he found himself struggling throughout the ward-round, feeling almost an outsider, with the houseman and Sister knowing the patients and their problems so well. He consoled himself that it was only a matter of time. He had been in this situation before, starting new jobs, doing locums. After a few days it would be as if he had never been away.

One thing that had surprised him was his first encounter with his old boss, Roger D'Arcy. He had asked him to come into the hospital the previous Friday, to 'have a chat about things'.

There had been a major upheaval in the Obstetrics and Gynae division with the sudden departure of Jeremy Greenwell to police custody. Simon knew a locum consultant was now doing Greenwell's work until a permanent replacement could be found, and he had assumed that he would be working with the new man. However, that was not the plan.

D'Arcy had welcomed him surprisingly warmly. The last time they had spoken to each other it had ended acrimoniously, to say the least. This time, as he entered D'Arcy's consulting room, feeling very apprehensive, he was greeted with an extended hand and a smile.

'Come in, come in. Sit down.'

Simon set himself on the edge of his chair.

'It's all right, there aren't going to be any angry scenes this time. I — ah — think I owe you something of an apology.'

Simon could not hide his surprise. He sat back a bit, and relaxed a little.

'On one of the last occasions we spoke,' continued D'Arcy, choosing not to comment on the look of astonishment on his junior's face, 'I more or less accused you of complicity in the disappearance of the Randall girl's histology report, and even of having something to do with Janice Marshall's death.'

Simon felt uncomfortable. 'Well, yes, but that's all water under the bridge now.'

'Thank you.' He cleared his throat. 'And as for the extraordinary business of your so-called epileptic seizure — well, I know all about that now, and I understand. It could have finished your career . . . correction, *I* could have finished your career, despite your negative EEG.' He seemed to be searching for the right words. 'The thing is, I don't feel I can leave it like that. I don't want any misunderstandings between us, no hidden animosity.' He paused, looking past Simon, avoiding his eye. He wasn't finding this easy. 'So I thought I should make sure beforehand that there are no hard feelings, so to speak.'

'Before what, sir?'

'It's Roger, remember? Before I ask you if you'd like to come and work with me again.'

Simon's response was genuine and immediate. 'I'd like that very much — er — Roger.'

D'Arcy looked relieved. 'So there won't be?'

Simon was getting confused. 'Won't be what?'

'Hard feelings, man!'

'Oh, no. No, of course not. I've forgotten about it already.' Simon could not help smiling. He hadn't dared hope for this.

'So?' D'Arcy spread his hands, obviously waiting for Simon to speak.

'I — I don't know what to say.'

'How about, "When can I start?"'

Simon's smile broadened. 'How about Monday?'

'Fine. Look forward to seeing you.'

And that had been that. A reconciliation. As he descended in the lift to go to Out-patients, Simon reflected that, despite all that had happened, things could be worse. His chest ached and his eyes stung whenever he thought of Kate, just as they were doing now. But life with the two girls was working out quite well. Pauline was fun, kept things moving, was terrific at jollying Gemma along. Simon was able to help Gemma too, supporting her when she tried walking, carrying her up and down stairs when needed. That was a great help, and gave her a much appreciated change of scene. Without Simon it had been a great performance, Pauline having to half-push or pull and half-carry Gemma, then go back for the wheelchair, which was also not easy. Simon could do it in less than half the time. They had an electric wheelchair on order, and soon she would be able to go out on her own.

'We're on the ground floor, doctor. Aren't you getting out?'

Simon came out of his daydreaming with a start, looking in momentary confusion at the staff nurse, standing there pressing the 'Open Door' button.

'Sorry — thanks. I was miles away.'

He walked slowly down the long corridor to the Out-patient Department, and despite the activity around him he was soon once more lost in thought.

He couldn't help but worry how long it was all going to run so smoothly. He had no great desire to go and live on his own at the moment — he enjoyed the company and support he was being given, and appreciated being fussed over, as both women did in their way. He was not flattering or deluding himself, he felt sure, but he was certain they both liked having him around. Pauline was a very nice person, and the little looks she gave him, the occasional touch of the hand, were genuine signs of friendship, he thought. Nothing more. Not yet, anyway. He couldn't cope with that, couldn't even entertain it. But with Gemma he had been more relaxed: joked with her more, played up to her more. He wanted very much to help all he could with her rehabilitation, and she was such a trier, he was full of admiration for her.

Thinking of her, he remembered that as he had left the house in Richborough Road that morning, Gemma had pushed a crumpled note into his pocket. He had given her hand a squeeze, brushed his lips against her cheek in a chaste kiss, and then responded to Pauline's good wishes in similar manner. He was so preoccupied with facing what he regarded as the ordeal of his return to work, that he had forgotten about the note until now. He took it out and read the message, oblivious of the bustle of people rushing past him.

Good Luck and God Bless
Hope your day's a success

Simon smiled, feeling warm inside, and walked on with more purpose and enthusiasm than he had felt for months.

It was now late August, and Simon had been back at work a week. The summer had not been a memorable one as regards the weather, but represented three months of his life that he would never be able to forget. And despite all that had gone before, this Saturday was going to be one of the most difficult days of them all.

He had thought and thought about what he should do, often lying awake until early morning. He had had seemingly endless talks — with D'Arcy and one or two other consultants in the hospital, and with Pauline and Gemma, too. He valued their opinion highly. They were his closest friends, his confidantes. There was no one else, now. He also valued Pauline's legal advice. He respected it, and if things went wrong, he could have need of it in the future.

The remarkable creature created by Ravensbourne and Greenwell, with Kate's unwitting assistance, was now seven weeks old. Simon still found it difficult to suppress the inner rage that threatened to rise up whenever he thought of how Kate had paid for their experiment with her life. At first, he had found himself fantasising about how he might avenge her death. Ravensbourne was dead — Kate had carried out her own retribution there — but her father lived on, soon to be released on bail by all accounts, free to enjoy the luxury of his home, the support and companionship of his wife. No doubt Greenwell would end up in prison eventually, but for how long? Simon had repeatedly pushed his thoughts of vengeance away, making a conscious effort to shelve them for a while, hoping that in time their intensity would fade. The distant dawn of hope for the rebuilding of his own life had helped keep the burning hatred under control.

These thoughts went through his mind once more as he took the lift up to the fourth floor, where he was to meet D'Arcy. He got out, went through the double doors of the Research Facility, and into the incubator room. D'Arcy had not yet arrived. There was only one nurse on duty, and Simon told her she could take a break.

He had only once been back to this room since that first occasion. He did not feel guilty any more about not visiting the baby, now he knew there was no flesh-and-blood link with either himself or Kate. He glanced into the incubator quickly, and could see that the infant was growing at a remarkable rate. He looked at the chart. It had weighed only eight hundred grams at birth, a pound and three-quarters. Now it was three and a half pounds, sixteen hundred grams, and the graph showed the weight gain was accelerating fast.

There had been little more understandable speech after the first reported incident, but the child nevertheless showed a prodigious degree of awareness. It responded to a number of commands, clearly comprehending them, and would try and indicate its needs to its carers with waves and a sort of sign language. Only when all else failed did it resort to vocalising, and this was very limited.

Simon had a private theory about that, which he had not shared with any of his colleagues. He thought the infant's awareness was even greater than it seemed, and that it could probably speak comprehensibly if it wished. He suspected that it somehow knew it would be better not to reveal all its abilities, in case that revelation should constitute a threat to its continued existence. It could not know that as far as Simon was concerned, it was already too late.

All was not well with the baby, however, despite its burgeoning powers. Something was still wrong with its lungs. Many babies born prematurely develop Respiratory Distress Syndrome, or RDS, whereby the transfer of oxygen into the lungs is impaired, because the lungs are as yet immature and not ready for breathing air. They lack surfactant, a substance that prevents the tiny air sacs in the lungs from collapsing. In many cases, after a few days' treatment and assistance with breathing on a ventilator, the condition resolves. Occasionally, however, the problem may persist for weeks, and even after surviving all that time, death sometimes ensues.

For all its physical and intellectual advancement, this infant was still suffering from RDS. It had even failed to respond to the recently available artificial surfactant, which was usually very effective. Nevertheless, there were signs it was slowly improving. The staff periodically switched off the ventilator, and serial measurements were made of the oxygen content of the blood. Originally it was only for ten minutes at a time, but now it was half an hour before the level became critical, and artificial breathing with oxygen-rich gases had to be resumed.

Simon was standing at one end of the incubator. He could only see the tiny but now well-covered body, the head was hidden by an oscilloscope. He thought that the baby was aware of his presence, for it kept moving to try and look around the obstruction. Simon stayed where he was. Foolish and weak though it might be, he didn't want to look this strange creature in the eye.

The door opened with a bang, making him jump. 'Sorry, Simon, didn't mean to startle you.' D'Arcy came over and gripped his upper arm firmly. 'How are you? Any second thoughts?'

Simon took a deep breath, looked at the Consultant's face, and was heartened by the expression of genuine concern he saw there.

'Lots of thoughts, but no change of mind.'

'It's a tough one, this. Never thought I'd find myself in this situation. Anencephalics, severe meningoceles, hopeless spina bifidas, yes, but this is different. Very different.'

They'd been all over this ground before, and Simon didn't want to open another debate, not now.

'I know, Roger. But I don't want to talk about it any more.'

'All right. Let's make the clinical decision for the record.' D'Arcy was troubled, but making an effort to be matter-of-fact, professional. 'Our considered opinion is that this infant is ready to go without the ventilator for long periods.'

Simon cleared his throat. 'I agree.'

'The pO_2 results may suggest we are being a little over-optimistic, but that is a matter of judgement.'

'That's my view also.'

'Let's just make a note to that effect.' D'Arcy picked up the case notes and scribbled quickly in them, before passing them to Simon. 'That's it, then, I'll leave you to it.' He touched Simon very briefly on the shoulder, then turned to leave. At the door he said, 'I'll instruct the nurses. They won't come in for an hour or so.' The door closed, leaving Simon alone.

He wasn't sure he could do it, now that it was time. He had thought about it so much, had convinced himself — no, he *knew* — that this was the right thing to do. He had done it before, it was true. There probably weren't many doctors of his seniority who hadn't had to face similar situations. Similar, but not the same. It was not the same as being confronted by a twisted, deformed caricature of a human baby, alternately grunting and squealing as if in pain, a throbbing mess of infected membranes bulging out where the back half of the head should be. There was no point in trying to prolong that sort of existence. But this . . .

Simon moved around the side of the incubator. The baby saw him immediately, and followed him with movements of the head and eyes. He was subjected to the same greeting he had received on his two previous visits — a snarling expression and a malevolent stare. This time it also made a hissing sound, like a cat. Simon shuddered, and averted his eyes. He had to move closer. The ventilator switch was on the side, below one of the incubator's entry ports. He briefly debated putting his hand inside. Should he try and make some sort of final contact with this deviant being?

The thought was fleeting. It was too late for that now. He reached out his hand, then withdrew it in terror as he touched the switch. For a moment he was overwhelmed with a paralysing fear, a fear that he was going to be struck by the same catastrophe that had befallen him when he had tried to abort Gemma Randall's foetus. He felt that same peculiar sensation, akin to an electric shock, go up his right arm, just as he had that morning more than three months ago!

Simon steadied himself, tried to control his over-breathing. He backed away, found a chair, sat down. Come on, he told himself. If you go on hyperventilating like that you'll pass out, even have another fit, like last time. You're OK, you're OK. He repeated the thought, over and over. Steady, steady.

After a full three minutes, he felt enough in control to glance back at the incubator. From inside a large pair of eyes looked out at him, and he could swear it was smiling, a mocking, toothless grin. Simon got slowly to his feet, his resolve returning, until an anger rose in him that gave him new strength. Memories of Kate, standing there, her lower abdomen slashed to ribbons; Kate talking maniacally to the freakish thing that now lay in the incubator; visions of the evil, grinning image on Gemma's scan. He knew no good would come from this unnatural being, whatever its phenomenal powers.

He looked around the room, saw the dressing trolley, found a pair of rubber gloves and put them on. He went up to the incubator and, without hesitation, pressed the ventilator switch. He felt nothing this time, perhaps because of the insulation of the gloves. The rhythmic humming died away slowly. Simon pulled off the gloves, threw them into a corner of the room, and turned to go. As he neared the door, he heard a strange, keening wail, that conveyed a mixture of fear and frustration. He knew he should not look back, but could not resist. From where he stood he could only see the upper part of the plastic dome of the incubator. All that was visible was a pair of tiny hands, opening and closing, the miniature fists grasping at the air in increasingly frenzied movement.

He turned away, bile rising in his throat, and hurried for the stairs, head down. In less than an hour the hideous experiment would be over.

* * *

Simon remembered little about the drive back to Pauline's. His mind was full of images — of grinning faces, bloodied bodies, tiny grasping hands, and a turmoil of emotions.

He parked the car badly, left it without locking it, and almost ran for the front door. The girls had been waiting for him, watching for him, and Pauline was there, opening the door as he approached. Simon hurried in and leaned back against the wall of the hallway.

Pauline could see how wretched he was. She felt so deeply for him, knowing what he had been trying to cope with over these last weeks, and now this. She made a move in his direction, wanting to comfort him in some way. Simon stumbled towards her, and then they were clinging to each other, swaying slightly, his head buried in her hair. At the end of the hall, Gemma watched from her wheelchair, sadness etching lines on her young face.

Pauline spoke softly, soothingly, gently stroking Simon's hair. At last he pulled away and gave an apologetic half-smile.

297

'Sorry about that.'

'Any time. It was my pleasure.' Pauline turned towards Gemma, anxious not to leave her out. She held out her good arm, and Simon went up to her. He leaned down and gave her a long, warm hug. He was so lucky. He needed both these girls right now, the sympathy and understanding he was getting from them was, he knew, far beyond the value of any drugs or psychiatric treatment.

He drew back, and saw that Gemma's eyes were shining, and Pauline was looking at him with a secret smile on her face. She held out her hand.

'Come with me.' He had no time to think as she led him into the lounge, and Gemma followed.

'Right. Sit there.' Pauline pointed to the sofa.

'What's this all about?' Simon looked from one to the other, sensed some sort of conspiracy, some joke of which he was as yet unaware.

'We've been saving a little surprise for you.' Pauline positioned Gemma's wheelchair in front of Simon, and then joined him on the sofa. 'We thought you might need something a little special today, to — well, take your mind off things. And so — ' she spoke in a motherly voice — 'are you sitting comfortably?'

A strange feeling came over Simon as he sat there in anticipation. These two had arranged something especially for him, knowing what a traumatic day it would be, and they were going to help him get over it. He was so fortunate. With the help of these two, he knew in that moment that he would survive.

He could hardly speak for emotion. 'Have you got me a present?'

'Sort of.' Pauline could see how affected he was. 'Come on, man, you don't know what it is yet.'

Simon sat back and prepared to receive his gift. He could not have guessed, then, at its immense value.

'Go ahead, Gemma,' Pauline instructed.

Gemma settled herself in the wheelchair, and took two deep breaths. Then, her face straining with concentration and effort, she opened her mouth.

Simon clutched at his chest in wonder as she spoke. Just one word. Harsh, husky and hesitant:

'Hi!'

33

The oxygen level in the blood was beginning to fall, and the tiny ribs were even more visible than usual as the chest muscles struggled to draw in more air. The frenzied movements of the arms had ceased, the brain somehow sensing that unnecessary exertion would deplete the available oxygen even faster. The baby's eyes, open wide, flicked from side to side, fear glinting in them as the remarkable intelligence beyond the optic nerves recognised the danger, struggled to hold on to its being.

There was a shiver, and the chest stopped moving. If there had been anyone there to watch, they would have thought death had come already.

But it was only a temporary reaction, a moment of revelation, of decision. Movement began again, and at the third increasingly desperate attempt, the infant managed to roll over. It was still for a moment, but then, very slowly, its puny muscles already weakening, the limbs worked laboriously in a crawling fashion until its body lay along the side of the incubator. The left arm lifted up, and began to scrabble at one of the rubber diaphragms, the movements getting more frantic until, almost by chance, the twiglike hand slipped through the opening.

There was an adjustment of position of the body, so that the arm followed the hand, hanging down out of the access port. The hand reached around, feeling blindly about, until it found what it was looking for. There was a paroxysm of movement, the whole body shuddering with a last, desperate exertion. All the creature's remaining reserves of energy were put into that one, final effort.

There was nothing more to be done. The tiny body flopped away from the side of the incubator, rolled onto its back, eyes closed. It was its ears that picked up and relayed the crucial message to the fading brain. The rhythmic hum of the ventilator broke the silence.